YESTERDAY'S SHADOWS

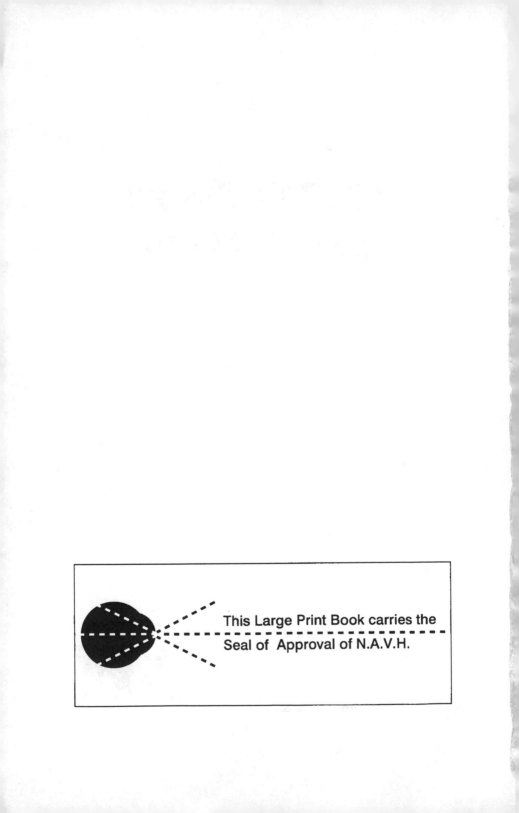

This Large Print Book carries the
Seal of Approval of N.A.V.H.

YESTERDAY'S SHADOWS

THE
PINKERTON LADY CHRONICLES 2

LEE RODDY

Walker Large Print • Waterville, Maine

Published in 2002 by arrangement with
Cook Communications Ministries.

The text of this Large Print edition is unabridged.
Other aspects of the book may vary from the original edition.

Set in 16 pt. Plantin by Minnie B. Raven.

Printed in the United states on permanent paper.

ISBN 1-4104-0037-9 (lg. print : sc : alk. paper)

To All My Family

with love and gratitude in this special year

CHAPTER 1

Laurel's violet eyes widened in surprise. "Are you serious?" she asked the bearded man behind the desk.

"Very serious, Miss Bartlett," the founder of the nation's most famous detective agency assured her. "It's exactly the kind of assignment you like, but safer. There is little possibility of your being in jeopardy there as compared to what you faced as a spy behind Confederate lines during the war."

Laurel squirmed uncomfortably. She didn't like to think of herself as a former spy. She considered herself a Union patriot who had done her duty for her country and her late brother who had died in the fighting.

Pinkerton didn't seem to notice her reaction. He continued, "But I'm confident you can handle it alone, just as you did in the war. However, you must understand that you will be two thousand miles from this office or any help from other operatives."

That would be a relief! Laurel thought. She resented Pinkerton's known tendency to have operatives spy on each other. "California," she mused, absently standing and straightening her hoopskirt. She liked working alone, and in California she wouldn't have to wonder if another agent was watching her. She walked to the window, thinking how this offer conflicted with the contents of the letter she carried in her velvet reticule.

Her emotions had been in turmoil since the mail came yesterday. After her last parting with Ridge Granger, she had not expected to ever see him again. But when the letter arrived, inviting her to visit him in Virginia, her strong attraction toward him weakened her resolve. The sudden prospect of being away from him for months confused her even more.

Outside the window, a brisk spring wind made Chicago pedestrians hang on to their hats. Breath from carriage and dray teams puffed into the cold air. The Stars and Stripes, symbolizing the reunited Northern and Southern states, snapped smartly under cloudy skies.

Returning to her seat, she said, "I hadn't thought about riding a stagecoach to Sacramento. I was waiting until the transcontinental railroad is completed."

"That's still about three years away, unless the present detractors succeed in stopping construction."

"It hardly seems possible for anyone to stop such a project, not with the government so solidly behind it."

"Even so, some companies fear financial ruin if the railroad goes through. That includes stagecoach and mail lines, steamships, freighters, and Alaskan businesses shipping glacier ice."

"Ice companies?"

"Yes. There are rumors that the Sierra Nevada snows could replace the glaciers, and it certainly would be a lot cheaper to have an ice supply closer than Alaska."

Laurel absently fingered the letter through her handbag. She could not tell Pinkerton the truth about why she was reluctant to accept the assignment. "I don't know . . ." she began.

He interrupted, "You're the most logical operative to send. It's unlikely that a woman would be suspected of being a detective. Posing as a newspaper correspondent will allow you to ask questions without arousing suspicion. Just be your usual charming self."

He reached into his desk drawer and pulled out a package. "Here. Take this home and read it. It will give you most of the details you'll need."

Laurel said with a trace of annoyance, "You seem pretty sure that I'm going to accept."

"It's got everything you want, Laurel. It will be like in the war when you worked as a spy."

Laurel flinched again at the last word.

Pinkerton caught the motion this time and added quickly, "I forget how you dislike that term. So call yourself an agent, operative, or detective — whatever you want. You are a very pretty, resourceful, and intelligent young woman. You knew how to charm military intelligence out of talkative Confederate officers, then get that information back to our Union forces. I'm sure you'll do well in Sacramento."

Laurel's annoyance eased at the compliment, but her mind was still on Ridge's invitation.

Pinkerton added, "You'll not only get paid by this agency, but, as you've done before, you can also earn extra money writing part-time for the newspaper. You might drop by Orville Seymour's office after you leave here. Tell him that you're thinking of going to California, but don't tell him why. Find out what kind of stories he'll pay you to write."

Laurel thoughtfully pursed her small lips.

She could use some extra income.

Pinkerton continued, "Just remember that, as always, you must not tell him or anyone that you're a detective."

Laurel silently rankled at the warning because it was one of Pinkerton's first rules of employment. Yet this necessity of keeping a secret meant she couldn't tell Ridge, and that troubled her conscience.

"I need a few days to think it over."

"Think quickly, then. The railroad people are anxious to find out whether there's a real organized conspiracy to stop the project. If it's not, then the trouble will blow over. But if it is a conspiracy, that's a problem. An agent must head for Sacramento as soon as possible."

Laurel sighed and picked up the package. "All right. I'll let you know in the morning."

Laurel walked outside the door and paused under the Pinkerton's all-seeing-eye sign bearing the words, *The Eye that Never Sleeps*.

Debating what to do next, she tucked Pinkerton's package under her arm and drew her cloak tightly around her shoulders. If she went to California, she would have to go by her father's house to get a small trunk for a prolonged trip. He would want to know why, and that would set off another disagreement.

I'm not ready to do that, she told herself. *So I had better go by the* Chicago Globe *and see what Mr. Seymour thinks about my writing stories from California.*

She hailed a passing hackney driver for the ride to the daily newspaper. Months ago, the publisher had agreed to let her work as one of the few female correspondents, paying her by the column inch for the stories that he used. Her writings about building the transcontinental railroad west from Omaha had been widely read.

Orville Seymour invited her into his office which was cluttered with stacks of newspapers and various other items. The distinctive smell of paper and ink could not override the odor of his dead cigar in a metal tray.

A sandy-haired man of middle age knocked on the door and stuck his head in without being invited. "We got that horse-whipping story," he announced, then left without waiting for a reply.

Caught up in the sense of urgency permeating the place, Laurel briefly told Seymour about possibly visiting California. "My uncle, Papa's only living brother, is ill and my father is not able to make the trip, so I may go."

Instantly, she regretted the lie. She had become proficient at such things during the war, but recently had felt guilt over such deceit.

The publisher had more skin showing on his receding scalp than on his face. A heavy gray mustache and matching bushy side-burns left only his clean-shaven chin showing above the tight white collar and broad-lapeled jacket.

He didn't answer, but his hazel eyes flickered from Laurel's face to the large glass window that gave him a view of the men moving very purposefully around the large editorial department.

Without looking at her, he commented, "I never knew any young and pretty woman who gets around as much as you do. Most of your friends must be married."

She resisted the temptation to snap the words that leaped to mind. "They are," she answered a little stiffly. She had the feeling that his tone held a hint of reproof. She made a motion as if to stand. "Well, I won't take up any more of your time."

"Hold on!" He turned to face her. "I guess all that spunkiness is what makes you a good correspondent. Give me a minute. I'm thinking."

Resettling into her chair, Laurel again

waited while his eyes probed hers. She held the gaze without blinking.

He finally spoke. "How would you like to tackle a really major story out there?" Without waiting for a reply, he rose from his squeaking swivel chair and walked to a large safe that stood against the back wall.

He continued, "I don't have anyone on staff to spare for this, but since you're going anyway, I'll take a chance." He paused, spinning the dial. When he opened the heavy metal door, he reached in and retrieved a package.

"This requires the utmost delicacy and discretion because it involves an unsolved murder case going back several years. The responsible party was never apprehended, but I've learned that a possible witness is now living in Sacramento. Find him and interview him. Try to get him to tell you what he saw and maybe identify the responsible person."

He handed the package across the desk. "Read through these files tonight and let me know if you're interested. But absolutely nobody is to know you have . . ."

He stopped abruptly as a bone-thin man with dark hair and sideburns paused in the open door. "Excuse me," he said, "but the press is broken down again, and . . ." He broke off upon noticing Laurel.

"Oh!" he exclaimed, "I'm sorry. I didn't see you, Miss." He shifted his gaze back to his employer. "Mr. Seymour, I didn't mean to interrupt, but you said to always let you know when the paper was going to be late."

"It's all right, Dick. Let me know when repairs have been made."

"Yes, sir." Dick backed out, his eyes darting from the publisher to Laurel. "Excuse me, Miss."

Seymour grumbled to Laurel, "I've ordered new presses, but it's too soon after the war to get them. Our present ones are old and tired. Now, as I was saying, nobody is to know what I'm giving you. After you've read the material, let me know if you're interested. If you are, and get the story, I'll give you a nice bonus."

Laurel reluctantly accepted the package. "I'm not yet sure that I'm going. Even if I do, it'll probably be a few days. Maybe you should keep this until —"

"No, you take it now," he broke in. "Read the material tonight. If you're not interested, return it to me before you go. But if you choose to follow up, you'll need this information in California."

Laurel placed the package on her lap beside the one Pinkerton had given her.

Seymour stood, indicating the meeting was over. "I must check on the press. See you tomorrow."

He was gone before she could protest.

The afternoon sun was shining over Chicago's skyline when Laurel walked outside with both packages and her reticule containing Ridge's letter. She was used to controlling her own life, and yet in the last few hours two men had unexpectedly thrust unusual projects upon her with the expectation that she would accept them. That, along with Ridge's letter, troubled her.

A desire to read it again prompted her to hail another hack for the short ride to her father's home. She slipped up the back stairs, carefully avoiding her father and Maggie, his long-time servant. In the privacy of the bedchamber where she had grown up, Laurel removed Ridge's letter from her bag. She hung it by the drawstring beside her cloak on the back of the door. Dropping the two packages on the high four-poster bed, she jumped up to sit on its edge. Her feet dangled above the floor.

In spite of how they had parted, she felt a warm glow seep over her as she sat under the bed's white canopy and thoughtfully reread Ridge's words.

I've been in your home and met your

family. As you know, I have none, but I very much want you to come visit me. I know it's presumptuous, but I want to show you where my ancestral home stood before the war, so we can have a better understanding of each other.

Laurel frowned, wondering again if he could be hinting at asking her to marry him. "No," she exclaimed to herself. "We can't even get through a few hours together without getting into a disagreement."

Aware that she had spoken aloud, she shook her head and let her thoughts continue. *Besides, we're so opposite in everything. He was a Rebel; I a Yankee. In fact, we have nothing in common. Well, except . . . why can't we just walk away from each other and stay away?*

Shaking brunette curls that bounced against her neck, she read on. *A wonderful woman who was my mother's best friend and my sort of honorary aunt has offered to open their home to you and your chaperon. I will meet you at the cars. Please wire me at the above address with date and time of arrival.*

Laurel whispered fiercely to herself, "He seems mighty sure I'll come!" She tossed the letter beside the two packages and glared at them. "What is it about all these men? They tell me what they want, and just assume I'll do it!"

She looked up at the sound of a knock at her chamber door. She reached out to slide the letter under a pillow, then checked herself. At twenty, she didn't need to act like a schoolgirl. "Come in."

Her father opened the door. Though sixty-one, there was no excess weight on his six-foot frame. His gray hair had receded to the middle of his scalp, however. He said, "Maggie told me that she saw you going up the back way."

Laurel carried the letter with her while walking over to give him a kiss on his clean-shaven cheek. "I just needed to think."

Hiram Bartlett had become wealthy by manufacturing iron wheels and other parts for the Union railroad's rolling stock used in the war. He regarded his youngest daughter with shrewd blue eyes. "Must be something serious."

"Nothing I can't handle," she assured him.

He slipped an arm around her and grinned. "If you ever have a coat of arms, that will be your motto."

Laurel smiled fondly at him. "Aunt Agnes always said I was born a rebel."

"My sister's unsolicited opinions have kept her a spinster, as I've often told her.

Speaking of rebels, Maggie told me that yesterday a letter arrived here from your Virginia friend."

That was true. The impertinent long-time Bartlett servant had brought it to Laurel, holding it between thumb and forefinger. The other fingers had been held out straight as if to avoid contamination. Maggie hadn't liked Ridge from the first time he showed up at the front door still wearing his Confederate cavalry uniform.

Laurel knew that her father's comment was intended to open a discussion which could only lead to another clash of wills. She didn't want that, so she replied, "I don't want to talk about it."

"That's fine, but just remember I love you, and I'm only trying to look out for your best interests."

"I know, Papa." She gave him another quick kiss on the cheek. "But if Harriet and Emma think I told you what was in that letter, they'll try to make you tell. When you won't, they'll be angry with you. So let's save both of us some grief and forget it."

A woman's voice from outside the open door asked, "Forget what?"

Laurel turned to see her oldest sister entering the room with dark eyes narrowed suspiciously. Emma was married with five preteen children, but her abrasive personality was similar to Aunt Agnes's.

Laurel said, "Nothing that need concern you, Emma."

Their father said, "Good afternoon, Emma. Did you bring my grandchildren with you?"

"Hello, Papa. No, they're at home." She turned back to Laurel. "I know what you were talking about." She pointed to the pages in Laurel's hand. "Maggie told me that you got a letter from that traitor."

Laurel bristled defensively. "He is not a traitor!"

"Now, now!" their father cautioned. "Let's remember you're not little girls anymore."

Laurel flared, "I'm not going to let her get away with misrepresenting Ridge's patriotism! He fought for the South because that's his home, and he believed he had a right to protect it. He lost everything in the world except his life, so watch what you say, Emma!"

She answered quietly, "No need to snap my head off. But there are lots of decent Union men back from the war. You know there's no way you and a Rebel could ever be happy together, so why not —"

"That's enough, Emma!" their father said

sternly. "The war is over! I will not have quarreling in this house over the past!"

Laurel gave him a grateful glance. "Thank you, Papa. Emma, I'm sorry about this." She snatched her cloak and reticule from the back of the door and pulled herself up to her full height of five feet and one-half inch. "I'll talk to you both another time."

"Why are you so defensive?" Emma demanded, following Laurel through the door and into the upstairs hallway. "What did he say in his letter that makes you get your back up like this?"

"It's none of . . ." Laurel caught her father's hurt, displeased look. She checked herself and took a deep breath. It would serve Emma right to give her another shock. "If you must know, he invited me to visit him."

Emma's eyes widened in disbelief. "No! You're not serious?"

Laurel started down the stairs. "Oh, yes! Furthermore, I'm thinking of accepting!" It wasn't something she had really considered, but in the heat of the moment, Laurel knew it would further irritate her over-bearing big sister.

Emma followed down the steps. "That would disgrace the family again as you did when you kept disappearing during the war!"

Laurel flinched at the old accusations. None of her family knew that she had been a Federal spy whose work took her behind Confederate lines.

"Stop it! Both of you!" their father ordered.

At the bottom of the stairs, Laurel turned to face her parent and sister. With forced calmness, Laurel declared, "I've told both of you before that I never did anything to disgrace our family. That's still true."

Emma asked more quietly, "Then why won't you tell us where you were all those times if you weren't dallying with some soldier?"

"Emma!" Her father spoke sharply. "She's of age, and doesn't owe either of us an explanation. Laurel, I take you at your word. Emma, that should be enough for you, too."

Laurel gave him a faint smile. "Thanks again, Papa. Now, if you'll both excuse me, I've got something to do."

Now I've done it! Laurel chided herself as she walked briskly along under leafless trees that had not yet begun to feel the hint of coming spring. After leaving home two years ago, she had rented a small apartment which a widow had built into her large old home during the war.

Laurel told herself, *Now that I've told Papa and Emma that I'm going to visit Ridge, I've got to go through with it. That means I'll have to have a chaperon. Even Papa wouldn't knowingly want me to go off alone to Virginia, but where can I get someone?*

By now Emma would probably already be on her way over to tell their middle sister, Harriet, about Laurel's scandalous plan to visit a man out of state, and a one-time Rebel at that.

That meant everyone at church would know, too, because Emma would find a way to spread the word there.

Raising her eyes, Laurel sought out the steeple of the church which she had attended as a girl. She had cut ties with her faith about five years ago, then made a recommitment shortly after meeting Ridge. Since then, her desire to live up to that commitment had conflicted with the deceit and downright lies that her secret detective work required.

Most of all, Laurel was uncomfortable with keeping the truth from Ridge. She had often asked herself how they could ever expect to have a proper relationship when she was dishonest in that area of her life? But she couldn't tell him, and that was an ir-

23

ritation to her conscience.

"Laurel! Wait up!"

The call from behind made her turn. She stopped as her father hurried toward her, buttoning his heavy coat.

"Something wrong?" she asked, starting toward him.

"I have to talk to you."

She had guessed why before they were close enough to speak in normal tones. She steeled herself to deal calmly with him.

She spoke first. "I'm sorry about that scene with Emma. I just couldn't keep quiet when she started saying things that were unfair."

"I know." He slipped her arm though his and continued walking the direction she had been going. "I'm not here to talk about that. A father still has to look out for his daughter, even when she's grown, and even if she does think she can take care of herself."

Light laughter bubbled from Laurel. "You sound just like Ridge. He's said the same thing to me a couple of times."

"I suppose he offered to do that?"

"Not really. I once teasingly asked him if he wanted that job, but he sidestepped a direct answer."

"Do you like him, Laurel?"

She hesitated before answering. "I'm very attracted to him. Oh, I know we're not at all alike, and we seem to always end up with some kind of disagreement and part in either anger or pain. But we always seem to get over those things and want to see each other again."

"Do you think he's an honorable person?"

"I've no doubt of it, Papa."

"Do you realize what it usually means when an eligible young man asks a woman to visit him?"

"I've thought he might be thinking of getting serious, but it's soon for that."

"Maybe for you, but maybe not for him."

Laurel stopped to look up at her father's eyes, now soft with concern. She admitted, "I hadn't thought of that. But I'm not ready, not sure, anyway, how I feel."

"You owe it to yourself to find out."

She cocked her head slightly. "Are you saying you think I should go?"

"How else will you learn how you really feel?" Her father started walking again.

Falling into step beside him, Laurel mused, "Knowing how you're always looking ahead, I suppose you've also thought about a proper chaperon. I have, too. My friend, Sarah Perkins . . . uh . . .

Skillens. She got married and probably is expecting a baby by now."

"Yes, she is," Laurel's father replied. "Didn't you hear from her while you were in Omaha?"

"I was too busy. I didn't write anyone except you, and you didn't mention the baby in your letters to me."

"You only wrote me twice in all that time." There was reproach in his voice. "Now Sarah and all the girls you grew up with are married, and most have started —"

"Don't say it, Papa!" Laurel broke in.

The same rebellious feelings that she had known for the last five years swept over her again. It was partly to show her father that she would not yield to his domineering ways that she had become a Union secret agent. Even though he didn't know about that, she had proven to herself that she was not like her sisters; she was her own person.

She continued indignantly, "My sisters and you are afraid I'm going to be an old maid like Aunt Agnes, but I won't. I just want to make sure I've found the right man."

"I'm sorry! I didn't mean to upset you," he said quietly. "In fact, while you were gone, I made up my mind to end this tension that's been between us."

She looked at him with softening feelings. "Really, Papa?"

"Really."

"I thought of the same thing in Omaha, but it's so easy to slip back into the old defensive emotions, like just now."

"We'll work on it together," he assured her. "I want us to be close, you and I. I don't doubt that one day you'll tire of running around and will marry some fine man who will make you happy."

She gave his arm a squeeze and whispered, "Oh, Papa, it's such a relief to find you open-minded and willing to talk to me, to really try understanding me."

"You're of age, so you can do what you want, but I love you and want to guide you without controlling you as I've tried to do in the past. That little scene awhile ago with Emma startled me, because for the first time, I saw myself in her. You're different, Laurel, and I don't want to change you, just help you if I can."

Taking a deep breath, Laurel said with relief, "I never really thought you approved of me."

"I sometimes didn't approve of what you did, like when you'd disappear for long periods during the war. But I always love you."

"You're going to make me cry."

He chuckled. "Don't do it yet."

She noticed his faint smile. "Oh? Why not?"

"Because your helpful sister has already gone to make arrangements for your traveling companion."

"Where would Emma get someone she approves of? Oh, no! Not Aunt Agnes!"

"She's not so bad —"

"Papa! She's a little old dried-up apple core of a woman with a bitter tongue. She'll drive Ridge away before I ever get a chance to talk with him!"

"I think that's what Emma hopes."

Laurel took a couple of agitated steps away, then spun back to face him. "Why am I concerned? Aunt Agnes won't go! She hardly leaves her house except for church."

"In spite of her tactless nature, Emma knows how to manipulate people. She'll convince my sister that the family's honor depends on her selfless devotion to duty. Agnes won't resist a challenge like that."

Laurel groaned, knowing her father was right. Aunt Agnes was the family's self-appointed guardian of morals, public and private. She would be the chaperon, and she would go prepared to keep a Rebel from ever getting too close to Laurel or disgracing the Bartlett family.

Her father put his arm around Laurel's shoulder. "Come back home and have supper with me. I'll walk you to your room later."

Laurel accepted, welcoming an opportunity to pursue continued restoration of her relationship with her father. The only irritation Laurel had was with Maggie's attitude. A matronly woman with graying brown hair, wearing a servant's black dress and white apron, she had been with the family so long she had grown impertinent. She didn't say anything, but repeatedly sniffed disapprovingly whenever Laurel mentioned Ridge.

When Maggie had cleared the table and retired, Laurel and her father moved to his library and sat down in leather chairs to talk more privately.

Laurel commented, "I never knew anyone who could say so much without opening her mouth."

"Don't let her bother you."

"I can't help it, Papa. Ridge told me what she said when he came here the first time before we had really met. He was wearing his Confederate uniform, so Maggie told him she was not going to talk to any Rebel, and if he didn't leave, she would set the dogs on him."

"We haven't had a dog since you were a girl."

"I know. Then when she brought me Ridge's letter, she carried it between thumb and forefinger and held it well away from her body, as though it were a dead mouse."

Laughing, Laurel's father said, "That's Maggie all right. You never have any doubts where you stand with her." Turning serious, he added, "I don't want you to have any doubts of where you stand with me, Laurel. I've been an autocratic father, but I love and trust you."

Laurel gave his arm a squeeze. "Thank you, Papa."

"You're of age, so you can go where you want, but because I love you, I just want to help."

She looked at him in thoughtful silence, wishing she could tell him about what she had done during the war, and that she was now secretly a detective. But that wasn't possible, and suddenly she felt more guilt. She was trying to live according to God's laws, and yet she was still living a double life and a lie.

"Papa," she said, "I'd love to stay and talk

freely with you, but I can't. Please take me home now."

He studied her in silence before nodding. "As your father, I accept you, no matter what you're not telling me. But if you're keeping things from Ridge, well, think about that."

Laurel's mental anguish increased as she and her father walked in silence the few short blocks to where she lived. She was in such deep thought that she was at her door before her father's startled voice aroused her.

"Laurel, did you leave your door open?"

"No, of course . . . oh!" She saw that the lock had been broken and the door stood half open.

"Stay back!" Her father cautiously approached and listened before striking a match.

Laurel moved up behind him so that when the light flared, illuminating the small room, she took one look and gasped. "Oh, my!"

The place was a shambles.

CHAPTER 2

Laurel's father hurriedly lit a kerosene lamp and carefully searched the room and closet. Laurel then picked her way through the mess of overturned furniture, opened drawers, and strewn clothing to begin an inventory. When she had finished, she shook her head slowly.

"Everything seems to be here: clothes, my watch, and even the two gold double eagles and a couple of greenbacks I had in my undergarments drawer."

"This doesn't make sense," her father said, righting a couple of chairs. "There's not a drawer that hasn't been dumped out, and not a thing that hasn't been opened and rummaged through. So if your watch and money weren't taken, whoever did this was after something else. But what?"

She replied honestly, "I can't think of anything."

"Could it have something to do with your periods of absence during the war?"

She considered that, but could not understand how anything from her war-time activities could be popping up now, a year after Lee surrendered at Appomattox. Yet that was possible because of the very nature of undercover work. There was always a minor fear that some of her spying activities would reach out from the past and touch her. That had happened with Ridge. It might happen again.

"I don't think so, Papa," she finally assured him.

"What about recently? Has there been anything that? . . ."

Laurel didn't hear the rest. *The package Pinkerton gave me!*

Her father prodded. "What?"

Laurel shook her head as her thoughts raced on. *No. Can't be. Nobody knows about that. But what about the one Mr. Seymour handed me? One man came in while I was there.*

"Tell me; what did you think of?"

"Oh, nothing, Papa."

"Don't tell me that!" His voice rose sharply. "I can see it in your eyes."

"I . . . I can't tell you."

"Can't, or won't?" There was hurt in his tone.

She hesitated as guilt again gripped her heart. She didn't want to even misdirect her father by manipulating her words, but she couldn't tell him about either package.

"Are you going to tell me or not?"

Her father's hurt tone touched her. She reached out imploringly. "It's something I can't discuss."

"Are you in some kind of trouble?"

"No, no, nothing like that," she said truthfully.

"We had such a good talk this evening, I hoped we had put our differences behind us. But I guess I was wrong."

"Papa, please try to understand —"

"Oh, I do!" he interrupted brusquely. "At least, I understand enough to know that you're shutting me out of a part of your life where I might be able to help you."

Laurel started to protest, but he turned toward the door. "Let's go talk to your landlady." There was sadness in his voice. "Then I'll walk you back to the house so you can sleep in your old room tonight. You can't risk staying here. Whoever broke in might come back and try to make you tell what you won't tell your father!"

That possibility troubled Laurel as she followed him from the room at the back of the house to the side door where she told her landlady about the break-in. She said she hadn't heard a thing. Neither had the newly-married couple who rented a room on the far side of the house.

Laurel, anxious to examine the packages

Pinkerton and Seymour had given her, secured her door and returned with her father to spend the night in her old bedchamber. Alone, she carried the lamp to the marble-topped nightstand and glanced at the packages on her bed.

She pulled off her shoes and swung her legs up on the bed without undressing. She reached for the package Seymour had given her. Only two people had entered the publisher's office while she was with him. Neither had stayed more than a few seconds.

The one who had mentioned the horse-whipping incident hadn't spoken to her. At that time, Laurel recalled that Seymour had not produced the package she now held. The man who had reported the press breakdown had come in just after the package was removed from the safe.

Could it be him? Laurel wondered, opening the package. She carefully removed a sheath of old newspaper clippings, recalling what Seymour had told her. *A major story requiring delicacy and discretion. An unsolved murder. A possible witness now in California who might be able to identify who was responsible.*

"Find and interview him," Laurel softly repeated Seymour's words. "Try to get him to tell what he saw."

She skimmed the old clippings, grasping the basics. Shortly after Fort Sumter was fired on in mid-April, '61, a Chicago wholesale meat processor named Oglesby who sold his product to the Union army had been found dead in his office. A passerby claimed in an anonymous letter to police that he had seen two men arguing with the victim before one struck him with a blunt instrument. Both men fled the scene.

The witness had never been located, but authorities had found a photograph outside the window where the witness claimed to have been standing. Police were unable to locate or identify the man in the picture, leading them to speculate that the letter might be a hoax. But it was considered more likely that the letter was true, and the writer had fled to parts unknown in fear of his life.

Disappointed in the meager details, Laurel finished the final clipping and sighed. The victim's name meant nothing to her, and obviously the breaking war news had forced the story out of future editions. But why had the editor saved the clippings in his office safe instead of the newspaper's normal story morgue?

She left the clippings spread on the bed beside her and lay down, gazing unseeingly at the white overhead canopy. *What connec-*

tion is there to this story and somebody breaking into my place trying to recover this package? There's nothing here that couldn't be found in the newspaper's own files. Or am I overlooking something?

She was intrigued, but an answer eluded her, so after a couple of minutes she sat up and started to replace the clippings in the envelope. They caught on something which Laurel shook out: a small photograph previously overlooked.

A thin-faced man with clean-shaven cheeks, no mustache, but rounded dark chin whiskers and heavy black hair falling across his ears stared back at her. He had an unusual amount of hair which seemed almost piled up on the right side. There was no identification except for the Union uniform with buttons down the front. He was obviously an officer, but Laurel couldn't make out the rank on his shoulder bars.

She decided that the uniform meant the portrait had been taken during the war, so this was not the victim. Probably the witness. But why was there no name on the photograph? Laurel had been around a newspaper office often enough to know that pictures were always promptly marked upon receipt. So why was there an exception here?

Well, it doesn't matter. When I tell Pinkerton

that I'm going to see Ridge, he'll withdraw his California offer. Since I'm going, I'll give this back to Seymour. But I will ask him about the picture.

Replacing it, Laurel glanced at the package Pinkerton had given her. Now that she wasn't going to take his assignment, there was really no reason to examine the contents of his package. Still, her curiosity made her open it.

There were several newspaper clippings about the origin and development of the transcontinental railroad. Separate printed biographies were included on the principal men behind the project. Laurel skimmed the familiar names connected with the Central Pacific in Sacramento and the Union Pacific in the mid-west.

Laurel didn't know whether any particular railroad company had hired Pinkerton, but that didn't matter. He wanted to know if there was a conspiracy to stop construction of the rails. Pinkerton had named five possible companies that would lose heavily if the railroad succeeded.

Laurel could easily understand how the railroad would hurt earnings of stagecoach and mail lines, steamship and freight companies. But the shipping of glacier ice from Alaska intrigued her. She had never been to

California, but she was quite sure that, unlike the perpetual Alaskan glaciers she had read about, snow in the high Sierra Nevada Mountains melted every summer. She puzzled over that, then read short histories of various companies and what efforts had been made to stop the railroad project.

Mostly, Laurel silently summarized her findings, *there have been several attempts to discredit the railroads, but nowhere do I see anything to suggest forcibly or illegally trying to stop them. This would be a hard case, so it's just as well that I've decided to turn down Pinkerton. Still, both this case and the story Seymour wants really appeal to me. Oh, well . . .*

Shrugging in resignation, she replaced Pinkerton's papers into the envelope and let her thoughts wander to Ridge. Had she made a mistake in deciding to accept his invitation? Would they get along, especially with Aunt Agnes there trying to end their young relationship?

Laurel prepared for bed and tried to read her Bible, but it wasn't a habit, and her thoughts kept drifting. She gave up, blew out the lamp, and slid under the covers. Tomorrow she would return both packages, then make plans to travel to Richmond with Aunt Agnes.

The cost would hurt Laurel, especially now that she would have no way of making extra money to replace her modest savings. Well, that couldn't be helped. She would wire Ridge when to expect them. Laurel fell asleep wondering if he was as concerned as she was about what would result from her visit.

Ridge Granger absently felt the saber scar that ran across the bridge of his nose and right cheekbone. He reached into his pocket and fingered the gold Indian head dollars there. Making a decision, he quit pacing the room he rented at Templeton Hall and walked out the door into the crisp night air.

"I wish she would answer," he muttered to himself, following the graveled path between rows of tangled ivy and box hedges surrounding the battle-shattered old farm house on Virginia's peninsula. He consciously tried to minimize the limp where a Federal minié ball had lodged in his left leg during his Confederate cavalry days.

He passed the frame section of the house which had been built forty years before. Invading Yankees had scorched its south side and burned all the outbuildings to the ground. On the north, the main part of the house was constructed of bricks. They had been added a couple of decades before General George McClellan and his hundred thousand blue coats had overrun the peninsula in a vain effort to seize the Confederate capital at Richmond in '62.

A slender older woman with gray hair parted in the middle and pulled back into a bun opened the front door just enough to peer out.

"Oh, Ridge!" she exclaimed with relief. "Please come in. I'm still not used to seeing a friendly face instead of those awful savages when there's a knock at my door."

"I came to pay the rent, Mrs. Ashby," he said, stepping into the room. He could not help but recall with pain the elegant furnishings and glistening silver serving sets that had graced the room when he and his mother visited here just six years ago.

Now only an old horsehair sofa with sagging springs and two battered ladder-back wooden chairs remained in front of the blazing fireplace. One coal oil lamp with blackened glass chimney cast a pale yellow glow from its wall bracket. The room seem darker and colder than it used to be.

Ridge pulled out the specie and began counting them into her hand.

She protested, "Oh, my, you don't need

to do that tonight. It's not due until day-after-tomorrow."

"They weigh my pocket down," he said with a grin.

"Thank you." She placed the coins on the mantle and smiled in understanding. "You mean you hoped that I might have heard something from your Yankee lady friend since you asked a few hours ago."

"Is it that obvious?"

"It is." She motioned for him to have a seat by the fireplace. "But you know there can't be any word before tomorrow, so maybe you'd like to talk with me instead."

She paused for the length of a heartbeat before asking, "Would you like some tea?"

"No, thanks, but I could stay a few minutes."

He waited until she sat on the end of the sofa nearest the fire before he eased into the wooden chair facing her. "It does get lonesome in my room," he admitted.

She adjusted wire-rimmed spectacles on her nose and picked up a faded dress from the sofa's arm. She slipped her finger into a thimble and plucked a needle from a pin cushion. "I wish your parents could be here to meet Laurel."

Ridge sighed deeply. "Yes. I wish they could too, but I'd still want her to meet you."

"What if I don't like her?"

He grinned, "You'd hide it like the Southern lady you are, and she would love you as I do."

"Save your sweet talk for her," she said, glancing at him over the top of her spectacles. "Tell me more about what you've been doing to help build that new transcontinental railroad out of Omaha."

"I'm not doing much to build it. Mostly, I do guard work to keep thieves from making off with railroad supplies and that sort of thing."

"Doesn't sound very exciting, Ridge."

"It isn't, but it's better than getting shot at by bluecoats. Besides, it pays well. But my only interest right now is in having Laurel get here."

"What if she doesn't come?"

"I try to not think about that."

"Even though she's a Yankee, she would be a fool not to try landing a fine, handsome man like you."

"Now you're teasing me again, as when I was a boy."

"Am I?" She lowered the sewing to her lap and studied him thoughtfully. "Let's see. You're just under six-feet tall and quite fit. Age twenty-two —"

"Twenty-three."

"Anyway, you've got nice medium-brown hair with a slight tendency to wave. Girls like to run their fingers through that. Even Varina . . . oops! Sorry!"

"It's all right, Mrs. Ashby," he said with a shrug.

Varina Owens had promised she would wait for him until the war was over. "She had a right to change her mind."

"She should have been horse whipped! Thomas Sedgeworth was twenty years her senior. But I guess the chance to marry into money was too much of a temptation. I mean, him being a widower with no children, Varina inherited it all."

Ridge shifted uncomfortably. "Let's change the subject."

She didn't seem to hear him. "I notice she didn't do that until after those savages from up north burned your place to the ground. But she doesn't know you as I do. I've told everyone that someday you'll get it back from those thieving Yankees, and you'll be more wealthy than Thomas Sedgeworth ever dreamed of being."

"Please," Ridge urged. "Let's forget it."

"I can't. When you two were growing up, everyone was sure you were just right for each other. Well, it may not be a very Christian thing to say, but what good did it do her to marry him? Not even married a year —"

"Please, Mrs. Ashby, let it go."

She heaved a heavy sigh before slowly nodding. "All right, but I know what it's like being a widow, although I was a lot older when my Harold passed on. Varina can't be much over twenty, and already alone and childless."

"She's nineteen, and that's the last word I want to hear about her or I'm going back to my room."

"Very well. I can take a hint." She resumed her sewing. "Is your Yankee lady friend concerned about your limp?"

Ridge didn't want to talk about that. Laurel had confessed to him that it was one of her war-time spying activities that had set up the Federal ambush which caused his leg wound. "She accepts it."

"You said she was a newspaper correspondent?"

"Yes, for the *Chicago Globe*."

"The only woman I ever heard about who did that sort of thing was Eugenia Benson, who worked for the *Illustrated Newspaper*. I first heard about her when she sketched the bombardment of Fort Sumter at the start of the war."

Mrs. Ashby paused, then asked, "What

kind of a woman goes off to do dangerous things like that?"

"Very special women, if they're like Laurel. Strong-minded, rather independent, self-reliant."

"You sure she's as pretty as you say?"

"Even more so, and saucy, too. Lots of spirit."

"With beauty and all those characteristics, I would think she'd be quite a handful."

"She is, but . . ." he trailed off as someone knocked at the door. "Who would come calling this time of the evening? Do you want me to get it?"

"Would you? Even though the war's been over a year, I still feel anxious, expecting it to be another one of those Yankees wanting to steal something else from me."

Ridge quickly crossed to the door as the knocking continued. He opened it and stared in surprise. "Varina!"

Varina Owens Sedgeworth's beautiful face was framed by golden Grecian curls which made her blue eyes seem larger than Ridge remembered. The traditional widow's veil had been thrown back so that the somber black mourning garment accented her fair skin and high cheekbones.

"Oh!" she exclaimed, drawing back

slightly, her right hand fluttering to her throat. "Ridge!"

He said nothing, but stared at her, aware of an old feeling that had so often roused him in their courting days. He watched the long, tapering fingers moving in that same slow way that had often caressed his cheek instead of her own white throat.

"Oh, mercy!" Varina exclaimed with a light laugh and a quick smile. "I wasn't expecting you!"

"Same here," he replied stiffly.

Mrs. Ashby called, "Ridge, either invite her in or step aside so she can come in before all the heat drains out into the cold."

"Sorry," Ridge apologized, opening the door wider. "Come in. I was just leaving."

"Oh, no, please don't let me run you off!" Her words were soft and low, carrying a hint of the slow speech pattern common to many well-bred young Southern women.

Ridge hesitated, feeling a mixture of longing and pain. "Let me take your cloak."

"Thank you." She turned so he could lift the heavy black garment from her shoulders.

He caught a faint fragrance of lilacs which had been so much a part of her.

The landlady said, "Please sit down, Varina."

"No, thanks." She turned her eyes toward the older woman. "I was on my way home when a wheel on my carriage came loose and began to wobble. I was fearful of an accident, so I stopped to ask if I could borrow your runabout to get home. I'll return it tomorrow."

"Certainly." Mrs. Ashby put her sewing aside and stood. "I keep a spare lantern on the side porch." She walked across the wooden floor and out of the room.

Varina called after her, "I really appreciate that."

Mrs. Ashby's footsteps faded, but she didn't answer, leaving Ridge and Varina alone.

For a few seconds, they stood in strained silence, avoiding each other's eyes.

"Well," Ridge finally said. "How've you been?"

She turned from seeming to study the room's meager furnishings to face him. "I'm getting by."

"I was sorry to hear about your husband."

"Thank you. It was such a shock, you know. Thomas had driven that same team and carriage for years before we were married. Then one night just before Christmas the wheel hit a hole in the road and overturned. The team ran away . . ." She sighed gently but didn't finish the thought.

Ridge had heard about the fatal head injury. Sedgeworth had been thrown against a massive tree trunk.

"How about you, Ridge?" Varina's eyes briefly rested on his facial scar, but she didn't look down at his leg. "Have you completely recovered from your war wound?"

"I'm as back to normal as is possible."

Another awkward silence followed with neither seeming to know what to say until Mrs. Ashby returned with a lantern. She said, "Varina, I wonder if your rearing included learning how to unhitch a horse from one carriage and harness it to another at night?"

"Oh! I hadn't thought of that."

Ridge caught a faint, unlady-like snort of doubt from the landlady. He quickly told Varina, "I'll give you a hand with that."

"Oh, I couldn't ask you to —"

"Nonsense, Varina!" the older woman broke in sharply. "Your hands would be torn up, not to mention the mess that would be made of your widow's weeds. Ridge, light this lantern and go along with her."

Nodding, he curled his fingers around the wire handle and accepted the match she also offered him.

"But first," Mrs. Ashby continued, "you

had better run back to your room and get a coat. It could be quite chilly out there before you get warmed up from all the changing that's going on."

Something in her voice warned him that she meant more than she said, but when he looked at her, she just smiled and said, "Hurry back."

He nodded and raised the glass chimney by the dry metal thumb latch. It squealed from rust and disuse. He struck the match, noticing Varina finally accept Mrs. Ashby's invitation to sit.

"I'll be right back," he said, stepping outside with the light and closing the door. He stopped in the crisp air while his mind raced back over the years with Varina.

Slowly, a strange feeling came over him. It was similar to what he had sometimes experienced on the night before he knew that he was about to ride into a battle with his cavalry troop where the outcome was uncertain. Taking a deep breath, he headed back down the graveled path.

"Laurel," he whispered, "you'd better answer soon."

CHAPTER 3

Even back in her childhood bedroom, Laurel couldn't sleep for hours. The more she thought about the break-in at her rented residence, the more violated she felt. The sense of defilement came from knowing that someone had handled her most intimate articles. But who?

When she went down to breakfast with her father the next morning, she found he had been thinking about the same thing. He waited until Maggie had served them and left the room before he brought up the subject.

"At the risk of having you think I'm interfering in the life of my grown daughter, I don't think you should return to your rented room."

There would have been a time that Laurel would have objected to this counsel, but not this time. "Maybe you're right. I'll look for another place."

"You could move back here. I'll help you."

She caught a note of hope in his tone and smiled her gratitude. "Thanks, Papa.

Maybe for a few nights until I can find something else."

"Good! I'll go with you to help straighten up the mess, then bring your belongings here."

"I appreciate that, but it will have to be later in the day. I've got some important errands to run first."

"Oh, yes, about your trip plans. Well, after you went to bed last night, I went over to talk to my sister about possibly being your traveling companion. She should arrive shortly."

Laurel smiled at the delicate way he had avoided using the word, chaperon. "All right, but it will have to be a short meeting."

"Don't be impatient with Agnes. For everyone's sake, she should go with you on this trip."

Laurel asked teasingly, "Even though she's got all the family's blessings to make sure my friendship with Ridge doesn't get patched up?"

"I'm on your side, remember? I think Harriet is, too, but she's not inclined to clash openly with Emma or your aunt."

"It's too bad that Harriet can't go, but with her little ones . . . If Mama were still alive —"

"I know," her father interrupted. "I still

miss Naomi, even after all these years."

Father and daughter lapsed into thoughtful silences before Laurel spoke again. "Don't worry, Papa. I'll try to get along with Aunt Agnes."

A short time later, Laurel was mentally prepared for the arrival of her reed-thin aunt. She blew in like a puff of cold wind, wearing her usual out-of-style clothes, and walking with her nose slightly elevated as though she smelled something unpleasant.

"Mercy!" Agnes exclaimed, turning cold blue eyes on her niece. "I've been thinking about what Hiram told me about the break-in at your room last night. I'm sure it was one of those philandering men you've consorted with."

Laurel felt her stomach lurch and bitter words erupted from her lips. "Aunt Agnes, you have absolutely no right to assume such a thing! I've told you before that I have not done anything to disgrace this family, and yet you insist on treating me like a scarlet woman!"

"Easy, Laurel!" her father cautioned, reaching out to grip her forearm. "Agnes, your remark was uncalled for. I admit having been judgmental during the war when Laurel kept disappearing, but that's over."

"Well, Hiram," Agnes finally said to her brother, looking away from him and back to Laurel, "in the interest of family harmony, I'll try to keep my opinions more to myself."

The possibility that Agnes might actually do that was so ludicrous that Laurel almost laughed in spite of the tenseness of the moment. Yet she replied in a controlled and respectful tone, "Thank you."

"Yes," her father added, "thank you, Agnes."

"You're both welcome, but . . ." she paused, a glitter of defiance in her eyes, "that doesn't apply if anything improper happens while I'm acting as chaperon."

Laurel said gravely, "I have no intention of letting anything happen to disturb your moral sensitivities."

Mollified, the older woman nodded. "Very well, then let's discuss the details of what's involved in this venture into Rebel country."

Instantly, Laurel rankled. "You will please not refer to the South as 'rebel.' The war is over; the Confederacy lost, and citizens there have taken the oath of loyalty to the Union. We are one nation again, so there is no 'rebel' country."

For a moment, Laurel thought her aunt was going to flare up again, but she took a slow breath and nodded. "Well, if you don't care for any of those nice Union soldiers who have returned from the war, then tell me more about your . . . uh . . . this Virginia man."

Hiram Bartlett said, "I'm sure Laurel has already told you about meeting him when he came here months ago, and I've told you I liked him even if Emma and Maggie didn't."

Agnes made an unlady-like snorting sound. "That's because he is the first one that Laurel couldn't wrap around her little finger. But I want to hear Laurel's thoughts about this man."

"Ridge," Laurel said crisply. "His name is Ridge Granger." She wondered if maybe her father was right about why Ridge was different. He was not subject to her easy smile and charm as other men were. But it was more than that, Laurel knew; there were many factors that attracted her to him.

She explained, "He was a third generation planter in his family. They grew tobacco until invading Union troops burned the house to the ground, destroyed the crops, and confiscated the property. His family is all dead."

"I see." Agnes scowled as though in thought. "But I don't understand why you're going to travel all that distance to see a man to whom you're not betrothed."

Laurel wasn't sure she understood that, either. Yet she had to see him in his own environment, with or without family. She had to know more about him, and the visit would give her an opportunity to meet people who had known him all his life.

Even Varina Owens, or whatever her last name is now. The thought surprised Laurel. But who else would know more about a man than the woman to whom he had been engaged? A conversation with Varina would be fascinating, yet Laurel's logic told her that she could not expect to have such a talk.

"Laurel?" Agnes interrupted her musings. "Aren't you going to answer my question?"

"I was just thinking about it. The truth is, I had not planned to go, but I have to, for several reasons, and all of them are personal. I trust you understand that."

For a moment, Laurel thought her aunt's sudden setting of the jaw meant trouble. But she relaxed and said, "I understand more than you know." Her voice was so soft that Laurel was surprised.

I wonder if she ever had a beau? I remember overhearing Papa once mention a man's name to her, but she jumped all over him, and he shut up.

Agnes added quickly, "Let's get to the point. My health is too fragile to undertake such an extensive trip for any other reason than to do my Christian duty by a member of my family. So I will go."

"I'm grateful," Laurel said, although she wasn't sure that she really meant that. If Agnes had turned her down, she would have a valid reason to decline Ridge's offer.

She continued, "I will pay your way out of money I've earned honestly, so I don't want any argument about that. Just tell me when you can leave."

"Tomorrow would be fine."

"Wonderful!" Laurel exclaimed. She would need today to return the packages to both Pinkerton and Seymour, pack, and make other last minute arrangements. "Now, if you will both excuse me, I'll check the train schedules to Richmond and wire Ridge."

Laurel was on her way to downtown Chicago with the packages when a wave of doubt overwhelmed her. *What in the world am I doing?* she asked herself.

Orville Seymour kept her waiting fifteen minutes and then glowered at her when she entered his smoke-filled office. "So," he said, putting his cigar into the ash try on his desk, "I see you've brought my material back."

She tried to ignore both the smell of smoke and his disapproving tone. "I'm sorry, but I've decided to go east for a while instead of to California." She extended the package toward him, but he did not reach for it. "I am curious about a couple of things, though," she commented.

"You mean the picture?" He reached for the cigar which emitted a thin blue line of smoke. He caught her disapproving look and replaced the cigar, then waved his hand through the smoke to disperse it. "That's the man I think might have witnessed the murder, or at least he has some knowledge about what happened. But he disappeared shortly after the event and hasn't been seen since then."

"Why doesn't the picture have a name on it?"

"Because I don't know his identity. I examined the shoulder insignia closely and determined that he was a colonel during the war. The reason I let you read all those clippings is because I recently saw a picture in a Sacramento newspaper that might be the same man. But he wasn't in uniform, so I can't be sure. However, if you went to the newspaper office there, maybe they could tell you where to find him. So I'm sorry you're not going."

"What did the newspaper say his name is?"

"It didn't. The picture was of a group of people, just a crowd gathered near the building of the railroad. But I know a former Chicago newspaper correspondent named Mark Gardner who's now working in Sacramento. He knows everyone and might be able to identify this unknown witness for you."

Laurel sighed gently. It sounded like a challenging case. Coupled with Pinkerton's secret assignment, a trip to California could be exciting. But seeing Ridge appealed to her more.

"Anyway," Seymour added, picking up the package and turning toward his safe. "If you change your mind, my offer still stands."

"Why are you so interested after all this time?"

Seymour didn't answer right away, but turned to open the safe. Laurel glanced through the large window at the men rushing around in the editorial department. Absently, she looked for the skinny dark-haired man called Dick who had entered the office yesterday when Seymour gave her the package, but he wasn't in sight.

A thought stabbed Laurel. Dick is the only one who saw Seymour give me that package yesterday. Could Dick have broken into my place to get it? He would have had more opportunities to steal it here . . . no, that's wrong. My room would be easier than breaking into a safe. My imagination is just running wild.

She briefly considered mentioning the break-in at her residence, but decided that Seymour might think she was accusing Dick. She had no reason to do that, so she waited silently for Seymour to deposit the package in the safe and close the heavy door.

He turned to Laurel and answered her last question. "My reason is personal."

"Meaning you don't want to tell me because I'm not going to try locating this missing witness?"

"What would be the point?"

"None, but why not hire a detective?"

"I've thought about it. The Pinkertons are the best, but they don't take murder or missing person cases."

Laurel was pleased that the agency was so well respected, yet she was slightly uncomfortable that even a knowledgeable person like a newspaper publisher had not guessed that was her occupation. She could keep secrets, but this one increasingly troubled her conscience.

Seymour continued, "Besides, it would cost too much to hire someone to travel two thousand miles to investigate a man who may or may not be the one in the photograph. And I can't justify sending a correspondent, so I'm right back where I started. Anyway, thanks for considering this."

Laurel left, glad to be out in the fresh air away from the cigar, although her curiosity was piqued about the mysterious missing witness. She made her way toward the all-seeing eye that marked Pinkerton's office.

She took the chair he indicated, but his eyes focused on the package even before she offered it to him.

"I'm sorry," she began, "but I've decided not to go to California."

He thoughtfully studied her face and absently stroked his beard before answering. "An employee does not usually turn down an assignment with impunity."

Laurel stiffened at the implied threat. "If you want my resignation, you've got it!"

Instantly, she regretted the outburst. She needed to support herself. Her hasty remark placed her income in jeopardy, and very few jobs were open to women.

Pinkerton leaned forward to rest his forearms on the desk. "That sounds as if you're seeking an excuse to leave this agency. Well, that won't work."

Laurel tried to suppress the sigh of relief that threatened to escape from her.

The famous detective continued, "You're a good operative, Laurel, with a solid record for achieving whatever goal I assign you." He hesitated before adding quietly, "Even though the railroad people are pushing me hard to get an agent off to Sacramento right away, I think you're the logical one to send. So I'll give you a few days to see your beau in Richmond."

She was startled. How did he know about that? she wondered, and instantly knew the answer. He spied on me! It was rumored among Pinkerton's agents that he sometimes had them kept under surveillance by fellow operatives.

She did not reply, but his eyes showed that he was obviously pleased by the reaction on her face.

He asked, "Well, how does that sound to you?"

It sounded fair, but she resented having someone check on her personal life. *How much more does he know?* she wondered. She chose her words carefully, hoping to show him where she stood and yet not close the door on continued employment. "I do not appreciate your looking into my private life."

A hint of smile showed through his beard. "It's your sauciness that distinguishes you from my other lady agents, but I assure you that I only do what I consider to be in your best interest."

"I don't see how my 'beau' as you put it, can be of any concern to anyone but me. Besides, he's not my beau; he's just a man I find interesting."

"Of course." Pinkerton's smile vanished and he was all serious business again. "Is there anything else you want to tell me?"

Laurel frowned. Was he hinting that he knew about the break-in last night? She had not reported the incident to the authorities, and so little time had elapsed it didn't seem possible he could have found out anything. *I wonder if he had something to do with it? No, that isn't Pinkerton's way.*

"Well?" he prompted. "Is there?"

She decided it was best to tell him about the break-in and to reassure him that nothing was missing. She said she had taken his package to her father's house, but she didn't mention that she had also had a package from Seymour.

"So," she concluded, "there probably is no connection, and you have the package back. It must have just been a coincidence."

He had stroked his beard and listened without comment, but Laurel could see concern in his eyes.

He said, "In this business, I've learned not to assume anything."

"Are you suggesting it might not have been coincidence?"

"I'm saying that it's safer to be concerned about many things, even those that might seem irrelevant."

"No one saw you give me that package yesterday, and I didn't tell anyone. So it's not logical that anyone broke into my place to recover it."

"I agree it's not logical. But as I told you in our meeting yesterday, there is a tremendous amount of money involved in the transcontinental railroad venture. Not just the profit the Central Pacific and Union Pacific stand to make, but those companies that are threatened by this project can lose their profits or even go bankrupt. That doesn't count the power that always follows money, and people hate to give up power once they've had it."

"You said yesterday that the jeopardy I would face in this case is nothing compared to what I had during the war. If I come back from Virginia and take this case, what risks are involved?"

"You'll be posing as a journalist, so, as before, you can ask questions without suspicion. The only possible danger would be if your real mission is discovered. But only you and I know that you're a detective, so how can anyone else find out?"

Laurel guiltily glanced away, knowing she had twice violated Pinkerton's strict rule about operatives keeping their occupation confidential. During the war, she had told her long-time friend Sarah, because Laurel needed Sarah's help with disguises and creating places to hide the military intelligence she gathered. Sarah had inadvertently let Laurel's secret slip to Ridge shortly after they met. To keep from losing him, Laurel admitted to Ridge that she had been a Union spy. But she had not told him about being a Pinkerton operative.

Laurel forced her thoughts back to answering Pinkerton's last question. "This isn't like the war where anyone caught spying faced hanging. If my California mission was discovered, how would that put me in danger?"

"Greed and power, Laurel. Those are really strong motivations. People sometimes take drastic action against anyone suspected of even threatening their means of creating great wealth and the power that goes with money. If the transcontinental railroad is completed, those men whose companies are threatened could be desperate, while the railroaders stand to become extremely wealthy and powerful."

"I hadn't thought of that," Laurel admitted.

"That's only looking at the corporate side," Pinkerton went on, his voice rising with enthusiasm. "But think of those other people who benefit if the railroad does go through. The whole future of this country depends on completion of rails connecting east and west. Think how many people will ride the cars to begin settling open land between here and the Pacific."

He paused, then rushed on. "It will be the end of the American frontier. Waves of immigrants will dwarf anything that has ever gone before. Cities will spring up all along the tracks because farmers and dealers can create profitable businesses through shipping their product by rail to distant markets. That means lots of money for countless people working in all kinds of occupations besides railroads."

Laurel could understand Pinkerton's enthusiasm for railroads because much of his income was derived from them. Yet from listening to her father over the years she knew that there was another side to each new enterprise.

She pointed out, "But others are threatened with going out of business and their workers losing jobs. Like those you mentioned yesterday: stage and mail coach lines, steamship and freighting companies, and even shippers of Alaskan glacier ice."

"That's true of them and other businesses. However, we don't know if they are involved in this obstruction case I'm sending you to investigate. It could be some other company. Of course, the railroaders already know where most of these companies stand, but it's crucial that the railroad people know all their opponents so they can take appropriate defensive action."

Laurel protested, "That sounds as if you're trying to place a heavy responsibility on me if I don't take this case."

"I'm trying to get you to see that you're the right person for this job. So I'll hold the position a few days until you return from Richmond. Fair enough?"

"Fair enough," Laurel agreed, standing.

Pinkerton also rose, saying, "Just a minute." He removed a small book from a shelf behind his chair. "You'll have time to read on the cars going to Virginia. Here. Take this. It'll help prepare you for Sacramento if you decide to go."

She accepted the book titled *A Brief History of Plans for a Transcontinental Railroad.* "All right," she replied. "Thanks. I'll let you know as soon as I can. Now I've got to send a wire."

She left to verify the train schedule for the next day, purchased two round trip tickets, and then stopped at the telegraph office. She wired Ridge the time of her arrival and train number, still concerned that she was doing the right thing. She wished she could see his reaction when he received the message.

Brickside Manor was one of the few grand old homes on the James River that had not been severely damaged by the invading Yankees. Ridge sat in a casual fan-backed chair under the ancient tulip poplar trees and gazed thoughtfully across the level lawn to the river's edge.

His companion broke the silence with a sigh. "It's been a long time, Ridge."

"A very long time, Griff," Ridge agreed,

turning to look at the young man with the heavy brush mustache sitting in the rolling chair beside him.

Ridge and Jubal Griffin had known each other since childhood. They were both about the same in build and height, but Ridge only limped from a war wound while Griffin would never walk again. He had returned from his infantry years in the Confederate army with a spinal wound which confined him to the chair.

Ridge reflected briefly on the fact that on humid summer days five years ago, he and Griffin had been fanned by young black servants who kept the flies and other insects away. That wouldn't happen now.

Ridge turned his head away from the peaceful water to admire the big house. The three-story brick structure with its great chimneys had survived without burning only because high-ranking Union officers had headquartered there, relegating Griffin's aging parents to one room on the top floor.

"I'm sure sorry they burned your house, Ridge."

"So am I."

"You going to try getting the land back to rebuild?"

"I've thought about it."

Griffin waited as though expecting Ridge to continue. When he didn't, Griffin commented, "Everyone expected you and Varina to be living there by now."

Ridge's jaw muscles twitched, but he didn't reply.

Griffin asked, "So when are you going to make up your mind?"

"Depends."

"On how your Yankee lady friend likes it around here?"

"I want her to see this whole area, and meet the people I've known all my life. See how she reacts."

"And how our people react to her?"

"That, too."

"What if it doesn't work out with her? Will you go it alone, or return to Omaha and follow the tracks west?"

Ridge ignored the question. He commented, "I'm very grateful to you and your parents for the hospitality extended to Laurel and her traveling companion."

Griffin looked down toward his stocking feet as though to avoid his friend's eyes. "They're as curious as I am about her. From what we've seen of Yankees, there's not much good we can say about them, so we're interested in how you found one that is different."

70

A slight frown touched Ridge's forehead. He studied his friend's downcast face, wondering if he was having regrets about having Laurel in their spacious home. "You can be honest with me, Griff," Ridge said evenly. "Are you or your folks having second thoughts about inviting her for these few days?"

"It's not that." He lifted his gaze to meet Ridge's. "It's none of our business, of course, but we wonder what would happen if you and this Northern woman became serious, really serious? Would she be happy among all of us? After all, there's probably not a family on this entire peninsula who hasn't lost at least one person to the invaders, or had someone return maimed. That's not counting what they did to most property."

He gripped the right three-foot-high wooden wheel and turned himself to face Ridge full-on. "We are a very polite culture, Ridge, but underneath the cordiality there will surely be bitterness, anger, or downright resentment. Are you both ready to face such attitudes?"

Ridge pondered the blunt words before answering. "I don't know. Naturally, I've thought about that, and tried to tell myself that if we care enough, we can overcome anything. Oh, I might lose some old friends, and that would hurt. But I could handle that. However, I'm not sure how Laurel will respond, or what I would do to protect her if she is rebuffed."

Griffin lightly brushed a forefinger down the heavy brush mustache. "There are those around here who believe you and Varina should still get together."

Ridge's forehead slid down into a scowl. "After what she did to me?" His voice was cold, hard. "No, Griff. I won't be made a fool of twice."

"I know how you must feel, but she can be a very determined woman."

"Oh, yes, determined to marry money when she got the chance, and to blazes with how I found out, or how I felt!"

"It was a terrible thing for her not to at least write and let you know before hearing it from the gossips in your outfit."

Ridge felt the old pain and shame begin to possess him. "Let's change the subject."

"Sure. But don't underestimate Varina."

In spite of his intentions to drop the topic, Ridge could not ignore his friend's last remark. "What are you trying to tell me?"

Griffin hesitated before answering. "Did you think that it was just coincidence that she showed up with carriage trouble last night outside your place?"

Ridge stirred slowly, shifting his weight to the chair arms as though to suddenly thrust himself up to his feet. He said harshly, "You'd better explain that, fast!"

"My mother heard it from some of her friends who —"

"Wait!" Ridge shoved himself upright onto the lawn. "Are you implying that Varina planned that, and that some of the other women knew of it in advance?"

Griffin paused before saying softly, "Don't be upset. She figures you've come back to regain and rebuild the plantation to what it once was. She is a young, beautiful widow with a practical side who —"

"That's enough!" Ridge turned and angrily stalked across the lawn to where his horse was tied. A fury suddenly burned inside him with an intensity he had not experienced since one of his cavalry messmates had read aloud from a letter he received from home. Varina had broken her word to Ridge and married Sedgeworth.

Griffin called, "I didn't mean to make you angry."

Ridge didn't answer but kept walking purposefully.

Griffin asked, "Where are you going?"

"To show somebody that I will not be manipulated!"

CHAPTER 4

Ridge had his fury over Varina under control by the time he rode down the peninsula and arrived at what was left of Hunter's Grove, the late Thomas Sedgeworth's plantation. He guided his horse along the gravel driveway under the ancient oaks now shattered by war.

Ridge dismounted in front of the two-story brick manor house with tall twin chimneys. The structure had five gables, seven identical upstairs windows, and six matching ones downstairs. He walked up to the unadorned door in the middle of the lower floor and pulled the bell. Thomas Sedgeworth had not been an ostentatious planter, although he once had the wealth to live any way he wanted.

High-ranking Union officers had lived there during the peninsula campaign, so the house showed no outward sign of the destruction which Federal troops had wreaked on the outbuildings. Most of those had been burned or torn apart.

An aging servant woman opened the door. Ridge recognized her as a slave who had been born and reared on that plantation. Unlike others after freedom, she had stayed on with her late master's new wife.

"Massa . . . uh . . . Mr. Granger!" she exclaimed, her smile showing in a warm welcome.

"Good afternoon, Tessie." He glanced beyond her, appalled at what he saw. Yankees had ransacked the interior of what had been a gracious home, destroying and defacing everything. The once-elegant curving staircase had splintered banisters. One newel post was missing. The parlor's wooden mantle was broken and the wall above blackened. A framed painting of Varina's grandmother had been smeared with soot. Chair legs were scratched and the cushions torn.

It was apparent that the war had left widowed Varina, like many Southerners, in dire circumstances with no resources to rebuild.

Breaking off his brief scrutiny of the interior, Ridge turned his eyes back to Tessie. "Is Varina home?"

"She down by da ribba." The smile widened. "She sho' goin' be tickled to see y'all."

Ridge was tempted to say that he doubted that, but he merely thanked her and walked around the house. His gaze swept the area.

The hedges were untended, the flower beds trampled, and all the peripheries were destroyed except for the necessary brick outhouse. The door sagged open, showing the small fireplace within.

In spite of the anger that had compelled him to rush here, Ridge suddenly felt concerned about Varina. She had never known anything but luxury in her growing-up years. Now, at not even twenty years old, she was widowed and in poverty. Yet she was proud enough that she had not given any indication of that in their brief meeting last night.

It was easy for Ridge to understand that her late husband had become like many men in the South: wealthy one day and financially ruined the next. Varina had inherited property without crops or laborers to work the land.

But, Ridge checked himself as his resolve softened toward her, *she has a roof over her head, and she still owns the land. That's more than I have.*

Instantly, he rebuked himself. He could regain everything if he wanted, but she couldn't, at least, not on her own. Before Ridge could rebuild, he would have to meet President Andrew Johnson's vindictive conditions against wealthy Southerners. Their property had been seized under the Union's wartime Confiscation Acts.

Ridge had choices, but Varina's only one was to remarry.

Ridge rounded the back corner of the house and saw her standing by the river, her back toward him. Without being aware of it, he caught his breath. She was a vision of antebellum beauty.

Almost from the time she entered her teens, she had been a striking girl. Now, she was stunning. She had replaced the black widow's weeds with a calico dress that accented her slender form and tiny waist. In spite of her money problems, she wore one of the new bustles just coming into style. The over-skirt was drawn up to show the pink-fringed petticoat underneath. No matter how poor she was, her pride managed to help her dress well.

Memories engulfed Ridge as he watched the long golden hair cascade down her back from under a wide-brimmed white hat. She moved one graceful hand there as a stray spring breeze grabbed the hat and threatened to blow it off. A moment later, Ridge caught her familiar lilac fragrance, and the memories became more painful.

As Varina moved gracefully toward the river's edge, Ridge started toward her, but stopped after one step.

His anger had vanished, leaving him strangely ill-at-ease. *I can't do it,* he told himself firmly. *I can't.*

Turning quickly, he retraced his steps across the untended lawn, around the house, and back to his horse. Ignoring the stiffness of his wounded leg, he mounted fast. Then he drummed his heels against the horse's flanks and galloped down the driveway under the war-torn trees. Reaching the public road, he thought he heard Varina's voice calling, but he did not look back.

When Laurel's errands were completed, she called on her childhood friend to tell her she was going to see Ridge. Sarah lived in the small frame home willed her by her late parents in one of Chicago's poorer districts.

Sarah, at twenty-two, was more buxom than ever in her approaching motherhood. Her dark hair, usually parted in the middle and severely pulled back in a knot, hung loosely over her shoulders.

As Laurel accepted the stiff-backed chair offered her in the small living room, she said honestly, "Sarah, you look positively wonderful."

"Thanks." Her gray eyes seemed to

shimmer with an inner light. She seated herself by the fireplace across from her guest before adding, "Except for my back aching, I have never felt better."

"When are you due?" Laurel asked.

"Middle of July." She reached out impulsively and took Laurel's hand. "This is the most marvelous experience of my life. I never dreamed it could be such a happy time. John, of course, is such a dear. He pampers me scandalously, but I love it."

Laurel had heard many of her friends speak of their feelings about the coming of their first child, but it had never touched her as it did with Sarah. As a plain-looking woman, she had never had many beaux. Laurel had been the opposite, yet she was the only unmarried one of those she had grown up with. That had never bothered her — until now. Abruptly, she wanted to get away from this environment of marriage and babies.

She freed her hand from Sarah's and said, "I can only stay a few minutes. I just got back in town and wanted to see you."

Sarah's eyes narrowed suspiciously. "You're off on another of your Pinkerton adventures, aren't you?" Without waiting for a reply, she added, "I read some of your pieces in the *Globe* about railroad building out of Omaha. I figured Allan Pinkerton had sent you there."

"It was an easy case."

"Did you see Ridge?"

"Yes. A few times."

"And?"

"Then he asked the railroad for time off to take care of some personal business in Virginia, and I came back to Chicago when I finished my case in Omaha."

"That's it?"

"Well, no, not quite. He asked me to come visit him so he could show me where his family's plantation had stood before the war."

A slow smile spread across Sarah's face. "That sounds serious."

"Not necessarily."

"But you've accepted, haven't you?"

"Yes. And at my family's insistence, Aunt Agnes is going with me."

Sarah laughed heartily. "That's funny." She choked off her laughter and leaned forward suddenly. "No, I'm wrong! That's bad! In fact, that's downright frightening! She will destroy any chance you and Ridge have of ever getting together."

"I would have preferred you as my traveling companion," Laurel admitted, "but when Papa told me about your baby, well, it was Agnes or nobody."

Sarah groaned and leaned back in her chair. "Oh, having her along is the worst thing! Unless —" she stopped abruptly. "Unless," she continued, "you have still kept any secrets from him."

Laurel didn't answer but looked away.

"I should have known!" Sarah exclaimed, throwing up her hands in disgust. "You haven't told him about being a lady Pinkerton, have you?"

"You know Pinkerton's rules on that. Besides, there's no reason to tell Ridge — at least, not yet."

Sarah warned, "If your relationship with him does get serious, you'll have to tell him, regardless of Pinkerton's rules. Not only that, how can you reconcile leading a double life?"

"I'm not leading a double life!"

"Aren't you?" Sarah asked quietly. "You were a spy during the war, pretending to be a Southern belle. Now you're a detective posing as a newspaper correspondent."

Laurel's conscience made her squirm uneasily. She was still unhappy that her sisters and aunt believed she had been dallying with soldiers during the war. Even now, she couldn't tell them the truth because of Pinkerton's rules.

Sarah continued, "I know what kind of a woman you are. I'm sure Ridge knows, too. But if he finds out that you've lied to him about what you really do —"

"I didn't lie!" Laurel broke in. "I told him I wrote for the *Globe*!"

"You're deliberately deceiving him! Where in the Bible does it say it's all right to do that?"

"You're starting to preach!" Laurel warned.

Sarah took a quick breath as though to reply, but slowly exhaled. "I don't mean to, but you are very special to me. I also like Ridge very much, and as I told you shortly after we met him, you shouldn't let him get away. That's why I want to see you be honest with him. Otherwise, you'll always be living under yesterday's shadows. Something could come out of them and hurt you worse than you can imagine."

"I am being honest. In fact, I'm not really sure how I feel about him. Sure, I'm very attracted to him —"

"And he is to you, too," Sarah broke in.

"Yes, I believe so. But until I know for sure how I feel, I don't want to tell Ridge about Pinkerton when it's not necessary. You know I can't work for him if I divulge what I'm doing. If I told Ridge something I shouldn't, and it doesn't work out for us, that would be even worse."

"You told him about your work in the war."

"That was different," Laurel said lamely. "I had no choice because of the circumstances."

"You always have a choice." Sarah's gray eyes locked onto Laurel's violet ones for a few seconds. "Well," Sarah added, changing her tone, "do you want to see the baby clothes I've been making?"

Laurel stood up. "Of course. Then I've got to get ready to leave for Richmond." She followed Sarah down the hall, but Laurel's thoughts were not on babies.

After Ridge received Laurel's telegram saying she was coming, he rode horseback to confirm the coming of his guests to Jubal Griffin and his parents.

Dismounting in front of the Griffin's three-story brick home, erected about 1750 in the classic Georgian style, Ridge hurried across the broad expanse of lawn toward his friend. He sat in his rolling chair outside the front door under great shade trees.

He asked, "How did your meeting go with Varina?"

Ridge had been expecting the question. "I

didn't speak to her." He produced the telegram to forestall any more questions. "Laurel arrives Friday afternoon on the cars. I want to inform your parents, and then I've got to ride into Richmond and get some decent clothes."

"Why waste your money that way? Save it, and borrow some of my clothes." He glanced at his useless legs, adding, "I won't need them."

"Thanks, but I —"

Griff interrupted, "No 'buts' about it. If you're going to regain your plantation, it'll take money. Railroad guards probably don't get paid so much that you can afford to waste what you earn. Show Laurel and her aunt a high old time, then save the rest in case you decide to regain your place."

Ridge hesitated, not wanting to borrow clothing.

Griff added quickly, "It's been five years since I last wore them, but they were new and stylish. Besides, nobody in the South today has money for new clothes. So I'd consider it a favor if you go through my closets and use what you want."

Ridge relented because he was practical, and Griff's suggestion made sense. "All right, if you insist, I'll see if I can find anything that will fit."

"Oh, anything I've got will fit you, but if you need a few changes, old mammy can . . . oops! Old habits die hard, you know. Now she's Aunt Betsy, but she can still fix anything."

"Thanks, Griff." Ridge laid a hand on his friend's shoulder. "I appreciate it."

"You can't bring two women and their baggage on horseback, so you'll need a carriage."

"I'm going to rent —"

"There you go, throwing money away again!" Griff shook his head in mock sorrow. "We've got one that the Yankees didn't steal because it was hidden in the woods. Take it, and the two sorry excuses for horses our Union visitors didn't take."

"Well," Ridge said, regretting that he could not meet Laurel with one of the matching teams and ornate coaches he had owned before the war. "Thanks, again."

"Glad to do it. Step inside and tell my parents, then let's you and I go down to the carriage house. I'll supervise the work while you clean up the carriage and curry the horses."

Ridge sensed that Griff was seeking a tactful way to again ask about Varina.

As heavy-set Aunt Betsy opened the door to Ridge's knock, he tried to anticipate how he would respond to Griff's questions. He didn't want to hurt his friend's feelings, but Ridge really didn't want to talk about it, with anyone.

The closer Laurel got to Richmond, the more her doubts grew about the wisdom of making this trip. Aunt Agnes had avoided adverse comments about Ridge, yet she had managed many negative opinions about Southerners, mixed in with complaints about the miserable conditions of traveling, especially south of the Mason-Dixon Line.

Northern railroads had suffered little war damage, but the South's lines had repeatedly been torn up. Rails had been heated over burning ties, then twisted around trees. Some lines had been repaired, but at times the two women had to leave the cars and take a stage to another rail line. Now, nearing the former capital of the Confederacy, they were on the train that would take them into Richmond.

Agnes looked out the window at the passing landscape while Laurel sat on the aisle seat and tried tuning out her aunt's incessant criticism. Laurel focused on what would happen with Ridge when they reached Richmond.

Would they still be drawn to each other as

strongly as before? How would his friends and neighbors treat her? What if someone recognized her from her spy work during the war? What if it didn't work out with Ridge, and she returned to Chicago in defeat? She would never hear the end of Aunt Agnes and Emma saying, "I told you so."

Going back to Chicago also meant she would have to take Pinkerton's assignment in California. Each time she thought about that, she remembered the ransacking of her room. She still could not believe that had been a random act by some burglar because nothing had been taken.

"Well," Agnes broke into her thoughts, "aren't you going to answer me?"

"I'm sorry." Laurel snapped her attention back to her aunt. "I was lost in thought."

"I said, 'Why do you suppose we've been passing mile after mile of tree stumps like those?'" She pointed through the window. "All the woods have been cut down."

Laurel's eyes swept the rural landscape. "I don't know for sure, but my guess is that they were used for firewood when the Union troops camped here. A hundred thousand men would need an awful lot of fuel for their campfires, their shelters, and so forth."

Agnes swiveled her head like an owl, eyes probing her niece's. "Why did you say 'the

Union troops' instead of 'ours'?"

"I don't know, but it doesn't matter."

"Doesn't it?" Agnes's voice was sharp, suspicious. "Are you starting to identify with these . . . uh . . . these people down here?"

Laurel's first reaction was to laugh because of the many times she had risked her life to gather military intelligence from "these people" during the war. Instead, she said, "The country is no longer divided. Before he was shot, President Lincoln said it was time to bind up the nation's wounds. So there are no longer 'our' people and theirs."

"You'll see that I'm right when we get there! Oh, they may spread their famous southern charm around as thick as molasses, but you can be sure that they're hiding their hatred for us!"

"I don't believe that."

"Then you're a little fool!"

Laurel's temper flared so suddenly that her aunt drew back even before Laurel spoke. "Don't you ever call me that again!" She jumped up in front of her seat.

Agnes asked, "Where are you going?"

"Anywhere!" In great agitation, Laurel stepped into the aisle without looking and bumped into a man behind her.

"I'm sorry," she said, turning briefly toward him.

She thought about Agnes's words as she paused to open the heavy door at the end of the car. *What if she's right? Maybe I shouldn't have come!*

An arm reached past her toward the door. "Allow me, Miss," the man said with a hint of southern drawl.

Laurel gave him an automatic smile. "Thank you." She looked a little more closely at the young man she'd bumped into just a moment before. She noticed that he was short and wore spectacles.

"My pleasure." He started to slide the door open, then stopped, looking closely at her. "Uh . . . I know this may sound trite, but haven't we met?"

She glanced at him again and shook her head. "I don't think so."

"Then please forgive me." He held the door. "I guess you just remind me of someone I met during the war."

Sudden alarm seized Laurel. She stepped onto the open platform and gripped the protective side railing. She watched the man with the specs start to open the door to the next car, then turn to look back at her. She looked off at the passing countryside until he entered the car and the door closed.

She frowned. *He did look somewhat familiar. I wonder . . .* A sudden chill rippled down her arms.

The fragrances of hay and polish mingled in Ridge's nostrils as he cleaned up the Griffin family's once-elegant black carriage with decorative gold striping.

Griff looked up from where he was sitting, wiping off a horse collar. "Have we been friends long enough that I dare risk again asking what happened when you went to see Varina?"

Ridge didn't want to be rude in light of his old friend's courtesy to him and hospitality for Laurel and her aunt. He vigorously rubbed the red wheel spokes to restore some of their pre-war beauty, while trying to avoid a direct answer. "When I'm finished, this carriage will glisten like new."

"All right," Griff said. "I get your message. It's none of my business."

Ridge stopped polishing to look at his friend. "I didn't mean that. It's just that I favor the Southern male code of not talking about women."

"I respect that in you Ridge, but being confined to this chair doesn't allow me the freedom to do very much except watch, listen, and think."

Ridge picked up another cloth and began polishing the carriage's gold mountings. "I wish it could be the way it was before the war."

Griff glanced at Ridge's leg. One bone had been splintered in a typical minié ball wound. "I wish the same for you." Hesitating, Griff added, "But there's no sense talking about what can't be changed. All we can do is talk about what might lie ahead."

"Hope for the future keeps me going, Griff."

"From what I hear, the same is true of Varina."

Ridge shot a disapproving glance at his friend but didn't reply.

Griff added quickly, "I'm not going to talk about it, but I thought you should know what some woman at church told my mother."

Ridge smiled and asked in mock shock, "Gossip at church?"

"You would horrify those women if they thought that was what they are doing. Instead, they mention these items in their prayer times. That way, they're talking to God and not gossiping. Anyway, it's whispered around that Varina again has her eye on you, and the women want her to have divine guidance."

Ridge said coolly, "I don't want to hear that."

"All right, but remember she's a clever and resourceful person. Always was. It should be interesting to see how she reacts to Laurel."

"I doubt they will even meet."

Griff placed the horse collar on his lap and asked softly, "Want to wager on that?"

Ridge ignored the question. "This carriage looks almost new. Now let's see if a curry comb will make these horses look like colts again."

As Ridge walked toward the horses, Griff called after him. "The next few days will be very interesting."

"I expect so," Ridge replied. "Very!"

Laurel hadn't even arrived, and already he could sense complications that he had not thought possible when he invited her.

CHAPTER 5

Laurel fell into thoughtful silence as she sat back down next to Aunt Agnes. The train eased through Richmond on its way to the depot. The man with the specs had reminded her of her final mission. It had taken her to the former capital of the Confederacy, just days before it fell to Union troops.

She was only distantly aware of her aunt's running commentary on the devastation which stretched in every direction.

"Oh, my gracious!" Agnes exclaimed, pointing. "Look at that!"

Following her aunt's pointing finger, Laurel's eyes briefly skimmed the blackened hulks of some nine hundred buildings that flames had destroyed. She closed her eyes against the ruins she had helped cause, but images of the burned tobacco warehouses and other buildings were instantly replaced by memories of what she had seen of the actual conflagration.

She tried to ease her conscience by reminding herself that the retreating Confederates had torched the city just before Union soldiers arrived. She had fled on

Sunday, April second, sure that the end of the war was in sight. Safely across the James River, she had watched the gigantic leaping flames reflecting off the black pall of smoke rising toward the sky.

Laurel had read later newspaper accounts of frightened women and children fleeing across the three bridges over the James River before retreating Confederate troops also burned those. She had read about looters roaming the streets, adding turmoil and wreaking havoc on a defeated people.

"Laurel!" Her aunt's sharp sound of disapproval made Laurel open her eyes. "I know it's a terrible sight, but you must see for yourself what these misguided Rebels brought on themselves!"

"Shh!" Laurel whispered, opening her eyes and glancing around nervously at the other passengers seated nearby. "Please be discrete!"

Agnes snapped, "Why? They lost the war."

"Isn't that enough?" Laurel demanded harshly.

"You're not very patriotic, my dear."

The remark stung Laurel. "Patriotic? You have no idea how patriotic I was!"

"Was?"

"And still am!" Laurel's tone held a keen

edge. It was a tremendous temptation to pour out her secret. She had been seventeen when her only brother was killed in action. That had driven her to apply to Pinkerton who had formed General McClellan's secret service operation early in the war.

Pinkerton turned her down, but after her eighteenth birthday, she reapplied and was accepted for clandestine work behind enemy lines. Having her patriotism questioned greatly distressed Laurel, but she managed to let her aunt's remark go without further challenge.

It was also helpful that the conductor walked down the aisle calling out, "Richmond next stop. Richmond."

Laurel sensed that she had made a mistake in coming. *But,* she told herself, *it's too late to think about that.* Even though the train had not yet come within sight of the station, she glanced out the window, searching for Ridge. *I wonder if it's going to be awkward, seeing him again — especially with Aunt Agnes?*

Ridge joined others on the wooden platform to wait for the cars' arrival. He tugged at the borrowed double-breasted brown jacket which ended about two-thirds of the way down his thigh. The gray beaver top hat and baggy trousers that were popular at the start of the war added to his discomfort. The plain tie troubled him most because he had worn nothing but a military uniform the past four years, except for a railroad guard's uniform the past few months. Still, he felt somewhat stylish and hoped Laurel would approve.

"Good afternoon, Ridge."

He turned around in surprise. "Varina!"

She laughed softly, a low, throaty sound that had always stirred him emotionally with its suggestive femininity. "You don't seem very happy to see me."

"Uh . . . no. No. I'm just surprised, that's all." He felt himself floundering like a boy caught in the act of doing something that wasn't quite proper. She was casually elegant in a walking-out dress and a lace-edged Stuart cap. He quickly asked, "Are you meeting someone?"

She shook her head, making the long golden hair worn in a waterfall style swing tantalizingly. "No, I came to check on a lost bag when I saw you."

Ridge doubted her excuse. He believed she was here to see what his Yankee lady friend looked like. He said, "It was nice seeing you, Varina." He turned to look down the tracks, hoping she would understand that he really meant that as a cue for her to leave.

She didn't seem to notice. "Tessie told me that you came to the house and asked for me, but I never saw you." Her tone was not accusatory, but he sensed that she expected an explanation.

"I can't explain now," he said, again looking down the tracks. The wood-burning locomotive with the diamond stack was just coming into sight around a curve about fifty yards away. "Please excuse me, Varina."

He started to move through the other waiting people but Varina startled him by slipping her arm into his.

She smiled up at him. "Tessie said she saw you start toward the river bank where she had told you I was. Naturally, I was pleased that you called, but I'm at a loss to understand why you left without speaking to me."

Ridge had pushed through the last of the crowd so that he and Varina were in the front row nearest the edge of the high wooden platform. He was annoyed that she still clung possessively to his arm as in years past.

"Varina," he said sternly, "I can't explain right now. Besides, it's not important."

The engine released puffs of steam as it rattled past, pulling the cars into position for the stop. Windows had been opened and some arriving passengers stuck their heads out to wave at people waiting on the high platform.

"I see." Varina said so softly that Ridge almost didn't hear her. There was a degree of hurt in her voice which he remembered from some of their courtship days when she didn't get her way.

"All right," he said brusquely, turning to face her again. "I was angry when I rode over to see you. But I got over it before I got close enough to speak to you. I'm sorry Tessie even told you I was there."

He freed his arm from hers and resumed searching the car windows as they crept past. Varina did not move, so he took a couple of steps away from her. He continued scanning the windows, but there was no sign of Laurel. He frowned. *Did she not come? Or is she seated on the other side of the car so I can't see her?*

Inside the car now stopped directly across from the platform, Laurel was shocked. She hurriedly stood and slipped into the aisle filling with other passengers.

Her aunt turned from the window seat to

ask, "Did you see him?"

"No!" she lied curtly, fussing with her reticule so that Agnes could not see the astonishment on her face.

"You don't have to bite my head off!" Agnes snapped. "Maybe he's delayed, but he'll be there when we get off."

Oh, he wasn't delayed! Laurel thought bitterly. *He has company, and I'm sure I know who!*

Many passengers had disembarked, momentarily making Ridge fearful that Laurel had not come. Then he saw her and an older woman each carrying small carpet bags. They stepped from the car, assisted by the conductor.

Ridge sucked his breath in sharply. Laurel was even more lovely than he remembered. A petite, pretty brunette with tiny nose and mouth, she wore a pale blue traveling coat and a diminutive hat set at a jaunty angle. Its decorative colored feathers reminded him of her saucy nature.

Ridge pushed through the crowd now flowing toward him so that he was at her side when she glanced around.

"Laurel!" he exclaimed, removing his hat and greeting her with a broad smile. He was tempted to imitate others who were sharing hugs and kisses, but one look at Laurel's female companion held him back. "You must be Aunt Agnes," he said, still smiling.

"I am Miss Agnes Bartlett, Laurel's aunt," she replied coolly, eyeing him with a disdainful expression. Ridge had been warned of her possible disapproval, but he was still unprepared for the implied rebuke. "Miss Bartlett," he corrected himself. "It's a pleasure to meet you." He replaced his hat saying, "Here, let me take those carpet-bags."

Agnes did not reply but surrendered hers along with Laurel's. Ridge spoke warmly to her. "It's so good to see you again."

Hurt and disappointed over what she had seen from the train, Laurel replied frostily, "Thank you." She did not return his smile.

He looked sharply at her, but she glanced away. *She saw me with Varina! But I can't explain in front of her aunt.* He pretended nothing had happened and asked pleasantly, "Did you both have a good trip?"

Laurel didn't reply, but her aunt said, "The cars weren't so bad, but the stagecoaches were miserable."

"I'm sorry," Ridge replied. "You'll soon have your own private room where you can rest in comfort. This way, please." He led the way across the platform.

Following half a step behind, Laurel noticed his clothing had a faint camphor smell, suggesting they had long been unused. Laurel's violet eyes swept his nearly six-foot tall frame. He was nice looking, clean-shaven, and the slight saber scar on the bridge of his nose and right cheekbone intrigued her. Even with his minor limp, he had an air of confidence. And, in spite of her displeasure over seeing him with whom she assumed to be Varina, Laurel felt the same stirring inside which he always seemed to arouse in her.

He pushed the waiting room door open with his foot and let the women enter. It smelled of stale cigars, spittoons, and smoke from the wood-burning stove. He set the carpetbags down by a long wooden bench, saying, "You'll both be more comfortable here than in the carriage. I assume you also have other baggage, so I'll get that and be right back."

As he walked away, Agnes observed, "I'll say this much for him: he seems polite and well-bred."

Still troubled over what she had seen from the train, Laurel chose not to answer. She glanced around at the crowd moving across the waiting room toward the outside door where carriages waited. She noticed that the same short young man with specs had stopped by the doorway and was watching her. He glanced away when she tried to make eye contact with him.

He was sitting down across the room reading a newspaper when Ridge returned. "I've arranged to have your two trunks placed in the carriage, so we can go now."

Laurel asked him, "Do you know that man with the spectacles?"

"That short fellow reading the paper? Name's Samuel Maynard. Why do you ask?"

"He spoke to me on the train, saying he thought we had met before."

Ridge chuckled. "He's getting bolder, although not very original. When we were growing up, he was the most shy boy on the peninsula. I guess the war changed that, because from what I heard, he became one of the best and most daring cannoneers in the South."

Laurel's heart skipped a beat. *Of course! He's the officer who showed me where the Confederates had hidden some of their cannons at Petersburg!*

In her role as a Union agent, she had chosen him as the most likely to respond to unusual attention from a seemingly-naïve Southern belle. To the envy of more self-confident young officers, she had subtly induced him to show her around the fortifications.

She had been startled when he walked her around the side of a mound of dirt and saw the big guns so well hidden that Union troops would have been right on top of them before they knew they were there. When she returned to Federal lines, she had passed that information on, but had never heard if her clandestine work had benefited the men in blue.

Laurel wasn't afraid, but she was concerned. *What will he do if he remembers me?* It was another reason to regret that she come to see Ridge. She let him give her a hand into the carriage, but instead of having a moment to look closely into each other's eyes, she looked away.

She's really angry! he thought. *This isn't the way I want to start our time together! I've got to explain about Varina as soon as possible.*

He was aware that Aunt Agnes had picked up on the apparent tension between them and she seemed pleased. Ridge would not give either of them the satisfaction of knowing he noticed anything amiss. He backed the team away from the hitching rail and focused on keeping an affable conversation going. "How is Chicago?"

"Not like this," Agnes answered, sweeping her hands in a broad gesture over the skeletal remains of the buildings that had been burned when Richmond fell.

"Virginia has great natural beauty," Ridge replied carefully. "However, except for the rivers, not much of that is as visible as it was before the war." He glanced at the sky. "I love springtime. Not too hot; not too cold; but just about perfect. Do you like it, Laurel?"

"It's warmer than Chicago," she replied briefly.

She didn't want to seem petulant, but she intended for him to regret his indiscretion by coming to meet her with his former fiancé on his arm.

He refused to acknowledge her coolness and drew Agnes into the conversation. She responded to the attention and seemed to delight in the poor start the others were making.

Despite his eagerness to get to Brickside so he could straighten out the misunderstanding with Laurel, Ridge drove slowly down the peninsula. He tried to spare the aging, mismatched bay and gray horses. They had not entirely shed their heavy winter coats, but he had curried them so carefully that there was some semblance of shine.

As they rode, they passed the blackened remains of buildings and stumps of countless trees which had denuded the green countryside.

Agnes motioned toward a pile of rubble which had once been the foundation of a house. Now only a chimney stood. She said, "I knew our valiant men had fought you Rebels hard —"

"Aunt Agnes!" Laurel broke in, her cheeks suddenly warm with embarrassment. "Please don't use that word!"

Agnes finished with a defiant tilt of her chin, "But I didn't know how desolate that would leave this land."

Laurel turned her face so that Ridge could see but Agnes could not. Laurel rolled her eyes up to suggest she was sorry but couldn't control her aunt's words.

"It's all right," he said softly to Laurel, glad to see any kind of thaw in her attitude toward him. "I bore the Rebel label with pride." He raised his voice slightly so Agnes could hear. "Yes, ma'am. A hundred thousand men can't surge back and forth over any piece of ground without doing a lot of damage."

"Back and forth?" Agnes asked, a challenge in her voice. "Who said our boys did that?"

"Well, since you ask," Ridge said, his tone hardening defiantly, " 'your boys' made various invasions of this peninsula. They all failed until the Petersburg defenses were breached. One invasion even got within five miles of Richmond before General Lee made the Union retreat. It was June and early July of sixty-two."

Agnes made a sputtering sound, but couldn't argue with the facts. Almost grudgingly, she said, "Well," then fell silent in sign of concession.

Ridge quickly moved to ease the tension. "I hope you two will be satisfied with the accommodations I've made for you."

"I'm sure we will," Laurel replied, giving him a brief smile in appreciation of his having politely but firmly held his ground against her aunt.

"Mr. and Mrs. Griffin, your host and hostess, are waiting to welcome you both, as is their son." Ridge explained how Griff had received a bayonet wound close to his spine so that he was confined to a rolling chair.

"After you meet them," Ridge added, "I'll help you get settled so you can rest this evening. Tomorrow morning I'll take you down to where my family's plantation was."

Knowing that might be their first chance to be alone, Laurel assured him, "I'm looking forward to that."

He smiled in approval, saying, "So am I." He waited for some further sign of friendliness, but she looked away. He continued, "Oh, the Griffins have invited some of their friends and neighbors to join all of us for dinner this evening, after you've had a chance to rest."

Laurel hadn't planned on that and would have preferred not to have such an event. But she was gracious. "That was very thoughtful of them."

Ridge sensed some reluctance in her voice. He said, "I hope you don't mind, but I didn't know about it until too late to notify you prior to your leaving Chicago."

Agnes seemed a little miffed. "I didn't bring proper attire for anything like that."

"Oh, it's nothing formal," Ridge assured her. He glanced at Laurel, remembering something she had told him about while they were in Omaha. Agnes's life revolved around her church. "Most of them are from church. I hope you'll find much in common with them, Miss Bartlett."

She perked up. "What kind of church?"

"Oh, various ones," Ridge replied evasively. "Baptists, Methodists, Episcopalians —"

Agnes interrupted. "Some broke off from

the North to form separate denominations. Our fellowship might be strained."

"I hope not," Ridge told her. "However, I'm not really familiar with such things. I figure that Christians are all believers, and I don't much concern myself with how they differ over some points."

Laurel surprised herself by again coming to Ridge's defense. "What does it matter, Aunt Agnes? We're not called to judge them, so let's just accept whoever they are and hope they'll accept us."

"Well," she said doubtfully, "I suppose it doesn't matter for one meal."

"Then it's all settled," Ridge declared, stealing a sideways glance at Laurel.

She caught his eye, but didn't smile, making sure he did not get off the hook so easily. "I'm looking forward to meeting your friends, Ridge." *Truthfully,* she added to herself, *I'm concerned about how they will receive me, and I hope Varina won't be there.*

Laurel exclaimed in wonder as the carriage turned down the tree-lined lane toward the Griffin family's stately three-story brick manor. It was in sharp contrast to many buildings seen on the drive down the peninsula. Ridge explained that Brickside had served as headquarters for

Union officers, so it had not been pillaged or burned.

After meeting the host couple and their son, and being given an orientation tour of the house, Ridge vainly sought for an excuse to pry Laurel away from her chaperon, but Agnes pleaded travel weariness, so she and Laurel were shown to their adjacent bedchambers on the second floor. Ridge had no choice but to wait.

Laurel refreshed herself from the flowered ceramic water pitcher and matching bowl on the marble-topped stand. *Perhaps, she told herself, I'm being silly. Ridge knows better than to let me see him with any woman on his arm, especially Varina. So maybe I should give him the benefit of the doubt until we can talk privately.*

She removed her traveling clothes, unpacked, and stretched out for an hour on a canopied bed. The hostess had said this bed came from England a century ago. Everything about the house had a history going back through the generations.

Before dressing for dinner, Laurel also had begun to get over her regrets of having come. Seeing Ridge had excited her, even though she was curious about the woman who had clung so possessively to his arm at the station.

Laurel let her mind drift to the man with the spectacles, wondering if he would place her as she had him. But even if he did, the war was over. Spies were no longer hanged. And if he did remember where they had met, he would have no way of knowing the military intelligence he had given her had been used against the Confederacy. Of course, if Aunt Agnes learned the truth, she would probably faint in dismay, but that didn't worry Laurel.

Her major anxiety was over what Ridge would say or do when they had a chance to be alone enough to talk privately, yet under Agnes's watchful eye. He certainly had not invited her here just to show her where he had been born and reared. Did he plan to propose marriage?

The thought gave her a warm glow, yet she also was afraid. She did not know how his friends would react to a Yankee in their midst, or whether Aunt Agnes would embarrass her. Laurel faced the prospect of dinner with some trepidation.

Dusk had begun to settle when Laurel heard the first horse and carriage arrive. Having changed her clothes and checked her appearance in the looking glass, she knocked on her aunt's door. Together, they slowly descended the graceful staircase.

Laurel enjoyed the feel of the polished black walnut banister as it slid under her fingers.

Ridge had spent the afternoon with his friend Griff, so both men came from the library to meet the women at the bottom of the stairs. Ridge's delighted grin brought a broad smile from Laurel.

After the four guests arrived and were greeted by the Griffins, Ridge stood by Laurel's side to introduce her and Agnes. Laurel made an attempt to remember each name, but even after visiting in the parlor she could only be sure that there were two couples, a widow and a widower. Each was gracious and the conversation was polite and casual. Even Agnes seemed to have caught the spirit, much to Laurel's relief.

Everything was still amiable when the freed woman announced dinner, and everyone adjourned to the dining room. The walls were a soft apricot color with twelve-foot ceilings a pale beige. A painting of Mrs. Griffin's paternal grandfather hung over the fireplace with its pale cream trim. The dark walnut sideboards matched the long wooden table set for dinner.

This is a real home, Laurel thought, turning slowly to scan the polished silver tea set on one sideboard, the tall candlestick, and the engraved candelabra in the center of the long table. *Ridge's house must have been like this. Even though it's gone, I want to see the site.*

Besides satisfying her curiosity, Laurel expected that Ridge would use that occasion to tell her whether he planned to try recovering the land and rebuilding the house, and how she fitted into his plans.

After everyone was seated, Jubal Griffin senior stood at the head of the table in his striped coat which fell to his knees. He adjusted the watch chain on his vest and asked the blessing.

Laurel didn't close her eyes, but bowed her head and studied the host. A distinguished looking man in his fifties, he had grown both mustache and sideburns, but shaved his chin. As the prayer continued, Laurel peeked at the hostess. She was slightly younger than her husband, dressed entirely in black, and had parted her graying hair on the right. This was in contrast to the other women guests who parted theirs in the middle and secured it in back of their heads. It gave them all a severe look.

"Well," the host said when he finished and the maid began serving, "I'm sure we would all like to hear about our charming visitors. Miss Bartlett, will you tell us a little something about yourself?"

Agnes astounded Laurel by saying, "There isn't much to tell, but I'm sure my niece and I would enjoy hearing about all of you. I understand you are all active church members, and so I wonder if it's true that some churches here in the South actually owned slaves."

"Aunt Agnes," Laurel said hastily, knowing that some churches had owned slaves, but it was a dangerous topic. "I'm sure there are more interesting aspects to churches down here that would be more appropriate to discuss."

Agnes gave Laurel a cold look to show her displeasure, but before she could reply, Ridge spoke up. "Griff, why don't you tell them about the revival that swept through General Lee's troops."

There was a quick murmur of approval from around the table, and all eyes turned to the far end of the table where Griff sat in his rolling chair. "It started in my company in early sixty-three. Before it was over, some 150,000 soldiers 'got religion,' including me."

Griff's mother urged, "Tell them about all the leaders who were included."

He nodded. "I think everyone knows about General Robert E. Lee's and Stonewall Jackson's faith. Perhaps they set the example for others. Some had already been believers who made recommitments of their lives, so I'm not sure which was which, but there were several generals like Joseph E. Johnston, Ewell, Hood, Bragg, and Hardee."

His mother prompted, "Don't forget Jefferson Davis."

Agnes exclaimed, "That traitor should be hung!"

An awkward silence fell over the diners as Laurel tried to think what to say to ease the sudden tension.

Again, Ridge came to the rescue. "Pardon me, Miss Bartlett, but perhaps it would be better if we did not dwell on the difference in our political views."

Agnes angrily impaled Ridge with a cold stare.

Laurel vainly sought words to end the conversation, but she saw that it wasn't necessary. Ridge locked his gaze on the spinster and held her eyes until she blinked and turned away. Laurel doubted that her aunt had ever been stared down by anyone.

"Young man, you are impertinent!" she snapped, throwing her napkin on the table and pushing her chair back. "Impudent!"

"Perhaps I am," he replied easily, his drawl seeming more noticeable, "so I beg your pardon. Please sit down again."

Agnes again turned her disapproving eyes on him, but he met them and again held them with his own.

"I want this to be a happy visit for you, Miss Bartlett," he said quietly. "I want you and Laurel to remember your time here as a delightful one. Please accept my apologies and let's enjoy our dinner."

Laurel held her breath and sensed that others around the table were doing the same as the contest of wills continued for several seconds.

"Well," Agnes finally said, again dropping her eyes, "since you apologized, I accept."

The sudden release of breath from the diners made the candles flicker on the table. But before anyone else could speak, Agnes tried to salvage some dignity from her defeat. "But watch your step, young man!"

Ridge grinned at her and said solemnly, "Thanks. I will. Now, would you please pass the salt?"

Laurel hadn't ever thought she would want to cheer someone for standing up to her haughty relative, but a glad cry formed in her throat. She gave Ridge a warm and radiant smile.

He winked at her, but it was so fast she

115

wasn't sure she had really seen it. Her bubbly personality returned, making her joyfully join in the discussion. Laurel had dreaded what Aunt Agnes could do, but for the first time in her life, it looked as if she had met her match. No matter what Ridge had in mind for tomorrow, Laurel was confident he would get her away from Agnes so they could be alone.

He surprised her when dinner was over and he pulled her chair back for her to rise. She felt his hand on hers, then a small piece of paper. Quickly closing her hands over it, she felt a rush of excitement. She was eager to be alone in her room to read his note.

CHAPTER 6

After Laurel lit the coal oil lamp in her bedroom, she held Ridge's note close to the glass
chimney and read by the small yellow flame.
*I must see you alone tonight. I'll wait by the back
stairs. Please try to come.*

Laurel's pulse raced and a warm pleasurable feeling swept over her. She also wanted
to see him alone, although she didn't like
the idea of slipping out in the night. Still,
she had done much more during the war
without anyone except Pinkerton and Sarah
knowing.

She waited half an hour for everyone else
in the house to have retired, then threw a
cloak over her shoulders, checked her appearance in the mirror, blew out the lamp,
and quietly eased down the hall past closed
doors. At the head of the back stairs, she
carefully placed her feet close to the wall so
that the steps would be less likely to creak,
and made her way downstairs.

The melon rind of moon barely gave
enough light for her to see him step away
from the shadows of an ornamental tree and
hurry toward her.

"Thank you for coming," he said softly, taking both her hands in his. "It means so much to me that you took this long trip in order to see where I grew up, and so I could share my dreams for that place."

Laurel's heart jumped. *Share his dreams?*

He added, "I was afraid you wouldn't come."

She didn't answer, but enjoyed the touch of his fingers on hers.

He released one of her hands but continued to hold the other. "Let's get away where we don't have to whisper." He led her away from the house along a path toward the well and water troughs she had seen earlier. She caught the fragrance of the smokehouse before he spoke again.

In a low tone, he said, "I had a terrible fright at the train station."

"Oh?" Laurel said noncommittally. She could still feel the distress of seeing Ridge waiting on the platform with a beautiful woman on his arm.

"Yes, I certainly did," he continued. "I looked at all the people waving at the windows and didn't see you. I was heart sick because I feared you had changed your mind and didn't come."

She was dying to know about his companion, but said coolly, "I was sitting on the opposite side of the car and couldn't get to a window, but I saw you."

He moaned softly. "I was afraid of that. You must have seen a woman with me and wondered who she was."

He glanced down at Laurel, but she said nothing. He added, "You probably guessed it was Varina."

She let her tone slip from cool to cold. "I guessed." *How could I forget the name of the woman to whom you had been betrothed?*

"Please don't be angry with me, Laurel. I didn't know she was going to be there. She came up to me and said she had come to pick up a trunk. I tried to walk away, but she slipped her arm through mine."

"I noticed." Laurel let frost edge her words.

"There wasn't much I could do without being rude."

Wasn't there? She's a recent widow, and others on the platform who knew her and Ridge might have noticed. The least he could have done was walk away from her.

Ridge continued eagerly, "I was so excited, looking for you, but when she did that, I thought you might see and misunderstand. That's why I had to see you tonight, to straighten this out right away."

Ridge stopped in the shadow of the

smokehouse and turned to face Laurel. "I have missed you so." His voice dropped to a husky whisper. "When I did see you leave the car, I wanted to take you in my arms and kiss you . . ."

He left his sentence unfinished, freed her hands and took her by both shoulders to pull her close.

Her heart seemed to gambol like a spring lamb, but she wasn't ready to let him off the hook so easily. She placed both hands on his chest and pushed. "Wait!"

He ignored her resistance. "I've thought about you day and night ever since the last time I saw you. Every moment was torture . . ."

"Ridge, please!" She stiffened her body and pushed harder against his chest. "Don't!"

He stepped back. "Why not?" he asked, his voice low and thick. "I thought you felt the same way . . ."

"I came here to find some answers." She moved into the moonlight. "I need time."

He stepped from the shadow of the smokehouse so the weak light from the moon fell on his face. His jaw had set and his eyes showed disappointment. "I thought the fact that you came here meant you already knew —"

Indignantly, she broke in. "I was afraid you'd think that! But I don't! I have countless questions, so I came to try to learn the answers to them."

"I see." The words were barely audible, but they were distant, as though he had retreated to some far place. "I see," he repeated. "Well, I guess my main reason for wanting to see you alone has been covered. I'll walk you back to the house."

She suddenly wished that he would take her hand again, but he didn't. She fell into step beside him, and walked in silence to the back of the house.

Only then did he speak. "Thanks for giving me a chance to explain about the train station."

She didn't want to leave with this tension between them, but she couldn't think of how to ease it. So she merely said, "I'm glad you told me."

He nodded. "We'll talk more tomorrow on the ride down to my old plantation. Well, goodnight."

He's hurt and angry, she thought as he walked away, leaving her miserable and wondering if she had made a mistake in not letting him do what they both wanted.

Laurel awoke the next morning feeling as

if a heavy lump lay on her heart. She hid her emotions during breakfast, forcing a cheery attitude so that her aunt and hostess could not guess how she felt. Afterward, at Mrs. Griffin's invitation, the three women toured the grounds while Ridge and Griff harnessed the team.

Mrs. Griffin led the way through the front door and onto the circular carriage drive. "The house is built in the classic Georgian style," she began. "The two smaller buildings on either side were added shortly after the original central structure. The building on the right is the kitchen. The other is the library. We are fortunate that it was not destroyed."

Laurel tried to appear interested, but concern over last night's disagreement made her fearful of an uneasy ride to see the site of Ridge's former plantation.

Mrs. Griffin turned around and motioned toward the water. "As you can see, the lawn sweeps right down to the river." She sighed heavily, adding, "We are so grateful that the soldiers did not cut down our beautiful trees. Perhaps that's because after the Seven Days Campaign in sixty-two, the Union wounded were laid out all the way from the house to the water's edge."

Laurel was suddenly interested. She had

not begun her clandestine work behind Confederate lines until January of 1864 when she turned eighteen. However, she remembered the excitement in the North when Federal troops, moving up this very peninsula, came within five miles of Richmond in late June and early July of 1862.

"Were there that many wounded?" she asked.

"Oh, yes. And we only got part of those. More were taken down the peninsula to Harrison's Landing," Mrs. Griffin replied.

"But it must be seventy-five yards to the river."

"I suppose it is, Laurel. Fortunately, the trees protected those wounded boys from the hot sun until they could be moved to hospitals."

Agnes asked, "How could you stand to be around such suffering?"

Mrs. Griffin shrugged. "There was no choice, so I helped tend the wounded."

"You helped Union troops?" Agnes asked in disbelief.

"Of course. So did many other women in this area. There weren't enough surgeons to attend to so many. Besides, in Christian conscience, we could not ignore their pain, regardless of what color uniform they wore."

"But," Agnes said, "you told us yesterday when we arrived that the officers took over all your house except for one room on the second floor. Weren't you angry?"

"Of course. My husband I were confined to that room except that we were allowed to prepare our meals in the kitchen. But that had nothing to do with wounded boys."

Agnes sniffed. "You can't blame the Union for doing whatever they had to do to put down the Rebellion."

Laurel saw Mrs. Griffin stiffen at the verbal barb, but she replied quietly, "I know Mr. Lincoln always called it a rebellion or insurrection, but we in the South didn't see it that way. We did what we believed we had a right to do."

Agnes snapped, "Whatever you call it, you're surely now seeing the biblical law of sowing and reaping most keenly demonstrated —"

"Look!" Laurel cut in, trying to stop her aunt's inflammatory words. "Here comes Ridge with the carriage."

He gave no indication of anything having occurred between Laurel and himself last night as he stopped the team in the driveway. He greeted Laurel and her aunt with a smile and stepped down to help them into the carriage.

"Mrs. Griffin," he said casually, "your son and I thought you might enjoy coming along with us. There's plenty of room."

"Well, I . . ." she began uncertainly while Ridge helped Agnes take her seat in the back.

"Please join us," Ridge interrupted, turning to her instead of offering his hand to Laurel as she expected.

"Well, if you're sure —" the hostess began.

Ridge interrupted. "Then it's settled. You can point out some of the sights to Miss Bartlett while I do the same for Laurel."

When both older women were seated in back, Ridge offered Laurel his hand. She whispered to him, "You and she had this already planned, didn't you?"

He grinned like a mischievous school boy. "I thought it was a good idea. Don't you?"

Her concerns over tension between them slipped away. She smiled and stepped up into the empty front seat. "I'll tell you later," she whispered back.

Ridge gently slapped the reins across the horses' backs and drove them toward the main road. Laurel was puzzled when he turned the team back toward Richmond.

She said, "Isn't this the way we came yesterday?"

"Yes, but it's also the way we start back to where we can cross the James."

"Over the river?" When he nodded, she said, "I thought your plantation was farther down this peninsula."

"No, it's across the James and south where the Appomattox flows into it."

"I thought that's where the war ended."

"That was Appomattox Court House. I'm talking about the Appomattox River. It's a superb spot, as you'll see."

Ridge was right, as Laurel saw at once when he turned onto the long lane of war-blasted trees where the sun glistened on a great body of water. "Oh, Ridge!" she exclaimed, straining to see ahead. "It must have been truly magnificent!"

"It was," he said gently. His gaze swept the thumb of land which jutted out into the confluence of the two rivers. The untended tobacco fields had only a few surviving broad-leafed plants still struggling to stay alive. Briars and weeds had overgrown the rest of the land. Except for great old oaks which lined the drive leading from the road, there were no other trees. Only countless stumps stuck up like miniature headstones along the spit of land leading toward two very tall brick chimneys. They stood at either end of what obviously had once been a great house.

126

The two women in the back had chatted somewhat amicably all the way, but now they fell silent as the team pulled the slow-moving vehicle toward the very tip of land.

Laurel felt tears suddenly forming behind her eyelids. "Oh, Ridge! I'm so sorry!"

He didn't answer, causing her to glance at him in alarm. His jaw muscles still twitched, but slowly that stopped and he thrust his jaw out and set it so hard she heard his teeth grind together.

"Mrs. Griffin," he said in a low voice that seemed about to tremble with emotion, "if you will kindly show Miss Bartlett around to the right, I'll escort Laurel the other way. We can meet back here when everyone's ready."

There was something so calmly confident about his manner that Agnes did not protest being separated from her charge. *Perhaps,* Laurel thought, *she knows there's no place here where I can be out of her sight.*

Ridge took Laurel gently by the elbow and steered her toward land's end. "The big house stood there." He pointed straight ahead with his free hand. "Between those chimneys. It was three stories. My grandfather built it for his bride before they were married. He made it with lumber from trees that stood before he cleared a few hundred acres for crops."

He used both hands to point on either side of the brick chimneys. "My father added a library on the left side and enlarged the kitchen on the right, much like the ones at Griffins' place. He had more than a thousand volumes, leather bound. He brought my mother here after they were married. My brother and I were born here, and someday I . . ."

His voice cracked, making him turn away in embarrassment.

Laurel stood uncertainly, then impulsively reached out and took his hand. She did not speak, but lightly held onto him while she gazed off over the rivers, allowing him time to compose himself.

"I'm sorry," he whispered, turning back toward her, his eyes bright.

She had never seen such sensitivity in any man, and it touched her to be a part of that moment. She said very quietly, "I understand."

He shifted his fingers, closing them over hers. "All my past is here, Laurel, except for the war years." His voice steadied and rose stronger. "Come on. I'll show you where everything was."

They walked together toward the blackened heaps of rubble. "The house and all the peripheries were wood, so they were either burned or pulled down for firewood. The rail fences, too."

Laurel pointed across the wide James. "Is that house over there your nearest neighbor?"

"Still standing and in a direct line, yes. As you saw, there were other houses near here on this side of the river, but they're gone, like this."

"Who's place is that across the river?"

When he didn't reply, Laurel turned to look up at him. She saw something in his eyes that made her wish she hadn't asked.

Finally he said, "It was Thomas Sedgeworth's."

"Now," she said, embarrassed because she had brought up the subject, "it's Varina's."

"Everything around here is yesterday," he mused, "or memories of the past. Even . . ." Again he broke off, his fingers closing hard on hers. He added in a voice choked with emotion, "over there."

They approached a small plot of land about a hundred yards from the house. Weeds and vines were taking over the area, but Laurel's mouth went dry at the sight of a single marble shaft sticking up in the center of the plot. The top had been broken off.

Even before she got close enough to read the inscription on the mud-splattered base, she realized that Ridge's parents were buried there.

Ridge explained, "The war killed them just as surely as it did my brother. The Federals overran this area, and destroyed everything."

Laurel winced as Ridge's fingers briefly closed down hard upon hers.

He continued in a low, hoarse voice, "My father died trying to stop the Yankees' vandalism, and my mother followed him, her heart broken."

Laurel's eyes misted so heavily that she could not see clearly, and she did not trust herself to speak.

"My grandparents and two of their children who died young are over there." Ridge pointed with his free hand, the other still gripping Laurel's. "The invaders even made firewood from wooden markers taken from those graves."

Pausing, he continued softly, "Some of the faithful old family servants are off to the side. Someday, I hope to have my brother's body brought from where he fell in battle. Someday . . ." he let his words trail off, then turned abruptly and led her away.

"There were some good things to remember, too." His voice brightened. "The spring parties, the sleigh rides in winter, the fun of my brother and me as boys having two great rivers to fish and swim in during hot, muggy summer days."

He circled back toward where the majority of field hand slaves had been interred near what had been the cabins he called "quarters." They passed what used to be the sick house, the toolshed, overseer's house, and moved on toward the barn, stables, then back toward the dairy, ice house, and smokehouse. They ended up at what had been the vegetable garden and orchard.

"That's about it," he concluded, releasing her hand and turning again to face the chimneys with the rivers reflecting sunlight beyond. He swept both hands in a broad gesture. "Not much left."

"You could rebuild." She was startled to hear those words come from her mouth, but she meant them.

He looked down at her with eyes full of tenderness. "I don't even own the land anymore. It was seized under the Union's Confiscation Acts."

"You could get it back, Ridge."

"You really believe that, Laurel?"

"With all my heart."

"Yes," he said so softly she barely heard

the words. "I believe you do."

He took a very slow, deep breath and held it for a long time, his eyes probing hers. Finally he nodded. "Yes, I know you do."

He took both her hands in his and gently pulled her toward him. She yielded, feeling her heart pounding with a depth of emotion she had never known. He released her hands and circled her waist with his arms. For the moment, Laurel felt she and Ridge were the only people in the world, and that world was theirs alone.

"Laurel," he said, his tone a pleasurable moan, "it would not be worth regaining unless you . . ."

He drew her close and bent his head. She lifted her face to his and closed her eyes, eager to feel his lips on hers for their first kiss.

"Oh, Ridge!" Agnes's voice ripped through the moment like a saw through wood.

Laurel and he turned toward the aunt who stood beside Mrs. Griffin. "Yes?" he asked with obvious irritation at being interrupted.

"Mrs. Griffin is unable to explain sufficiently how milk and other dairy products were kept cold in this southern heat. Would you clarify it for me?"

"Be right there," he called. He dropped his voice and released Laurel. "She's got eyes like a hawk, but neither she nor anyone else is going to keep me from having time alone with you. Will you have dinner with me tonight?"

"I'd like to, but Aunt Agnes —"

"I respect your family's wishes," he interrupted with a wry smile. "I'll invite her and Mrs. Griffin but arrange for separate tables."

Laurel turned warm eyes upon him. "I like that."

"Good! Now let's go where I can answer your aunt's question, and then get back across to the peninsula."

There were no nearby hotels or fine dining rooms, so Ridge took the three women to a modest peninsula home overlooking the James where a widow had opened her house to diners in an effort to support herself.

"Like it?" Ridge asked Laurel after the hostess seated them in a small semi-private alcove overlooking the river. The door remained open to the main dining room where Mrs. Griffin and Agnes could be seen, but were too far away to overhear the young couple's quiet conversation.

"It's lovely," Laurel assured him, glancing around at the fireplace flanked by two wooden cupboards, then back to the table for two in front of the garden window.

"It used to be a small library. Mrs. Brisbee converted it after her husband and three sons died."

Laurel glanced sharply at Ridge, who explained quietly, "The boys were lost during the war."

"All three?"

"Yes. There probably isn't a house in all of Virginia that didn't lose someone: husband, father, brother, son. . . ." He paused, then rushed on. "A couple of servants stayed on as freedmen, so they do the cooking and help. But enough of this." He pushed the single candle aside to reach across the table and gently take Laurel's hand in his. "Let's talk about *us*."

Us. The word sounded strange and yet somehow, it was right, too. *Not you, not me: us.* She asked, "Where shall we begin?"

"Anyplace. Such as what you've been doing since I last saw you in Omaha."

"There's not much to tell."

"Sure, there is. We don't get Chicago newspapers down here; are you still a correspondent?"

She nodded, but before speaking she felt

his hand tighten on hers and his eyes suddenly shifted from hers into the adjacent dining room.

His startled look made Laurel whirl around.

A strikingly beautiful woman gracefully entered the larger dining room. She approached the table where Agnes and Mrs. Griffin were seated. Laurel started to turn back to ask Ridge who she was, but suddenly she knew.

It was the same woman Laurel had seen clinging to Ridge's arm at the train station. *Varina!*

Ridge muttered, "What is she doing here?"

Laurel wondered the same thing while she watched Mrs. Griffin obviously introduce Agnes. Laurel could not hear the conversation, but Varina slowly turned toward the small alcove. She smiled at Ridge and Laurel, then glided toward them.

Laurel heard Ridge make an angry exclamation under his breath. Laurel caught her breath and tensed, watching Varina as she seemed to almost float toward them.

Up close, Varina was even more striking than she had seemed at the train. She wore a pale yellow dress with scoop neck, puff sleeves with soft ruffles showing flawless bare arms. A black velvet ribbon accented her white throat. The attached full skirt hid her shoes. Long blond hair, pulled back and caught at the crown, created cascading curls at her slender neck. She was as beautiful as any woman Laurel had ever seen.

Fleetingly, Laurel remembered in Chicago wishing she could have a chance to talk to Varina about Ridge. Now Laurel regretted that his once-promised bride-to-be was before her. Why was she here, coming directly toward Ridge and her? Laurel didn't know, but she didn't like it.

CHAPTER 7

Laurel couldn't take her eyes off Varina as she stopped beside the table. Her smile was still in place as though laced there. Laurel heard Ridge's chair scrape on the floor as he pushed it back and stood politely.

"Pardon my interrupting," Varina said in a low, throaty tone, her eyes flitting from Ridge to Laurel. "Ridge, I just had to come meet your Yankee friend."

He cleared his throat as though to make the introductions, but Varina didn't wait. Her pale green eyes touched Laurel with a brief, appraising look. "You must be Laurel."

"I am." Laurel's voice sounded more crisp than she intended.

"I've heard so much about you," Varina said softly.

Laurel reluctantly asked, "Won't you sit down?"

"No, thank you. I can't stay. The reason I'm here is because I'm giving a dinner party tomorrow for a few friends. They would like to meet you, so I trust that you and your aunt will come. And of course, you, too, Ridge."

"That's very thoughtful of you." Laurel forced a smile. "My aunt and I appreciate your hospitality, but our time is very limited. So please excuse us."

"Oh, I'm so very sorry. Perhaps another evening?"

"I don't think it's possible," Laurel cut in quickly. "Thank you, anyway, Varina."

"Of course." She looked at Ridge. "That's too bad. While you were at the party, I wanted to show you some drawings and plans I've collected as ideas for the home you want to build."

"What?" Ridge exclaimed.

Laurel saw that he seemed as startled as she was.

Varina told him, "You know, things we've talk about. I knew how important this is to you, so I was just trying to help." She turned to Laurel. "I hope you have a pleasant stay in Virginia."

Varina moved gracefully away, leaving behind a faint lilac fragrance.

A chill raced through Laurel. She gave Ridge a pained look across the table. *I thought he had only told me about those house plans!*

Grim-faced, he met her eyes. "My family home still stood when I left during the war. It was destroyed when I returned. Since then, several people know I've dreamed of rebuilding, but I never discussed that with Varina. Laurel, I want you to know that what I said to you about rebuilding was very special between you and me."

She met his eyes, hoping he would not see in them the lingering pain she felt. "Obviously," she said with forced control, "some special ties still exist between you and Varina."

"Don't say that, Laurel! Don't you see what she was trying to do?" There was a hardness in his voice.

"She was being polite —"

"Don't be naïve!"

Laurel recoiled in surprise and more pain.

"Think about it!" Ridge said angrily. "You and I are off in this little private place when Varina shows up. How did she know we were here? What was her real reason for coming? Do you think she really wanted to invite us so you could meet some of her friends?"

Those questions had not occurred to Laurel. "You think she deliberately . . . ?"

"Oh, yes!" he broke in, then fell silent as the matronly freed woman showed up to take their order.

Laurel suggested Ridge order for both of them so she could mull over the incident with Varina. It didn't make sense to Laurel for Ridge's former fiancé to go out of her way to be nice to his new lady friend. Most couples who broke up avoided each other.

She shook her head. *Even if that's why Varina showed up, maybe it's for the best. I wonder if I could ever be comfortable down here? I'm an outsider, not a part of this culture or Ridge's world. The past could keep coming back to haunt me.*

Ridge asked, "Why are you shaking your head?"

Laurel roused herself, aware that the server had gone and Ridge was looking across the table with a slight scowl. "Oh," she said, "just thinking."

"About what Varina said? Forget it. She hurt me once, but that's over. Besides, she never made me feel the way you do."

In spite of her torn emotions, Laurel felt her pulse start beating faster.

He stood up. "Tomorrow, I'll show you the house plans and get your opinion about them. Meanwhile, our food won't be ready for a while. Let's take a walk."

"Aunt Agnes won't —"

"You leave her to me," he interrupted, helping pull out Laurel's chair. "I'll show you around outside."

He told Agnes where they were going,

140

that Laurel was safe with him, and that they would be back before their meal was served. Agnes had no time to protest before Ridge led Laurel into the night air.

The sliver of moon reflected off the broad river, making a silvery path that seemed to lead from them to the far shore. The fragrance of the James was fresh and clean as Ridge took her hand and led her along a barely-visible path running along the river bank.

Her heart raced, but warning bells rang in her mind. *He's wonderful, but I don't belong here. It's not just my past, but what I've sensed about the people. Even Mrs. Griffin. She's very cordial, but inside she must resent me because I'm a Yankee, and because of what we did to the South. I suspect they all feel that way. I doubt that I would ever really be accepted as Varina would, even if Ridge and I could work out our differences.*

"Where are you?" Ridge asked.

"What?"

"You didn't hear a word I said, did you?"

"I'm sorry. My mind wandered."

"That's fine! I'm speaking from my heart, and you're not even listening!"

"Please don't be angry."

"I'll try, but I guess there's no use continuing to express my thoughts until I know what's on your mind."

She hedged, saying, "Oh, it's nothing, really. Let's talk about something else."

He released her hand. "You're deliberately avoiding what we both know should be our topic of conversation." His words were short, crisp, edged with disappointment.

"You're upset." There was enough moonlight for Laurel to see that his jaw was clenched.

"Don't you think I have reason to be?"

She gently laid her hand on his arm. "I don't want us to quarrel."

He made no move to cover her hand with his. "It seems to me that's about all we do. I can't stand to be apart from you, but every time I try to tell you what I feel, you find an excuse to push me away."

"I don't mean to do that, really, I don't. But if we stay here, I'm afraid we're going to make things worse."

"Fine! Our dinners should be ready. Let's go back inside." He turned back toward the house.

She didn't move. "If we go on feeling like this, we'll have a miserable time eating dinner together."

He stopped and nodded. "You're right. Forgive me for speaking out of turn."

"There's nothing to forgive."

He took her hand. "It's just that I've been thinking about you every waking moment since I last saw you, and I had so many things I wanted to say. But I guess they'll have to wait."

I do want to hear what he has to say, but is that just my vanity? The more I think about it, the more I don't feel things could ever work for us.

She felt the pleasant tingle of his hand, and a silent anguished thought pricked her. *But if that's so, why can't I accept that and just walk away? Why does my heart ache at the very thought of never seeing him again?*

He led her back to the two older women, giving them a broad smile. "See?" he said to Agnes, "your niece has survived these few minutes alone with a Rebel, and she's none the worse for it."

Laurel tried to smile at his humorous tone, but she caught her aunt's probing glance. Something in those eyes warned Laurel. *She knows something happened. There's a triumphant look as if she's thinking, "I told you so!"*

Returning to their seats, Ridge spoke casually. "Have you found a church in Chicago since Omaha?"

Matching his tone, she explained, "My family has always worshiped in the same

143

one since I was a little girl. I intend to start attending again. How about you? I mean, you told me earlier that your church had been burned in the war."

"It's been rebuilt. I've gone a few times."

They fell silent as their food was served, giving Laurel a moment to reflect on the continuing conflict of conscience over misleading him about the secret of her real work.

Well, I guess that doesn't really matter now because there's no way our relationship is going to last beyond this visit.

Laurel looked down at the plate the server had placed before her. "This looks and smells delicious."

"Southern cooking," he said with a grin. "Nothing better anywhere. Try some."

She took a bite and savored the flavor. "I believe you're right."

As they both enjoyed their meal, Ridge said, "Now, let's make our plans for tomorrow."

A slight frown touched Laurel's forehead. *Why prolong this?* she wondered. *I've got my answer; it's not going to work, so why don't I just tell him I'm heading back to Chicago on the first available train?*

Thrusting her logic aside, she asked, "What do you have in mind?"

"How about a picnic?"

"That's sounds wonderful, but I'm afraid that Aunt Agnes isn't much of an outdoor type person."

He laughed. "Good! Then maybe she'll stay home and we can be alone together."

Laurel found herself wanting to laugh with him even though she was fighting back the thought of having to tell him that she was going to return to Chicago.

"I don't think Aunt Agnes will do that, but I'll accept, anyway." She said it cheerfully, hiding what she must do. *Tomorrow,* she decided. *I'll tell him I'm going home.*

Laurel came down for breakfast the next morning with a heart full of misgivings. She had never felt such a strong attraction for any man, yet her mind urged her to face up to reality. *Make a clean break. Go home. Take the California assignment. Get on with my life and let him do the same with his.*

Mrs. Griffin greeted her pleasantly. "Sit down, Laurel. I'll pour us some coffee."

Laurel was not in the mood for talk, but she accepted her hostess's suggestion and took a chair at the table. She said conversationally, "I appreciated your being so gracious to my aunt at dinner last night."

"We found lots to talk about." Mrs.

Griffin set a cup of hot coffee in front of Laurel. "Oh, I almost forgot." She turned back to the sideboard. "There's sugar and cream if you like." She set the small containers before Laurel and sighed softly. "I'm still having a hard time adjusting to these changes."

"Changes?"

"Yes. Little things. Before the war, servants would have poured the coffee and stood behind our chairs to spoon in sugar, pour cream, or do any other little service." Sitting down opposite Laurel, she continued, "Now, except for, . . . well, almost all the Negroes are gone, and I've had to learn to cook and do things I never expected to do."

"You never learned to cook?"

"There was no reason," Mrs. Griffin said sadly. "I'm still trying to adjust. But this is nothing compared to what many women face. At least I have a husband. It's not as bad as Varina's situation."

Laurel was uncomfortable with the subject, so she quickly asked, "What did you and Aunt Agnes talk about?"

"Everything from the weather to the differences between the way she and I live. But after Varina showed up, your aunt wanted to know all about her."

Laurel again tried to steer the conversation away from the uncomfortable subject. "Aunt Agnes and I deeply appreciate your hospitality."

Mrs. Griffin continued as if she hadn't heard Laurel. "She is very discerning. She correctly guessed that Varina is in a tight spot financially."

"I don't know if we should talk —"

"I'm not gossiping my dear. I'm just telling you what your aunt told me. She figures that Varina married a man who was wealthy one day, but a pauper the next. She was right.

"You see, Laurel, all the Confederate money Tom Sedgeworth had — like many other Southern men — was absolutely worthless when the Union won the war. Only those few who had gold survived the change from Confederate money to Federal greenbacks. Tom might have recovered if he lived, but as it is, Varina was left with only the house and no way to keep it up."

"Mrs. Griffin," Laurel said, shifting uneasily in her chair, "I sympathize with Varina's problem, but I don't feel right discussing it."

"I'm just trying to show you what it's like for many Southern women who lost a husband in the war, or any other way. There are very few ways for a widow to support herself, so the most logical option is to remarry. Your aunt knew that. That's why she said Varina has set her cap for Ridge."

"She what?" Laurel blurted without thinking.

"Oh, you needn't worry, Laurel. Varina has always been a bit of a schemer, but Ridge is no fool. That's why even though he has no money now, all of us who have known him since he was a boy know he'll find a way to get it. You believe that, too, don't you?"

"Yes, but —"

"Somehow," Mrs. Griffin rushed on, "he'll rebuild his family house. And in spite of the way your aunt feels about Ridge, he'll get what he wants, so you and he can be happy together."

Agnes entered, still looking sleepy-eyed, ending the conversation between Laurel and Mrs. Griffin. But Laurel still mulled those thoughts over when Ridge picked up the three women for their picnic. He drove a short distance down the James to the shade of a great oak overlooking the river, produced a huge basket prepared by his landlady, and spread a cloth for everyone.

"I also brought two sets of house plans," he told Laurel, producing them from the back end of the carriage. "All of you ladies are welcome to help me decide which one you like best. Do you want to look at them now, or enjoy our meal first?"

Agnes and Mrs. Griffin asked to see them now. Ridge looked questioningly at Laurel. She didn't want to look at house plans of a man who seemed intent on having her become a part of those plans when she was so unsure of how she felt. Even if she did expect to share his life, she would rather have discussed the plans privately.

She realized he was looking expectantly at her, so she reluctantly nodded. "Let's see them now."

He unrolled one set and had each woman hold down a corner. He held the last one.

Laurel caught her breath at the splendor which the artist had depicted. It showed a magnificent square, two-story white frame building enclosed within a series of glistening ivory-colored marble pillars that extended along two sides of the house. White railings with perpendicular supports connected the columns. A long porch obviously separated these from the dwelling which was set back several feet.

"This is called Classical Revival style of architecture, with ancient Greek and Roman influences," Ridge commented.

"It's very popular in the Deep South. Laurel, do you like it?"

"It's breath-taking," she admitted, scanning the rest of the building with its four brick chimneys and a flat-roofed cupola with windows on top. "It truly is."

Agnes declared, "Only a very wealthy man could build that, let alone pay for the landscaping or other things."

Mrs. Griffin smiled. "Ridge can do anything he sets his mind to. Why, even when he was a boy —"

"Excuse me," he interrupted with an embarrassed clearing of his throat. "If you're ready, I'd like to show you the other set of plans."

Laurel lowered her eyes, hiding the pangs of doubt that darted through her mind. It was a far more grand home than she had ever dreamed of, but it wasn't for her.

"This one," Ridge said, spreading the second sheet, "is more modest."

"Not by much!" Agnes declared.

Ridge continued, "This will be made of brick. It's also two stories and only has six pillars in front instead of eighteen. But, unlike the first one, there's a railing on the second floor balcony and none on the bottom. See the three dormer windows and twin chimneys?"

The two older women exchanged comments, pointing to features drawn on the paper, but Laurel looked at Ridge.

He asked, "Do you have a preference?"

"Uh . . . I . . . we need to talk privately."

He studied her face thoughtfully for a moment, then stood and offered his hand to pull her up. "Ladies, if you're hungry, please feel free to go ahead. Laurel and I are going to take a walk."

"What's wrong?" he asked when they had strolled far enough away that the two older women couldn't overhear.

She hesitated, unable to think how to properly express her troubled thoughts. They rolled and tumbled over each other like winter storm waves on Lake Michigan.

She knew that he had invited her down to see how she, a Yankee, reacted to the idea of living in the post-war south. She had come because she wanted to be near him, to even possibly hear a marriage proposal. He might even make that today. But she had seen enough to know that it would take more than tremendous attraction to make them happy. It wasn't just Varina, who was obviously still romantically interested in Ridge.

He said, "Please tell me what's bothering you."

"It's hard to know how to begin."

"Jump in anyplace; grab a thought and drag it out so we can consider it together."

Again, she paused, the mad whirl inside her head tangling with her heart strings.

He asked, "Is it because I have no money for all the dreams I've shared?"

"Oh, no; it's not that."

"Then what? Do you want to hear the rest of my dreams right now? I was saving some of them for later, but I could —"

"No, no. It's not that, either."

"Then what is it?" He paused a heart beat before adding, "You must know I love you. . . ."

She glanced up at him so suddenly that he left his sentence dangling in the air. *I love you. He has never said that before.*

For a long moment, she stared into his eyes, her pulse throbbing, her mind spinning, but not in harmony.

I care very deeply about him, but is it real love? Love that would survive the problems that I would face living as an innocent-looking woman among these people, when my spying helped cause the deaths of their men, destruction of their homes, land, and even their economy?

"Please," he pleaded, his voice low, his eyes filled with questions, "don't shut me out! Tell me what's in the secret part of your heart!"

Secret! I haven't told him the truth about my role as a Pinkerton lady detective. My conscience bothers me about that, both because I'm being dishonest with him and because of my spiritual convictions. I'm not breaking the commandment about bearing false witness, yet I'm bending it all out of shape.

She broke eye contact with him. "I'm so mixed up!" she exclaimed, turning away from him and stepping behind the thick trunk of a giant oak.

He didn't speak, but came up behind her and gently placed both hands on her shoulders. She felt shivers race from his fingers and over her entire body. Then she sensed rather than felt his head tip toward her. His breath, warm and pleasant, caressed the back of her neck. Then his lips gently touched her.

"Don't!" she whispered, pulling away, and instantly regretting it. She didn't want him to stop, yet it was not right for her to want more and not be willing to give in return.

"Sorry," he said curtly, his hands falling away from her shoulders. "It's just that you drive me out of my mind, and then pull away from what I think we both want."

She turned to again face him, her back against the tree's rough trunk. "I told you I was mixed up."

"Let me hold you," he said huskily. "Maybe you'll find the answers in my arms." He pulled her close, murmuring, "I've wanted to do this almost from the time we met, and I want to do it for the rest of my life."

She started yielding to his gentle pull, but when he bent to kiss her, she stiffened and held back.

"Now what?" he asked, eyes sparking angrily.

"It's . . . it's too soon," she said weakly.

"How so?" Frustration edged his voice. "You know how I feel about you. Don't you feel the same about me?"

She wanted to whisper that she did, and started to relax her stiff body, but checked herself. "Don't ask me that," she replied.

His hands fell away from her, but she saw in his eyes that he felt rebuffed.

"I'm trying to understand you, Laurel," he said bluntly. "I can't get you out of my mind or heart, but neither can I figure out why you seem to feel that way about me one minute, then you push me away the next. Is there something about me that you don't like?"

"No, of course not."

"Then why do you keep pulling back? Is there something you're not telling me?"

She didn't answer, which seemed to make him pounce on that silence as affirmation. "So that's it. Then get it out in the open right now so we can resolve this."

"It's about —" she stopped abruptly.

"About what?" he demanded. "Is it because you might not feel comfortable living in the South where resentment is still high against Yankees?"

"Yes, but my mother followed my father wherever he went, as long as they could be together. I always planned to do the same someday when I . . ." She didn't finish that thought, but ended lamely, "but this is different."

"How different? Don't you love me?"

"I . . . think so, but . . ."

"Don't stop in the middle of a sentence, Laurel!"

She again skirted the truth. "I have to return to Chicago."

"No, you don't. Stay so we can work things out."

"I can't. I have a possibility of being sent to California to . . . to write stories about building the transcontinental railroad from the Pacific end."

She avoided mentioning Pinkerton, which bothered her conscience even more than before. *I'm misleading him again! No, call it what it is: I'm lying!*

He exclaimed, "Not California!"

"Yes, and I think it's best for me to take that assignment because it doesn't look as if I really fit into your life."

He stepped close to look directly into her eyes, but he didn't touch her. "Now I'm beginning to see it." He did not raise his voice, but it had great intensity. "You are still the reckless young spy —"

"Shh!" She glanced around in alarm, but the tree at her back prevented her from seeing either of the other women.

He plunged on, his tone harsh and disapproving. "You can't resist a challenge, can you? You prefer excitement and adventure to staying where we can get to know each other better, to have what most normal women want!"

The remark stung Laurel so hard that a natural tendency to defend herself made her snap back. "You mean a woman like Varina! Well, she's available again!"

Ridge drew back as though slapped in the face. Laurel watched his eyes burn with sudden fury. "Fine!" His tone hit hard although he still did not raise his voice. "You go to California and write your stories! I wouldn't want to stand in the way of whatever makes you happy!"

He strode angrily away, the limp barely noticeable.

Laurel called, "Wait! Where are you going?"

"To be alone!" he said over his shoulder. "Mrs. Griffin can drive you back to her place. Griff can take you to the cars and see you off to Chicago. I'm sorry that I was so mistaken about you, Laurel! Good-bye!"

She watched him stalk off across the open ground toward the main road. Slowly, tears leaked unnoticed down her cheeks. This wasn't what she wanted. She started to call after him, but he was too far away to hear her.

It's over. He's gone.

"Gone!" she whispered aloud, closed her eyes, and dropped her face into her hands.

CHAPTER 8

Laurel had expected to feel better when the hackman stopped his horse in front of the Bartlett's brick house. Instead, she felt even more sad than she had been on the stagecoach and railroad trip back from Virginia.

Laurel paid the driver after he deposited both small trunks on the front porch. Agnes complained as he walked away, "You should have wired my brother as I wanted. He would have met us at the cars with a carriage and saved the price of that hack."

Laurel didn't reply. She pulled hard on the doorbell cord and waited for the housekeeper to answer.

Laurel had stoutly refused Agnes's suggestion that they wire the family to meet them at the train. Laurel didn't want to be confined to the carriage with any of her family while Agnes triumphantly chronicled the news that Laurel and Ridge had broken up.

Agnes mumbled, "What's taking Maggie so long?"

"She's probably upstairs."

Instead of the housekeeper, the door was

opened by Laurel's older sister, Emma. Laurel suppressed an inward groan. Emma's dark eyes quickly moved from Laurel to Agnes. Laurel knew without looking that the expression on her aunt's face gave Emma the news she wanted.

"So," she said cheerfully, "you're back." She called over her shoulder, "Papa, they're home."

Greeting Emma was always a little stiff because she, like Aunt Agnes, didn't like to be hugged. However, Laurel's father spoke cordially to his sister and gave Laurel a warm embrace. "Welcome home," he said, his shrewd blue eyes probing her violet ones.

She gave him a kiss on his clean-shaven cheek. "Thanks, Papa. It's good to see you."

"You, too." He smiled fondly and released her. "I'll have your trunks brought in."

Emma said, "Papa, they should probably be put in my old room." She turned to Laurel, adding, "yours is a real mess. Right after you left, somebody broke in and tore it apart."

"Mercy!" Agnes exclaimed. "A burglary here?"

Laurel stared in surprise at her sister, then swung around to look at her father. "No!"

"It's true. Maggie was at choir practice and I was visiting friends. When we returned, your bedchamber here looked like the rented room where you had been staying. We've not cleaned it up yet, because we wanted you to see if there's anything missing."

Laurel caught the tinge of reproach in his voice and realized he was hurt. She had refused to tell him anything after her rented room had been ransacked. He had protested that she was shutting him out of a part of her life. "Papa, I'm so sorry!"

"Are you in danger?" he asked.

"Not that I know of." She turned her eyes on each of them. "Apparently someone thinks I have something he wants, but I don't."

Her father gently touched her shoulder. "We can talk about that later. Right now, I'm sure you both would like to clean up and rest after your trip. Then you can tell us all about it."

Emma asked, "How was the visit with your beau?"

"I saw you and Agnes exchange glances," Laurel replied coolly. "You already know the answer. Now, if you'll all excuse me, I'm going to clean up."

She left them, intending to see for herself what the intruder had done to her old room. A second break-in concerned her. *Somebody has gone to a lot of trouble, but why?* She hurried upstairs, but even before she was out of

160

earshot, she heard Agnes drop her voice as the others gathered around.

She'll gloat the rest of her life over this, Laurel thought. *And Emma will join her, but I don't think Papa will. I think he liked Ridge.* She opened the door to her old room, surveyed the mess, then closed her eyes. She thought bitterly, *Welcome home, Laurel!*

Shortly after the offices underneath the sign reading, *The Eye That Never Sleeps* opened, Laurel had told Allan Pinkerton about the break-in at her father's home.

"Not a thing was missing that I could see," she said. "I can't think of anything in either of those packages that would cause anyone to break in twice. Especially after I returned Seymour's package to him at the newspaper, just as I returned yours before I went South."

Pinkerton thoughtfully stroked his full brown beard. "Whoever did this may not know that you returned the packages, so when you didn't return to your rented place, he struck at your father's."

Pinkerton leaned back in his chair and looked across the desk at her. "Did you just come here to tell me about that, or to take the case in California?"

Laurel suspected he already knew the

answer. He was a keen observer of human nature, and even though she had tried to be her usual self, she was afraid that he had somehow picked up a subtle clue to her emotional pain over breaking up with Ridge.

"This seems like a good time to go, so how soon do you want me to leave?"

"How long will it take you to get ready?"

"I'll need to make travel arrangements by rail as far as possible, then take the Wells Fargo stage from there to Sacramento. So, a few days, at most."

"Good!" He stood up and came around the desk toward her. "We've already lost valuable time, and that's making the railroad officials anxious. While you do what you must, I'll try to puzzle out who's broken into your room, and whether it's my package they want, the one Seymour gave you, or possibly something we've overlooked."

"I appreciate that." She left and headed toward the Chicago *Globe*.

Orville Seymour kept Laurel waiting, as he had before. She avoided painful thoughts of Ridge by spending the time focusing on the break-ins. Her searching eyes quickly located the middle-aged man who had stuck his head into the editor's office when Seymour had given her the package. There was no sign of the skinny, dark-haired employee who had reported the press breakdown. She realized that he might be in the press room.

Those break-ins must have some connection with one of those packages, and most likely the one that Seymour gave me with the photograph of the missing witness, she concluded, *but why? And who knew I even had it?*

Nobody had been in Pinkerton's office when he gave her the parcel, or when she returned it. At the *Globe*, two men had briefly spoken to the editor the day he gave her his package. One man had entered the office just as it was being handed to her. She didn't recall anyone being present when she returned it to Seymour.

But, she reminded herself, *any number of other people could have looked through that big window and seen Seymour hand it to me.*

Seymour finally admitted her to his glassed-in office which smelled of cigar smoke. His heavy gray mustache bobbed as he explained brusquely, "I'm short of time. What can I do for you?"

"I'll be brief. There's been a change of plans," she told him from across his cluttered desk. "I'm going to California as soon as possible. Do you still want me to write railroad stories and try to locate your missing witness?"

"Of course. You want his picture and the files now?" He turned in his squeaking swivel chair toward the large chest-type safe against the back wall where he kept the package.

"No, thanks. I'd rather wait until just before I leave. I've still got to make traveling arrangements."

Seymour retrieved a stub of cigar from the ash tray but replaced it when Laurel unthinkingly wrinkled her nose. "I'll light up after you leave," he said. "Anything else for now?"

"No, nothing," she replied casually. She rose, glancing through the large plate glass window overlooking the bustling editorial staff. "What was the name of that very skinny man with dark hair and sideburns who came in here when we were talking the other day? I think you called him Dick."

"Dick Morton. Don't tell me he appealed to you?"

She smiled and waved the idea away. "I don't know any of your staff, but I had seen him when he came in to say the press was broken down. So I was just curious when I didn't see him today."

"He quit a few days ago. Well, I guess he did. He didn't show up for work for two days, so one of the staff checked on him at his boarding house. The landlady said Dick suddenly packed and left. Didn't leave a forwarding address." Seymour turned suspicious hazel eyes on her. "Why do you ask?"

"Idle curiosity," she replied, but her interest rose. Dick was the only one in the office when Seymour had given her the package. Now he had mysteriously vanished. It might be coincidence, so she asked, "How about the other man who came in and said something about a horse-whipping story?"

"I don't remember."

"He was middle-aged, sort of sandy-haired with sideburns. He stuck his head in the door without knocking. I saw him out there awhile ago."

"That has to be Henry Gooch. Say, young lady, you're mighty curious today. What's going on in that pretty head of yours?"

Laurel flashed one of her most charming smiles. "Just female curiosity. See you in a day or so, Mr. Seymour."

Laurel took a hack to see Sarah, who welcomed her with a glad cry and a quick hug before leading the way into the parlor.

Sarah carefully lowered herself into a straight-backed chair across from the sofa. "Please sit down," she said. "I'm dying to know about your visit with Ridge."

Laurel heaved a deep sigh. "It didn't work out, so I came back here."

"Oh, I'm sorry! You two are so right for each other! I hoped you'd return as his betrothed. What happened?"

"There are several problems. The culture, for one thing. I just don't think I'd fit in down there. Then I ran into a man who said he remembered me from somewhere, but he couldn't remember where."

"You mean from the war?"

"Yes. I did recognize him. He was a junior officer I met on my last trip into the Confederacy."

"Did he finally remember you?"

"No, but it wouldn't have mattered, really. He has no way of connecting what he told me with what later happened. Still, it bothered me."

"I can see where it would."

"It seems something from the past is always popping up to give me trouble," Laurel admitted.

"What else besides that man?"

"Oh, just the way I felt around those Southern women. They were hospitable and kind to my face, but I had the feeling they were thinking about all their men who had died because of the Union."

"And you felt guilty about your part in helping defeat them?"

"Especially that."

166

"Your conscience shouldn't bother you over that any more than soldiers' do because they killed in battle. The war meant everyone had to do whatever was possible, which is what you did."

"I tell myself that, but I still feel guilty somehow."

"Let's go back to you and Ridge. What happened? Another woman?"

"Why do you assume that?" Laurel asked a little abruptly.

"Because I've known you since we were little girls, and I can see the hurt in your eyes. To me, that suggests another woman. Did he replace the girl who was going to marry him after the war, but didn't wait? What was her name?"

"Varina, but this isn't about her."

"Then who?"

"Nobody. Ridge and I just couldn't work things out."

"Did he ask you to marry him?"

"Not in so many words."

"Did he say he loved you?"

Laurel slowly nodded. "But I told him it was too soon, and things escalated from there."

"For pity's sake, Laurel! Don't make me drag everything out of you! Start from the beginning and tell me the whole story."

Reluctantly, Laurel complied, concluding with her final moments with Ridge. "What really hurt was when he got angry and said something about me not wanting what most normal women want."

"Ouch!"

"Then I lost my temper and told him that he meant some woman like Varina."

"You didn't!"

"Worse! I reminded him that she was available again. He told me to go to California and write my stories. He wouldn't stand in the way of whatever would make me happy! He walked away, and I didn't see him again."

"Oh, Laurel, I ache for you both, because he must be hurting, too."

"I suppose so. But it's over, and I'm going to California." Laurel decided not to mention the break-in at her father's place.

Sarah shook her head, "I think you're afraid to let yourself love Ridge or anyone else."

"Afraid? No, that's not true!"

"I think it is. On one hand, you want to remain the daring, independent woman who does what she wants. But on the other hand, you're thinking that all the girls we grew up with are married and have children, or are expecting." Sarah glanced at her swollen middle. "You keep running away from love."

"That's not true, either!" Laurel abruptly stood. "I've got to be going. There's a lot to do before I leave for California."

Sarah rose with an effort. "Don't leave while you're upset."

"I'm all right."

"Are you going to have a traveling companion, or go alone as you did in the war?"

"Alone. I don't have a choice."

"How about your aunt?"

"She complained all the time on this trip, so she wouldn't like traveling to California. Besides, I don't need her or anyone else."

"Your father and sisters will have a fit, especially Emma. Please find someone. That's a very long, dangerous journey for a pretty woman our age who is all alone."

"Thanks for your concern, but I can take care of myself."

Sarah threw up her hands in mock despair. "Oh, how many times have I heard that from you?" Without waiting for a reply she added, "Before you go, come with me to the kitchen. I had an urge to bake today, so I made some pastries even though I can't eat them because of the baby. You'll do me a favor by taking some with you."

Dusk was settling when Laurel left with a

sack of Sarah's pastries. Laurel walked absentmindedly, deep in thought over some of her friend's observations. *Is she right? Am I afraid to love?*

A few blocks from Sarah's, Laurel roused from her reveries at the sound of someone running up behind her.

She spun around, startled to see a man rushing toward her. "Watch out!" she shouted, and tried to jump aside, but it was too late.

The runner bumped into her, spinning her around so she dropped both her handbag and the pastry sack. She fell backward, arms flailing in a vain effort to stop her fall. She landed in a high hedge and cried out in pain as sharp twigs and branches closed about her. Instinctively, she closed her eyes to protect them.

When she opened them again, she was startled to see that the man was running down the street, carrying both her handbag and the sack of pastries.

Laurel continued to her father's place, hoping to slip in the back door and up to her room where she could wash the blood off her hands and face without being seen. But the housekeeper saw her enter, stared at Laurel's bloody face, and screeched in alarm.

"Shh! Maggie, be quiet!" Laurel hissed, hurrying toward the back stairs. But it was too late. Her father rushed toward her just as she put one foot on the stairs.

"Laurel! What happened?"

"It's nothing, Papa. I'm just scratched. Come upstairs so I can clean up and I'll explain."

"Maggie," he said, "get some water for her," and he followed Laurel to her old room.

She headed for the dresser mirror, and told her father about the street attack. She was finishing her story as Maggie arrived with a pitcher of water.

"Here," the housekeeper ordered in the same authoritative voice she had used when Laurel was growing up. "I'll clean you up." She poured some water into the wash basin on the bedside stand, adding, "You tell us what happened."

"I've already told Papa all there is to tell," Laurel replied. "Somebody ran up behind me and snatched my handbag and a sack of pastries Sarah had given me."

"Could you describe him?" Laurel's father asked.

"No, not really. It happened so fast, and it was nearly dark." *But,* she thought, *he was sort of thin, so it could have been Dick Morton, but I can't accuse him because I'm just not sure.*

Maggie dipped one end of a wash cloth into the basin of warm water and gently began washing Laurel's facial scratches. "Wickedness!" Maggie muttered, clucking disapprovingly. "There's so much wickedness in the world that not even a young girl is safe anymore!"

"That'll do, Maggie," Laurel's father said gently. "Now, young lady, this settles it! I know that you're in some kind of danger. I must know what it is so I can help protect you."

"Papa, there's no danger. The man who grabbed Sarah's sack must have thought that what he wanted was in it. He didn't try to hit me after I fell. He did not ransack my rooms when I was home. So he's not after me, but he wants something he thinks I have. The trouble is, I don't have anything. It's a mix-up of some sort."

"Whoever's bothering you isn't mixed up about where you are," he replied. "I don't want you sleeping in this room tonight, so you'd probably better stay with one of your sisters, or Agnes."

Laurel didn't want to stay with either of her sisters and their children, and certainly not with her aunt. Flinching as the water contacted her broken skin, Laurel protested, "I don't want —"

He broke in. "All right. Not your room, but use one of your sisters' old ones. Emma had your trunk put in hers, so you could sleep there. I'll keep watch outside that door until we understand what's really going on."

Laurel recognized that her father's iron will had dropped into place and there was no way of getting around it. "All right," she said with a sigh.

"That's my girl." He turned to the housekeeper. "Maggie, I'll finish this. You go make sure Emma's old room is ready."

Maggie muttered in a mimicking tone, " 'Maggie, get some water. Maggie, get a room ready. Maggie, do this, do that.' A body can be run to death —"

"Please, Maggie," her employer interrupted, gently taking the wet cloth from her. "Save your opinions until you're alone."

Laurel took the cloth from her father's hands. "I'd better do this," she said as the older woman left, still grumbling.

"I don't know why I put up with her sass," Laurel's father lamented. "She gets worse ever year."

"She's the best housekeeper we ever had," Laurel reminded him, carefully tending to the scratches on her hands. "Papa," she continued, her tone hardening with resolve, "I'm going to California."

He stared in disbelief. "Why would you do that?"

"Business, work, certainly not pleasure."

"You mean to get far away from Ridge." When she didn't answer, her father said sadly, "I recognize that tone of voice from when your stubborn streak turned up in your teen years. I guess your mind is made up?"

"It is."

"Who's going with you?"

Laurel hesitated before saying, "Nobody."

"No! Absolutely not! That's two thousand miles from here. I won't have it!"

"Papa, you know I'm of age, so please don't make it difficult for me. I'm going."

He didn't say anything for several seconds. Finally he nodded. "I love you with all my heart, even if you are a very stubborn young woman."

She grinned at him. "I inherited that from you."

"I guess I have to plead guilty. But I've got a little bit of mule-headedness still left in me, so I'm going to ask you to honor my . . . uh . . . request."

She eyed him suspiciously. "What's that?"

"Don't go alone. Take someone with you."

"I've thought about it, but nobody's available."

"I'll get somebody."

"Like who?"

"Your Aunt Agnes."

"Oh, no! Papa, it was bad enough having her with me on the trip to Virginia. Besides, if we went all the way to California, one of us might do something drastic to the other." Laurel added quietly, "Anyway, she won't go."

"I know how to make her go."

"Oh, Papa! Please don't even ask!"

He interrupted, "You agreed to honor your father on this. I'm going to hold you to that."

She groaned. "If I didn't love you so —"

He interrupted with a pleased laugh. "Good! Now tell me more about this trip you and Agnes are taking."

CHAPTER 9

Having made up her mind to leave for California did not entirely relieve Laurel about the two break-ins and searches of her rooms. Whoever had done that, and snatched her purse and a bag of pastries on the street, might strike again.

Laurel tried to lessen the likelihood of that happening by refusing to accept either of the packages from Pinkerton or Seymour until the day she planned to leave. She still sensed some jeopardy, so she hurriedly made preparations for the Sacramento trip.

Laurel wanted to see Sarah once more before she left, but she soon regretted that decision because Sarah's blunt words further hurt Laurel's already fragile feelings. She sipped from a rose-patterned teacup while sitting across from Sarah in her spacious kitchen.

"Are you sure you're not making a mistake?" Sarah asked softly. She shifted her weight on the straight-backed chair to ease her advancing pregnancy. "Ridge loves you. Instead of going off to California, shouldn't you swallow your pride and write him?"

"No! He's the one who walked away!"

"I can understand how you felt, but what about him? He bought those house plans to share with you. That shows he is very serious, yet you pushed him away!"

"That's not true!"

Sarah's voice softened. "Isn't it?"

"I told you, it was his choice!"

Sarah interrupted. "For pity's sake, Laurel! He was obviously leading up to asking you to marry him, so do you think he chose to lose you?"

Laurel sat her cup on the table and forced herself to speak calmly. "I know that you care about me, but this is a decision I have to make for myself. I've made it."

Sarah leaned toward Laurel with some difficulty and took Laurel's hand. "We've been friends too many years to let honest differences of opinion come between us."

"I'm not angry with you, Sarah, but I have to go. There's still the packing and making arrangements with Aunt Agnes." Laurel stood and started down the uncarpeted hallway toward the front door.

Sarah followed, saying, "As soon as you're settled, send your address. I'll write when the baby's born."

"The baby." Laurel stopped in front of the massive framed pictures of Sarah's late parents and glanced at her swollen abdomen. Laurel loved the challenge and danger of her work, but she was also torn by a desire to have a husband and family. She told Sarah, "I pray the baby is healthy."

"Thank you." Sarah lightly touched the dark wooden frame of her mother's photo. "I'm sorry she and Papa won't ever get to hold their grandchild."

The plaintive note in Sarah's voice caused Laurel to impulsively reach out and hug her. "I'm sorry, too."

Sarah nodded. "At least you'll have one grandparent for your baby, if you ever get married. I hope you won't let Ridge get away."

"Thanks, but I'm capable of making my own choices."

"I know. You always have been. But I don't want you to end up like Agnes."

The words stung Laurel. "I'm not ever going to be like her!"

"I hope not, but I remember my mother telling me that Agnes used to be different."

Laurel's eyebrows lifted. "I've known her all my life, and she's always been the same as she is now."

"That's how I remember her, but my mother hinted to me that Agnes had a beau when she was young."

178

It was hard for Laurel to image that being true of her brittle aunt. "What happened?" Laurel asked.

"My mother wouldn't talk about it."

Laurel reflected on the fact that neither her father nor his sister had ever said anything about Agnes' younger days. Laurel wondered if it was a family secret, or just a sensitive subject.

Defensively, Laurel declared, "Well, that doesn't matter. I've always had many suitors."

"Have you ever felt about any of them as you do about Ridge?"

Laurel didn't answer, but the question echoed in her mind long after she said good-bye to Sarah.

Ridge fumed as he knocked at the front door of Templeton Hall and waited for Mrs. Phoebe Ashby to answer.

I was a fool! he fiercely told himself. *I should never have walked away from Laurel like that, leaving her to be embarrassed by riding back to Brickside, especially with her aunt. That woman must have congratulated herself all the way to Chicago, thinking she caused us to break up.*

Mrs. Ashby opened the door slightly and peered out, then swung it open and invited her tenant in. Her gray hair hung loosely down her back. "Forgive me for not being properly prepared to receive visitors," she said. "My arthritis has made my fingers swell this morning, so it's hard to put up my hair." She motioned toward the horsehair sofa and two battered ladder-back wooden chairs in front of the cold fireplace. "Please sit down."

"No, thanks. I can't stay. I just came by for a couple of reasons, and especially to say how sorry I am that you didn't get to meet Laurel."

"So am I, but I understand that young lovers do have these kinds of spats. My late Harold and I did that back in our courting days, but it turned out fine. We had forty-one years together. You and Laurel will —"

"Excuse me," Ridge broke in, "I don't feel much like talking about that."

"Of course. I'm just sorry for you that it had to end the way that it did."

Ridge wasn't surprised she knew the story already, but he felt a twinge of annoyance. He was sure that whoever had shared the news had felt she had not done it as gossip, but as a way to ask Mrs. Ashby to pray for Laurel and him. Everyone rationalized his actions, even as Ridge had been doing about letting his anger make him walk away from Laurel.

His landlady continued, "At the risk of speaking out of turn, I urge you to wire her at once."

"I appreciate your suggestion and concern, but by now, Laurel is probably making final preparations for her trip to California."

"California?" Mrs. Ashby's eyebrows shot up in surprise. "I hadn't heard about that."

Ridge regretted his slip, but now he knew that Mrs. Griffin and Laurel's aunt had been too far away to overhear any of the details of their quarrel. He felt compelled to add, "She has an assignment to write about the Southern Pacific's progress in helping build the transcontinental railroad from Sacramento."

"Oh, my! All the way out there!"

Shrugging, Ridge shifted to his second reason for talking to his landlady. "I'm going back to work for the Union Pacific out of Omaha, so this is to give you notice that I'll vacate my room in the next few days."

"Oh, Ridge!" Mrs. Ashby's hands fluttered like a wounded bird. "Please don't! Oh, I know I'm sticking my nose into something that's none of my business, but you should stay here with us. Where your roots are! You can rebuild —"

"I'm sorry, but I have nothing left here. No reason to stay. Now, I'm sorry to disappoint you, but that's the way it is. Goodbye, Mrs. Ashby. You're a good friend."

Laurel left Sarah's home with a sense of sadness that dogged her all the way back to her father's home.

Sarah's coming motherhood made Laurel vaguely aware that she envied her friend. Sarah had a husband, a home, and would soon have a baby of her own.

Now, unexpectedly, Laurel thought of the plans for the grand house that Ridge had shown her. *What a lovely home!* Laurel thought. *It would be everything a woman could want. Room for husband and children. And a garden.*

Laurel frowned. *A garden? Why did I think of that?*

She had grown up in Chicago where the only gardens she had seen were in little pots on window sills. But suddenly she could see herself in a wide-brimmed hat digging in the earth, looking up from her flowers and seeing the waters of the Appomattox and James Rivers blending less than a hundred yards away.

Stop it! I know that would never work for us! That decision is already made, so don't think about it again!

Laurel tried to obey her stern reprimand, but suddenly she felt an ache that she could not quite explain. Even the usual excitement about going on a dangerous mission could not arouse Laurel the way she expected.

In her bedchamber, she continued packing. "What's the matter with me?" she muttered to herself.

Her father's voice came from the open doorway behind her. "Who are you talking to, Laurel?"

"Nobody. Just thinking out loud, I guess."

He seated himself on the vanity bench in front of her mirrored dresser. "About what?"

"Oh, nothing and everything," she said evasively, absently placing clothes in her trunk.

"About him?"

"Ridge?" Laurel shook her head. "That's over. No sense in dwelling on that." To avoid any further discussion, she asked, "Did Aunt Agnes ever have a beau when she was young?"

"Why don't you ask her?"

"And have my head snapped off? No thanks, Papa. But I am curious."

"She wouldn't like me telling about such things."

"But couldn't you at least tell me yes or no?"

"I guess I could answer that. Yes. But if you want details, ask my sister."

"No thanks, Papa. It's going to be a long trip, and she's difficult enough to get along with as it is. I'm not going to unnecessarily risk her acid tongue."

"That's a good decision."

"I'm still curious about how you got her to agree to accompany me on this trip. I wouldn't have believed it was possible. How did you manage that?"

He grinned at her. "That's a secret."

"Oh, Papa! Don't tease me. I'm not a little girl anymore."

"I just knew what to say to her so that she wouldn't refuse."

"Well, if Ridge were going to be out there, I could see where Agnes might be challenged to do what she went to Virginia to do. But there's no man in my life, so that's not why she's going with me. So why?"

"Ask her."

Laurel laughed lightly. "You're terrible, Papa!" Then she added soberly, "Surely she doesn't think she can protect me from whoever broke into my rooms and snatched my things on the street?"

"It's not that. But I'm glad there hasn't been another attempt since that street attack. That's the only good reason for having you so far away; whoever was bothering you won't be able to do it out there."

"That's true." She closed her trunk. "Well, Papa, I'm ready to go."

He didn't answer, but stood quickly and walked over to hug her tightly. They stood that way in silence for several minutes. Then her thoughts jumped and she remembered Ridge holding her.

Involuntarily, she shivered, not knowing why.

In companionable silence, Ridge sat in a fan-backed chair beside Griff in his rolling chair while both gazed toward the river. A light breeze rustled leaves on the hundred-foot-tall tulip tree sheltering them.

Griff pensively stroked his heavy brush mustache and broke the stillness. "My mother told me about the house plans you showed her, Laurel, and Agnes on the picnic. Does that mean you're going to apply to President Johnson for amnesty?"

Ridge's jaw muscles twitched with anger. "Reclaiming my plantation is no longer important. There's no reason."

"You could go after Laurel. Make up with her."

"Leave her out of this."

"All right, but look at it another way: You owe it to yourself to regain that property. You've got to do it for your own sake. Otherwise, you'll either keep running off somewhere, like back to Omaha, or you'll stay here and end up marrying someone instead of the woman you really want."

Ridge glared at Griff. "I have no intention of marrying anyone."

"Many a man has felt that way, but ended up married anyway. And every woman in this area knows that Varina is interested in you again."

"She lost that chance during the war when she married Sedgeworth. I won't be made a fool of twice."

"My mother tells me that the women are betting on Varina."

"Well, they'll lose. Now, let's drop it."

Shrugging, Griff said, "Fine. But I wish you'd consider getting your plantation back. All you have to do is comply with the oath requirement and apply to the President for a special pardon."

"I won't do it! The Union took everything I ever had: my parents, my brother, and four years of my life. Under their Confiscation

Acts, they seized the land that was my inheritance, then burned the place to the ground. After the war, I returned to nothing. Nothing! I will not give up my pride and go crawling to Johnson!"

"My father didn't feel he had to 'crawl.' He petitioned the President directly, as required, and got Brickside officially returned to him."

"I have no quarrel with what anyone else does. But I'm convinced that Johnson deliberately put in those exemptions, including those of us whose property was worth twenty thousand dollars. He blames us for the war, and he's determined to make us grovel to get our own land back. Well, I won't do it!"

"I see." Griff turned to gaze toward the river and spoke without turning to look at Ridge. "What would you have done if things had gone differently with you and Laurel?"

Ridge shifted uneasily in his chair. "I had not made up my mind."

"But," Griff said, turning toward Ridge, "you must have at least thought about it. It's the only way you could have gotten that property back to build the house you had planned. Right?"

Ridge didn't answer. Before Laurel arrived, he had decided that if she had agreed to marry him, he would explain the circumstances to her. If she wanted him to petition Johnson, Ridge would have done it. But not now.

Griff asked, "Are you going to answer me?"

"No."

"What will you do instead?"

"I'm thinking about returning to the railroad."

"You're sure that's the right thing to do?"

"I'm sure." Ridge stretched his legs out ahead of him, easing the discomfort in his wounded left one.

"I wish you were as sure about some other things as you are about going back to Omaha."

Ridge glanced at his friend. "What does that mean?"

"It's none of my business, but I have to risk saying it at least this one more time: Go after Laurel."

"That's not something I want to discuss."

"I know, but I saw the way you looked at her during dinner that night she arrived. I liked her. I don't know what happened on that picnic except for what little my mother told me, but I know you didn't show Laurel those house plans without figuring she was part of them."

Ridge's voice took on a bitter edge. "She loves excitement and adventure too much to care about a home and family."

"Maybe she's frightened. You defended her at the table that night when her aunt kicked over a hornet's nest with her uncalled-for remarks, but I wonder how Laurel felt."

Ridge raised his eyebrows and looked hard at Griff. "Embarrassed, I'm sure. What else would you expect?"

"You're right, of course, but I also think she was probably wondering how she, as a Yankee, could live here among all of us Southerners so soon after the war. Almost everyone lost a husband, a son, a father, a brother —"

"She lost her only brother," Ridge broke in. "He was barely sixteen."

Ridge did not want to tell how he had found the dying teenager on the morning after a battle. The boy had given Ridge a letter which Ridge promised to deliver after the war. That had led to Ridge meeting Laurel, but that was too personal to talk about.

Ridge added, "There's no point in going on with this subject."

"All right. I've said what I felt I should. But I've also been thinking about something else." Griff patted the wheels on his chair. "I'm never going to be able to leave this thing to make a living, but I have an idea on how to do that without my legs. I also have some gold hidden away, so if I had a partner with legs, like you, he could take that money and invest it so that we would both eat regularly. How about it, Ridge? You willing to listen?"

"Just because I don't have any money now doesn't mean I'm not capable of earning it on my own."

"I'm fully aware of that. In fact, I don't know anyone who doubts that someday you'll be a wealthy man."

Even Varina, Ridge realized. *That's why she's apparently thinking of me again.*

He told Griff, "I never thought of being partners with anyone, but if I did, you'd be someone I could trust. So what do you have in mind?"

"Land speculation." Griff's eyes lit up with excitement. "Wherever the transcontinental railroad goes, towns will spring up. Open land now worth little or nothing will be worth more money than anyone can count. The one who goes in now with gold can buy land where the railroad's going to pass, then sell it for a huge profit."

Ridge pursed his lips. "I remember

reading about how the first land speculators in San Francisco did that back in the Gold Rush Days. Made millionaires of them. But the railroad . . . ?"

"Push this chair into the house, and I'll show you what I've worked out."

"Well," Ridge said cautiously, "I'll look, but I'm still planning on returning to the railroad and following it as the tracks are laid westward to California."

"Fine. All I'm asking is that you hear what I have to say first. Fair enough?"

"Fair enough," Ridge agreed, and stepped behind the rolling chair, but his thoughts were on Laurel.

After having to change trains five times from Chicago and then take a ferry across the Missouri River, Laurel and her aunt reached Omaha on Sunday morning. There they transferred to the stage coach depot. It was crowded with waiting passengers and friends or well-wishers who had come down to see others off to California.

Laurel had dressed stylishly in gray traveling clothes. Her cloak-coat with a bell-shaped dress flared out less than hoopskirts. There wasn't room on a stage for the popular skirts. A ribbon-trimmed bonnet accented her face, causing men in the waiting room to steal glances at her.

Laurel used her right foot to push the small carpetbag along the wooden floor toward the agent receiving the three-hundred-dollar fare per passenger. Foot contact constantly confirmed the bag's location while allowing her hands to be free except for the reticule hanging from her left wrist.

There had been no further break-ins or street attacks in Chicago, and it seemed highly unlikely there would be any in Nebraska Territory. Still, Laurel was concerned because the two packages given her by Pinkerton and Seymour were now in that carpet bag.

After paying the six-hundred-dollar fare for their two passages, Laurel shoved the bag to a nearby bench and sat down with Agnes to wait for the call to board.

Agnes complained under her breath, "I don't know why you insist on keeping that thing with you instead of letting the driver put it on top with our trunks. It's not as if you're carrying gold, you know."

Glancing around to make sure that no one seemed to be listening, Laurel replied softly, "I feel more comfortable having it with me."

She still assumed that whoever had ransacked her rooms and knocked her down on the street was after the unidentified photo, but she couldn't be sure. Neither was she sure that her assailant wasn't among the passengers riding trains from Chicago to here, or mixing with those waiting to board the coach for Sacramento.

Agnes mused, "I do hope we have respectable companions. The idea of being in that tiny little coach for fifteen days and nights with seven total strangers frightens me. You can see from the bags they're carrying which ones are going on the trip."

Laurel had tried to ignore most of her aunt's constant complaints. She said with forced cheerfulness, "I'm sure they'll all be respectable."

"I don't know." Agnes sounded doubtful. "See those two women over there?" When Laurel glanced at them, Agnes continued, "You can see they're from rustic backgrounds. Why, they're not even wearing proper traveling clothes."

"My guess is that they're poor women, maybe widows, who don't have much of this world's goods."

Agnes sniffed disdainfully, "They have enough to pay for this trip. Oh, there's someone respectable looking." She indicated a short, slender man dressed entirely in black. He was balding with a brown handlebar mustache and a goatee streaked with gray.

"He must be a minister," Agnes observed. "He's carrying a Bible."

"Could be," Laurel replied without interest.

"Oh, there's that distinguished looking gentleman I saw on the train when we left Chicago. He's quite attractive, and I think he's waiting for this stage."

Laurel glanced briefly at a tall, well-dressed man in his middle twenties. She noticed a full head of wavy black hair and a handlebar mustache with a slight twist or curl upward at the ends. "Please, Aunt Agnes! Don't start being a match-maker."

Agnes seemed not to have heard. "He's probably a businessman. I wonder if he's married."

"I don't care to know." Laurel shifted her gaze to a clean-shaven man in his middle fifties. A full head of silver hair covered the tops of his ears. "There's a man who reminds me a little of Abraham Lincoln, except he doesn't have a beard. Not quite as tall, either."

"Looks more like that traitor, Jefferson Davis."

"Shh!" Laurel glanced around in alarm,

but no one seemed to have overheard Agnes. "Even out here, you've got to watch what you say."

"I'll speak my mind whenever and wherever I want!"

Laurel sighed. No matter how she tried, Laurel found it difficult to put up with her aunt's outspokenness.

A loud shout from outside startled everyone in the room so they turned as one toward the sound. Through the window, Laurel glimpsed two men quarreling near the coach's front wheel.

"What's going on?" Agnes asked anxiously.

Laurel stood up to look, but she was too short to see over the heads and shoulders of almost everyone else in the room. The shouting changed to a scuffle with the sound of blows. Laurel took a couple of steps away to try for a better view, but everyone was taller than she, so she dodged until she could see outside the station.

She could only discern several men trying to break up the combatants. "Whatever it was is over," she told Agnes, turning back toward her seat.

Laurel started to sit down, then instantly froze. "Where's my bag?"

She glanced around in alarm and

glimpsed a shabbily-dressed man running toward the back door with it under his arm. "Stop!" she cried, running after him. "Stop him, somebody! He's stealing my bag!"

CHAPTER 10

In half a dozen flying steps, Laurel caught up to the man running away with her carpetbag. Behind her, she heard Agnes scream and others in the crowded waiting room shifting to watch the unexpected drama.

Laurel swung her handbag with all the strength of her diminutive five-foot body, striking the back of the fleeing man's head. He ducked but kept running. "That's my bag!" she cried, using her free hand to snatch at it while again smashing the handbag across the thief's shoulders. "Drop it! Drop it!"

Someone brushed against her from behind, sending her off balance. Assuming this was an accomplice, she shifted her attack to him and took an awkward swipe at him with her makeshift weapon. He blocked the blow with his left arm and dashed past her.

In two long steps, the man crashed heavily into the escaping thief. He staggered, dropped the bag, but kept running. Another man rushed by Laurel and chased after the thief, but he dashed out the back door and leaped upon a waiting horse. Both men who had attacked him watched him frantically spurring away.

The first man picked up Laurel's carpetbag and brought it back to her. She recognized him as the well-dressed one she had earlier guessed was a businessman.

"You're mighty handy with that reticule," he said with a grin. "You sure surprised him, and me, too."

Conscious that the waiting passengers had crowded around, Laurel flushed. "I'm sorry I hit you, but I thought you were trying to help him."

"That's perfectly understandable, Miss." He paused, then repeated the last word as a question. "Miss?"

"Laurel Bartlett." She raised her eyes to meet his dark brown ones. "Miss Laurel Bartlett of Chicago."

"Bushrod Pomeroy, lately of your city but heading back to Sacramento." His gaze swiftly and discretely swept her from head to toe and back again.

She turned to the man who had helped save her bag.

He was the older man who she thought resembled Lincoln. "I'm grateful to you, too, Sir," she said with smile.

He gave a slight, courtly bow. "My pleasure. May I present myself?" When she nodded, he added, "Horatio Bodmer of Springfield, Illinois." He glanced at Agnes who had come up to stand beside Laurel. "I'm a widower on my way to California to see my only son."

"Gentlemen," Laurel said, "may I present my aunt, Miss Agnes Bartlett?"

"How do you do, Mr. Bodmer?" she said formally, then beamed at Pomeroy. "I am grateful for your quick action."

He shrugged. "It was nothing. Miss Bartlett," he said to Laurel, "may I carry that carpetbag onto the coach for you?"

Laurel was unwilling to let the precious contents out of her sight. It seemed implausible that there was any connection between what had happened in Chicago and here, but she didn't want to take any chances with the bag.

"No, thanks. That's very kind of you, Mr. Pomeroy, but I'm used to it. Thanks again for your help."

"You're welcome. Well, if you'll excuse me, I've got to make sure my bags are aboard our coach."

"I'll go check on mine, too," Bodmer said. He bowed slightly to the women and walked away with Pomeroy.

Laurel watched as the crowd parted to let

them pass. They acknowledged the compliments with brief nods.

Agnes whispered, "It's a good thing he was around just now. Rather handsome, don't you think?"

"I didn't really notice," Laurel replied, but knew that wasn't quite true. He was probably in his middle twenties, stood about five-ten and was nicely built. She added, "Mr. Bodmer is very courtly. Did you notice how he looked at you?"

Agnes brushed that remark aside. "Mr. Pomeroy is very charming. Protective, too, and quick. Did you see how fast he moved? If he hadn't, your bag would be long gone by now."

"Aunt Agnes, he's probably married, so please quit trying to interest me in him."

"I wasn't! I was just commenting."

"Well, you can stop." Laurel carried her carpetbag and reticule to the bench and sat down again.

Agnes joined her, saying, "You don't suppose there's any connection between what happened just now with the break-ins back home, do you?"

Laurel had already thought about that. "Just a coincidence. If it wasn't, then whoever unsuccessfully tried in Chicago would have had to know when I would be in

Omaha, be waiting, and set up the fight as a diversion. It was just a random act, so forget it."

"I suppose you're right, but why did he try to take your bag instead of anyone else's?"

"Maybe it was because mine was closest to the door."

The two ladies heard the call to board. Laurel glanced out the front window as the driver opened the stagecoach door and offered his hand to help one of the older women aboard.

The sight triggered the memory of Ridge's touch when he assisted her into a carriage. She remembered the sensation with pleasure, then shook her head.

Don't think about him! Focus on what I've got to do in Sacramento!

Her logical mind tried to do that, but her heart would not listen. She rose with her carpetbag and handbag to follow Agnes toward the waiting coach.

For the first time in days, Ridge felt at peace when he sat in church next to his friend Griff. He had slid from his rolling chair into the end of a pew. Their strong baritone voices blended well on the opening hymn, reminding Ridge of when they had been boys and his brother was still alive, all singing in the choir.

The memory made Ridge sigh regretfully. When the music ended, he stared thoughtfully at the flickering candles on the altar. The Union invaders had burned the original wooden building with its beautiful stained-glass windows, but volunteers had rebuilt the sanctuary. Even though it lacked the biblical window scenes, it was still a place of serenity and peace.

Ridge was vaguely aware that there was a stir among the other parishioners behind him as late-comers were seated. He didn't look around, but Griff turned his head, then gently jabbed Ridge in the ribs.

"Don't look now," he whispered, "but when you can, casually look back and across the aisle near the door."

Nodding without interest, Ridge lowered the kneeling rail in anticipation of the prayer, but his mind had drifted to Laurel. With an effort, he mentally slid into reflections on Griff's business proposition. He was undoubtedly right about the money to be made in land speculation along the route of the transcontinental railroad. Now was the right time to get involved, too. But Ridge wasn't sure that's what he wanted to do, at least, not unless he could put in matching funds.

At the rector's call to prayer, Ridge slid out of his seat to kneel on the padded rail. At the same time, he turned his head for a quick glance back. He was just in time to look straight into Varina's pale green eyes.

Startled, Ridge's gaze lingered, taking in her white short-sleeved dress that accented her perfect figure, yet in a discreetly modest way. Her golden hair was parted in the middle, tied in braids, and twisted to form a crown on her head. She reminded Ridge of a drawing he had seen of a mythical goddess.

She held his eyes for a second longer before giving him a faint smile, then knelt so that only the top of her head showed above the backs of the pews.

When the prayer ended and Ridge resumed his seat, Griff leaned forward slightly. "See why my mother says the women around here are betting on Varina?"

"This means nothing," Ridge whispered back. "This is her church, same as ours. She's got a right to be here."

Ridge knew that was true, but he was unable to focus on the rest of the service. When the benediction was pronounced and everyone began filing out the front door to shake hands with the rector, Ridge avoided looking back at Varina. Instead, he held the rolling chair while Griff eased back into it.

"Would you prefer us going out the side door?"

The thought had occurred to him, but hearing it verbalized made him shake his head. "No, of course not."

"Then let's head up the aisle where she's waiting."

Ridge tried to tell himself that Varina should be treated just like any other parishioner, but he could not make himself act that way. There were too many bitter-sweet memories; now mostly bitter. He shoved Griff's chair ahead of him until they came even with the pew where Varina waited alone. Her faint lilac fragrance made the memories more hurtful.

He managed to speak normally. "Good morning."

"Good morning to you both," she replied with a smile. "I trust you're both well?"

"I am," Griff answered, adding, "Ridge, I can roll myself out from here. You take your time."

Ridge was tempted to protest, but he could not be rude. "I'll be out in a minute, Griff."

Ridge and Varina stood in awkward silence for a few moments after Griff had gone and the last stragglers passed with a friendly word of greeting. Ridge was aware that the older women looked knowingly at each other or hid understanding smiles behind their fans.

Ridge finally asked, "How've you been, Varina?"

"Let's not pretend," she replied, reaching out to lightly rest long graceful fingers on his forearm. "We have known each other too long to be awkward about our feelings. We can still be friends."

Ridge pulled his hand away. "Friends? No, we can't, and what do you know about my feelings?"

"Don't sound so accusatory. I know you were hurt, and I'm sorry. I wouldn't have done that for the world."

"No." His tone was suddenly cold. "No, you did it for less — for a lot less: money that's now gone!"

A mist showed in her eyes, but her voice remained calm. "Please, people are watching, so let's not prolong this. We need to talk, so couldn't we? . . ."

"You might need to talk," he rudely corrected her. "I don't."

"Shh! Please keep your voice down. You were always so kind and considerate, and I don't think you've changed. Please, Ridge!" Her lower lip trembled slightly before she added, "Meet me about two this afternoon at the place where we used to go."

No! leaped to his mind, but a single tear appeared in the corner of her left eye, then slowly slid down her flawless cheek. "All right," he said, regretting the words. "I'll be there."

"Thank you." Her voice dropped to the throaty huskiness that he remembered so well. "Thank you."

She pushed by him and walked gracefully down the aisle, away from the front door and the cluster of parishioners who seemed to be engaged in small group discussions, but clearly had been waiting to see the outcome of the meeting between the two former lovers.

That was foolish! Why did I agreed to do that?

Ridge squared his shoulders, involuntarily breathed in the lilac fragrance, then walked as casually as possible toward the front door.

A few hours west of Omaha, Laurel had become used to the Concord stage swaying on its leather thoroughbraces. These had often been touted for their comfortable ride, but nothing had prepared Laurel for the close confinement of nine passengers seated inside.

There were three rows of seats each accommodating three passengers. Laurel was squashed in the middle of the forward-facing rear seat with Agnes on her right and a matronly woman on the left.

Agnes said under her breath to Laurel, "These are too tight quarters. I'll never make it to Sacramento."

"You'll be all right," Laurel said, studying the other seating arrangements.

Directly in front of her, in the center of the coach between the two doors, a folding bench for three was hinged so that it could be flipped up out of the way when not in use. Now it was occupied by an untidy young man sitting next to the left-hand door with Pomeroy in the middle directly in front of Laurel. Bodmer sat next to the right-hand door ahead of Agnes. Laurel's and Agnes's knees barely cleared the back of that seat. The men sitting there had their backs supported by a broad strap somewhat like a shaving strop.

In the backward-facing front seat, from Laurel's left, a tired-looking woman sat by the window. The small man in black sat next to her in the middle. A stocky man in a slouch hat occupied the other window seat. Knees of those in the front and center seats almost touched.

The man in black with the Bible in hand raised his voice. It was in sharp contrast to his small stature. "Since we're going to be traveling in such a tight space, perhaps we should introduce ourselves. I'm Lyman Villard, a minister of the Gospel." He turned expectantly to the woman next to him.

Laurel didn't pay much attention and so missed most of the names as each person in turn introduced himself or herself. Then they broke into small conversational groups with those closest to them, but Laurel deliberately avoided eye contact with everyone.

That was especially true with Pomeroy, who repeatedly tried to engage her in conversation. Agnes encouraged this by discreet jabs in the ribs. When Laurel refused to be drawn into a dialogue, she noticed that he often turned as if to look out the window, but she knew he was really stealing looks at her.

Agnes also avoided talking with Bodmer, the man who resembled Lincoln. Soon both men gave up and began chatting with those in the front row. But Laurel noticed the man in the right corner didn't join in. He remained silent and aloof.

Agnes began complaining again. "It's bad enough having to travel on the Sabbath, but

I'm not sure I can stand fifteen days and nights of this. Especially when there's no stopping for anything, day or night. Well, except changing teams every twelve miles. Even then, there's not time to get off."

The six-horse teams averaged slightly more than five miles an hour heading across the Great Plains of the Nebraska Territory, rising toward the tablelands. The horses were changed every twelve miles or so, and a fresh team was brought on.

Laurel had tried to tune out the incessant carping so she could concentrate on her California objectives, but that was hard to do.

She tried to reassure her aunt from the material she had read before starting the trip. "The driver has to average a hundred and twenty-five miles every twenty-four hours. But every forty-five miles, there's a way station where we can refresh ourselves."

"That's eight hours!" Agnes exclaimed indignantly. "If I'd known that, I would never have come."

Pomeroy twisted around in the swing seat. "Excuse me for butting in, ladies," he said with a friendly smile, "but you'll soon get used to it."

"Really?" Agnes leaned toward him.

"Have you made this trip often?"

"Too often. But a businessman has to put up with some inconveniences now and then."

Agnes asked, "Does your wife mind your being away from home so much?"

Embarrassed, Laurel gently kicked her aunt's foot.

"I'm not married," he replied.

"Really?" Agnes almost seemed to purr. "My niece and I have never been west before. Any information you can impart to us would be welcome, wouldn't it, Laurel?"

Courtesy required Laurel to at least nod, but she flushed with humiliation and lowered her eyes. She nodded without speaking. There was nothing subtle about Agnes now, any more than there had been when she set out to destroy Laurel's relationship with Ridge.

"Is Sacramento your destination?" Pomeroy asked, his gaze inviting both women to respond.

Agnes glanced at Laurel as if to prompt her to answer, but she didn't. Agnes said, "Yes. My niece is a correspondent for the Chicago *Globe*. Perhaps you've read some of her stories?"

"I may have. What do you write about, Miss Bartlett?"

Trapped into responding, Laurel replied, "In the past, I've written about the Union Pacific Railroad building west out of Omaha. Now I'm going to do the same for the Central Pacific building eastward."

Her dual life had never troubled her much before making her recent Christian recommitment, but now her conscience was pricked again. Her correspondence work wasn't the real reason for her trip.

Pomeroy said, "I'm not a railroad man myself, but I am acquainted with some of the principals in the CP. If I can be of assistance in any way —"

"That's very kind of you," Laurel broke in, "but I have already made other arrangements." She added a quick smile because she appreciated his saving her carpetbag. It wasn't his fault that Agnes was trying to be an instant matchmaker. And he was good looking.

Agnes said quickly, "Oh, but if she does need other contacts, where could you be reached?"

"Aunt Agnes!" Laurel muttered angrily. "Please!"

"My office is on Front Street near K where the railroad started. Pomeroy Company. It's easy to find."

"Railroads!" The man in the left swing

seat made a spitting motion out the door window. Laurel had heard him tell the driver upon boarding that he wanted to sit next to the window so he could enjoy his quid. He had been told that spitting was prohibited. When the passenger grumbled that he couldn't go eight hours without a "chaw," the driver bluntly warned: "You chew, you walk."

Laurel joined all the others in looking at him. He was about twenty-five, and wore a battered kepi forage cap with the tattered remains of a butternut-colored jacket. His untidy blond beard was stained with ugly brown tobacco juice.

"Railroads!" the bearded one repeated with a snort. "They're going to ruin lots of businesses." He had a soft southern accent.

"Why do you think that?" Pomeroy asked pleasantly, turning to face him.

"I'll tell you why, Mister. . . ."

"Pomeroy. Bushrod Pomeroy."

"Lorenzo Hodges, lately of South Carolina, and proud to have fought for the Confederacy. You a Yankee?"

"From Illinois. Lately captain of artillery."

Hodges snorted again. "I thought so. All you Yankees speak with a nasal sound that rubs a man's ears wrong."

"Gentlemen, please!" Agnes interjected. "As my niece often reminds me, the war is over. Please, in deference to the four of us ladies present, a civil discussion about the railroads would be appreciated."

The men began a lively discussion on the pros and cons of the transcontinental line. Laurel breathed a sigh of relief, glad to escape the conversation so she could mentally review her various objectives in reaching California.

First, I've got to find out for Pinkerton who's behind the efforts to stop the railroad, if there is indeed an organized conspiracy. Then I've got to locate Mark Gardner and see if he can identify the man in the photo that Seymour gave me.

She glanced down at the carpetbag between her feet at the bottom of her seat. *I wonder if that man in the picture really is a witness to murder.*

If that was true, Laurel could understand if the killer was the one who had tried to get that photo from her. He couldn't risk being identified. With the picture, he might locate the witness. If the stakes were high enough, another murder was possible. But whoever it was, he was back in Chicago. She could forget him. Then she frowned, remembering the attempted theft in Omaha.

No! There's no possible connection. Yet a silent voice seemed to mockingly ask, *Are you sure?*

She heard Hodges vigorously defending the same basic companies Laurel already knew would be hurt by the coming of the railroad. She didn't care to hear more because there was no likelihood that the South Carolinian knew anything of value. She again focused on her objectives.

I hate misleading these men and my aunt about what my real job is, but Pinkerton is strict on his rules.

She took a deep breath. *That's it. Two things that must be done, and as quickly as possible.*

Her mind leaped, unbidden, to another goal. *No, there's one more thing. I have to forget Ridge.* She glanced at Pomeroy and nodded to herself. *No time like the present to start.* She leaned forward to listen.

Ridge was standing by his horse, still castigating himself for having agreed to meet Varina when she drove up in her carriage. He unconsciously sucked in his breath. She was beautiful, he had to admit. Laurel was pretty with a tiny nose and small mouth and a flawless figure for one so petite. Varina was four or five inches taller, with a face and form so perfect that she again reminded him of some mythical Greek goddess.

Careful! he warned himself, going to help her down.

"Shall we walk along the river?" Varina asked, her green eyes silently pleading for him to agree.

"Of course." He turned toward a small path worn on the bank. They had played here as children and walked along this same path during their late teens. Ridge was confident she had chosen to meet him here to remind him of those happy times together.

He asked, "What did you want to talk about?"

"I don't know where to begin." She raised her hand in an uncertain motion, then dropped it so it lightly brushed against his.

Ridge pretended not to notice, although the touch also brought back memories from before the war. "Why not come right to the point and say it straight-out?"

She looked reproachfully at him. "You sound angry."

"I've been angry and hurt, but I'm over that."

"You don't sound that way."

"I'll try to keep my tone more to your liking."

She stopped, causing him to do the same.

"Are you trying to quarrel with me?" she asked, her green eyes searching his face.

He took a slow breath and let it out. "Maybe I was being a little defensive. I'm sorry."

She started walking and he fell into step beside her. "Ridge, I made several mistakes while you were away fighting the Yankees."

She waited, but when he didn't answer, she continued. "I got lonely, very lonely. Thomas was one of the few men not away with the army, well, except for the ones too old to fight. Thomas was also lonely after losing his wife. So we began just talking, and . . ." she shrugged, leaving her sentence dangling.

"You think I didn't get lonely?" His voice rose. "You think riding with a bunch of horse soldiers, tearing up Union railroad tracks, burning bridges, sleeping on the ground, and being in the hospital with a leg wound kept me from getting lonely?"

He turned and took her by both shoulders as if to shake her while the painful words continued to pour out of him. "You think I didn't feel lonely when your letters slowed, then stopped coming altogether? You didn't even write to let me know that you were breaking our engagement to marry Sedgeworth!"

She protested softly, "You're hurting me."

"Sorry." He released her. "When I look back, I can see that you always did what you wanted. Most of the time it didn't matter, but you finally went too far. So it's good that I was away when I learned you were married."

"Ridge, I'm sorry!" There was a tremor in her voice. "I am truly sorry, but I can't change the past."

He turned to look across the river. "I know. I didn't expect to say all this, but then, neither did I expect us to ever again have a private conversation."

She took a step to stand so close that her arm brushed his. "I said I made several mistakes. One of those was in not waiting for you."

"I don't want to hear that, Varina."

"But I have to say it. Please try to understand."

"I don't," he said bluntly. "I probably never will."

"You said in church that we couldn't be friends. Did you mean that?"

"Yes, at least, not as we used to be."

"Not even like when we were growing up, and before we began courting?"

"I've thought about that. We just sort of

seemed to drift together. I suppose we were encouraged by everyone else who seemed to think we would get married."

"We could still do that."

He frowned, gazing down at her with a wrinkled brow. "Get married?"

"I've never gotten over you, Ridge." Her words were so soft they were barely audible. "I never will. I hoped . . . I still hope that if we talked like this, you might say you felt the same."

"Don't say any more, Varina."

"I'm know I'm being very brazen, but it's the only way I know to possibly undo the terrible mistake I made. Do you understand that?"

He took another slow breath before answering. "Yes, I believe I do, but I don't feel the same anymore."

Varina dropped her eyes. "Is it Laurel?" When he nodded, she asked, "Do you love her?"

"Very much."

"So why did you walk off and leave her at that picnic?"

So it was true that everyone, including Varina, had heard about that. He told her, "I was a fool."

"But she went back to Chicago, which suggests that she doesn't love you. Are you

218

going to spend the rest of your life pining for her?"

Ridge felt his jaw muscles twitch. He reached out and took both of Varina's hands in his. He saw the sudden flicker of hope in her eyes, so he quickly shook his head. "Don't misunderstand. You're a beautiful woman, and most men would be proud to be your husband. But . . ."

"But not you," she broke in quietly.

He released her hands. "Thanks for suggesting we have this meeting, Varina. It's helped me clarify my thinking, and I hope it's done the same for you."

"You're going after her?" There was a hint of sad resignation in her voice.

"Yes, I am. I planned on returning to the railroad, but I've changed my mind."

For a moment, they stood facing each other in silence. Then he saw tears in her eyes, but before he could say anything, she suddenly stood on tiptoes and kissed him lightly on the cheek.

"Good luck, Ridge. But if it doesn't work out —"

He interrupted, "Good-bye, Varina."

He swung around and walked purposefully away.

CHAPTER 11

After the heated discussion about the railroads, conversation in the stagecoach had died down to an uncomfortable silence. The little man in black cleared his throat, drawing all eyes to him. "As I mentioned before, I'm a minister, and this is the Sabbath. Our only possible place of worship is this traveling conveyance. If you're all agreeable, I would like to say a few words."

The woman sitting next to him in the backward-facing front seat exclaimed, "That would be lovely, wouldn't it?" She turned for confirmation from the three women in the back seat.

"Absolutely," Agnes said emphatically. "But a hymn or two would help us establish a worshipful attitude." She fanned some of the fine dust sifting in through the open windows. "Lead on, Reverend Villard."

Hodges, the former Confederate soldier protested, "I don't want no part of your caterwaulin'."

Pomeroy said, "But surely you have no objection to the rest of us joining with Mr. Villard?"

"I'm ag'in it," Hodges growled.

Pomeroy commented, "I'm sure we all regret whatever caused you to feel that way, but let's see about the rest of us. All in favor of the preacher's suggestion raise their hands."

Laurel's hand went up along with all the others, except Hodges and the man with the slouch hat who had not spoken except to give his name. All eyes turned to him. His hand slowly went up.

"Majority rules," Pomeroy said. "Lead on, Pastor."

Laurel joined in singing *Blessed Be the Tie That Binds* as she studied the preacher. Balding, his mustache blended with a heavy goatee. Both were streaked with gray. She guessed he was only about five foot four. He seemed as mild-mannered as anyone she had ever known, but when the singing ended and he began his homily, a power showed in his voice even though he did not raise it.

"Perhaps I can just give you a bit of what I plan to talk about to my new congregation in Sacramento.

"There is a divine principle not unlike the physical law of gravity," he began, opening his Bible. "It is summed up in just seventeen words. 'Be not deceived; God is not mocked: for whatsoever a man soweth, that shall he also reap.' Galatians six-seven."

Laurel fidgeted uncomfortably. She didn't want to hear a sermon on that topic. It made her think of Sarah's warnings, and the fact that everyone on the stage now had a false sense of who she really was. Her aunt had said Laurel was a newspaper correspondent because she didn't know that she was really a Pinkerton detective. There was nothing wrong with being one, but perpetuating the lie was wrong.

I lied to Aunt Agnes, Laurel realized. *Indirectly, I did the same thing to Ridge. Yet I have to do that under Pinkerton's rules. Now all these people . . .*

She forced herself to stop thinking about that. She could not ease her mind by rationalizing. She noticed the little minister looking beyond his small congregation to focus his sharp eyes on Laurel.

She squirmed as he warmed to his subject, pointing out that nobody doubted that if he planted potatoes, he would not harvest roses.

"Neither," Villard said, "could he sow deceit and expect honesty in return."

"Amen!" Agnes said softly, causing Laurel to glance sharply at her. Agnes considered herself to be righteous, a regular

222

church goer and a staunch defender of morals, both public and private.

She's a hypocrite, Laurel thought. *So how is the law of sowing and reaping proven in her life? She's getting away with it. So am I.*

With her conscience somewhat relieved, Laurel heard the rest of the sermon with less discomfort, but she could not be completely at peace.

Ridge entered the barn at Brickside where Griff was trying to groom one of the horses while sitting in his rolling chair. Griff dropped the curry comb into his lap and wheeled the chair toward a manger where Ridge stood.

"I've been thinking about your offer," Ridge began. "I appreciate it, but I have to decline for two reasons. I can't because I wouldn't feel right not risking an equal amount of money as you. I also feel uncomfortable about being in business with a friend, especially a good one."

"I was afraid you'd say that, Ridge. But I assure you our friendship would stand, even if our venture failed. I've lost more in life than a little gold. I hope you'll change your mind."

"To tell the whole truth, I couldn't concentrate on any business right now, not the way it would be necessary to be successful."

Griff studied him with thoughtful eyes. "Something has happened since I last saw you?"

"I went to see Varina."

"Did you talk to her this time, or walk away again?"

Ridge caught the hint of humor in the question, but he ignored it. "Your mother and the other ladies were wrong about Varina and me. I told her that I'm going after Laurel."

Griff's eyebrows arched. "Oh? How did she take it?"

"As well as can be expected, I suppose."

"I see. When are you leaving?"

"As soon as possible. I've got to write Laurel's father and ask him where Laurel will be stopping in Sacramento. She must have left him some sort of address."

"Probably. Then you're just going to show up on her doorstep without letting her know you're coming?"

"Something like that."

"What if she isn't glad to see you?"

"I'll stick around until she changes her mind."

Griff warned, "If you don't win her over, you're going to end up with a terribly painful heartache."

"I've suffered pain before. Besides, I'm not going to lose her."

Griff nodded slowly, absently playing with the curry brush for several seconds. Finally he said, "What if Varina is as determined to make you change your mind as you are to make Laurel change hers?"

Scowling, Ridge asked, "Why do you even think of such a thing? It's over between us; I told her that, and she accepted it."

"Did she?" Griff asked softly.

"What else could she do?"

Griff hesitated, then said, "Some of us see a side of Varina that you never could. It was evident to us, even as children, but not to you. She is more than just a beautiful woman. She gets what she wants."

Ridge asked sharply, "Are you suggesting that she still intends to get me?"

"Don't get defensive! No, I'm not suggesting anything like that. I'm just reminding you, as a friend, that you should not underestimate her. That's all."

"Thanks, but you needn't worry." Ridge shoved himself away from the manger where he had been sitting. "Well, I've got to get moving." He extended his right hand. "You're a good friend, Griff. I appreciate you."

"You, too." Griff gripped Ridge's hand

225

firmly. "If you ever change your mind about being partners in the business venture, my offer's still open."

"Thanks, I'll remember. Well, I'll drop you a note from Sacramento and let you know when the wedding is going to be."

"Sure," Griff said as Ridge walked away. "Sure."

Shortly after the devotions had ended, the driver stopped at the next way station. The passengers, stiff from sitting so long in confined and cramped quarters, eagerly disembarked. Laurel retrieved her carpetbag from where she had placed it on the floor behind her feet and next to the seat.

Agnes asked, "Why do you insist on dragging that with you every place? It's bad enough to carry a handbag."

"I just feel more comfortable hanging on to it," Laurel replied, watching the other two women hurry toward the tiny "necessary" building in back of the small, desolate station. "You go on with them. I'll wait inside."

As Agnes followed the other women, Laurel started toward the front door of the low-ceilinged building when she felt a hand close beside hers on the carpetbag's handle. Instantly, she whirled, swinging her handbag back with the other hand.

"Easy!" Pomeroy exclaimed, jerking his hand back. "I was just going to help you with that!"

She gave him a quick smile. "I'm sorry. I guess I'm still jumpy after that man tried to steal it in Omaha."

"You must have something very valuable in there," he commented, walking with her to the front door.

"Just my personal effects that won't fit in the handbag, including my writing essentials."

"I see." He opened the door for her, allowing her to enter a dark, very rustic room. The fragrance of coffee mingled with the stench of perspiration and spittoons. It took all her will power to keep from wrinkling her nose.

"These way stations usually serve beans. Want some?"

"If that's all there is, yes, please."

As he started to turn away, the former Confederate turned from where he had rushed to be first at the counter. He held up a cup of coffee and a couple of small squares. "Ain't nothing but hardtack. The owner says that supplies didn't get here. You ever eat hardtack?" he asked Laurel.

"No, I haven't."

"Only way to make them soft enough to chew is like this." He plunged one into a cup of steaming coffee to soften it, adding, "Worm castles. That's what we called them in the army."

Laurel didn't want to know why. "I'll just have coffee." She turned toward the counter where most of the other male passengers were already lined up.

"I'll get it for you," Pomeroy said. "Have a seat. I'll be right back."

Laurel thanked him and sat down on one of the rough benches in front of a homemade table. She hoped Hodges would leave, but he sat down uninvited across from her.

"What's a purty little filly like you doin' way out here?" He stuck moistened hardtack in his mouth and sucked noisily on it. Fresh drops of coffee fell among the old chewing tobacco stains on his blond beard.

Trying to avoid getting into a discussion, Laurel glanced up as the minister entered. "Oh, Pastor, that was a most thought-provoking sermon."

"Thank you." He studied her with eyes that seemed to probe into her very thoughts. "I noticed that you seemed to be interested. I trust that the message touched you."

Laurel hesitated. "I found it helpful."

"Preachers," Hodges grumbled. "I seen

plenty of them in the war. Chaplains, they called theirselves. I seen a many of them turn tail and head for the rear when the shootin' started. Reckon you had a nice little church in some safe place, huh, preacher man?"

"Mr. Hodges!" Laurel exclaimed. "Have some respect."

"A man's got to earn my respect, Miss. Same with you women." He grinned through the untidy beard. " 'Course, you got my interest right fast."

"Brother Hodges," the minister said quietly, "won't you be more comfortable at another table?"

The veteran scowled and set his cup down so hard on the table that the coffee sloshed over. "You too good to eat with me?"

"No, I'm just trying to be considerate of everyone present, Mr. Hodges."

"You got more grit than brains, preacher. If you wasn't so blasted little, I'd —"

"Mr. Hodges!" Pomeroy interrupted, returning with two cups of coffee and some squares of hardtack. "I do believe you'd be better off outside."

Hodges leaped to his feet, his face contorting in anger, but stopped when he saw Pomeroy standing quietly, his eyes hard.

"I need a chaw anyhow," the veteran

muttered, and walked toward the door with his coffee and hardtack. He brushed by Agnes who had just entered.

Agnes smiled in approval at Pomeroy, then rushed up to the table. She gave Laurel a quick glance, then turned to the two men. "Mr. Pomeroy, I commend you for standing up to that ruffian. Reverend Villard, you were very brave to face him down that way."

"Thank you. With the Lord's help, I faced worse as an army chaplain."

Pomeroy handed Laurel's coffee to her, then set his down beside her and placed the hardtack over the top of the cup to be softened by the steam. He asked Agnes, "Would you like some coffee and a cracker?"

She smiled and nodded. "Yes, thank you." As Pomeroy walked away, she turned back to the little preacher. "You were a chaplain?"

"Three years."

"Which army?"

"Confederate."

Agnes's demeanor changed. "Oh, I see."

"I was pastoring in Missouri, not taking sides," he explained quietly. "But when President Lincoln sent troops to try keeping that state from seceding, Union troops seized the church property and threw me in jail. They claimed I was a Rebel whose property was subject to seizure by the Union. I tried to explain that it wasn't my church, but it didn't do any good. Finally, they let me out and I signed up as a chaplain."

Laurel asked, "You said three years in the army?" At his nod, she added, "I have a feeling that you were not one of those who went to the rear when the fighting started."

"I tried never to shirk my duty to my God or my fellow soldiers."

Agnes asked, "Were you ever wounded?"

Villard was slow to answer. "Five times."

Laurel's eyes opened wide. "But you still stayed in the ranks?"

"It was my place to serve the Lord."

"I think a Confederate chaplain's views would make good reading," Laurel commented. "Would you let me interview you for the newspaper?"

"Thanks, but I would rather not."

"Why not?" Laurel persisted. "I think it would make a great story."

Pomeroy returned with Agnes's cup, nodded politely to her but looked at Laurel. "Perhaps while the stage is stopped I might be able to answer some of your questions about the railroads. We could finish our coffee outside."

Laurel suppressed a frown. Her independent nature did not respond well to being interrupted, and especially in what she perceived as an effort to control her time. She started to decline, but Agnes gently nudged her foot under the table.

"That's a good idea, Laurel. It will help you to get a head start on your Sacramento assignments."

"I'm sure you're right, Aunt Agnes, but I want to be alone before the stage starts again. Pastor, I hope we can talk some more later on."

To forestall any further discussion, she reached under the table and retrieved her carpetbag. After giving everyone a brief smile to show she didn't mean to be rude, she headed toward the front door.

There she suddenly stopped, aware for the first time that the man with the slouch hat had been silently watching her from across the room. She turned so quickly that she caught him looking at her carpetbag. He glanced up, caught her eye, then instantly looked away.

Who is he? He said his name was Walker, but he didn't say if that was his first or last name, or where he was from. Why is he so stand-offish? Was he watching me, or am I just imagining things?

She visited the small facilities in back of the desolate way station and she returned to find the hostler moving a fresh team into place in front of the stage. The stocky driver in his long duster gave the horse handler a final word of instruction and tipped his dusty hat to Laurel.

"I hear tell you're one of them lady newspaper correspondents I heard about. That right?"

"You may have read some of my articles in the Chicago *Globe*."

"We don't get that one out here, but if you're looking for stories, your readers might like to know something about these stage coaches. After all, if what I hear about the transcontinental railroad is true, these here coaches may soon be a thing of the past."

From the appreciative way he looked at her, Laurel figured he wanted an excuse to talk with her. "I would be happy to interview you, Mister . . ."

"Evans, Hugh Evans."

"How do you do? I'm Laurel Bartlett. But when will you have time for me? I understand we keep moving, day and night, not even getting off the coach to sleep."

"That's right, Miss Bartlett, but if you don't mind riding up front with me, we can move and talk."

Laurel cast a doubtful eye on the high box, and then down at her long skirts.

"Don't worry," he said, understanding her concern. "You wait until everyone else is inside, then I'll climb up and reach a hand down to help you up. Best seat in the whole world. As soon as everyone's finished eating, I'd be glad for your company."

"Then I accept," she said brightly. "I'll go tell my aunt."

Outside the door of the way station, she realized that Walker had been watching her. She walked directly up to him where he squatted on his heels, smoking a pipe.

She stopped in front of him. "Mr. Walker?"

He stood and removed the pipe from his mouth. "Yes?"

Her impulsive act had caught her without an excuse for approaching him, but she was used to improvising. "I heard you introduce yourself on the stage," she began, using one of her disarming smiles, "but I didn't catch whether that's your Christian or last name."

"Last. It's Albert Walker."

She quickly studied him with practiced eyes that took in details. Hazel eyes, square jaw, strongly built with big hands and a quiet, self-assured manner of speaking. He reminded her of some detectives she had known in Chicago. She wondered if he was armed.

"How are you enjoying the trip so far?"

"Fine." He spoke the one word softly, but stopped.

Laurel was surprised. Men usually began fawning over her as soon as she showed an interest, but Walker's eyes seemed to cloud with suspicion. She tried again.

"Have you been to California before, Mr. Walker?"

"No."

Suspecting she had made a mistake in a direct approach, Laurel tried to think how to gracefully exit her awkward situation. "I guess you heard I'm . . . I'm a newspaper correspondent."

Careful! She silently lashed herself for the slight hesitancy. Leading a double life hadn't bothered her until recently. Lies had come easily to her, and her actions had made them believable.

"I heard." He knocked the residue from his pipe and scraped dirt over them with his foot.

"I'm looking for good stories," she continued, trying to sound sincere. "On a long trip like this, I would like to interview everyone in hopes of finding some stories my readers will like. I wonder if you —"

"No," he interrupted. "I don't have anything worth writing about."

"Sometimes people don't recognize a story the way a correspondent does, Mr. Walker." Laurel felt herself floundering. She had never met a man who didn't want to talk about himself, especially when it afforded him an excuse to impress a pretty young woman. "Perhaps if we could chat sometime. . . ."

"Thanks." Walker shoved the pipe into his pocket. "The others are coming out of the station, so we'd better get aboard."

"Yes, of course." She expected that he would at least walk with her to the stagecoach, but instead, he walked off briskly, leaving her embarrassed and bewildered.

Agnes hurried up to Laurel. "It's time to get back on the coach."

"You go ahead. The driver asked me to ride up in the front with him."

"You scandalize me, Laurel! You really do!"

"Oh, Aunt Agnes! Nothing's going to happen when a man is driving a six-horse hitch!" She thrust the carpetbag into her aunt's hands. "Please take this. I can't climb up with it and my handbag. Place the carpetbag on the floor as I do, and don't let it or my reticule out of your sight."

"What's in this thing?" Agnes took the carpetbag but eyed it suspiciously. "What are you not telling me?"

"Nothing you need to know. Now, please, do as I ask." Laurel hastily moved toward the front of the coach.

The driver looked down from his high box. "I'll give you a hand up as soon as everyone else is aboard."

"Thank you." She waited while her aunt eased into the back seat and the folding bench was lowered into position between the two doors. Pomeroy gave Laurel a quick smile before he entered to take the center position. Bodmer followed him while Hodges slid through the other door.

"Reach your hand up to me," the driver instructed. "Then hang on to your bonnet, Miss Bartlett."

She was barely seated beside him when he released the brake, called to the leaders, and the stage lurched ahead. Laurel had always enjoyed adventure, and knew she should be enjoying this experience. Yet the incident with Walker had somehow left her feeling uneasy.

Mrs. Phoebe Ashby opened her front door and called to Ridge as he started to walk around the house to his rented room.

"Oh, Ridge, I've been watching for you. This wire came for you awhile ago."

His heart jumped. *Laurel! She changed her mind!*

He grinned with anticipation as he skimmed the message. After reading the first couple of words, he scowled and glanced at the signature. "Tomkins," he read aloud.

"What?" his landlady asked from the door which she had started to enter.

"That's the name of the man who sent the wire. He's chief of detectives for the railroad."

"Bad news?" Mrs. Ashby inquired anxiously.

"Nothing like that." Ridge's voice held a hint of his disappointment that the message wasn't from Laurel. "Tomkins is the man I've been working for in Omaha. He has an emergency job he wants me to handle."

"Oh. I hoped it was from your Yankee lady friend."

"Me, too." He shoved the sheet into his pocket. "Mrs. Ashby, I've already told you that I'm vacating my room. I'll ride into the village to wire my answer to Tomkins. Then I'll leave tomorrow."

"Oh, my! You just paid the rent. Come inside. I'll give you back —"

238

"Just keep it. Now, please excuse me."

After Mrs. Ashby went inside and closed the door, Ridge walked a few steps then re-read the wire.

I could use the money, he reasoned. The sensible thing would be to meet with Tomkins. But in his heart, Ridge had made a firm decision.

He was going to Sacramento to find Laurel.

CHAPTER 12

Laurel had brought her writing materials to interview the driver, but quickly discovered that was it impossible to write on the swaying, tilting coach. She needed one hand to keep her bonnet from blowing, and clung to her precarious seat with the other.

Evans spoke above the drumming of the six-horse hitch and creaking of the coach. "It's a lot less crowded up here than inside with nine people."

"It was really tight," Laurel admitted, aware of how very darkly tanned he was under his sweat-stained hat, and how deeply his face was furrowed by weather.

"You've got the best seat," he continued. "When we're carrying valuable cargo, and when we come to Sioux territory, the shotgun messenger rides where you are."

"Sioux?" Laurel asked, feeling motion sickness starting. "You mean Indians?"

"Don't worry. We'll be in Pawnee territory for a hundred and fifty miles. They're friendly. Some even work as scouts for the Union Pacific. But when we reach Sioux and Cheyenne lands, we'll have a guard aboard."

"Cheyennes, too?" Laurel glanced around. "I've heard that both those tribes are blood-thirsty savages."

"They're just defending their traditional hunting grounds, mostly against what they call the iron horse."

"Iron? . . . Oh, you mean the train. But I haven't seen any railroad tracks since we left Omaha."

"Indians don't often bother stages anymore. They've turned to attacking small parties, like survey crews. Track laying gangs are now well armed and the army stays close. We're not likely to be bothered."

"Oh." Laurel was relieved, but her skin felt clammy. She hoped she wouldn't embarrass herself by getting sick.

He looked sharply at her. "You all right?"

Reluctantly, she admitted, "I'm slightly queasy."

"Happens to some folks who ride up here. Helps if you look out in the distance instead of up close, and try to think about something else."

"Thanks. I'll try that." She shifted her gaze to the seemingly-endless high prairie. "It's a lonely country."

"Right now it is, but have you heard that there's talk of this territory maybe becoming

241

a state next year? If it does, it would be the thirty-seventh."

"Yes, I've heard. The country's growing fast, but I can't imagine anyone wanting to live way out here."

"I heard tell that some folks say when the railroad is complete from Omaha to Sacramento, everything between the two places will be full of people. You believe that?"

"It's difficult to imagine."

"Not everyone likes the railroad. Like Pomeroy who sits in front of you in the coach. Have you met him?"

"Briefly. You say he doesn't like railroads?"

"He sure doesn't. He's ridden this stage a couple of times, so once I invited him to ride up here with me. He told me why, but that's all I'd better say. You might ask him about it. Could make a story for your newspaper."

Laurel's interest instantly spiked. "Thanks. I'll do that. But I rode up here to interview you. How did you start driving stage?"

Ridge sent two wires. He told the chief of railroad detectives that he was on his way to California, but would stop in Omaha to see him. In the second telegram to Laurel's father, Ridge said he was going to see

242

Laurel. When he checked into a Sacramento hotel, he would wire again, asking that Laurel's address be sent to him.

The next morning, Ridge boarded the first of several trains he would ride toward Omaha. Each segment of the journey would take him closer to Laurel. Somehow he had to convince her that they really belonged together.

By the time the stage driver stopped to change teams, Laurel's nausea had passed. Still, she was glad to descend from the high box and return to her seat inside the coach, curious to know more about why Pomeroy hated the railroad. He might provide the opening for her to solve her Pinkerton case.

As the stage rolled again, Agnes asked, "How did your interview go with the driver?"

"Oh, fine. I had no idea that these horses are all specially trained and paired, and all have different duties. There are what's called wheelers, swing team, and leaders. Oh, and every harness is very complex, and made to fit one particular animal."

Agnes asked doubtfully, "You think readers will be interested in that?"

"I hope so, especially if I put in what Mr. Evans told me all about how the coaches are made in Concord, New Hampshire. That's why they're called Concords."

A twinge of conscience again nipped Laurel. She did not plan to write that story, but she was caught in a role which she had to play out to protect her real objective.

Pomeroy turned in his seat to face Laurel. "I enjoy hearing someone sound enthusiastic about her work."

"I enjoy it," she assured him with an encouraging smile. "Riding up on the box was fascinating. I suppose you've ridden there?"

"Yes, once. I travel this way fairly often."

Laurel saw her opening. "On business?"

He nodded. "It's a hard trip, but it has to be done."

"It'll be easier when the railroad is complete."

Pomeroy's face hardened. "*If* it is."

"I didn't think there was any doubt."

"Some companies oppose it because it'll ruin them."

Laurel asked naïvely, "Oh? How's that possible?"

"Because they can no longer compete. Take this stage line, for instance. If that transcontinental railroad goes through, stage coaches will be forced out of business. Steamship companies will suffer, as will freight lines, toll road operators, and so forth."

Laurel raised her eyebrows. "I'm sorry to hear that. But isn't there anything that can be done about it?"

"There has been a lot of resistance, especially by some Democratic newspapers in San Francisco. But most of it has just been sniping at the railroads without any organized effort to stop it."

"I trust that your business isn't among those?"

He hesitated, but Laurel kept her eyes focused on his, her interest urging him to continue.

He said, "If you'd like, I could tell you more at the dinner stop."

"I'll look forward to it."

"Good! You ladies get a table and I'll bring your dinners to you."

Laurel glanced at her aunt. She was smiling to herself.

When they disembarked at twilight, Laurel and her aunt headed though the dusk toward the way station's two lanterns that marked the entrance. Agnes lowered her voice. "Now you're showing some sense about a man."

Laurel's heart protested, *I'm not interested in him as a man. I'm doing a job, that's all.* Ridge's image floated into her mind. *No!* she upbraided herself. *That's over and done with. It would never work for us.*

"Miss Bartlett?" A voice behind made both women turn around to see the little preacher. "One moment, if you please." When they stopped, he approached and looked at Laurel. "I notice that you take that carpetbag with you everywhere you go. Please allow me to help."

"That's very kind of you, but I'm used to it."

"Laurel!" Agnes said sharply. "If you can't trust a man of the cloth, who can you trust? Let him help."

Laurel hesitated, then smiled her thanks and held the bag out to him. "Just while we're off the stage."

"You may put your mind at rest," Villard assured her, motioning for the women to proceed him inside.

I shouldn't have done that, Laurel reprimanded herself as she and Agnes entered the building. *He's all right, but both those packages are in there.*

Her eyes located the uncouth ex-Confederate Hodges and the silent man who called himself Walker. He sat down across the table from the minister as he placed her carpetbag under the table between his feet.

I'm being silly, she reproached herself. *But*

246

if anything did happen to those packages, I'd be lost. I'll not do that again.

Laurel and her aunt had barely sat down at a corner table by a tallow candle when Agnes whispered, "Here comes that man who sits next to him in the coach."

"Bodmer," Laurel said quietly. "Horatio Bodmer. I've seen him glancing at you when you weren't looking."

"He can keep his eyes to himself!"

"Shh! Be nice to him."

"Pardon me, ladies," Bodmer said, shifting his gaze to Agnes, "but if I'm not being too forward, I would be honored if you joined me at my table."

Agnes's hands fluttered like frightened doves. It was obvious that she was not used to such invitations. "I have to stay with my niece. Mr. Pomeroy is join—"

Laurel interrupted, suppressing a grin. "It's all right, Aunt Agnes. You can see us from anywhere in here."

Bodmer nodded his appreciation to Laurel before smiling at her aunt. "I'm honored," he told her, offering his hand.

Obviously flustered, the older woman hesitated, then slowly reached up and allowed him to assist her to her feet. She gave Laurel a sort of wide-eyed, almost panicky look before he slipped her arm through his and led her across the room to another table.

Pomeroy returned to Laurel with three big bowls and three cups on a tray. "Has your aunt left us?"

"She accepted Mr. Bodmer's invitation to join him."

Pomeroy looked down at the tray. "The owner of this establishment informs me that our bill of fare consists of coffee and beans seasoned with a little fatback. Beans are commonly served at these places. So I brought some and hope you can eat them."

"They're not my preference, but I imagine they're better than hardtack."

Having missed lunch, Laurel found the boiled beans quite tasty. Some heavy home-made bread helped, although it was served without butter. The coffee was very strong.

As their meal progressed, Laurel prompted Pomeroy, "How does the trans-continental railroad threaten your business, Mr. Pomeroy?"

" 'Mister' sounds so formal. Please call me Bushrod."

"Very well. And call me Laurel."

"Laurel. That's a pretty name."

"Thank you." She steered him away from getting too friendly. "You were saying about your business?"

"Oh, yes. Well, I have an interest in a California toll road and a freight line."

"I think I understand. Trains can carry bigger loads faster than oxen or mules, and trains can't be made to stop and pay a toll every few miles. Right?"

"Right. That will become true across two thousand miles from Omaha to Sacramento. Of course, my companies have no grandiose plans, but neither do we want to be put out of business, especially by greedy railroaders using government money from greedy congressmen. Greed! That's what's going to ruin lots of businesses."

"Government money which you can't get?"

"Not a cent."

"That doesn't seem fair."

"It's extremely unfair. But there's so much money involved in the railroad that corruption goes all the way from voters who are paid in gold to cast their ballots a certain way, right on up to many elected representatives in Washington who are bribed. Even President Lincoln was flimflammed."

"Is that all possible?"

"It's actually happened!" Pomeroy suddenly put down his spoon. "This frustrates me and makes me angry, so let's talk about something else."

It was a temptation to urge him to continue, but Laurel sensed this was not the time to push. "Of course," she said, "I can understand how upsetting it must be."

"Perhaps we can discuss this another time?"

She was intrigued, especially about how Lincoln had been involved, but she didn't want to lose Pomeroy as a source of information.

Flashing one of her most disarming smiles, she agreed. "I'll look forward to it."

Out of habit, she moved her foot, expecting to feel the familiar weight of the carpetbag. In sudden panic, she realized it wasn't there. "Oh!" she exclaimed in alarm, and started to bend over to look.

Pomeroy asked, "What's the matter?"

"My carpetbag! It's . . . Oh! I forgot! The preacher has it." She looked to where he had been sitting across from Walker. Walker was still there, but Villard was heading toward the door. *He doesn't have my bag!*

"Excuse me!" she exclaimed, and rushed away from Pomeroy. Dodging tables, chairs, and some passengers, she darted up behind the little man. "Pastor Villard! Wait!"

He spun to face her. "Oh, Laurel! My!"

he cried, "I almost forgot your bag!" He scurried toward the table.

Laurel followed and saw Walker straighten up from reaching under the table. Her carpetbag was in his hand. Her heart leaped in sudden fright. Everything she needed for both her assignments was in there.

He turned, extending the bag to Villard. "You forgot this."

Laurel sighed in sudden relief as the minister thanked the usually-silent passenger.

Villard apologized to Laurel, saying, "I am truly ashamed of my dereliction. Please forgive me."

She quickly scanned the bag. It was closed and looked undisturbed. "That's all right. I'll take it now." Turning to Walker, she said, "Thank, you, too."

He shrugged and nodded but didn't say anything.

A sense of near-panic lingered, even after the carpetbag was safely behind Laurel's feet and the stage rolled again through the darkness. She didn't blame the minister for his lapse. She alone was responsible for the bag.

To forget the incident, she leaned close to her aunt and whispered, "What did you think of Mr. Bodmer?"

Agnes arranged the two blankets she had brought to cover herself while asleep on the stage. "There's nothing to think about. We just talked."

Laurel wasn't sure whether her aunt's cool tone meant she was being her usual self, or if she was trying to hide any hint of having enjoyed herself. "What about?"

"Nothing important. How about you and Mr. Pomeroy?"

"He was charming and friendly. We had a good visit."

"I saw you smiling at him. Do you like him?"

Laurel said evasively, "We're going to talk again."

"Good!" Agnes' tone clearly showed that she was pleased. She settled down into her blankets before adding, "I wonder what the preacher and that man Walker were talking about."

Laurel tried to find a comfortable place to rest her head on the back seat cushion. "About religion, I guess."

"I'm sure the minister would have done that, but I'm surprised that Walker even sat by him. After all, he was slow to raise his hand to vote for hearing a sermon. He hasn't said more than a dozen words since we got on this stage. So why would he even go near the minister?"

Yes, why? Laurel visualized Walker straightening up from reaching under the table. *How long had he been under there? Was it long enough to reach inside?* . . .

Laurel sucked in her breath, then bent over, reached down under the blankets and opened the bag. She felt inside with trembling fingers. One package. Two. She let her breath out in a soft rush.

Agnes raised her head from the back of the seat cushion. "Why the sigh?"

"No reason," Laurel murmured. She gently closed the carpetbag and replaced it under her feet. "Go to sleep."

Bringing her hands out from under the blankets, she adjusted the blankets around her shoulders. Satisfied, she tried to find a comfortable place to lay her head against the back of the seat cushion.

Laurel tried to look beyond the shadowy figures of Pomeroy and Bodmer sitting in the jump seat ahead of her. In the darkness, she could not discern the man who called himself Walker. *Who is he? Why does he stay aloof from the rest of us passengers? Why doesn't he ever join in any of our conversations?*

Had he really just been helpful in retrieving the carpetbag for the forgetful preacher? It would have been impossible to steal the bag in a roomful of witnesses. Suddenly, she sat upright. The photograph! He might have hidden it on his person without being seen.

Agnes grumbled, "Now what?"

"I just thought of something." Laurel again reached down and opened the carpetbag.

"Stop threshing around."

"In a minute." She identified the photograph by feel. Gripping it hard, she silently said an impromptu prayer of gratitude and resolved to not again let the bag out of her sight.

Agnes whispered, "I hope you're not wasting time thinking about that Reb . . . uh . . . Ridge."

"No, I'm not." Laurel closed her eyes, but sleep eluded her. She wished her aunt hadn't mentioned Ridge, for she found herself thinking of him. *He's probably with Varina. Well, I don't care!*

She slapped her open palm down hard on the back of the seat cushion. *Why don't they make these more comfortable? I don't think I can stand fourteen more nights of this.*

She again struck the cushion, but the image of Ridge and Varina lingered as the team ran on through the night.

★ ★ ★

Laurel didn't have an opportunity to approach Walker until the lunch stop when she saw him finish his food and go outside to smoke his pipe. She told her aunt she was going to the "necessary" room, then took her carpetbag and walked out, wanting to speak with Walker.

The new driver was talking to a heavily armed stranger just beyond where Walker leaned against a post. Laurel started past him, then turned as if in alarm.

"Oh!" she exclaimed to him. "Surely the driver isn't going to let that armed man ride with us!"

Walker puffed on his clay pipe without replying.

She took a couple of steps closer to him and tried again. "You don't think that's going to happen, do you? I mean, those guns . . . and we're all unarmed. At least, I think we are."

"He's the shotgun messenger." Walker's voice was low and flat, without inflection. "He's our protection."

"Protection? From what?"

"Indians."

Laurel played her innocent part carefully, opening her eyes and making nervous motions with her hands. "Are there

Indians around here?"

Walker removed the pipe from his mouth. He motioned toward the open countryside. "I heard that after we get about a hundred and fifty miles out of Omaha, we'd be in Sioux territory. Guess we're there."

That confirmed what the first driver had told Laurel yesterday, but she played innocent. "Do you think we're in any real danger?"

"I wouldn't worry, if I was you."

She called on her practiced ability to flash a friendly smile. "You must have traveled this way before. I mean, to know so much about everything out here."

She saw the flicker of caution in his eyes. He stuck the pipe in his pocket and tipped his hat. "I got to go."

He turned and walked around the side of the way station, leaving Laurel frustrated. *I moved too fast! I scared him off! But there's still time before we get to Sacramento.* She frowned and shook her head. *Strange man!*

With the armed guard on board, the stage continued safely toward the great deserts. Pomeroy continually tried to engage Laurel in conversation in the coach and to serve her at meal stops. She managed to keep him at arm's length by playing her role as correspondent.

She interviewed all passengers as possible personalities to write about for the Chicago *Globe*. Agnes repeatedly encouraged Laurel to be nicer to Pomeroy, but she in turn prodded her aunt to quit being so cool to Horatio Bodmer. Only Walker avoided Laurel. Even though he sometimes briefly answered other passengers' questions, he never engaged in real conversations.

Finally, as the last section of Nevada Territory desert slipped by and the soaring Sierra Nevada Mountains loomed ahead, Laurel again approached him.

"I don't mean to ignore you, Mr. Walker," she began as he puffed on his pipe after a meal stop, "because I would be happy to interview you for the paper."

She waited for a response, but he tamped his pipe with the end of a burned matchstick and was silent.

"Of course," she continued, "as I've told all the others, I can't guarantee that the story will be published. The editor decides that. But I would . . ."

She let her words trail off as he politely touched his hat brim, nodded, and walked away.

What's going on with him? she silently fumed. *Who is he, really? What's he hiding? I'm running out of time to find out.*

★ ★ ★

Walker was the only person on the stage Laurel had not charmed when they reached the seven-thousand-foot summit of the Sierras. While a fresh team was led into place for the downhill run toward Sacramento, Laurel casually moved away from the main cluster of passengers. They stood staring across the canyon where railroad crews could be seen working.

Laurel neared Walker when a puff of smoke across the canyon was followed moments later by the sound of the explosion. She asked, "Is that blasting I hear?"

"Must be."

"Even powder doesn't seem powerful enough to even make a dent in that mountain. Why, look at all those huge boulders! It's only what's sticking up that we can see. What must it be like where those men are working?"

"It's probably the same: Granite. Hard, hard stuff."

Encouraged by the few words from the taciturn man, Laurel asked, "Exactly what are they doing over there?"

Pomeroy came up so silently behind them that Laurel didn't hear him until he spoke. "They're starting to drill a tunnel almost seventeen-hundred feet long, right through solid granite."

Laurel controlled her annoyance at the interruption. "Really, Mr. Pomeroy? That does sound impossible." She looked to Walker, "Don't you think so?"

He shrugged. "Excuse me," he said, and walked away.

She struggled to control her sudden anger at Pomeroy for having interrupted her conversation with Walker.

Pomeroy said bitterly, "There's too much money at the end of that tunnel for the company owners to let anything stop them, even if it costs the lives of countless workers. Those Chinese chip away with hand tools, but average only seven inches to a foot a day."

"Chinese? I heard that railroad workers are Irish."

"They do predominate on the Union Pacific out of Omaha, but the Central Pacific uses Chinese workers."

Still irritated at Pomeroy's interfering with her plans, she turned back toward the stage. He joined her.

"I'm looking forward to accompanying you to an elegant restaurant when we reach Sacramento."

After nearly two weeks of being confined in the stagecoach with him, Laurel wasn't really interested. But Agnes had pushed her so hard to be nice to him that Laurel reasoned accepting his invitation might be a way to keep Agnes satisfied. And Pomeroy did seem to have some knowledge of what was happening to the railroads. Laurel needed whatever information she could get.

She still was annoyed with Pomeroy for driving the silent Walker away, but she forced another smile for Pomeroy. "After my aunt and I get settled in our hotel, I would appreciate something besides beans and hardtack."

He grinned. "I can hardly wait to reach Sacramento."

Neither could Laurel, but for another reason. Two weeks of travel had given her too much time to think of her times with Ridge. Now she could forget by focusing on her two work objectives.

The stage reached its final terminal at the foot of K Street right beside the Sacramento River. For more than a dozen years, it had been the transportation center for the capital city. Sailing vessels and stage coaches had been first. In January, 1863, Governor Leland Stanford turned the first spade of dirt there, signaling the start of construction for the Central Pacific Railroad. It was now inching east into the Sierras. Trains ran as far as tracks had been laid while Chinese laborers continued daily to chip away a scant few inches of the mountain's granite heart to lay still more railbed.

Laurel joined the others in anxiously peering out the stage windows at people waiting to welcome the new arrivals. She was startled to see a bone-thin man with sideburns standing at the back of the waiting crowd.

"Morton!" she exclaimed.

"What?" Agnes asked, gathering her blankets and handbag for disembarking.

Laurel didn't answer. She watched Morton suddenly turn away from the crowd and enter the station. There was no doubt. He was the same Dick Morton who had seen Seymour hand her the package containing a photograph of the missing witness.

What's he doing here?

CHAPTER 13

With the last train left behind on the east side of the Missouri River, Ridge crossed on a ferry and entered Omaha. The former river port now throbbed with new life as the jumping-off point for the Union Pacific Railroad.

Ridge threaded his way through crowds of men seeking work. They were a very mixed lot. Former soldiers wearing parts of blue or gray uniforms mingled with freed slaves in tattered clothes. There were many accents, dominated by Irish immigrants.

Deep dust in the roads was churned up by countless ox-drawn and mule-drawn wagons transporting freight from the Missouri River to the rail yards. The teams passed shops where railroad cars were being built. Essential rail construction components were stored in larger buildings. Smaller, quickly built housing for railroad workers helped give the community a frontier atmosphere.

Near the U.P. depot where a wood-burning locomotive stood on the tracks facing west, Ridge approached an office made of a canvas tent and rough boards.

Ridge stuck his head in the door where Tomkins scowled over a stack of papers piled on a packing crate now serving as a desk.

"Ridge Granger!" the chief railroad detective exclaimed, pushing his chair back to reach his right hand across the desk. "Glad you're back! Shove some of that junk off that chair and sit down!"

After shaking hands, Ridge hurriedly explained, "I really don't have time. As I said in my wire, I'm on my way to Sacramento. But I owe you the courtesy of coming by to say why I'm doing that instead of coming back to work for you."

"That's more'n most do," Tomkins admitted. "Can't keep men from moving, but set a spell anyway."

Nodding, Ridge obeyed, his eyes sweeping Tomkins.

Unlike Jack Casement, the former Union brigadier general who performed his U.P. construction boss duties with a bullwhip and a pistol, Tomkins's appearance testified to his background as a bare-knuckle brawler. He was about the size and shape of two hogsheads set on end. His hook nose had been broken and grown back crooked. However, his huge hands suggested he had given more than he ever took.

"You know me," Tomkins began, leaning back in his chair. "I'm blunt as a club. So why are you going to Sacramento?"

"It's personal."

"A woman, huh?" Tomkins slammed a massive fist down on the desk. "More important than money?"

"This one is."

"You serious?"

"Very."

"Last I knew, Ridge, you didn't have two coins to rub together, 'cept what you got paid here."

It was none of Tomkins's business, so Ridge didn't answer.

"All right," Tomkins grumbled, "I'll talk, you listen. I watched you when you were here before, Ridge. I consider myself a pretty good judge of men, and I figure you're going to get whatever you set out to do. That's why I wired you to come. It's hush-hush, but a lone man with a shotgun recently robbed this railroad of a payroll of a hundred thousand dollars in greenbacks."

Ridge gave a low whistle.

"I want them back," Tomkins continued, "and you're the best man for the job. I'll pay you a thousand dollars to recover it, then keep it all quiet. What'd you say?"

"Laurel's worth more than money to me."

Tomkins's eyes narrowed thoughtfully. "Tell you what: I'll have my neck in a sling with the stockholders, but they're spending millions, and most of that belongs to the federal government. You catch that scoundrel and I'll go five percent of what you recover."

Ridge hesitated. It was tempting. It wouldn't buy the house for Laurel, but it was a start. Still, money wasn't as important as she was. Ridge shook his head and started to stand.

Tomkins leaped up, his face suddenly flushed with anger. "Do you realize what you're turning down?"

"Yes, I do. I appreciate your offer, but I don't have time to go looking —"

"Wait!" Tomkins's anger faded from his face as quickly as it had erupted. "There's one thing more you need to know. Our Pawnee scouts followed that thief's horse tracks almost to Sioux territory. There's no doubt he's riding straight to California. Sacramento's the first big town between here and there."

Ridge slowly sank back into his seat but didn't speak for nearly a minute. Tomkins waited until Ridge nodded. "You've got a deal. Give me the details."

★ ★ ★

Agnes fussed at Laurel while their luggage was loaded onto a hotel omnibus near the waterfront. A wood-burning locomotive rested on the tracks just a few feet away from the river.

"What's the matter with you?" she demanded. "Why did you go off by yourself instead of staying with me when they were unloading our bags from the stagecoach?"

"Nothing that concerns you."

"Don't tell me that, Laurel! Something happened when you looked out the stage window. It bothered you so much that you were almost rude to Mr. Pomeroy when he was saying good-bye. You shouldn't have done that."

"I didn't mean to be rude to him. I was preoccupied. Now, let's please forget it."

"I think you're keeping something from me." Agnes stepped up into the omnibus and exclaimed, "Oh, Pastor Villard! I didn't see you get on."

"Sisters," the little minister replied, standing. "You seemed to be in such deep conversation that I didn't want to intrude." He patted the long board seat beside him. "Please join me."

Laurel was glad that no other passengers from the Omaha stage were on the omnibus.

Fifteen days and nights had given her all the close time she wanted with them, although she was still very curious about the silent Walker.

The omnibus driver clucked to his team and began reciting a brief history of Sacramento and pointing out the historic sites as the omnibus pulled away from the waterfront. It was here that construction of the Central Pacific Railroad had started just three years ago.

This railroad was the dream child of Theodore Judah, called "Crazy Judah." He couldn't get the necessary financial backing for constructing a railroad over the Sierras because everyone claimed that was not possible. Judah had eventually succeeded in interesting four merchants in a venture to open a wagon road to the rich Nevada silver regions.

Wagon road? Laurel mentally repeated. Pomeroy had said he owned an interest in a freight line through those mountains. Laurel needed more information about this business. She would ask him when he took her out for dinner.

The driver's voice droned on. Judah's concept for the railroad was finally grasped by those four men. Mark Hopkins, Collis Huntington, Charles Crocker, and Leland

Stanford were now known as the Big Four. They had formed the Central Pacific Railroad Company in 1861, the same year Stanford was elected California's Republican governor. The partners forced Judah out before he died.

Agnes leaned close to Laurel, "Are you listening?"

"Very definitely."

The driver continued, "Each of the Big Four is unique; real interesting characters. Personally, I think Charley Crocker is the most fascinating. You should meet him, ladies."

Laurel nodded. She would like to meet this man. But when the omnibus left the intriguing waterfront behind, Laurel found the driver's recitation less than interesting. Her thoughts flashed back to seeing Morton from the stage window. She vainly tried to tell herself she was mistaken. But she was positive that the skinny man who had seen Seymour hand her the package in Chicago had also seen her arrive in Sacramento.

The two break-ins and the street attack had all followed that Chicago incident. But was it coincidence, or was there a connection? As soon as possible, Laurel decided she had to ask the local newspaperman whom Seymour had named as a possible contact. Mark Gardner supposedly knew everyone. Maybe he could not only identify the unknown man in the photograph, but he also might know Morton.

Agnes fanned herself with her hand. "My, it's hot! But notice it's very dry heat, not muggy like back home."

Laurel hadn't noticed. She glanced around, but was not impressed with Sacramento. It was a community at the confluence of two great rivers: the American and the Sacramento. These waters merged and flowed on through the great flat valley to blend with the Pacific Ocean through the San Francisco Bay Area.

Following the influx of gold seekers in forty-nine, Sacramento had grown up haphazardly as the state's capital. Disastrous floods had been partly controlled by levees. But in the late spring of 1866, the winter rains had stopped and hot, dry weather dominated.

When the narrative ended, Agnes moved to the seat across from the driver to ask questions, leaving Laurel and the minister alone in the middle of the vehicle. Laurel sighed with relief.

Villard commented, "I know how you feel."

She looked at him with uncertainty. "What?"

"Your sigh. I feel the same relief in being off that stage after two weeks of day and night travel."

"Oh, yes. A great relief."

She wondered if the minister had noticed her aunt's increasingly critical attitude toward every passenger except him and Pomeroy. Agnes had constantly urged her to respond more to Pomeroy's attentions. Laurel cultivated him as a possible source of information, but resisted any personal involvement. Pomeroy didn't seem to notice her reserve, so Laurel hid an internal tension that was almost painful before the stage ride was over.

Villard said, "Miss Bartlett, I hope you'll attend one of our services at the church which has called me to be their pastor."

"I'd like very much to do that."

"Should I look for you next Sunday?"

She hesitated, remembering the way his brief words in the stagecoach had touched her. She wasn't sure about hearing a sermon that would trouble her conscience. "I'll try," she finally said.

"I'll pray that you make it." He took a quick breath before saying, "I am still embarrassed over your carpetbag."

"Don't be. No harm was done."

"If I may speak frankly, I've watched you for two weeks now, and I sense that something is troubling you. If that's so, and I can help . . ."

"Oh, thanks, Pastor, but I'm used to taking care of my own problems."

"I suspected as much. However, life is a journey of faith. We must all eventually reconcile the conflicts between Christian values and our secret selves."

Laurel shifted uncomfortably, sensing that he had somehow discerned her silent internal struggles.

He added softly, "There comes a time in everyone's life when our own strength is not enough. I trust that won't happen to you, but if it does, please remember that the Lord is our strength. Call on Him. Of course, I'm available for counseling if you wish."

"Thanks, I'll remember." She glanced ahead, eager to be away from the preacher whose insight into her troubled mind bothered her in a way she could not explain. She started to stand. "There's my hotel. It's been very nice knowing you, Pastor."

"May I pray for you?"

She smiled as the omnibus stopped in front of the wooden Traveler's Hotel. "Of course, Pastor Villard. I would appreciate that."

Laurel followed her aunt into the lobby which seemed crowded with heavy dark furniture that had been shipped around the Horn. The ever-present smell of cigars and brass spittoons made Laurel sorry she had booked this hotel. But at least she was sure of having a room upon arrival.

Agnes approached the desk and spoke to the balding man waiting there. "My niece and I have reservations under the name of Bartlett."

The clerk turned the heavy book toward Agnes. "Please register. Oh, I believe there's a message."

A spurt of anxiety surged through Laurel as the clerk turned to a row of cubbyholes on the wall behind him. Only her father knew her hotel destination, so the wire had to be from him.

The clerk turned around with the wire. "Which of you is Miss Laurel Bartlett?"

"I am." She glanced first at the last word. "It's from Papa," she told Agnes.

"Is he all right?"

Skimming the few words, Laurel felt her face warm.

"Well?" Agnes demanded impatiently.

Laurel licked her lips and hesitated before

answering in a quiet voice, "Varina asked him for my address here, so Papa gave it to her."

"You didn't tell him about her?" Agnes asked.

"There was no need." Laurel silently added to herself, *Why did Varina want to know my address? She has no reason to write me, and I certainly won't answer her.*

The clerk cleared his throat. "If you ladies are ready, I'll have the baggage taken to your rooms."

"We're ready," Agnes replied.

Laurel nodded, then followed the bellman and Agnes.

Why in the world would Varina want my address here?

The question threatened to tear open wounds Laurel had thought were beginning to heal.

No stagecoach was due for two days, and time was so important that Tomkins provided sturdy mounts for both Ridge and a former Union cavalryman named Philotas O'Brien. Tomkins had confided to Ridge that O'Brien was a dependable second man from the railroad's staff of detectives. He wasn't a leader, but Ridge was. Tomkins had cautioned Ridge not to mention his percentage arrangements for recovering the payroll. This led him to believe O'Brien was only being paid his regular salary, plus traveling expenses.

They rode along the newly laid railroad tracks out of Omaha armed with revolvers plus repeating Spencer and Henry rifles. Tomkins had explained that a lone rider would be an easy Indian target on the open plains, but two, obviously well-mounted and armed, might be avoided. The Sioux and Cheyennes focused their attacks on those obviously connected with the intrusive railroad, like surveyors and tracklayers. Even so, Ridge and the big, red-faced Irishman rode warily.

He asked Ridge, "You really think there's a chance of catching this outlaw?" He had no trace of Irish brogue because, as he told Ridge after Tomkins introduced them, he was first generation American. His parents had fled Ireland's potato famines in the 1840s.

"It's possible," Ridge explained, "mainly because he probably won't expect pursuit. When he hits Sacramento, it's likely he'll get reckless in spending some of that money. We ask around, keep our eyes open, and hope we luck out."

"You married?" O'Brien asked, his eyes

habitually scanning the plains.

"No. You?"

"Was. Smallpox carried her off with our baby boy."

"I'm sorry." It always seemed like such an inane thing to say.

"Don't look back, but we've got company."

"Indians?"

"Small party. Could be hunting, or could be looking for an easy target to attack."

Ridge didn't want to be delayed in getting to Sacramento. First he would see Laurel, then he would try to find and recover the money. He told O'Brien, "You have experience in dealing with them. What do you suggest?"

"We ride on like we don't know they're there. See what they do, but keep a sharp eye out ahead. We don't want to be ambushed."

Ridge nodded calmly, but he felt his muscles tighten just as they had each time his cavalry troop prepared to engage invaders of Virginia's sacred soil.

It was tempting to imitate her aunt and lie down on a real bed to rest, but Laurel was too perturbed for any such luxury. She fretted over seeing Dick Morton at the stage depot in Sacramento, and learning that Varina had wanted her address.

Laurel told Agnes that she was going out. Her aunt muttered disapproval, but Laurel closed the door to the adjoining room and opened her carpetbag.

There was no sense carrying it, she decided. She argued with herself about the propriety of first working on Pinkerton's assignment. But that would take time. Conversely, it would only take a few minutes to learn if Mark Gardner knew Dick Morton, or if Gardner could identify the man in the picture Seymour had given her.

She closed the carpetbag, placed it on a shelf in the small clothes closet, slid the photograph into her reticule, and walked downstairs. With the aid of a rough map the hotel desk clerk drew for her, she easily found her way to the *Sacramento Sentinel.*

The pleasant smell of ink and newsprint greeted her before Gardner came out to the front desk. His eyes brightened at the sight of her.

"Well, what a surprise!" he said with an appreciative grin. His pale blue eyes swept her from bonnet to shoes. "I'm not used to having pretty young women ask for me, but I could get used to it."

Laurel lowered her eyes in what she

thought was the appropriate response to his compliment. He was just over average height, with wavy hair so blond it tended toward whiteness. He was certainly nice looking, if a bit brash.

She raised her eyes to meet his. "My name is Laurel Bartlett, from Chicago. A mutual friend, Orville Seymour of the *Globe* suggested I contact you."

"Seymour?" Gardner's face sobered. "I used to work for him. How is he?"

"He's fine." Glancing around, Laurel asked, "Is there someplace we can talk privately?"

The newsman's grin returned. "There's no such thing for the likes of a reporter like me. We're all in a giant pen like sheep. But I feel lucky. Come on. I'll risk a few minutes at the nearest restaurant." He seized her hand and hurried out the door so fast she had a momentary fear of being swept off balance.

He continued holding her hand. "So, Miss Bartlett . . . it is 'Miss' Bartlett isn't it?"

She nodded, feeling slightly breathless from his unexpected exuberance and impertinence.

"I thought so. You've got that unmarried look." He stopped suddenly, his fingers still firmly on hers. "Say, you're not one of those lady correspondents are you? Seymour didn't send you out here to get my job, did he?"

She regained her composure and laughed lightly. "No, you don't have to worry about that, Mr. Gardner."

"Mark. Call me Mark, and I'll call you Laurel. That all right?"

It really wasn't because it was too much familiarity too soon, but she needed a favor, and then she would not see him again. "All right," she agreed.

"You want some coffee or something?"

"No, I just want to talk."

He opened the door to The Brown Jug, a small, informal cafe tucked into a niche between two retail stores off an alley. Gardner did not release her as he called to the man behind the counter, "I'm working on a big story, so don't bother us for a year."

He did not release Laurel's hand until they passed a few male customers and slid into a booth at the back.

"Now, Laurel, tell me all about yourself. Start at the beginning and don't leave anything out." He paused briefly, then smiled, adding, "You've got sixty seconds."

She laughed with genuine delight. "Mr. Gardner —"

"Mark. Remember?"

"Mark," she repeated. "Are you always so impetuous?"

"No, but I'm working on it. Now, you were going to tell me about yourself."

"No, I wasn't." She let her voice firm slightly. "I need your help. Will you be serious and hear me out?"

"It's against my nature, but maybe just this once." His tone sobered. "How can I help?"

She had three questions to ask: about the source of anti-railroad sentiment, the identity of the possible murder witness, and unexpectedly, what Gardner knew about Dick Morton. She began with the photograph.

Lifting it from her handbag, she held it across the table for him to see. "Do you know this man?"

Gardner glanced down and nodded. "Sure. That's Ira Phillips. He was a few years younger then, but that's who it is. Why do you ask?"

Laurel evaded the question while her hopes bubbled up. "When's the last time you saw him?"

"Yesterday. Why?"

Taking a very deep breath, Laurel slowly exhaled before answering. "Where can I find him?"

"He lives over near Chinatown by the

river. I could take you there."

"Oh, thanks, but I need to see him on a private matter. Can you give me his address?"

"No, but I can draw a map. However, you should have an escort to go to that area."

"I'm not afraid. Now, I have two more questions."

"It'll cost you," he said with an easy smile. "Dinner with me tonight at the best restaurant in town."

"Thank you, but I have other plans."

Gardner asked hopefully, "Perhaps another time?"

She didn't like being rushed. "How about drawing that map for me right now?"

He teased, "Does that mean you're thinking about another time?"

"The map," she said with mocking severity.

"Walk back to the paper with me and I'll give it to you."

She agreed and they walked outside again. She said, "Seymour tells me you know everyone. Do you know Dick Morton of Chicago?"

"Really skinny fellow with dark hair and sideburns?"

Laurel nodded hopefully. "Does he also live here?"

"He recently arrived, but you don't want to know him. We worked together at the old *Bulletin* in Chicago for awhile, but he got fired. He's a gambler and a cheat, an all-around no-good scoundrel. I'm surprised Seymour hired him. Anyway, how come you know anything about him?"

"I'd rather not say. Do you know where he lives?"

"No, but I can find out. Come by here tomorrow about this time and I'll try to have your answer. No, wait. I don't want these other men to start competing for you until I get a chance to know you better. Better meet me at The Brown Jug."

Laurel reluctantly agreed because she saw no other alternative to getting the information she needed.

At the *Sentinel*'s front counter, he quickly sketched directions for finding Phillips's house.

She thanked him and put the paper in her handbag.

"You've been very helpful," she said, turning to leave.

"Not yet. You said you had three questions."

"The third one will have to wait until tomorrow."

Gardner protested, but she was firm. She

said good-bye and walked back toward her hotel. Her step was light because she felt good. Far above her expectations for being in town so short a time, she had two important questions partly answered. She had seen Morton from the stage window, and she knew what Gardner thought of him. She had identified Ira Phillips as the possible murder witness. Tomorrow she would begin working on her Pinkerton assignment. Right now, she had earned the right to stretch out on a real bed.

Across from her hotel, she waited for a heavy dray wagon and a team of huge draft animals to pass. Through the dust kicked up, she noticed someone exit the hotel's side door. Something familiar about him made her take a second look. He was walking away, but she recognized the well-built figure and slouch hat of her fellow stagecoach passenger, Walker.

Strange man, she thought again. *I wonder if he's stopping at the same hotel?*

She climbed the stairs and started to unlock her door, ready to take off her shoes and stretch out to rest before telling her aunt that she was back. But as Laurel inserted the long key into the lock, she stopped and sucked in her breath. The door was ajar. She shoved it open with her foot, gripping her handbag as a possible weapon.

It wasn't necessary. The room was empty, but it was also a total mess.

"Oh, no! Not again!"

She dashed across to her leather trunk. The lid had been thrown back and its contents strewn over the floor. Her collapsed carpetbag had been dumped on the bed and both packages ripped open. The papers that Pinkerton and Seymour had given her were scattered on the bed and over the floor.

The photo . . . oh! She remembered it was in her handbag. She quickly thrust her fingers in and touched it for reassurance. *Still there!* She closed her eyes in a brief moment of relief, but they instantly popped open. *Aunt Agnes!*

Laurel turned to the connecting door and frantically pounded on it with her open palm. "Aunt Agnes! Aunt Agnes! Are you all right? Answer me!"

CHAPTER 14

Laurel stopped pounding on the door to her aunt's adjoining room and grasped the knob, but it turned in her hand. Agnes jerked the door open, her eyes showing fear. "What's the matter?" she demanded sleepily.

"Thank the Lord you're all right!" Laurel exclaimed.

"Why shouldn't I be? I just dozed . . ." She looked past Laurel and saw the mess. "Oh, my! What happened?"

"Somebody broke in. Didn't you hear anything?"

"No, I was so weary I slept soundly." Agnes hurried across the floor, trying not to step on the scattered old newspaper clippings and paper. "What did they take?"

"I haven't looked yet, but there's nothing for you to worry about. I'll run down to the lobby and ask to have the police come."

While waiting for the police, Laurel inventoried her trunk and carpetbag. Nothing was missing, indicating to her that the intruder only wanted the photograph which she had taken with her.

Agnes said, "This is just like Chicago! Twice somebody broke into your room, but didn't take anything. What's going on?"

Laurel said evasively, "Perhaps the authorities can figure —" She interrupted herself as there was a heavy knock on the door. "That's probably them."

Two uniformed officers examined the room and took a report. Laurel did not mention seeing Walker. She didn't want to name him as a possible suspect just because she had seen him leaving the hotel. Her suspicion fell on Dick Morton, but she did not mention him, either.

Agnes reported the two similar Chicago incidents, but the officers shrugged that off as not likely to have any connection. They left after declaring that the responsible party seemed to be a professional who successfully entered Laurel's room without breaking the lock. It was obvious to Laurel that there would be no real follow-up detective work. She would have to do that for herself.

When they were alone again, Agnes returned to the question she had asked earlier. "I still want to know what's going on. Just because those men didn't think there was any connection with Chicago doesn't mean I don't. So what aren't you telling me?"

"I told you: it's nothing to concern you —"

"I'm not so sure!" Agnes interrupted. "I want to know the truth. Does this have something to do with your strange absences during the war?"

"No, it doesn't."

"Then what is it? Why would somebody come two thousand miles to rummage through your things again? And that's not counting the time your handbag was snatched when you were walking along the street. So what's this really all about?"

Laurel hesitated, not wanting to tell about either of her two assignments.

Agnes argued, "I don't believe you're telling me all you know. Whoever did this must have been desperate to risk breaking in during broad daylight with me right next door. If he knew we were together, he could have attacked me! So I have a right to know what's going on."

Laurel decided she had to make some explanation. "If there is a connection to Chicago, it's because someone's trying to find something they think I have."

"Do you?" Agnes's voice rose sharply.

A denial formed in Laurel's mind. It would be so simple to say, "no," but that would compound the lie she lived daily, professing to be a correspondent while actually being a secret detective.

Agnes seized on the hesitation. "So you do! You have something that important! What is it?"

Even though Seymour had not put any restrictions on her work as Pinkerton had, Laurel's basic nature was to keep things to herself. She said, "It doesn't have a thing to do with you, but to make you feel better, I'll get rid of it."

"Yes, get rid of it right away. But wait! How will whoever's after it know that you don't have it anymore?"

It was a question Laurel couldn't answer.

Agnes rushed on excitedly. "If he hasn't found whatever it is in your possession, then he'll think it's on your person. Is it in your reticule?"

"Yes, but I'm not going to risk having it stolen. I'll pin it to my chemise."

"What if he's so desperate he might murder you to get it?"

"Aunt Agnes! Be reasonable! Nobody's going to try anything like that, especially in daylight."

"Well, he could murder you in your bed tonight! Maybe me, too! Oh, I wish I hadn't come on this trip!"

Me, too. I didn't want her involved in this. "I'll go take care of it right now."

"Don't leave me here alone! I'll go with you."

"Sorry, but I must do this by myself. If you'll feel safer, wait in the lobby."

Alone in her hotel room, Laurel knew the safest place for the photograph would be in a bank. But she might need it to be positive when she saw Phillips. She wrapped the picture in a handkerchief and pinned it to the inside of her chemise.

Satisfied, Laurel consulted Gardner's map, then left the hotel and walked south, away from her destination. She periodically stopped as if looking in store windows, but the glass reflections showed nothing suspicious about any of the people on the streets.

She remained cautious, turning east for a couple of blocks before finally following the map north toward the river, ships' docks, and railroad and stagecoach terminals. She could see Chinatown to the west and the poorer white neighborhood nearby, but she didn't head there until she was confident nobody had followed her.

Walking gave her time to think. Even though she had seen the mysterious and silent Walker leaving the hotel, Laurel thought Dick Morton was more likely to have broken into her room. He had seen Seymour hand her the package with the photograph. Morton was watching in Sacramento as though he had been expecting her to arrive. But how did he know that? Why did he want that photograph so much?

The most logical reason, Laurel assured herself, *is that Morton must have killed that man in Chicago. He somehow knew that Seymour had a picture of the witness who could identify him. Morton got a job at the paper, but couldn't get into Seymour's safe. When Morton knew I had that photograph, he tried to get it back. Now he's here in Sacramento, still after it.*

She shook her head. *Or am I wrong, and Walker's the one who broke in just now?*

She sorted out what facts were clear. Dick Morton or Walker wanted to find the missing witness, whom Gardner had identified as Ira Phillips. His life was in danger because he alone could identify the man who had killed Oglesby in Chicago. There were only three ways to locate Phillips.

First, Laurel realized, the photograph could be stolen from her, then used to inquire around until someone recognized Phillips and knew where he lived, as Gardner as done for her. Or the murderer might know that she had talked to Gardner, and get him to tell where Phillips lived. The third possibility was to follow

289

her when she went to see him.

An uneasy conclusion intruded in Laurel's mind. *Regardless of who killed Oglesby, maybe somehow my own life is in jeopardy. Well, it won't be the first time.*

She took a final casual look around, feeling slightly uneasy because of Gardner's warning about going alone. It wasn't that she was afraid of the people; it was more the fear of the unknown. How would Phillips react to being confronted with something from the past like the Oglesby murder?

She was relieved to find Phillips's small, plain shack on the edge of the ramshackle area. Dogs barked from several neighbors' houses, and she caught glimpses of furtive movements at nearby windows. Stepping up on the broken boards of Phillips's front porch, she glanced around apprehensively, knocked expectantly, and waited.

There was no sound from inside the house. She tried twice more and was about to leave when the door squeaked open a few inches. Part of the face and head showed, but it was enough. She was facing the man in the photograph, except he now was graying at the temples.

"Mr. Phillips, a mutual friend —"

He interrupted, "Who're you? What'd

you want?" There was suspicion in the quick questions.

"A mutual friend in Chicago sent me. I want to talk to you about something very important."

"Don't know nobody in Chicago!"

Laurel ignored the denial. "Won't you please step outside for a moment so I can explain?"

"I ain't comin' out. How'd you find me?"

"Orville Seymour asked me to —"

"Seymour?" Fear sprang into Phillips's eyes. "Don't he never give up? He's as bad as they are."

They? A tingling feeling raced through Laurel. She explained, "He's trying to help you. He gave me your photograph. I . . . I'm afraid your life might be —"

"No! He can't find me! Now, go away!" He started to close the door, but she quickly stuck her handbag between it and the jamb.

He? They? Was he confused? In desperation, Laurel tried a new tactic. "Wait! If I found you, so will he. I want to help you. Please, let's talk."

Slowly, the door opened enough so her reticule fell free. "You're right," he said hoarsely. "Even after all this time and all these miles . . ."

Elated, Laurel interrupted, "Then talk to

me! Tell me the whole story, right now. That's the best way to protect yourself! Let the truth come out!"

"Got to think," Phillips muttered. "Got to think. You come back later. No, wait! They might follow you! Where'd you live? Maybe I'll send word where to meet me."

Laurel protested, "But now would be —"

"Quick! Where'd you live?"

"I'm stopping at the Traveler's Hotel, but —"

"Now go 'way," he interjected. "Got to think." The door closed firmly.

The puckering feeling stayed with Ridge as he and O'Brien casually rode on as if they weren't aware that a small party of Indians was following them.

O'Brien mused, "There's a little rock out-cropping ahead. Make a run for it if they start shooting."

Ridge nodded. "Did you see how many there are?"

"About half a dozen. We can handle them with these repeaters unless they have the same."

"Whatever happened to bows and arrows?"

"They traded them for white man's rifles."

There was only the sound of the two horses' hooves and the wind blowing over the waving grass. Ridge watched the outcropping, hoping it wouldn't be a place where blood would be spilled. But if it came to that, he intended to survive and go on, earn the reward money, and make things right with Laurel.

Four years of war had taught him how to let his mind wander to pleasant places while his cavalry mount carried him toward an engagement where he might die. Now, in the endless western wilderness, he filled his mind with the reservoir of his heart, with memories of Laurel.

He relived the moment of their first time alone in Richmond. In the shadow of the smokehouse, he had whispered of his desire to take her in his arms and kiss her, how every moment away from her had been torture.

That was nothing compared to the agony he had carried with him over later walking away and leaving her at the picnic. *I can't blame her for saying it's too soon, and she wanted to be sure how she felt. I was a fool to let her get away! But this time . . .*

O'Brien's voice roused Ridge from his reverie. "Here they come!" He kicked his horse into a hard run.

Ridge did the same before looking back under his arm at the Indians whooping wildly and charging hard on fast ponies. Then Ridge leaned low over his horse's neck, ignoring the stinging dark mane in his face as he raced for the rock outcropping.

Excitement gripped Laurel as she took a circuitous route back to her hotel, occasionally checking to make sure she had not been followed. So many things had happened so quickly that her thoughts collided with each other. She forced herself to be calm while sorting those thoughts.

Phillips is frightened for his life because he's the missing witness to a murder. He ran away back then, but I found him. Now he's afraid that whoever killed Oglesby is desperate enough to murder him.

She frowned. *Killer or killers? He said "them," then "he." Is there more than one involved?*

She checked again to make sure she wasn't being followed, then began grappling with the questions that tumbled in her mind.

Morton must be one of them. He's the most logical person to have broken into my things. No, wait! Why do I assume that? If there are two people, who's the other? Walker? How do

I know what he did?

Laurel frowned. *What about the man who tried to steal my handbag on the streets of Chicago, and the other man in Omaha? I got a quick look at them, and don't think they were the same man. Yet they must all fit in this. But how?*

Agnes was still waiting in the hotel lobby when Laurel returned, but she wasn't alone. The tall, gaunt man who resembled Lincoln stood up from where he had been sitting across from Agnes.

She said, "Laurel, you remember Mr. Bodmer from the stagecoach?"

"Of course. It's good to see you again so soon."

"I was walking by when I saw your aunt sitting here," he said. "We've had a good visit."

Agnes added, "I told him about the break-in, and all."

"All?" Laurel repeated, her voice registering disapproval. She didn't want any of this known.

"I'm a discrete man," Bodmer assured Laurel. "Your aunt needed a friendly ear, so I provided it, but nothing will leave my lips."

Laurel wanted to believe him. "Thank you. It's very important that no one else knows of this."

Agnes asked, "Did you get rid of that item?"

Laurel blinked. *The photograph!* "Oh! I forgot!"

Agnes leaped up from her chair. "You didn't!"

"I'm sorry. I had to do something very important, and I became distracted." She glanced at the tall case clock against the lobby wall. "I'll do it first thing in the morning."

Bodmer said, "If I'm not out of line in suggesting this, perhaps the hotel has a safe where your item could be secure. Of course, I don't know what it is, but I'm assuming it's not too big."

"That's a very good idea, Mr. Bodmer. I'll check on that right now."

He said, "I have an appointment, so I'll visit with your aunt for a couple more minutes, and see you later."

Laurel lifted her hand in a brief farewell gesture to Bodmer. She approached the desk where the clerk sat. "Do you have a safe here?" she asked.

He rose, nodding. "We can accommodate you, Miss Bartlett."

"Good. I'll be right back." She entered the ladies' lounge off the lobby, removed the wrapped photo from her chemise, and carried it to the desk clerk. He placed it in the safe and handed her a receipt, saying, "Oh, that reminds me. You have a message." He turned to the cubbyholes and retrieved a small envelope.

She had been surprised to have her father's wire waiting when she arrived, and now she was puzzled about who else would have sent her a message. She didn't recognize the handwriting of her first and last names on the envelope.

She opened it after stepping away from the counter.

There was only a single line.

"Will call for you and your aunt at 7:30 tonight for the best dinner in Sacramento. Bushrod."

Laurel suppressed a groan. *Not tonight!*

Agnes came up and asked, "What is it?"

Laurel handed over the letter which her aunt skimmed, then looked up and smiled. "That's wonderful!"

"No, it's thoughtless. I need a good night's rest in a real bed. Besides, he's being too forward. It'll serve him right to eat alone."

"Now, Laurel, don't be like that. I thought from the way you started being nice to him that you were interested."

"I tried only because you kept urging me to!"

"I'm only looking out for your best interest. You should be flattered that he extended this invitation so soon after our arrival."

Rebellion made Laurel declare, "I'm not going!"

"If you're still thinking of that Reb—"

"Don't say it!" Laurel interrupted. "That's over! And I don't want to talk about it any more."

"Then act like it's over. Go to dinner with Bushrod."

Laurel opened her mouth to again refuse, but two thoughts leaped into her mind.

I could start working on Pinkerton's assignment by asking Pomeroy more of what he knows about efforts to hinder the railroad, and I need to make sure Aunt Agnes doesn't interfere. I think I know how to do that.

"Very well, Aunt Agnes," she said. "I will, on one condition. We invite Mr. Bodmer to join us."

"What?" Agnes exclaimed indignantly. "What a ridiculous suggestion! Besides, he had to leave for an appointment."

"I know you would die of embarrassment before you asked him, so I'll contact him and do it for you. It'll be my idea. You two can sit nearby. . . ."

"You're being impertinent!"

Shrugging, Laurel turned to the clerk. "May I leave a note for someone?"

Agnes protested, "What are you doing?"

"Leaving word for Mr. Pomeroy that I'm indisposed."

"Wait!" Agnes gripped Laurel's writing arm. "I have no interest in Mr. Bodmer."

Laurel smiled triumphantly. "And I have none in Bushrod Pomeroy, so that makes us even! But I've watched him for two weeks, and it's obvious that he has some interest in you. Now, last chance: my way, or yours?"

In the scant shelter of the outcropping, Ridge lay prone, his forty-four caliber Henry repeating rifle resting in the crevice between two rocks. Two feet away, O'Brien again checked his fifty-two caliber Spencer while six braves sat on their ponies just outside of effective rifle range.

"They going to wait us out?" Ridge asked quietly.

"Can't tell, but I noticed they all have percussion carbines. They can see we've got greater firepower. I can fire fourteen rounds in a minute, so between us they know their chances of getting us before we get them is pretty slim. Anyway, I don't want a fight if we can avoid it."

"Me, either. I'm anxious to get to Sacramento."

The big Irishman grinned at him. "To recover that payroll or to see your lady friend?"

"Both."

Watching the mounted braves still parleying among themselves, Ridge asked, "Is there anything else you haven't told me about this man who stole the payroll?"

"You know as much as I do. Skinny, with dark hair and sideburns. He entered the railroad car with a shotgun shortly after it arrived."

Ridge nodded, remembering the rest. The gunman had surprised and disarmed the guard and the clerks, then made one tie up the others. The robber tied the last man himself, stuffed the greenbacks into his saddlebags, but left the gold. He had obviously known its weight would slow him down. He had escaped on a good horse.

O'Brien commented, "He took a mighty big gamble, doing that right in Omaha."

"So far, it's paid off for him." Ridge tensed, peering toward the Indians. "They're turning back."

"Maybe they figured we weren't worth their losses, or it could be a trick. Let's wait to make sure."

Ridge fretted as the braves rode out of sight. He was glad it was apparently ending peacefully, but he regretted the lost time. Laurel's image tormented him, making him anxious to again see her in person.

Minutes later, O'Brien observed, "They're gone. Let's mount up and make as much time as possible before we have to camp for the night."

For her dinner engagement with Pomeroy, Laurel had deliberately chosen the least attractive of her dresses.

The two-piece brown silk taffeta was slightly out of style but still practical. Laurel thought its only drawback was that it emphasized her tiny waist.

She reasoned that she didn't want to encourage Pomeroy's personal interest. At the same time, she had to keep his attention while asking questions to elicit any information he might have which would help her solve the Pinkerton case.

The reflected glow of the setting sun on the broad Sacramento River provided an ever-changing panoramic view of commercial scows, lumber steamers, and fishing boats through the windows of Sacramento's best restaurant.

Pomeroy had reserved a semi-secluded

table in a corner just a few feet from the fast-flowing river. Aunt Agnes and Horatio Bodmer were seated in the center of the main dining area out of hearing. Laurel wasn't surprised that Agnes seemed a bit stiff and cool toward Bodmer, although he didn't seem to notice.

After the waiter left with their order, Pomeroy asked Laurel, "Do you like my choice of a restaurant?"

She looked past the kerosene lamp. It was turned so low that it cast a romantic glow which she tried to ignore. "I like it very much." She glanced out the window. "I'm surprised how close we are to all that water."

"This is nothing compared to the periodic winter floods. We're on a levee, but sometimes the river rises so high the whole town is flooded. When Governor Stanford was inaugurated, he climbed out of a second story window into a rowboat to attend the ceremonies."

"That must have been quite a sight." She sensed an opening to guide the conversation toward her goal. "Isn't he one of the so-called Big Four in building the Central Pacific Railroad?"

"Yes, along with Mark Hopkins, Charles Crocker, and Collis Huntington."

302

Noting the sudden hard edge to Pomeroy's tone, Laurel commented, "Do you think they can be stopped from finishing that line?"

"No, not now." Pomeroy leaned back in his chair, his face grim in the weak lamplight. "The most powerful men in other companies that would be hurt by this railroad joined with the little businessmen to oppose it. That included telegraph companies, rival local railroads, private toll roads, and all the stage lines, not just Wells Fargo. They all failed."

Laurel forgot about her aunt and Bodmer as she sensed Pomeroy moving in the direction she wanted him to go. "I imagine that made those men frustrated and angry."

"Of course. I was, too. Still am, in fact."

Pomeroy's voice dropped so that Laurel had to lean forward to hear. She asked, "Is it really hopeless for all those men, and you?"

"I'm afraid so. In looking back, I think it was already too late when the Big Four and some others completed the Dutch Flat and Donner Lake Wagon Road Company. That was two years ago this month."

"I don't understand what a wagon road has to do with this railroad."

"Originally, Theodore Judah — I told you about him on the stagecoach — couldn't get anybody to believe that a railroad could actually be built over the Sierras. But he did convince the Big Four that it was possible to run a wagon road over a route Judah had surveyed. The object was to open up transportation to Nevada and the silver mines of the Comstock Lode which was discovered in 1860."

Laurel kept her eyes focused on Pomeroy's to show she was very interested.

He continued, his voice low but filled with a rising intensity. "San Franciscans were outraged, calling it 'The Great Dutch Flat Swindle,' but it was built anyway. This forced stages and freight wagons onto the railroad's own road. Now rails are being laid over that same route. So the Big Four will get more wealthy and powerful, and lots of businesses like mine will be ruined."

She watched him close his eyes as if in pain, so she waited until he opened them again. An intense flash of strong emotion in them startled her, making her involuntarily draw back.

"Greed," he said hoarsely. "Greed! But there's a price . . ." He stopped so suddenly his head jerked. He looked at her for a fraction of a second as if he had forgotten she was there. "Forgive me, Laurel. I got carried away."

"There's a lot more to building a transcontinental railroad than most people imagined, including me."

He said softly, "I didn't bring you here to talk about that. I want to know about you." He reached across the table to let his hand lightly touch her fingers.

The movement brought a mental flash of Ridge's hands touching hers. Slowly, she withdrew her fingers from Pomeroy's. She demurred, saying, "I told you pretty much everything on the stage." *That's certainly not true!*

He seemed not to notice that she had pulled away. His gaze quickly swept down from her face and back again. He dropped his voice. "You're very lovely."

She didn't want the conversation to go that direction. "Thank you," she said, glancing around for some excuse to change the subject. Darkness had settled so that there was only a shimmer of lamp light on the river rushing by.

Pomeroy abruptly stood and came around to pull her chair back. "Come on. I'll show you around outside before our dinners arrive."

She started to protest, but he took her hand firmly and pulled her to her feet. To avoid a scene, she let him lead her toward the rear exit. She looked toward her aunt, who gave her a quick smile of approval.

Pomeroy still firmly held Laurel's hand as he guided her through the door and onto a long, narrow wooden porch overlooking the water. Out of the corner of her eye, she saw someone furtively duck around the corner of the building. But it was enough for Laurel to recognize Walker. *He's been standing here watching!*

Pomeroy said softly, "A warm June evening and this view helps make a pretty sight for a pretty lady." He gently moved her ahead until her waist touched the top guard rail.

"It's very pleasant, Mr. Pomeroy, but our dinners —"

"Bushrod," he interrupted from behind her. "It's Bushrod. Remember?" He released her hand but immediately placed both of his hands on her shoulders. His face brushed her hair. He whispered, "Laurel, I have wanted to have you alone since the moment I first saw you."

When Ridge had held her in his arms, she had felt herself wanting to yield, but this was different. She pulled away from Pomeroy and turned toward the door. "I'm sure our dinners must be ready by now."

He didn't move, so she opened the door

and stepped inside before turning back to face him. She again caught that same intense flash of emotion in his eyes that she had seen before. This time, it frightened her.

He stepped toward her. "I'm sorry, Laurel. I hoped that you felt the same way I do. Forgive me?"

"Of course." On the way back to her table, she passed within a few feet of her aunt and Bodmer. Agnes looked up, her eyes widening in surprise.

Laurel hurried on, trying not to be upset with the bold and unexpected move Pomeroy had made, and especially with the strange flash in his eyes.

Her mind jumped. How long had Walker been standing in the dark, watching? A slight shiver rippled over Laurel's shoulders and down her arms.

CHAPTER 15

Dreams filled Laurel's first night in a bed after riding in a stagecoach day and night for two weeks. She and Ridge were walking along the James River where the moon made a shimmering path on the water. Her heart raced as it had then.

He's wonderful, but . . .

The words echoed in her mind, followed by their brief quarrel. He said he was speaking from his heart, and she wasn't listening. She protested that she was, and raised her face to his. She trembled, anticipating their first kiss. Her eyes closed. She felt his gentle hands on her cheeks and his warm pleasant breath.

Her eyes popped open. The barely perceptible valley breeze drifted through her open second-story hotel room window and caressed her face. The rattle of early-morning dray wagons and the heavy-footed plodding of draft horses floated in from the streets.

She sighed, staring at the ceiling. *Why can't I even escape from him in my dreams?*

Laurel allowed herself to stretch luxuriously, wishing she could sleep longer. Flashes of yesterday's various encounters flickered through her mind, especially dinner with Pomeroy and seeing Walker lurking in the shadows. *There's plenty to do today, so I may as well get at it.*

Before she slid off of the high bed and pulled on her dressing gown, she went over what she had already done toward completing her two assignments.

She realized that she should have felt good about things, but she was troubled. More than that, she sensed danger. The intuition was something she had learned to heed during her spying excursions in the late war.

After deciding not to disturb her aunt, Laurel dressed and walked downstairs. She smiled at the desk clerk on her way to the small hotel restaurant. She had barely been seated when a barefoot boy of about twelve in ragged homespun hurried up to her.

"You Miz Bartlett?" he asked, running a dirty hand across his sunburned nose. When she nodded, he said, "Here, a man give me two-bits to hand this to you."

Phillips! She took the folded paper and started to reach into her reticule for a coin, but when she looked up, the boy was gone. She unfolded the smudged note and read the scrawled capital block letter printing:

NOON TODAY FRONT & K STREETS

There was no signature, but that didn't surprise her. *So he's decided to talk. But how much will he tell me? Did he see who murdered Oglesby? Was there only one person or two?* She would know in a few hours. Meanwhile, she had things to do.

She reclaimed the photograph from the desk clerk's safe and returned to her room to again pin it to her chemise. Stopping before her aunt's adjoining door, she heard her snores and decided she was really tired and should not be awakened. Laurel scribbled a note saying she would be out most of the day but would return in time to have dinner with her.

Carefully checking to make sure she wasn't followed, Laurel circled the downtown area and finally entered the *Sentinel*'s office. The morning activity was in marked contrast to the quietness of yesterday afternoon. The man at the desk summoned Mark Gardner who rushed out looking preoccupied.

Upon recognizing her, his facial features instantly changed. "Miss Bartlett!" he exclaimed with a broad smile. "I didn't expect you until later. But you're a welcome sight anytime."

She ignored the compliment. "I'm sorry to bother you, but I needed to know something before our appointed meeting time."

"We're on deadline, so I can't leave right now, but I can give you one quick answer to your question of yesterday. I haven't yet found out where Dick Morton lives. I'm sorry, but I thought I had time before —" He interrupted himself. "Oh, did your uncle find you?"

Laurel blinked in surprise. "My uncle? I don't have an uncle."

"Ah! I suspected as much. Are you in some kind of trouble?"

"No, why? What's this all about?"

"Shortly after you left yesterday, a man came by claiming he was your uncle. Said he got separated from you after you both arrived on the stage. He claimed he forgot which hotel you were stopping in."

"What did you tell him?"

"I told him the truth. I don't know where."

She interrupted. "What did he look like?"

"Oh, let me see. Stocky, square jaw, small mustache and a quiet way of speaking. Slouch hat."

Walker! But he knows I'm at the Travelers! I saw him leaving there. She asked Gardner, "Did he say anything else?"

"He asked if you had shown me a certain photograph. I told him no."

"Thank you!"

"You recognize him?"

"Sounds like a man who was on the stage from Omaha with us. He said his name was Albert Walker, but that's about all I know about him. He said very little the whole trip."

"If you're in some kind of trouble because of this man . . ."

She said hurriedly, "It's nothing I can't handle."

Gardner's eyes lit up. "I should have guessed you might say something like that." Grinning, he added, "Oh, yesterday you said you had three questions. You've still got one coming. Seems to me that now maybe I've earned the right to again ask to call on you. Let me show you around Sacramento. I'm off tomorrow. Then you can ask me your last question, and any others you might dream up in the meantime."

She gave him a teasing smile. "I'll give you an afternoon when you give me Dick Morton's address. By the way, where's Front and K Streets?"

"That's the transportation terminal area, trains and stages, where your stage ride ended yesterday." He cocked his head at her. "Why? Are you meeting some other man there?"

"That's a secret," she said, smiled again, and left.

Laurel had plenty of time before her meeting with Phillips, so she looked around casually but carefully without seeing any sign of being trailed. All the while, her resentment toward Walker grew. *Who is he, really? Why is he following me?*

There was one way she might find out, but first she had to get rid of the photograph. It had served her purpose in locating Ira Phillips, but she didn't want to risk Morton or Walker or anyone else getting it. That could lead them directly to the missing witness, just as it had done for her.

Not seeing any sign of being stalked, she entered the nearest bank and arranged to have the photograph placed in the safe. At the heavy outside bank doors, she paused as though retying her bonnet while actually scanning the street for any indication that Walker or Morton was waiting. She didn't see either of them, but was pleased to see the small preacher just alighting from a buggy.

She walked outside and approached him as he tied his horse to the hitching rail. "Good morning, Pastor. It's good to see you again so soon."

He tipped his hat and returned the greeting. "I'm glad we ran into each other, Miss Bartlett. I have the information you wanted about when I'd give my first sermon. Eleven o'clock Sunday at the Capital Bible Church." He pointed. "It's just a few short blocks from here. You can see the belfry just beyond those streets."

"I plan to attend. Something you said on the stagecoach has been troubling me, so I hope I'll find some answers during your sermon."

He absently patted the horse's muzzle. "I thought I noticed that first Sunday morning in the stage that you seemed a little disturbed. Uh . . . if it's important, I have a little free time right now. Perhaps you'd like a cup of coffee with me?"

It was tempting to consider informal counseling, but even that would require sharing the truth about her dual life and the spiritual battle going on inside of her. "Oh, thank you. I'd like that, but I have an appointment coming up soon."

"Of course."

They talked for a few minutes before he

entered the bank and she slowly sauntered down the street. She had only gone a short distance before she glimpsed Walker across the street and well behind her. *Well, let's find out something.*

She rounded the corner of a brick building with iron shutters over the doors and windows, a holdover from the Forty-niner days when periodic fires swept through most California communities. Out of Walker's sight, she waited against the side of the rough bricks.

He turned the corner and abruptly turned away, but she hurried toward him. "One moment, Mr. Walker!"

He turned and politely touched his hat. "Oh, Miss Bartlett. I didn't recognize —"

"Stop it!" she snapped, locking his hazel eyes with her angry ones. "Why are you following me?"

"Following —"

She cut him off, her voice sharp and hard. "I said, stop it! I know what you're doing. Now I want to know why, and I want to know right now!"

His eyes did not waver from hers, but steadily met their challenge. "And if I don't tell you?"

She blinked, taken off guard, but only for a second. "Then I shall summon an officer and charge you with behavior unbecoming to a decent man."

It was his turn to blink. "You wouldn't dare!"

"Oh, wouldn't I? One scream and I'll have half of Sacramento here, ready to protect me." She opened her mouth wide as if to shriek, but he stopped her.

"Wait! Wait!" He glanced around apprehensively as she slowly closed her mouth. "All right. I'll tell you, but not here. Let's go someplace —"

"Oh, no, you don't! It's here and now, or I'll start screaming."

"All right! All right!" He took another quick glance around, then lowered his voice so much that she had to lean forward to hear. "You are in great danger, and I'm trying to protect you; that's all."

"Danger from what?" she challenged.

"You've stumbled onto something that threatens some people with a great deal to lose. They'll kill you if they have to."

She hid her concern by demanding, "What makes you think that? How would you know such a thing?"

"I can't tell you, but it's true."

"I don't believe you! Prove it!"

Walker shrugged. "Twice they broke into your place in Chicago, and yesterday they tried at your hotel, trying to get something you have."

"It was you who broke into my room yesterday afternoon, Mr. Walker! I saw you leaving the hotel just as I returned."

"No, I'm not the one who broke in."

"Then how do you know about it?"

"That's not important. Anyway, you can think what you want, yet that won't change the facts. Do you have any idea of the next logical thing they'll do?"

She didn't answer, but waited with a growing sense that she knew what he meant.

"They'll figure you've got it on you, and they'll come for it. You know what could happen then. So I've been trying to keep an eye on you in hopes of preventing it. But I can't be with you every moment."

She eyed him suspiciously. "Why should you do that?"

He shrugged. "That's not your concern. But I assure you, this is the truth."

Laurel licked her lips in an involuntary action. She believed him, but by nature and training she was a loner; one who was accustomed to taking care of herself. "You have to admit what you're saying about protecting me doesn't make any sense at all."

"It doesn't have to. You've been warned. So if you'll excuse me . . ." He touched the brim of his slouch hat and walked back around the corner and out of sight.

Wait! She silently urged, but stopped the word before it escaped her mouth. Shaken, uncertain, and with countless questions suddenly nagging to be answered, she slowly headed toward the waterfront. In a few steps, she was again confident that she could take care of herself.

But now her scheduled noon meeting with Phillips had taken on a new dimension, and she didn't like it, didn't like it at all.

Ridge and O'Brien came to a small settlement at about noon. They stopped at the weathered trading post to water their horses, refill their canteens from the well, and talk with the owner. Ridge asked the question posed many times before to anyone encountered on their western trek.

"Have you seen a skinny man with sideburns pass through here recently?"

The negative response had been so common that he had come to expect it, but this time the unshaven trading post owner nodded. "Reckon ye must mean the one who came through maybe three, four weeks ago. He give me some brand new greenback bills on account'a he claimed he didn't have no gold or silver."

Ridge and O'Brien exchanged meaningful looks before Ridge asked casually, "Greenbacks scarce this far west?"

"Scarce as hen's teeth. Well, sometimes I see some that's been crumpled an' beat up before they git out here. But brand new ones that ain't even been crinkled none, well, now, that's diff'rnt, don'tcha know?"

Ridge suspected that the owner didn't get much company and was likely to be talkative. Quickly, he commented, "I don't know that I've seen one that fresh. You still got one he gave you?"

The owner snorted through his nose. "Got two. Cain't git rid of 'em. Folks hereabouts don't cotton much to paper money. 'Specially us who fit fer the South." He shook his head. "We learned our lesson the hard way. One day back home we had our Confederate scrip an' the next day, we had scrap. Lots of us drifted west. Wasn't much left fer us to stay behind nohow. Why? You like to see one o' them greenbacks?"

"Would you mind?"

"Mind?" Turning to a small box under the counter, the owner noisily pushed some gold and silver coins aside. "Mister, I'd be plumb tickled to trade if'n you got some specie like I got here." He lifted a handful of coins and let them trickle through his fingers before handing a five-dollar bill over to Ridge.

He and the big Irish detective examined it loosely, felt the crispness, and nodded together.

Ridge told the owner, "I wouldn't mind trading with you. I could consider it like a souvenir."

"You got a half eagle?" the owner asked. As Ridge nodded, the man exclaimed, "Hand it over and ye've got yerself a deal."

"Well, now," O'Brien said, "I might as well trade you for the other one."

"It's a twenty. Gimme a gold double eagle fer it."

That transaction completed, Ridge asked, "Did this fellow have any more of these?"

"Couldn't rightly say, but he didn't seem to mind handing these over. Claimed he didn't have nothin' else."

Ridge and O'Brien nodded together and started out the door before the Irishman turned back. "I don't suppose he mentioned his name or where he was heading?"

"No name, but come to think of it, he mentioned bein' saddle sore an' asked if they was a stage stop near here. I tol' him they's one two hours ride thataway."

Ridge and O'Brien followed the man's pointing fingers. West and slightly south.

The owner continued, "He was a right talky kind. I guess ridin' alone makes a body hanker fer somebody to talk to, don'tcha know? Well, I'm obliged to ye fer stoppin' by. Hope you enjoy them greenbacks."

The two men started to walk out into the sunshine before the owner called after them. "I jist 'membered somethin' that feller said about a friend o' his'n works on a newspaper in Sacramento."

"He say which paper?" Ridge asked.

"Don't think so. But I reckon they cain't be too many of them."

The two riders waved their thanks and mounted.

O'Brien asked, "What do you think, Ridge? Is it worth heading for the stage stop in hopes our suspect said something there that'll help us find him?"

Ridge hesitated. He wanted to see Laurel more than catch the payroll robber and claim the reward. He also had not ridden so hard and fast since the war ended more than a year ago. He admitted, "The truth is, I'm in favor of going straight on to Sacramento, but I'm saddlesore. Also, if we catch the stage, we can roll day and night."

"Sounds good. If the suspect did switch to a stage, he didn't have to stop to sleep again. He's had plenty of time to be in Sacramento long before now."

"He might not stay there very long, but go on down to San Francisco to spend that payroll. Let's check that stage stop."

The men kicked their mounts into a lope while Ridge tried to think what could be done with their horses if they did get an opportunity to switch to a stagecoach.

Shortly before noon, Laurel arrived by a roundabout way at the foot of K Street. She was puzzled as to why Ira Phillips would have chosen to meet her where there was so much activity. People were everywhere: workmen with teams, women with parasols, and even small boys chasing stray dogs. All except the latter seemed to have some business with the various kinds of transportation connected with this terminal.

Laurel moved casually, occasionally glancing around to make sure she wasn't followed, then letting her gaze sweep over the area. Why hadn't Phillips's note been more specific than "Front and K Streets?"

A faint column of smoke drifted up from the cone-shaped stack of a wood-burning locomotive while dray wagons backed up to the open-sided box cars to load or unload cargo. Nearby, a fresh six-horse hitch was being led toward a waiting empty stagecoach. Just beyond those, on the far side of the levee, a river steamer lined with passengers waited to shove off. To the east of that vessel a scow loaded with gravel was just edging into the current while a lumber schooner edged toward the wharf.

Laurel began focusing her attention on the men. She had not seen Phillips too well because he stayed behind the door while they talked. Still, she was confident of being able to recognize him. He would not likely be active, like the workmen. Rather, he would probably be off by himself. She wandered on, anxious to find him so she could ask what he knew of the Chicago murder.

A boy of about ten with tousled hair and freckles ran toward her. He looked up and squinted at her with brown eyes. "The man you're lookin' for is over by the river, behind those barrels."

She thanked the boy, gave him a dime, and began moving toward the oversized barrels stacked four high. She glanced back, but it was difficult to be sure if Walker was among the countless men moving about the area.

Laurel walked away from the train and stage depots, following the rough boardwalk built along the shore. The noise of commerce faded behind her as she passed vessels on her left and sideless dray wagons on her right. The barrels were not close to any of the other cargo waiting to be loaded onto a vessel or a dray wagon. There was nobody around them, either.

She became apprehensive as she neared them without seeing anyone. She tried to assure herself that nothing could happen in daylight and so close to all the human activity. Still, Walker's warning echoed in her mind.

"You're in great danger. You've stumbled onto something . . . people with a great deal to lose. They'll kill you. . . ."

From fifteen feet away, she circled wide around the stacked barrels and turned toward the river to see if Phillips was waiting on the other side of them.

Nothing! Nobody! Could this be a trick? She vainly looked back in hopes of seeing the boy who had brought the message. She shook her head in disappointment and turned away from the river to again circle the barrels on the wharf side.

"Come closer." The voice was deep, almost booming.

She whirled around but saw nothing. Then she realized why the voice was so strange. *He's in a barrel.*

Carefully, ready to pick up her skirts and

run if necessary, she approached until the voice came again.

"That's far enough."

She stopped, trying to pinpoint which barrel. "Mr. Phillips?"

"Who else you expecting?"

"Show yourself so I can be sure."

"Don't tell me what to do if you want to know what you asked me yesterday!"

"All right. I'm listening."

"First, look around and make sure nobody's close."

She obeyed. "Nobody. You can speak freely."

"Now turn to face the river and pretend you're just looking around."

Again, she did as told, but she stood so she could see the barrels out of the corner of her eyes. "All right," she said. "Tell me."

"I'll make this fast, then you get out of here and don't look back. Don't never come near me again because they'll kill me if they can."

"All right, but give me the whole story; don't leave anything out, and I won't bother you again."

"Fair enough. Well, it was back when the war was still on. I guess you heard that. Anyway, there was two of them killed Oglesby that night. I saw one real plain, but not the other. Dick Morton was the one who clubbed Oglesby. . . ."

He stopped when Laurel involuntarily sucked in her breath.

"What's the matter?" he asked, his voice barely audible. "Somebody coming?"

"No, no! It's all right. It just startled me to hear that name."

"Morton?" When she nodded, Phillips continued, "He saw me and chased after me with that club. The other man was shouting at him not to let me get away, but I did. Came to Sacramento to be safe, but now —"

Laurel interrupted. "What about your photograph? How does that figure in this?"

"I just got it that day and was going to send it to my mother. Must've dropped it. But Morton didn't find it; the police did. Somehow Seymour found out about it, and the story ran in the Chicago *Globe*. They said the name of the witness — me — was being withheld by the police. But that wasn't true. That was to protect me. The only person who really knew was Seymour. He got hold of the photograph and Morton found out about it. But Morton still didn't know my name."

"How does Seymour fit into this?"

"Don't you know? He was my father-in-law. Was, before my wife died of diphtheria in the war."

"Oh!" Laurel's surprise was genuine. *So that's why Seymour said it was personal!* "Mr. Phillips, why did they kill Oglesby?"

"I don't know for sure, but I heard them arguing with him just before the shooting. Something was said about selling spoiled meat to the army, and Oglesby wanted to stop. Said it wasn't right to do that to our troops, but Morton and this other man said he was a fool.

"If they didn't sell it, the other man said, they could go broke and lose all their money. Oglesby said he wouldn't do it, and that's when it happened. So that's all I know, except I'm reduced to living in a shanty and hiding in a barrel to talk to you. Now, you better go and make sure nobody sees you leave. Don't get yourself killed."

"I'll be careful, and I'll do my best to help you so you can live a normal life again, but I can't promise."

"I know. Just get out of here so I can do the same."

Laurel forgot about lunch as she carefully but hurriedly returned to her hotel. She was happy to find a note from her aunt slid under the adjoining door. "Have gone sight-seeing. Wish you had wakened me so we could have gone together."

Sorry, Aunt Agnes, but I'm glad I didn't. Now I can write in peace.

Laurel sat down at the small dressing table in her room and began composing a report to Seymour. It would be expensive to wire, but mail would take too long. She figured the editor would be so glad to receive the information that he would reimburse her.

It took her a couple of hours before she was satisfied that the message was both as complete and brief as she could make it. She had located Ira Phillips who told her that he had witnessed Dick Morton and an unknown accomplice kill Oglesby after a quarrel. She concluded with a request for Seymour to wire her with his opinion of whether she should tell the local authorities or let him handle everything from Chicago.

Again exercising caution to make sure she wasn't followed, she found the telegraph office and handed her written message to the operator. He read it, before gawking at her through wire-rimmed glasses.

"You understand, sir," she told him with her most severe look, "that this is highly confidential. If any of this gets out, I'm sure you'll understand that I will have to go to your superiors. I wouldn't want to have to do that."

"Miss, I need my job too much to tell anybody what I send or receive. Don't worry about this."

Somewhat reassured, Laurel headed for The Little Brown Jug, but waited outside until Mark Gardner arrived out of breath.

"Sorry I'm late," he began, "but the editor sent me on a drowning story, and I was delayed getting back." He smiled at her as he opened the restaurant door. "I got that address for you, so when are we going to dinner?"

"Dick Morton's?" she asked, following Gardner back through the admiring glances of the few male patrons lining the front counter.

"That's who you asked for. Oh, and I hope you've already been to see the man in your photograph: Ira Phillips. If not, you're too late."

She stopped abruptly, a sickening feeling suddenly surging over her. "Too late?"

"Yes. He was the drowning victim."

CHAPTER 16

Laurel listened in shocked silence while Mark Gardner told her what little he knew about the death of Ira Phillips. Shortly after one o'clock, some boys playing along the Sacramento down river from Chinatown reported a body caught in some exposed tree roots.

It was too soon for a medical examiner's report, but there were no signs of foul play, leading police to theorize Phillips tripped and fell into the deep, swift water. Laurel couldn't help suspecting that there was more to this than an accidental drowning. She felt some guilt because she suspected that she may have been responsible for putting Phillips in danger.

Gardner concluded, "His body would probably have been swept all the way down to the delta if the high water hadn't washed away some of the riverbank, exposing the roots that snagged on his clothes. Otherwise, his death wouldn't have been known for days, maybe weeks."

Laurel placed an elbow on the table and rested her head in her hand, partially blocking Gardner's view of her eyes. She was sure that Phillips had not drowned, but had been murdered.

The logical sequence of events flashed in her mind. In spite of how careful she had been, someone followed her, probably Morton. He had undoubtedly watched as she stood by the stacked barrels, seemingly by herself. He had waited until she left and Phillips emerged from his barrel. He had gone back past the transportation hub toward his home near Chinatown. Near there, in the willows and cottonwoods, the fatal attack would have been screened from sight and the body dumped into the river.

Gardner commented, "I didn't think this would upset you so much. I'm sorry."

"I'll be all right in a minute." She let her thoughts race. *Whoever did it must believe Phillips told me about the Chicago murder. Now I'm the only one who could testify against them, so they'll come after me. . . .*

Gardner broke into her thoughts. "Maybe you'd better go lie down. I'll call a hack." He started to stand.

She had many questions to ask, but knew that now was not the time. She offered an excuse for her reaction to a stranger's death. "I'm just so shocked."

"Does that mean you saw him?"

Laurel needed time to think, and long ago she had learned to not tell everything she knew.

"Yesterday," she admitted. "I followed your map to find him, but he told me to go away."

"I'm not surprised. He's known to be a kind of recluse and rude." Gardner spoke with dignity, his usual bantering manner gone. "I can understand why you're so upset. I still think you should go back to your hotel and lie down." He stood, adding, "I'll get that hackney."

This time, Laurel did not object.

An hour after leaving the trading post, Ridge's horse began to limp. Stopping and dismounting, Ridge checked the animal's right front hoof and leg while O'Brien watched anxiously from his saddle.

"I don't see anything," Ridge announced soberly, "but I can't risk riding him any more."

He looked around hopefully for any sign of other people, but there was nothing except the vast empty loneliness broken only by the low moaning sound of wind bending the high grass.

O'Brien also looked, standing in the stirrups and shading his eyes against the slanting sun's rays. "Not a thing in sight," he declared. "Nothing but nothing."

Ridge's eagerness to reach Laurel gnawed at him with a sharp, fierce intensity, but his immediate concern could mean life or death. A man afoot in the wilderness was a prime target for big trouble.

Countless men and women had walked to California, but they had wagons with provisions, and water. He had a canteen, weapons, and saddlebags with food. He had counted on that lasting until he could replenish his supplies.

O'Brien stepped down before asking, "Now what?"

"Well, that stage way station should be somewhere off to our left."

"You could ride double with me that far." O'Brien reached a hand down. "Swing up behind me."

Moments later, settling behind the big Irishman's saddle, Ridge found himself fretting at the delay and the uncertainty of when and how he would get to see Laurel.

Gardner rode with Laurel to the hotel where she thanked him and promised to meet with him later. She entered her room, and listened at the adjoining door before sighing with relief. Agnes wasn't back.

Laurel removed her shoes and stretched out on the high bed to consider her situation.

I'm not just going to sit around waiting for Morton or whoever killed Phillips to do the same to me. But I can't accuse Morton without proof. Besides, Phillips said Morton didn't act alone. So who is his accomplice? Morton could catch me off guard because I have no idea who else is involved.

She needed a plan to stay alive. That included watching out for possible suspects.

"Suspects," she mused aloud. She made a short mental list. *Besides Morton, there's Walker, even if he did warn me of danger. Maybe he just did that to make me trust him. I can watch out for both of them, but who's the one that Phillips saw with Morton when Oglesby was killed?*

He could be here in Sacramento, but how could she protect herself from a nameless, faceless phantom? She frowned, wondering if there could possibly be a connection with the man who had attacked her on the Chicago street and escaped with the bag of pastries that Sarah had given her. Her frown deepened as she thought about the man who had tried to steal her bag at the Omaha stage stop. Could it all be connected somehow? She needed to find out.

And what if it really was an accidental

drowning? Am I frightening myself unnecessarily?

Her thoughts jumped. Pinkerton was paying her to find out if there really was a conspiracy to stop the railroad. She had been sidetracked into devoting her time to Seymour's assignment, although he would be paying for each publishable column inch she wrote. So far, that was nothing. Now she needed to send him a wire regarding Phillips's death, but that would wait. Saving her life was the new top priority.

The safest thing would be to leave for awhile; maybe go to San Francisco where I couldn't be found. But I can't do that until I've finished Pinkerton's case. Besides, how would I explain any of this to Aunt Agnes?

Laurel suddenly sat upright on the bed. *Where is she? Her note said she was going sightseeing, but that was hours ago. She should have been back by now.*

Laurel slid off the high bed and reached for her shoes. Agnes had been right about Laurel keeping something from her that could put them both in danger.

Now Laurel had two lives to fret about.

Ridge and O'Brien reached the stage way station just before sunset. They saw several horses in the corral behind the main building, so it was impossible to know if one of them had been left by the payroll robber. Ridge asked the heavy-set hostler if he had a horse for sale.

The man who had introduced himself simply as Shavers studied Ridge's lame mount with a knowledgeable eye before replying. "Can't do it. The company would have my hide if I was to sell you one of their hosses. I got my own riding mustang, but he's not for sale, neither."

"Do you have another horse besides him that doesn't belong to the company?"

Shavers rubbed his stubbled beard. "Well, a rider came in here a spell back with his hoss plumb tuckered out. Sold him to me and took the stage, but that hoss ain't in no shape to travel. You best wait for the next stage."

"When will that be?" Ridge asked.

"Tomorrow mid-morning." The hostler walked around Ridge's horse, shaking his head.

O'Brien protested, "We can't wait that long!"

"Mister, you ain't got much choice," Shavers pointed out. "You can't ride at night, even if you had another hoss." He briefly lifted a battered wide-brimmed hat, allowing uncombed and greasy gray hair to show. "Now, if you men got cash money, I got beds and hot coffee."

Ridge asked, "Can we take a look at your mustang?"

"You can look 'til your eyes hurt, but I ain't selling."

"We heard you," O'Brien growled, "but let's take a look anyway."

"Suit yourself. Come on, I'll show you."

Shavers stood on the lowest fence rail and pointed toward several horses bunched together on the far side of the enclosure. "Them's all company hosses 'cepting my mustang and that sorrel. That's the one the man sold me."

Ridge asked, "Was he dark-haired, skinny, and wearing sideburns?"

"Sure was; didn't have much more meat on him than an old buffalo skeleton. Why? You know him?"

"Know of him," Ridge replied carefully. "Did he happen to mention his name to you?"

Shavers shook his head. "Don't remember. He might have. He talked a lot. Said he was from Chicago; I remember that."

O'Brien asked, "Did he say where he was heading?"

"Might have. There was no reason to remember, though. Why?"

Ridge didn't reply, but parried, "You said he sold that sorrel to you?"

"Sure did. He gimme a bill o' sale, too."

Ridge smiled. "I thought he might have. His name will be on it!"

Shavers slapped his thigh. "Never thought of that!"

Ridge tried to conceal his eagerness. "Can we take a look at it?"

"Don't see why not. Now, le'mee see . . . where did I put that?"

O'Brien said impatiently, "You don't know where it is?"

"I'll have a look soon's I get the chores done."

Ridge gave O'Brien a satisfied smile, then turned back to Shavers. "I'll pay top dollar for your mustang."

Shavers' tone hardened. "I told you he's not for sale. Now you can't walk to California with that limp. It's getting dark, and I got things to do. Why don't you both spend the night and then you'll only have a few hours to wait for the stage?"

O'Brien turned to Ridge. "What do you think?"

Ridge took a deep breath. His heart ached at again being delayed in finding Laurel, but he nodded. "We have to wait to see that bill of sale. Besides, like the man says: We have no choice."

The hotel desk clerk shook his head in answer to Laurel's question. "No, Miss Bartlett. I haven't seen her since she left this morning with a gentleman."

Laurel's eyebrows arched. "What gentleman?"

"Why, the one who was sitting here last night with your aunt and you. Tall, looked a little like Lincoln, only without the beard."

Laurel nodded with relief. "Horatio Bodmer. Did they say where they were going?"

"They didn't speak to me. They met here and left."

"About what time was that?"

"Oh, maybe nine-thirty or ten."

A glance out the door at the lengthening shadows made Laurel's concerns come rushing back. *He could be the man involved with Morton. No, that's silly. Bodmer's a gentleman!*

She turned back to the clerk. "I've heard about the lawlessness in California, and how the vigilantes dealt with it because the law couldn't. How safe is it? . . ."

The clerk's quick chuckle interrupted her. "That was right after the gold rush back in forty-nine. Sacramento has changed. It's safe to go most places, but . . . excuse me if I'm speaking out of turn, but unescorted young women . . . well, why take a chance?"

After considering that thought, and deciding that her aunt would surely be back shortly to have dinner, Laurel returned to her room.

She looked out the window as darkness settled, and tried to concentrate on solving the various problems that tormented her. The most important one was trying to stay alive while finishing her assignments.

In the war, she had always been able to achieve what she was commissioned to do behind Confederate lines. She did it alone many times, and always returned safely. She could do this, too. But in the South, she knew everyone was an enemy who would hang her if caught. Here, except for Morton or maybe Walker, she didn't know her enemy.

There's no sense sitting here, she told herself. *I've got to start eliminating suspects. She stood, trying to steady her resolve. I'll offer him — or them — some bait, which I sure can't afford to lose.*

She stopped at the front desk to leave a message for her aunt that she was going to a nearby restaurant for dinner. Then, taking a deep breath, Laurel walked outside and into the soft glow of gas street lamps. She resisted looking back, but felt confident that at least Walker was following her. Or maybe Morton. That made her shiver.

On Gardner's map she had noted his simple sketch of the state capitol and the large, open square around it. She assumed it would be landscaped with trees and shrubs, so she walked slowly down Tenth Street, passing P and O Streets toward N where the capitol grounds began.

She did not plan to take any unnecessary risks, but thought that her direction would offer her stalker some hope of moving close enough that she could identify him without peril. She passed a tiny grocery store where dressed chickens or ducks hung in the window under signs which she assumed were Chinese. Boxes, barrels, and baskets of fresh fruits and vegetables were displayed on the boardwalk. The strange smell of unknown herbs filled her nostrils, but she barely noticed.

Ridge's image suddenly appeared in her mind's eye, unbidden and unexpected. Her heart began to speed up as it had that night at Brickside when he had slipped her a note. The memory of that warm pleasurable feeling returned. She tried to stop the re-membrance, but it was useless. The thoughts swept in, randomly, swiftly.

She had slipped out that night to meet him, and slowly melted at his explanation about meeting her at the cars with Varina clinging to his arm. His words were soft and real in her mind. *I wanted to take you in my arms and kiss you. . . .*

"Laurel?" The man's voice behind her shattered her reverie. She whirled around, startled that she had let her attention wander even momentarily when she was on such a precarious mission.

He had stepped out of the little store with a small sack in his arms, but the street light didn't reveal his features until he moved away from the door toward her.

"Laurel? How are you feeling?"

"Oh, Mr. Gardner!" she exclaimed with relief. "You startled me."

"Please call me Mark. You're looking better than when I last saw you this after-noon."

"I'm fine now, thank you, Mister —"

"Mark," he reminded her, coming close so the street light fell fully on his face. He was grinning. "I'm very glad to see you," he said soberly, then quickly added in his ban-tering way, "saves me a trip to your hotel and possibly being thrown out for trespassing where only decent folks go."

She tried to match his mood. She said with smile, "You haven't ever been thrown out until you've been thrown out by my Aunt Agnes."

Gardner glanced around. "An aunt, huh? Where is she?"

The question sobered Laurel. "I . . . I don't know. She went out with a gentleman friend —"

"Which is what you should be doing right now," he interrupted. "Don't you know that night air is bad for pretty young women? Anyway, what are you doing out here?"

She considered that before saying, "You wouldn't believe me even if I told you."

"Try me." He took her hand and slipped it through his while holding the bag with the other. "Have you had dinner? Don't try to fool me. I have a hidden gadget in this bag that squeals like a pig caught under a fence when someone lies to me."

She laughed with delight. "I wouldn't risk scaring the whole neighborhood. No, I haven't had dinner."

"Good. Now you've got no excuse to put me off as you've done before. The best place in town is down by the river. Let's jump in a cab and enjoy the evening." He led her to the street and looked up and down. "Here comes one now." He signaled the driver, then turned to smile at Laurel. "If you're hungry, reach into the bag and grab a carrot. It's not as romantic as flowers, but it's the thought that counts. Isn't that right?"

A delighted laugh burst from Laurel's lips. "Why, Mr. Gardner — I mean — Mark, are you telling me a carrot can tell when a person's lying?"

"Shh!" he looked around and whispered as the cabriolet driver reined in his horse at the curb. "This is a special Chinese carrot. But don't tell anybody, or the price will go sky high at Wong's. There are many Chinese merchants in Sacramento, but he has the freshest produce, and he's the only one with talking carrots."

"You're incorrigible!" she told him as he helped her into the vehicle with the folding leather hood. "You really are."

"That's the nicest thing anyone's ever said to me." He slid into the seat beside her. "Driver, I have the honor of escorting the prettiest woman in the world to dinner at Delmonicos. No, I'm in the wrong city. So take us to the Golden Slipper. It's Sacramento's version of the original."

Mention of the Golden Slipper made Laurel wince. Pomeroy had taken her there, and she had seen Walker hiding in the shadows. "Uh . . . could we go someplace else?"

"Bad memories, huh? You've been in town less than forty-eight hours and somebody has already hurt you."

"Not hurt. It's just . . . well . . . something else."

"Which is none of my business, and I should have known that." His tone turned somber. "I apologize."

"It's all right."

"Then we won't think about it anymore. Driver, take us to Maxie's."

"But don't go straight there," Laurel blurted, then bit her tongue. Gardner might misunderstand, but it was too late now.

He seemed to understand that she was embarrassed, so he didn't comment. Instead, he told the driver, "Go by the capitol, and then give us a brief circle tour of downtown before we reach the restaurant."

"Thanks, Mark," she said gratefully.

He glanced down at her, his eyes warm with concern. "I'll be serious if you insist, but it's against my nature."

"I understand, but I don't feel like being serious now."

He used his open palm to make an imaginary swipe across his face. "Your wish is granted. Besides, you still have one question to ask me. Is it a serious one?"

"Very serious, but I'll save it for dinner."

As the carriage turned at the next intersection, Laurel thought she saw someone quickly step back in the shadows away from the gas street light. She couldn't be sure, but it didn't matter. Her quick glance up and down the street showed no other hack at a stand or moving. Unless whoever it was had a horse saddled nearby, there was no way he could follow her and spoil her dinner.

Maxie's was inland, but it was close enough to the water that from their window table Laurel could see lights on the ships snugged up against the wharf. The faint flicker of carriage lamps briefly lit up a stretch of darkness, reminding her of fireflies back home in Illinois.

"So," Gardner said after they had finished their dessert and were sipping coffee, "have I answered that third question to your satisfaction?"

"You've answered that one and many more." She paused, reflecting on their brief conversation about Phillips, what more he knew about Dick Morton, and more extensive discussions on building the transcontinental railroad. She added, "You don't believe there is any organized effort to stop building of the Central Pacific or the Union Pacific?"

"As I said, lots of businessmen hate it, but there's no conspiracy that I know about, and I poke my nose into lots of places. It's an occupational hazard, but so far, nobody's broken it, although I've had a few offers for a free poke at my nose."

She gave him a faint smile but did not reply. In a way, she was disappointed. His opinion matched Pomeroy's. Of course, it was too early in her investigation to notify Pinkerton that her trip seemed to be an expensive but unfruitful one. She needed to dig deeper, including asking what Gardner knew about Pomeroy. To do that, she again had to nudge her conscience aside.

"I didn't tell you the whole truth when we met," she began, studying his face in the candlelight. "Orville Seymour pays me to be a stringer for him, so I'm looking for stories."

"You're a newspaper correspondent?" There was genuine surprise in his voice.

"Oh, I'm not in competition with you. I write only for the Chicago *Globe*. I hope you

don't mind that I didn't tell you that earlier."

"Why should I mind? A lady newspaperman! No, I'm wrong. Nothing about you
reminds me of a man, except that I'm glad
I'm one and I'm here enjoying your company."

She lowered her eyes but instantly raised
them to head off any further personal comments. "I need to know as much about the
Central Pacific as possible so I can write
good stories. Would you answer other questions, or did I use up all of mine with the
original three?"

"Tell you what, Miss Newspaper Lady,
let me take you on a picnic tomorrow and
I'll answer as many questions as you can ask
on the car."

"Car? You mean carriage?"

"No, I mean car. The C.P. runs excursion trains from here up into the Sierras as
far as track has been laid. Sometimes the
smoke and cinders from the engine blow
back into the passengers and burn holes in
their clothes, but if you're willing to put
up —"

"I'm willing!" she interrupted, excited at
the prospect. "What time?"

"I'll have to check the train schedule,
then leave a note at the desk in your hotel.

I'll bring the picnic basket with everything we need."

She frowned. "There's one possible problem. My aunt insists on going wherever I do, so she might . . ." She stopped when he cocked his head and looked suspiciously at her. "Oh," she added quickly, recalling what she had told him earlier, "she obviously doesn't know I went to dinner with you." She glanced around. "She should be back at the hotel by now, and I need to be there, too."

"So Cinderella suddenly sees the clock start to strike midnight, and she's got to run, huh? Well, I've enjoyed this evening so much I don't want to jeopardize my chances of having another with you."

He motioned to the waiter for the check, then stood and came around the table to Laurel. "So let me see if I understand what you're saying. Tomorrow, you would like me not to mention tonight, and you'd also like to see if your aunt throws me out the way you warned me she could. Well, the rose is worth chancing the thorn."

She demurely lowered her eyes, but when he pulled back her chair, it was suddenly Ridge doing that at Brickside. She shook the thought away and let Gardner take her hand and lead her out into the night air.

Laurel's concern for her aunt made her quiet. She was relieved when the cab slowed in front of the hotel and Laurel glimpsed her aunt and Bodmer in the lobby, their backs to the street.

"Oh, Mark," she exclaimed, turning to him, "would you mind letting me off at the side entrance?"

"You just saw your aunt, huh?" As Laurel nodded, he added, "I'll go in with you. There's no need for you to get in trouble. It's my fault I took you off alone."

"Oh, it's not that."

"Then it must be the man she's with. Is he the one who hurt you?"

"He's my aunt's friend. Now, please, do as I asked."

"As you wish. Driver, the side entrance, please."

When the carriage stopped, Laurel said, "Thanks for a lovely time."

Gardner stepped out and held up a hand to assist her down. "I'll walk you to the door."

"That's not necessary, but thanks anyway."

"It's rather dark around here, and the nearest street light is down on the corner. I'd better —"

"I appreciate it, but I'll be fine."

"Then I'll wait until you're inside."

"Thanks. See you tomorrow."

She entered the side door and was surprised at how dim the kerosene wall lamps were. She started down the long hall toward the stairs, but turned to wave at Gardner. The cab had already pulled away.

As Laurel started to turn around toward the stairs, a shadowy figure leaped from the stairwell. Before she could react, he was behind her. His hand clamped hard across her mouth. Lamp light reflected off a long-bladed knife.

CHAPTER 17

Laurel struggled against her attacker but stopped when the knife point touched the side of her throat. Waves of intense fear rippled over her entire body. Her eyes turned sharply toward the blade, but all she could see was a gloved hand that held it, and the dark form of a man with a hat behind her.

A man's voice whispered hoarsely, "Give me that photograph!"

Photograph? She unsuccessfully tried to turn frightened eyes to see his face. She glimpsed only part of a white handkerchief and the hat brim pulled down over his forehead.

"Don't look at me! Where is it?"

Frantically, she looked away, glimpsing the long empty hallway. She tried to shake her head, but the knife point pricked her skin. She froze while the ripples of terror continued.

"Don't be a fool!" he growled. "I want it!"

Desperately, Laurel tried to explain, but only a muffled sound escaped through his fingers over her mouth.

He said gruffly, "I'm going to release my

hand just enough for you to answer me. But if you try to scream, it'll be the last thing you ever do! Understand?"

She managed to nod slightly, and felt the fingers slowly lift.

The hallway door directly opposite opened, giving Laurel a fragment of hope, but her attacker instantly pulled her close and thrust his face down over hers.

She tried to pull back, but it was useless. Out of the corner of her eye, she saw an older couple step out into the hallway, glance Laurel's way, then close their door and walk down the hallway.

The woman clucked disapprovingly, speaking just loudly enough that Laurel could hear her. "Kissing in the hallway! Young people today have no shame!"

Laurel was sure that was the impression her attacker had meant to convey.

"All right," he muttered, raising his head but keeping the knife at Laurel's throat. "Let's try again."

The fingers relaxed just enough for her to say, "I don't have it!"

The fingers clamped down hard. "Then where is it?"

"Take that knife away," she whispered when the grip again relaxed.

"Don't tell me what to do! You've got it

on you! Hand it over or I'll have to look for it!"

The fingers relaxed a bit, giving Laurel a moment to summon her courage and protest, "No, I don't, and you'll never find it if you hurt me! Move the knife away!"

He hesitated briefly, then drew the blade back. "Last chance. Otherwise, I'll take you outside . . ."

He broke off as someone dashed from the stairwell toward them. Laurel caught a glimpse of a short club in the other man's hand. It smashed down on the knife hand, sending the blade clattering to the floor. Her attacker released her and grappled with the second man.

Laurel's survival instincts took over. She raised her long skirts and ran screaming down the hall toward the lobby. She burst through the door to find Bodmer talking to Aunt Agnes and the desk clerk.

"Two men are fighting! One's got a knife!" Laurel cried, pointing back the way she had come.

The clerk reached under the counter and produced a short-barreled pistol. He raised a corner of the counter, stepped from behind it and started running across the lobby toward where Laurel had pointed. Bodmer followed.

Agnes threw her arms around Laurel. "There's blood on your throat! What happened?"

Her hard breathing and racing heart made her unable to answer. She freed herself from Agnes's arms and touched the cut spot on her neck. Her finger came away sticky.

Agnes quickly examined the cut. "The bleeding has stopped, so it's not serious. But how did it happen?"

"Tell you in a minute," Laurel puffed, pivoting to look toward the door to the hallway. There was the sound of voices, but no noise of a struggle and no shot. She hurried toward the door, ignoring her aunt's warning.

Cautiously opening it, she was relieved to see the clerk and Bodmer coming back toward her.

"They got away before we got there," the clerk said, shoving the gun into his waistband. "All we found was this." He held out a slouch hat toward Laurel.

It's Walker's!

Bodmer looked down from his great height to ask, "What happened?"

"That's what I've been asking," Agnes said, hurrying up to join them. "And where have you been, Laurel?"

"Wait!" the clerk exclaimed, "I want to hear, too, but first I've got to call the police."

As he ran toward the lobby, Laurel sighed heavily and steeled herself against the tirade she knew would follow when Agnes heard the story.

To the officers, Agnes, and Bodmer, Laurel recounted the chance meeting with Mark Gardner and an unchaperoned evening. Agnes glared at Laurel but didn't say anything in front of the others. She told of the attacker's demand for a photograph which had been placed in a safe. She offered to give it to the officers later, but she didn't offer an opinion as to why it might be important. It was essential that she keep some facts to herself because an unknown assailant was stalking her. He might have friends in the police department. This decision caused another conscience twinge, but Laurel ignored it in the interests of self-preservation.

She, Agnes, and Bodmer confirmed that Walker's slouch hat had been found at the attack scene. But had he been her assailant or her rescuer? If he had been her protector, why hadn't he returned after chasing off the adversary? She had not recognized her assailant's voice, and her defender had not spoken.

After the officers and Bodmer left, Agnes vehemently berated Laurel. "You could be killed, and maybe me, too! What's so special about that photograph? I demand to know what's really going on."

"I can't tell you," Laurel replied, and retreated into silence. Ignoring Agnes's continued verbal assault, Laurel moved a trunk and a chair against Agnes's outside door. Back in her own room, Laurel locked the hallway door, but didn't brace it. She thought was it unlikely her assailant would return that night.

Her head ached from all the excitement and deepening mystery as she wearily prepared for bed. She blew out the lamp and slid into bed in the darkness while considering many questions and some hard, cold realities.

I had a narrow escape. It's probably not over, either. He could be back with that knife, and this time there might be nobody to save me.

The questions piled on top of each other and became so entwined that she had difficulty trying to separate them. Some questions went unanswered while possible explanations to others readily came to mind.

If Morton had been the knife-wielder, why would he have wanted the photograph? If he was the one who followed her when she met with Phillips, the picture was no longer needed to identify him. And Phillips was dead now, anyway, so who would need it?

"Ahhh!" Laurel groaned. Her thinking was going in circles. She needed to take action to find the answers, and that meant plain old hard work: asking questions and following up on what she learned. But that couldn't start until she reviewed her goals and set priorities.

Most important, I've got to stay alive and protect Aunt Agnes while I try to solve this mess I'm in. I've also got to make sure there's no railroad conspiracy so I can complete my Pinkerton assignment. To protect my detective work, I'd better write some stories for Seymour. I must also look for Morton and try to discover the identity of his accomplice.

Feeling better, Laurel turned over and tried to sleep, but something still nagged at her. *I'd better go hear Pastor Villard on Sunday.*

She closed her eyes, but Ridge's image appeared in her mind. *Forget Ridge!* she told herself sternly. *The best way to do that is to become interested in someone else, like Pomeroy or Gardner. But how can I do that when I've got all these other problems?*

She finally slept without thinking of an answer.

Her morning got off to a bad start when she told her aunt of the planned train trip and picnic with Gardner.

"I'm not going!" Agnes snapped, setting her coffee cup into her saucer so hard it cracked.

"I'm not asking you to go," Laurel replied quietly, glancing around to see if any of the restaurant's few other customers were looking. "But I'm going, and you're welcome to come along if you want."

"After what happened last night, I think we should get on the next stage bound for Chicago! That way, we might save both our lives."

Patiently, Laurel explained, "I can't go now because I have things to do here first. But I'll help you pack if —"

"No! I can't go back alone and you know it! I promised my brother that I'd look after you. It's my Christian duty!"

"Your duty is to save your life if you're afraid of losing it, Aunt Agnes. I can take care of myself. . . ."

"Stop! I get so tired of hearing you say that! But you're wrong! Nobody can always take care of themselves all the time. But in our arrogance, we think we always can, and that's when we make mistakes! You're heading that way right now unless I can stop you."

Laurel stared in surprise. There had been anger in her aunt's tone, but there was also compassion. "I'm touched, Aunt Agnes. I really am. But I don't want you to risk your life for me."

Agnes dropped her head over her cup for a few seconds. Slowly, she looked up with tears glistening in the corners of her eyes.

Laurel reached across the table and gripped Agnes's hand. "Why the tears?"

"Foolish tears!" Her voice trembled. "Tears from a foolish old woman who remembers what it was like to be young and confident, to make decisions that seemed right at the time, but instead led to a lifetime of regret."

Momentarily, Laurel thought her aunt referred to some youthful indiscretion, although it was hard to imagine straight-laced Agnes being guilty of that.

Agnes shook her head. "It's not what you think. I was in love, very much so; but we were going to wait, so that's not why I'm weeping after all these years."

Laurel's eyebrows shot up. She had not

thought of her aunt ever being in love. *But what happened?* Laurel wished she knew, but she didn't want to pick at an old emotional wound which had unexpectedly been reopened.

"Surprised you, didn't I?" Agnes asked, raising the napkin to dab at the corner of her eyes. "But I once knew what it was to love, to lose, to hurt. Oh, yes, I know."

Laurel waited expectantly, eager to hear more, but only if the information was volunteered.

Agnes dropped her napkin on the table, indicating she had regained control of her emotions and the moment had passed. She wasn't going to elaborate. "Come on," she said, pushing back her chair, "We'd better get ready for the picnic trip with your new male friend."

There was time for Laurel to wire Seymour a second time before Gardner arrived. She walked the few short blocks to the telegraph office while puzzling over her aunt's remarks.

What did she mean, "I once knew what it was like to love, to lose, to hurt"? Why did she tell me that after never once before hinting at anything like it? Was she trying to tell me something — maybe about Ridge?

He appeared in a memory kaleidoscope of

rapidly changing scenes: The first time they met. His initial anger when he learned that her war-time spying had cost his brother's life and given him a permanent limp. The way they made up. More recently, him standing on the Richmond train depot with Varina. Him showing her plans for the grand house he hoped to build. Standing with him under the great oak by the James when he first confessed his love for her. His reaction when she protested it was too soon for her. . . .

Too soon? No. Too late. How many times do I have to remind myself that it's over between us? Laurel shook her head. *Did something like that happen to Aunt Agnes that she now regrets? If so, why would she have tried so hard to discourage my relationship with Ridge? Or could she be testing me?*

Waiting for the stagecoach was annoying because of the delay in finding Laurel and trying to catch the railroad's payroll robber. At least he was supposed to be heading for Sacramento, so Ridge had just one destination. There was an advantage to taking the stage, because it would roll twenty-four hours a day, making much better time than he would riding horseback.

Ridge shifted his thought to immediate

concerns: arranging to have their horses left behind, and waiting for the hostler to find the bill of sale with the payroll robber's name on it.

Rising early the next morning, Ridge and O'Brien sat down with some of the strongest and worst coffee either had ever tasted. Ridge asked the hostler, "Did you find that bill of sale?"

Shavers looked up from where he was making slapjacks that didn't look any better than the coffee. "Not yet, but I know it's around."

O'Brien groaned, then exclaimed angrily, "We don't have time —"

"Easy!" Ridge cautioned, laying a warning hand on the Irishman's arm. "Mr. Shavers, we'd be in your debt if you can find that bill of sale before we have to leave."

"I'm studying on where it might be," Shavers said.

O'Brien muttered into his coffee cup, "Might not help us anyway. He could've used another name."

"Yes," Ridge agreed, "but maybe this far away from civilization he might have felt safe to use his own. At least we'd have a name to ask around."

Ridge turned to the second concern. He said to the hostler, "Mr. O'Brien here will

363

be coming back this way in a few weeks, so we'll pay you to keep both our mounts until then."

"Mister, you must think I ain't got a brain in my head. Neither of you will ever come back, and I'll be stuck with two hosses and no bill of sale. In this country, that could get me hung."

O'Brien snapped, "Having one you can't find might also get you hung!"

"I'll find it," Shavers growled.

To ease the tension, Ridge said, "You misunderstand us about our horses. We'll sign a paper showing you're just boarding them for us. We'll also pay you half now for doing that. You'll get the rest when Mr. O'Brien returns."

Shavers frowned. "What happens if you don't git back? I keep them hosses?"

Ridge looked at O'Brien, who nodded. "You do."

Shavers flipped the cake, which wasn't even brown on the bottom. "You said half now. How much is that?"

"Whatever's fair," Ridge said. "Then we'll take the stage on to Sacramento."

Shavers scratched his head without stepping back from his cooking. "Greenbacks or gold?"

"Greenbacks," O'Brien promptly said.

"Too bad. If you'd said gold, it'd be a deal."

Ridge and O'Brien exchanged glances before Ridge asked, "How long before the stage comes?"

"You're in luck," Shavers replied, lifting the cakes onto a plate. "I made a mistake yesterday. I forgot they changed the times. The stage will be here in an hour."

Ridge produced a double eagle and saw Shavers's face light up with delight. "Here's your gold. Take it, then get us a pen and paper, then we've got a deal. Right?"

"Right! For a twenty-dollar gold piece, you've got a deal." He took the coin with one hand and extended the unsavory-looking plate of slapjacks with the other. "Who wants to eat first?"

Ridge grinned at O'Brien. "You start. I'll write out our deal and we'll both sign it."

Shavers said, "I'll be right back." He hurried into the small lean-to while O'Brien gingerly took a bit of the sorry breakfast. He made a face.

From the lean-to, the hostler whooped joyfully. "I found it!" He rushed back into the room holding pen, inkwell, and two pieces of paper. "Bill of sale!"

Ridge set his cup down so hard the coffee

slopped over. He leaped up and took the sales document.

O'Brien seemed to be glad to stop eating, for he joined Ridge in peering at the signature. "Dick Morton."

"Dick Morton," Ridge repeated softly. He sat down and wrote out the agreement on the horses, his mind jumping to Laurel and how soon he would see her.

Laurel's questions still tormented her when she returned to the hotel after wiring Seymour. She mentioned that Phillips was found dead, but said she would write a story with details and send them by mail.

As she passed the front desk, the clerk stopped her, saying she had a message. It was from Bushrod Pomeroy.

There's a dinner meeting of important railroad officials next Tuesday. I'll call for you at 7:30.

She should have been glad about the opportunity, but she bristled at the tone.

Who does he think he is to just assume I'll be waiting? She crumpled the note, threw it into the lobby wastebasket, and started to walk away. Then she stopped. *If he's so against the railroads, why would he be in a meeting with railroad men?* Intrigued, she retrieved the note from the wastebasket so she could think about that more later.

Then Laurel shoved all thoughts of Pomeroy aside to focus on the pressing problems still facing her. Mark Gardner might help with some of them.

Before boarding the Central Pacific's excursion train with her aunt and Gardner, Laurel noticed that Agnes was strangely subdued. She was even cordial to Gardner while Laurel casually but carefully looked around for any indications that Walker or Morton might be following.

Once aboard, Agnes chose to sit in the very front seat, well out of hearing range of anything Laurel or Gardner might say. Laurel assumed that was to encourage the newsman's interest in her.

Laurel was not satisfied that she was not being trailed until the train left the flat valley behind and began climbing into the foothills. Heavy black smoke and cinders from the engine drifted into the open car windows.

As they began their ascent into the hills, Laurel said, "Last night after you left me, I was attacked by a man with a knife."

Gardner immediately dropped his usual light-hearted manner and soberly probed for details. She revealed only what she deemed necessary. The subject was thoroughly discussed, with Gardner concluding that on Monday he would talk to the police beat reporter. If there were any new developments, Gardner would let Laurel know.

In what she hoped would be considered a change of topic, she asked, "Have you seen Dick Morton lately?"

"No, not for a few days. Why?"

She seemed not to hear his question. She asked, "Do you know any of his associates?"

"No, but in working my beat, I've seen him several times at a run-down grog shop near the waterfront."

"What's the name of that place?"

"Shanghai Joe's, but you mustn't go down there. It's no place for a lady. Why do you want to know about him?"

"I can't say at this time, but trust me. I need to know everything you can tell me about him."

"I've already told you just about everything I know."

"How about Ira Phillips? Any further news on him?"

"No. Won't be until a routine autopsy is completed, but it seems to be a clear case of accidental drowning."

"What do you know about Bushrod Pomeroy?"

Gardner cocked his head to look at her with a hint of suspicion. "I said that I'd answer all your questions, but I'm beginning to wonder if that's why you're with me today. I hoped it was for more personal reasons."

Realizing she had been too direct, Laurel said, "Please forgive me. I have a lot on my mind."

"It's not very flattering to have you thinking of someone else when I'm right here beside you."

Laurel recognized that he was fishing for information, so she gave him a reassuring smile. "My interest in those men is business, not personal."

Gardner smiled in relief. "I should have known that, but I'm glad to hear you say it. However, I can't imagine why Chicago readers would want to read about Morton or Phillips. Maybe Pomeroy because of the local angle."

Laurel tried to slide unobtrusively into the opening Gardner had just left. "How so?"

"Well, he's a speculator. Invests in various businesses. But he's not very good at it. County records show he's lost a lot of money, especially in supporting a wagon road from Sacramento through Placerville toward the Comstock Lode in Nevada."

"Placerville?"

"A foothill community farther east from here. That road goes around the south end of Lake Tahoe whereas the one built by the CP circles the north end."

"The Dutch Flat and Donner Lake Wagon Road?"

"That's the one. The train we're riding followed the original wagon road that Theodore Judah laid out."

"And the Big Four of the Central Pacific now own?"

"Right. After forcing Judah and Daniel Strong out."

"Strong? I don't think I've heard that name."

"He was a druggist in Dutch Flat, about fifty-five miles northeast of Sacramento up in the Sierras. He's the one who told Judah about a kind of pass through these mountains that Judah later used to build the wagon road."

"When was that?"

"Back in 'sixty, so six years ago. This railroad was also conceived in Strong's drugstore."

"Both Strong and Judah were forced out?"

Gardner grinned. "My first editor used to

say, 'Big fish eat little fish.' In humans, it's called 'greed.' "

Laurel sensed she might be on to something. She asked, "You think Pomeroy is greedy?"

"Yes, but he doesn't have the business sense that the Big Four possess. For example, when I worked for Seymour in Chicago before the war, I learned that Pomeroy borrowed money to invest with a meat-packing company. He would have lost his shirt if the war hadn't come along."

Laurel's interest grew rapidly. "But he didn't?"

"No. Like lots of unscrupulous men, his company sold inferior products to the government. The companies made big profits, and the fighting men got stuck with the bad items. In this case, it was spoiled meat."

Laurel made a face.

Gardner continued, "I'll say one thing for Oglesby, the man who ran the company. He opposed the idea, but I guess greed finally got to him, too. Maybe that's what got him killed."

The tidbits of information were like pieces that would fit into Laurel's puzzle. She found it hard to keep her voice calm and casual. She prompted, "Killed him?"

"Clubbed to death, but as far as I know,

the case is still unsolved." Gardner took a deep breath. "Enough about that." He looked out the window. "We're coming up on Cape Horn. You afraid of heights?"

"A little, why?"

"Well, just ahead there's a community called Colfax — just recently changed from Illinoistown. Nearby, there's a nearly perpendicular stone cliff called Cape Horn. It rises nearly 4,000 feet above the American River. There was no way around it, so last summer the Chinese railroad workers were lowered in baskets to use hand tools and blasting powder to chip a narrow ledge on the face so they could lay tracks on it."

"Blasting powder?" Laurel exclaimed in disbelief.

"Black powder is all there is besides hammers and hand-held drills. But if you're wondering how the Chinese set the charges and then got hauled up to safety in their baskets before the explosion, well, they didn't always."

The image of a premature blast made Laurel close her eyes. "Those poor men!" She opened her eyes.

"Yes, poor is right. It was proven here that no Caucasians or any other race could do as much work in twenty-four hours, day after day, as the Chinese. They also work cheaper, earning twenty-five to forty dollars a month. The CP imported thousands, so about ten thousand are now working on this road."

Gardner paused and glanced out the window. "Speaking of this road, by last month, the Chinese had carved a narrow ledge on Cape Horn for a roadbed wide enough to lay these tracks."

"The tracks we're on right now?"

"The very same. Come on! Let's go out and stand on the observation platform to have an unobstructed view."

He started to stand, but when Laurel hesitated, he spoke quickly to save her any possible embarrassment.

"On second thought, we can see just as well from here. We're going to be on the cliff side, so you may not want to look down. In fact, you may want to close your eyes and think of something else."

Slowly, the train approached the massive mountain and the point where the cars would travel four thousand feet above the river. Laurel could see it below like a thin silvery ribbon. Ahead, there was a long, narrow scar which had been gouged into the mountain's granite face. The roadbed seemed no wider than a string, and appeared to end just inches short of the sheer drop-off. If the train jumped the track . . .

Laurel tried not to show her fear as the small engine crept toward the frightening spot. She closed eyes and tried to think of something else.

Who attacked me last night? If it was Morton, he didn't need the photograph, so it must have been the man whom Phillips told me was with Morton when Oglesby was murdered. Morton. Why hasn't he been seen lately?

She felt the car slowing as Gardner said quietly, "We're here. Cape Horn. It's an incredible site. If you can, look down."

Laurel forced her eyes open. She glanced out the window and gasped. There was nothing below except four thousand feet of space.

She suddenly reached out and clutched Gardner's hand. He started to smile, but stopped when she instantly released him, embarrassed.

"I'm sorry," she whispered.

"Don't be. It's a scary sight." He reached over and gently interlaced his fingers with hers. "We can be scared together."

She managed a wan smile before turning back to look out the window at the incredible emptiness spread out below. Gardner still held her hand, but she found herself wishing it was Ridge's. It somehow generated a tingle that could not be explained. Her mind retreated from the fearful precipice to remember Ridge walking away. But it had been her choice to leave Virginia.

Sarah's warning also came to mind: ". . . you're going to end up a bitter old woman like Agnes."

Then Agnes's own words about herself: ". . . decisions that seemed right at the time, but instead led to a lifetime of regret."

CHAPTER 18

Gardner gently squeezed Laurel's fingers. "Well, you have now safely passed Cape Horn. Are you going to write about this experience for your Chicago readers?"

"You think they would like it?"

"Absolutely! People are fascinated with trains, so if you even come close to describing what you saw, felt, and thought just now, it could be a great piece."

She smiled. Gardner had no idea what thoughts had jumped into her mind. *A lifetime of regret . . .*

He continued, "I can suggest another strong feature idea. The tunnels. You know about them?"

"A little. From what I understand, the workers only make a few inches of progress each day. That sounds as if it would take forever to cut through the mountains."

"The CP doesn't have forever. Government payment is made for each mile of track laid, so the easy money will be made in the flat deserts of Nevada and Utah, beyond these Sierras. The company has to get there fast."

Laurel began to nod. "You're right. That would make a great story, but first, I'll write about Cape Horn."

Gardner released her fingers. "I hope you do, but that's enough talk about work. Now I'd like to talk about you." He leaned closer. "You have beautiful eyes."

She stiffened slightly at the unexpected comment.

"Thank you."

"I've never seen violet eyes before. They're —"

"Mr. Gardner," Laurel said firmly, "I think we had better talk about the railroad again." She glanced toward her aunt who was looking out the window. Laurel hadn't seen her look back at all during the entire trip.

Gardner drew back. "I'm sorry, Laurel. I don't want to offend you, but I really do want to know you better. I guess I was in too much of a hurry. It was too soon."

Too soon! She had said those same words to Ridge when he bent to kiss her. Now it was too late.

"Laurel?" Gardner's voice brought her back.

"Oh, I'm sorry. I was just thinking." To prevent him asking other personal questions, she urged, "Tell me about your work."

He shrugged in defeat, then smiled and returned to his bantering style. At their picnic, he explained his newspaper job. Laurel tried to listen, but it was an effort. She found him attractive and easy to be with, however, she was glad when the train returned to Sacramento.

Gardner hired a hack and dropped Laurel and her aunt off at their hotel. Entering the lobby, Laurel asked her, "Why were you so quiet today, up front by yourself?"

"I didn't want to spoil your day, and he seemed like a nice young man. So I enjoyed the scenery and did some thinking."

"What did you think about?"

"Something that happened a long time ago. It's nothing to talk about now."

The desk clerk called, "Ladies, one moment, please."

They approached the counter where Agnes was handed a message and Laurel received a telegram. She opened it and skimmed the few words. Seymour simply acknowledged receipt of her wire and was waiting details by letter.

Aunt Agnes quickly scanned her message. She frowned, crumpled it up and turned to the clerk. "When he comes back, tell him I'm indisposed." Whirling about, she walked rapidly toward the hallway.

"From Mr. Bodmer?" Laurel guessed, catching up.

"Yes. I didn't mind talking to him on the stage, but I was trapped into going with him to chaperon you and Mr. Pomeroy, and on that day of sight-seeing. But that's as far as my interest goes."

"I should think you would be flattered."

Agnes stopped, her eyes and voice filled with anger. "Do you think I've never had a beau in my whole life?"

Laurel hesitated, unsure what to say.

"I can see it in your eyes; you think I didn't. You think I should leap at a chance to have one now, even if he is as plain as Horatio Bodmer."

"I didn't mean that at all! And he may not be handsome, but he's a fine gentleman."

"Don't change the subject! You don't think I've ever loved a man, do you? Or that one could love me?"

Laurel was taken aback. It was hard to imagine Agnes being in love.

"Believe it or not, Laurel," Agnes continued in a quieter tone, "I was once betrothed —" She broke off abruptly and hurried toward the stairs. A sound like a single sob followed her.

Laurel waited, then deliberately stayed a few steps behind Agnes as she went to her room. *So that's what she meant about a wrong decision and a lifetime of regret.*

How long ago must it have been? Agnes was in her middle fifties now. Many girls were married at eighteen, so courting usually began earlier. About forty years ago, Laurel realized, and Agnes still hurt over a lost love.

That won't happen to me! Laurel told herself. *I've always had lots of beaus.* She tried to stop her thoughts there, but couldn't. *Yet not one of them ever made me feel as Ridge does. Have I made the same mistake Agnes did — a mistake I'm going to regret the rest of my life?*

On the way to church the next morning, Agnes didn't say a thing about her unexpected outburst at the hotel. Laurel didn't ask. She enjoyed the hymns, but Pastor Villard's sermon was about the Prodigal Son. She had heard the story many times, and this was without any new insights. She drifted back in memory to Villard's stagecoach topic of sowing and reaping. That theme still troubled her.

Afterward, she shook hands with the little preacher at the door. She managed to quietly ask if she could talk to him privately sometime soon. He said he would be glad to see her anytime next week. She wondered how much she should tell him to help ease her conscience.

Laurel took Pomeroy's note from her handbag and re-read it: "There's a dinner meeting of important railroad officials next Tuesday. I'll call for you at 7:30."

Laurel wanted very much to attend, but Mr. Pomeroy had to be shown she could not be taken for granted. At the hotel desk, she wrote beneath his words: "I am used to being asked, not told."

Satisfied at the tone of her note, she left it at the desk for him to read when he came to pick her up.

Early the next morning, Laurel found a copy of the *Sentinel* outside her hotel room door. Gardner's byline on a front page story reported that Phillips's autopsy showed he had died from a blow to the back of his head. His body had been thrown into the river in an apparent effort to make it look like an accidental drowning.

Laurel wrote a story for the Chicago *Globe* with details of the death. She tied in Phillips's Chicago background to give the story a local angle. After addressing an envelope to Seymour, she mailed the story before telegraphing Seymour to watch for it.

She also wired Pinkerton. She told him

that she had been unable to find any proof of a conspiracy to stop the railroad, but was still working on the case.

Leaving the telegraph office, Laurel reflected on the significance of the murder. Phillips had been killed right after she talked to him. She felt some guilt about that. If she had not missed seeing someone following her to the meeting, he might still be alive.

The photograph baffled Laurel. She assumed that whoever had killed Oglesby in Chicago was limited to a couple of ways to find the only witness to that crime.

One way was to take the photograph from Laurel to identify the witness. The alternative was to follow her after she used the photograph to identify and find Phillips. Obviously, that had been done.

She reasoned, *if I'm right in assuming that Morton was responsible, then he no longer needed the picture. Therefore it couldn't have been he who held a knife to my throat and demanded the photograph. That indicates two men are involved; probably the same ones connected with the Chicago murder.*

Phillips told me that he had seen Morton as one of the men who killed Oglesby. But if these same two men are here in Sacramento, why didn't the one who attacked me know that Phillips had already been found and murdered?

After locking herself in her room, Laurel made a list of possible suspects, starting with Dick Morton. At the *Globe*, he had seen Seymour hand her the photograph of the missing witness, who turned out to be Phillips. Her rooms had been ransacked twice, and someone had assaulted her on a Chicago street. Morton was waiting at the stage terminal when she arrived in Sacramento. Did he know she was coming, or was it pure coincidence?

Either way, Phillips had identified him as a killer, but who was his associate in crime? She could watch out for Morton, but how could she protect herself from the unknown person? Making a mistake could cost her life. Then she studied the next name on her list: Walker.

She had met this strangely silent man on the stagecoach. He had since followed her in Sacramento. When she accosted him, he warned her that she was in danger.

His hat was dropped at the scene of the knife attack. But that didn't prove he had tried to kill her; maybe he was the man who rescued her. Besides, what motive did Walker have to murder anyone, including her?

On the other hand, if he had been her defender, why hadn't he come back to explain how he happened to arrive on the scene just in time to save her life?

There was also the possibility of an unnamed third party. Maybe it was the man who had attacked her on the streets of Chicago, or, more likely, Morton's unknown accomplice whom Phillips had glimpsed at Oglesby's murder.

Laurel decided that was certainly possible, but she could not think of whom he might be, or of any motive.

She reminded herself that Pinkerton paid her a salary to complete an assignment: Find out for sure if there was a conspiracy to stop the railroad. Seymour had only asked her to learn the identity of the man in the photograph. That sideline job had unexpectedly filled her time and threatened her life.

Laurel folded the list and put it in her handbag. She reminded herself, *You're a detective. Solve both cases, and do that while you're still in good health.*

She left the hotel by a side door, then crossed the street and circled back to see if anyone might be waiting to follow her if she left through the lobby. Seeing no one, she tried another way to make sure so she didn't make the same mistake which led to Phillips's death. She began walking away from the river, periodically looking back.

Carriage and saddle horses were tied to hitching rails in front of stores. In the street, hooves of heavy draft horses threw up clouds of dust with each step. Pedestrians sauntered along the boardwalk. There was no sign of anything suspicious, but she kept changing directions every few blocks.

She had noticed several churches representing various denominations, but paid no attention until she came to a small white frame structure with a bell tower marked with woodpecker holes. The round ends of acorns from the nearby clumps of oaks showed where the birds had driven the nuts into the holes last autumn. The sign in front confirmed that this was where Lyman Villard was the new pastor.

This seemed like an opportune time to speak with the pastor. With a last reassuring look behind, she followed the sound of voices from the open front door. Climbing the steep wooden steps, she entered and stopped. It took a moment for her eyes to adjust from the bright July sun to the unlit interior. A couple of matronly women dusting the polished pews directed her to the pastor's study. She passed the slightly curving mourners' bench in front of the pulpit and found Villard in a cramped study with two men building book shelves.

The pastor welcomed her warmly and dismissed the two men who left the door open and began nailing something a few feet away behind the choir loft.

Laurel came directly to the point of why she had come. "I can't stop thinking of what you said on the stagecoach about sowing and reaping. For reasons I cannot disclose, I must keep a business secret that seems to be in conflict with my Christian commitment. Well, recent recommitment."

The little preacher nodded. "Recent?"

"Yes. I had wandered away from my faith in my teen years. I don't want to do again, so I need some guidance in how to ease my conscience about my dual life."

Villard raised his eyebrows. "How is it dual?"

"Oh, nothing illegal or anything like that, Pastor. It's just that my employer demands that I don't disclose what I do."

"I never heard of a newspaper requiring that of a correspondent."

Taking a deep breath, Laurel said, "I do write for the paper, but that's not my real job. It's something my aunt told people on the stagecoach because even she doesn't know what I really do. Not that's it's illegal, you understand. But being thought of as one thing when I'm really another makes me fearful that I might be heading for a harvest that I don't want."

"Let me make sure I understand. You're involved in deceit, but you really want honesty."

That was a little blunt, but Laurel nodded.

The pastor continued, "It's apparently not only in your job life, but in your personal life as well. I'm judging that from the fact that your own aunt has obviously been deceived in at least part of your personal life."

"That's true, and that's what troubles me most."

"You mean, misleading your aunt and possibly other family members?"

"It's more than that, but . . ."

He waited for her to finish, but when she didn't, he asked, "Does that have anything to do with a young man?"

An anemic smile touched her lips. "You are very perceptive. Yes and no. Actually, it's over between us, but part of the reason is that I didn't tell him the truth, even though my conscience kept nudging me."

The minister leaned back in his chair and regarded her in thoughtful silence for several seconds. Finally he said, "I'm sure you're a very bright young lady, but I wonder if you're overlooking something."

"Oh? What's that?"

"I suspect you came in here expecting a future harvest, but you have already reaped one."

She stared. "I've already . . . ?"

"Yes, by your own admission. But the break-up with your beau is only the first crop. What do you expect to gather from what you're continuing to plant?"

Laurel protested, "But I can't stop!"

"Can't? Or won't?"

"I need my job! I like my job! I don't know what else I could do besides that."

"Off-hand, I can think of two possibilities. You could truly become a newspaper correspondent." He paused, then added gently, "Or you could marry."

Laurel took a shuddering breath. "It's too late."

"How do you know?"

"It's a long story."

"Well, if it's truly too late for this young man you obviously favored, there are always many other eligible bachelors around."

I don't want any of them! The thought exploded in her mind, but she drove it away. "Yes," she admitted, "I've already met a couple since leaving Chicago."

"Only your heart can advise you about what's right in the area of marriage. Just remember that continuing in deceit will always bring the same unwanted results you've already known. It's just a matter of time."

Laurel thanked him and started to rise, but he asked if he could pray for her. She nodded and sank back down into her chair, her heart and her mind warring with the choices that she alone could make.

She walked back in a pensive mood. She had expected to feel relieved after sharing part of her concerns with the minister. Instead, he had created new distress by pointing out an obvious truth that had eluded her. Yet she didn't know how to change her circumstances and end the bedeviling problems that swirled around her.

Nearing the hotel, she roused herself and remembered to look around. Two men stood by the entrance to an alley between adobe brick stores.

She looked again. *Walker — and Hodges.*

They seemed engrossed in deep conversation and didn't look at Laurel. She turned into the recessed entry to a haberdashery and watched the men's reflection in the glass window. They faced each other and gave no indication of looking around. Convinced that they were not waiting for her, she continued toward her hotel.

I haven't seen Morton for days. I wonder why?

Bushrod Pomeroy was waiting in the lobby when she returned. He rose quickly and stopped her just inside the door. "I am so sorry about my note," he began. "I didn't mean to be so presumptuous. Please forgive me."

It was a temptation to keep him off balance, but she didn't feel right about doing something that involved more deceit. Besides, he was good looking, charming, and just might help her forget Ridge.

"Mr. Pomeroy," she said with a warm smile, "you caught me when I'm in a forgiving mood. I accept your apology."

"I'm glad! Now, I don't know of any new upcoming meetings of railroad executives, but if I'm not pressing my luck, may I please have the honor of escorting you to another dinner? Your aunt is also invited, of course."

For a moment, Laurel hesitated, remembering the way he had twice shown flashes of emotion at their first dinner. The second display had frightened her, although he had quickly apologized. But her job required her to take risks. She might be able to elicit information from him.

That included what Gardner had said about Pomeroy having been an investor in Oglesby's meat company. If she accepted Pomeroy's invitation, she might be able to lead him to talking about that subject. Besides, with her aunt along, it would be safe.

She gave Pomeroy a warm smile. "That sounds lovely."

"How about Saturday night, eight o'clock?"

"I'll look forward to it."

Agnes had remained aloof and withdrawn all week. She now surprised Laurel by telling her to have dinner with Pomeroy without her. That momentarily upset Laurel's safety plan, but she reminded herself that she had safely gone behind enemy lines in the war. She had nothing to fear from Pomeroy in a public restaurant. *In fact*, she told herself, *I'm glad Aunt Agnes won't be along. I want to be open to developing a new relationship with Pomeroy.*

The Golden Slipper featured a string quartet on Saturday nights, a feature which Laurel found delightful. That, combined with the soft lights and the moonlight reflecting off the Sacramento River, created a romantic atmosphere. That wasn't what Laurel had had in mind, but it was seductive, and she let herself relax.

I wonder if it's possible to deliberately fall in love with someone? Well, here's a chance to find out.

Pomeroy was his usual charming self, never taking his eyes off of her and encouraging her to tell him all about herself. At first, she tried to turn the tables on him, but he deftly reversed them until she found herself conversing comfortably with him. Even though the pastor's words still stayed with her, she skillfully avoided any indication of her spy background and detective work.

When she exhausted the safe topics of her family background, a pleasant silence settled over them.

Pomeroy finally broke it. "I didn't want to ask, but since you haven't mentioned it, I hope you won't mind if I bring up the story in the local newspapers about you being attacked."

She hadn't wanted think about that, but it was only natural that Pomeroy would care. Still, it destroyed the sentimental mood. She tried to blunt his interest by saying, "There's nothing to add to what the story said."

"You couldn't identify either man?"

"No. It all happened so fast, and I was frightened."

"You wouldn't recognize his voice?"

"No. It was muffled by a mask."

"I see. Is there anything that you remember which didn't come out in the newspaper?"

She hesitated, *Why is he asking all these questions?* She briefly considered the logic. *It's understandable. I would probably be doing the same if he had been attacked.*

She recalled that Walker's hat had been recovered at the scene. However, the police apparently hadn't released that information to the press. She tried to hedge by simply shrugging off Pomeroy's last question.

Pomeroy said, "The paper mentioned a photograph the attacker demanded. I didn't understand that."

Although given as a statement, Laurel understood it was intended as a question. "I guess it's a mystery," she said evasively.

"I guess so. Are you afraid whoever attacked you might do it again?"

"I've thought about it."

"I would be honored to hire a private guard to protect —"

"Oh, no, thanks," she broke in. "I'm sure I'll be all right."

"I hope so, but there seems to be more unpleasant news than usual." Pomeroy leaned closer and spoke across the candle.

"The papers reported a man named Phillips was murdered down by the river. At first, it was thought he drowned."

Laurel was becoming uncomfortable with the unpleasant subject, but she needed all the information she could get. She turned the questions away from her and back to Pomeroy. She asked, "Did you know the victim?"

"I never met him."

"How about a man named Dick Morton?"

"Can't say that I do. Why do you ask?"

"I was just curious because I saw him in Chicago and then at the stage depot when our coach arrived. Since you came from Chicago, I thought maybe you'd met him."

Pomeroy chuckled. "Chicago's a big city. I'm sure you didn't know everyone there any more than I did."

"You're right, of course."

"I wish you would reconsider my offer to hire —"

Laurel knew she had to stop this subject. She broke in quickly, but with a little smile, "Are you trying to frighten me?"

"Oh, no, of course not. It's just the coincidence of that death and your attack. . . ."

"Please! I don't want our evening spoiled."

"Neither do I." He turned toward the musicians before asking her, "If you have a favorite selection, I'll have them play it for you."

"That's very thoughtful of you, but I would rather sit and listen to you. Tell me about your background, before you became a businessman."

Pomeroy shrugged. "There's not much to tell."

Laurel tried a more direct approach. "I've heard that you once invested in a meat-packing business in Chicago."

"I've invested in many businesses, but you wouldn't be interested."

Laurel detected a note in his tone indicating he didn't want to talk about that. She prompted, "I'm a good listener."

"I'm sure, but that's a dull topic. On the other hand, I've got some stories from my childhood that might at least be entertaining."

Laurel realized that he was not going to tell anything that she really wanted to know, so she nodded. "Tell me about them."

She tried to listen as he told amusing anecdotes from his childhood, but Laurel wasn't really listening anymore. The mood had been shattered, and she was glad when dinner was over and Pomeroy escorted her back to the hotel. He saw her to the lobby door.

"I've been saving a little surprise for you, Laurel. I've been trying to set up an appointment for you to meet Charles Crocker. He's —"

"I know!" she broke in. "He's one of the Big Four!"

"Right! He's really quite a character."

"So I've heard!" Laurel was excited at the possibility of meeting the man who supervised building of the Central Pacific in the field. He would be able to tell her whether he thought there was an organized conspiracy against the railroad.

"Once a month," Pomeroy continued, "he rides among the men on horseback carrying saddlebags filled with a hundred and fifty dollars in gold and silver coins to pay the men. Well, I'm hoping he'll let you watch him do that, and then give you an interview for your newspaper. Would you like that?"

"Of course! I'd love it!"

"So shall I firm up the date he's going to do that?"

"Of course. Just tell me when and where."

"I'll let you know. Your aunt is also invited to come along, but those canyons are rough, so part of the trip will have to be on horseback. I assume you ride?"

"It's been awhile, but yes. I can do it again."

"Then it's all set except for the date."

Laurel's spirits surged back from where they had dipped after Pomeroy's earlier questions about the knife attack and photograph. She left him and hurried across the lobby before the clerk stopped her.

"Oh, Miss Bartlett, a letter came for you earlier, but I missed you before you left a while ago."

"Thank you," she said, taking the envelope. She caught a faint fragrance of lilacs as she glanced at the unfamiliar handwriting, then touched the flap. "It's been opened!" she exclaimed.

"Uh . . . yes, but I didn't do it," the clerk said.

"Was it open when delivered?"

"No, Miss Bartlett. It wasn't."

"Then who opened it?" she demanded firmly.

He lowered his head. "I . . . I can't say."

"That sounds to me as if you know who did."

"Well, yes, but please don't ask me anything more."

"It is a serious breach to open private . . . !" she began, then caught herself. *Aunt Agnes!*

She spun around and started across the lobby, her anger rising with each step. Then she again caught the faint fragrance from the envelope. She stopped, and stared at the envelope.

It's from a woman. Laurel impulsively lifted it and sniffed. *Lilacs? Who wears . . . Oh!*

Stepping to a big overstuffed chair near one of the coal oil lamps, Laurel extracted the single sheet with fingers that suddenly began to tremble. The words leaped up at her.

My dear Laurel. Although we only had a brief time to get acquainted while you were here, I thought that you would like to know that Ridge and I are betrothed. . . .

The letter slipped unnoticed from her hands as a violent pain stabbed her heart. She bent forward at the waist, closed her eyes and unconsciously started rocking.

She vaguely heard the clerk's voice. "Are you all right?" She didn't answer. He asked, "Should I call your aunt?"

"No!" She looked up at him through tears she didn't know were there. "No! I'll be all right. Please . . ." She dropped her head and let the tears fall freely.

She was vaguely aware that others were passing through the lobby, but she didn't care. She retreated deep into her mind, as far as she could get from the pain. But she could still faintly hear, as from a great distance, the clerk's low voice saying she had received a letter with bad news.

Laurel had no idea of how long she sat there, torn and bleeding from wounds nobody could see. Finally, very slowly, she sought to replace the heartache with reason.

Why am I carrying on like this? She scolded herself. *It was over before I left Virginia. I knew that. I've told others that, but I guess I didn't believe it. Well, I was a fool. Like Aunt Agnes. But I'll not end up like her. The preacher was right. The are many other eligible bachelors around. Besides, Varina's letter shows Ridge didn't really love me, even if he did tell me he did.*

She was aware that someone else had entered the lobby and stopped instead of going on through. She heard the low rumble of a man's voice, and the clerk's reply.

She didn't care. Let them stare. She had already made a worse fool of herself than she was doing now.

"Laurel?"

The voice seemed far away. She ignored it, her eyes closed, her head still on her lap.

"Laurel, please! Look at me!"

Startled, she slowly raised her head

enough to look through the tears. She made out the outlines of two men. She started to order them away, then froze. She brushed the tears from her eyes and looked more closely.

"Ridge?"

"What's the matter?" he replied, reaching out to take both her hands in his.

She stiffened in sudden fury and jerked her hands away. "What are you doing here?" she demanded hotly.

"What do you think?" he asked tenderly, again reaching for her hands. "I came to see you!"

In sudden fury, she leaped to her feet. "That's the cruelest thing I've ever heard! Go back to her and leave me alone! Forever!"

She whirled around and ran blindly toward the hall, Varina's letter forgotten on the floor.

CHAPTER 19

Laurel slammed her hallway door shut and collapsed brokenly in the big chair. Jerking her feet up under her, she curled into a tight ball. The tears still flowed, but they had changed from tears of pain to anger.

How could he do that to me? How could he?

She heard the connecting door to Agnes's room open and her aunt's voice. "Laurel! What on earth?"

She interrupted, "Go away!"

"Don't speak to me that way!" Agnes snapped. "I know I shouldn't have opened your mail, but that's no excuse for your rudeness!"

Laurel cried, "This is not about the letter!"

Agnes stopped beside her chair. "Then what is it?"

"Him! He . . . he . . ." A knock on the hallway door stopped her. "If that's him, send him away!"

"Send who away?" Agnes asked.

The knocking sounded again, harder. Ridge called, "Laurel! Please let me in! We have to talk!"

"Never!" she jumped up and looked around for some place to run, but there was only her aunt's room. That wouldn't help.

Agnes exclaimed, "Laurel, I don't understand what's going on! Who is at the door?"

"Him! Him! Send him away!"

"Him who? You're not making sense!" Agnes turned to the door. "Who's there?"

"Ridge Granger. Please let me in. I must talk to Laurel."

"I don't want to talk to you!" Laurel's voice shot up. "Go back to her and leave me alone!"

"This is ridiculous!" Agnes said, opening the door. Ridge stood there with O'Brien behind him. "Well!" she said, "this is certainly a surprise!"

"Sorry to show up like this, Miss Bartlett," he said, then looked past her to Laurel. "If I'd had any idea I would upset you like this, I would have found another way. But I was so anxious to see you."

Laurel stared at him with mixed emotions. Even though he had hurt her terribly, she felt the same inexplicable tingle of excitement he always generated in her. She was aware of how wonderful he looked in spite of rumpled traveling clothes and weariness in his face. But her anger made her lash out. "I don't want to see you!"

"I don't understand," he said, extending the letter. "Oh, you dropped this downstairs."

"Throw it away! No, take it back to her!"

"What *are* you talking about?"

"Don't play innocent with me! Leave me alone!"

He turned bewildered and imploring eyes on Agnes.

She said, "Didn't you read the letter?"

"Of course not. I just brought it up."

"I've read it," Agnes admitted. She turned to Laurel, "So have you, obviously. Perhaps Ridge should, also."

"I don't care what he does as long as he goes away!"

"Read it," Agnes ordered Ridge crisply.

Laurel watched him nod, unfold the single sheet and glance at it. His eyebrows shot up and his mouth dropped. "I can't believe it!" he exclaimed softly, almost to himself. "Griff warned me, but I never imagined . . ."

He started toward Laurel. "This is a lie! Do you understand what she's trying to do?"

Laurel drew back, but he dropped the letter and seized both of her hands. She tried to pull them free, but his grip was firm.

"Laurel! Laurel!" His voice was almost a groan. "I am not betrothed to Varina! Don't you see? This is exactly what she planned! Well, it won't work! I love you and only you. Neither she nor anyone else is going to keep me from making you realize that we belong together!"

Laurel's mouth suddenly felt dry and her throat seemed to constrict so she couldn't breathe. Twice in the last few minutes everything had turned topsy-turvy. She was so totally confused that she could only gape at him.

She heard her aunt say, "I'm Agnes Bartlett."

"Philotas O'Brien. Ridge and I traveled from Omaha together. We didn't mean to —"

"It's all right," Agnes interrupted. "Why don't you and I go down to the lobby and leave these two alone?"

Laurel came out of her trance-like feeling. "Aunt Agnes!" she cried in surprise and shock.

"Oh, all right. We'll all go, but you two find a quiet corner while Mr. O'Brien and I get acquainted."

Laurel gazed up at Ridge who looked perplexed at Agnes's unusually friendly attitude toward him. Laurel's heart melted at his tender expression. She said softly, "Yes. Maybe we should talk."

Ridge led her to a far corner of the lobby where she apprehensively seated herself on a Victorian circular sofa. He sat across from her in an upholstered wing chair. Out of hearing across the lobby, Agnes and O'Brien settled down at opposite ends of a serpentine-back sofa.

Laurel was emotionally fatigued after the whiplash of Varina's letter and Ridge's appearance. She was glad that Ridge gave her a few minutes to collect her thoughts, while he commented on how different Sacramento's dry heat was from Virginia's hot, humid June weather.

Slowly, she sorted out her confused feelings.

Ridge leaned toward her. "I regret with all my heart having walked away from you that day at the picnic. I have anguished every moment since you left before I could apologize for being such a fool." He gently touched her fingers. She tensed them but did not resist.

"When I came to my senses," he added, "I knew we belonged together. That's why I'm here. I'll do whatever it takes, including waiting until you feel the same way."

He paused, obviously waiting for her to

reply. She vainly tried to think of the proper response.

He urged gently, "Please say something."

She nodded, but remained silent while her thoughts raced on. She recalled her many weeks of misery over their turbulent relationship, and the vain efforts to forget him. Her heart ached to respond in kind to his deep feelings, but she didn't want to get hurt again.

Agnes saved Laurel from having to answer by walking over and saying, "Mr. O'Brien tells me you men haven't eaten, and he's starved. We're going down the street to a restaurant. You two want to join us?"

Laurel leaped at the opportunity for some extra time before replying to Ridge's plea. She had dined with Bushrod Pomeroy, but she replied, "I'd like coffee."

Ridge hesitated, obviously preferring to have Laurel alone awhile longer, but he finally nodded. "Sounds good. I had forgotten about missing dinner."

He and O'Brien returned to the front desk where they had checked their rifles and pistols. They registered to assure a bed for the night, then walked outside with Laurel and Agnes. The women sipped coffee while the men had their first quality meal in nearly two weeks.

Laurel listened while Ridge recounted how he had been told to find a newspaper man in Sacramento named Mark Gardner who would know where Laurel was staying.

"But," Ridge told her with a grin, "it was obvious that he didn't want to. I'm sure he has his eye on you."

"So does Bushrod Pomeroy," Agnes murmured.

"Aunt Agnes!" Laurel exclaimed. "Please!"

Ridge raised an eyebrow. "It seems I got here just in time, but the competition for you is understandable."

He saw that Laurel was ill at ease, so he looked at Agnes. A faint hint of smile touched her thin lips. He expected that she would be her usual cool, disapproving self toward him. Instead, so far she had been cordial. He didn't understand her change of attitude since Virginia, but he liked it.

She prompted, "You were telling us about your trip."

Ridge nodded and told about starting to Sacramento, stopping in Omaha, meeting O'Brien, and the railroad's reward for recovery of the stolen payroll.

Looking across the small table at Laurel, he added, "You know what I'm going to do with my share of that reward when I get it?

It's going toward building that house for you, for us."

Embarrassed, she lowered her eyes. He was being a little too bold in front of others. She was delighted to see him, but she hadn't been formally asked to marry him, and she wasn't in a hurry for him to do that. She wanted to be sure that the high emotion she felt was going to last. She didn't want to again protest, "It's too soon."

Agnes seemed to sense her niece's discomfort. She quickly asked, "Did Laurel tell you about the knife attack made on her?"

Ridge's face blanched. "What?"

"It's true," Agnes said, and told how the attacker had thought Laurel possessed a certain photograph, how the police now had the picture, but had been unable to find the assailant.

Ridge asked for details, his face and voice showing such concern for Laurel that she felt protected and safe. She fidgeted at having to only mention her assignment from the *Globe*. It seemed she was always being forced slightly deeper into her role of newspaper correspondent.

She thought that if she had been alone with Ridge, she might have disclosed her real work as a Pinkerton detective. But even if she did break the company rule and tell Ridge, it would have to be in private.

So the moment slipped away and vanished when O'Brien, who had been largely silent, spoke up.

"Ridge and I have a possible lead on who stole the railroad's payroll. He was supposed to be headed for Sacramento. Name's Morton."

Laurel gasped. "Dick Morton?"

Ridge nodded. "You know him?"

"I had seen him at the newspaper in Chicago, and then when Aunt Agnes and I got off the stagecoach here in Sacramento. I asked Mark Gardner about him."

Agnes exclaimed, "Morton? Was that what made you go dashing off without even saying good-bye to Mr. Pomeroy the day we arrived in Sacramento?" At Laurel's nod, her aunt asked, "How do you know this Morton?"

Laurel briefly explained.

Ridge straightened up, his tired body suddenly alert with interest. "Does he know where I can find Morton?"

"Gardner told me that he often frequents a place down by the river called Shanghai Joe's."

"Where's that?" Ridge demanded, glancing at O'Brien who was grinning like a delighted schoolboy.

"Beyond Chinatown. But Gardner told me never to go there because it's a disreputable place, and dangerous."

The big Irishman had said little while eating, but he dropped his fork with a clatter. "It'll be more dangerous for him when we catch up with him, huh, Ridge?"

Laurel had the distinct impression that O'Brien loved a fight. She was grateful that he was there for Ridge, who was a good-sized man, but the limp from his war wound made him slower on his feet.

"Let's hope so," Ridge replied. "In the morning, let's look for him and hope he's not spent all that payroll."

"He may not be around here," Laurel pointed out. "I haven't seen him for some days."

Ridge said, "I was afraid he may have gone on down to San Francisco. But we'll still look at Shanghai Joe's."

"Be careful!" Laurel exclaimed, knowing that Morton had murdered Oglesby in Chicago and almost surely had killed Phillips.

"There's no need to worry," Ridge assured her. "I didn't come all this way to let some bandit stop me from spending the rest of my life with you."

Laurel's secret made her throat constrict,

but all she dared say was, "He . . . he might be a killer."

"O'Brien and I will be very careful," Ridge replied.

Laurel wanted to tell him more, but couldn't.

It was after midnight when she returned to her room and prepared for bed. She blew out the lamp and fretted in the darkness about Morton. She must see Ridge alone before he and O'Brien left. She could at least tell him enough to make him very cautious with Morton.

When she awakened the next morning, she was irritated with herself for oversleeping. She hurriedly dressed and scurried down to the front desk.

"I'm sorry, Miss Bartlett," the clerk replied in answer to her question. "Both those gentlemen left about an hour ago."

Laurel walked across the lobby on legs that suddenly seemed to go weak. She sat down in the nearest chair and whispered an earnest prayer for Ridge and his friend.

Shanghai Joe's was an unpainted wooden structure sagging on the south bank of the Sacramento River a couple of miles out of town. Ridge and O'Brien vainly looked for someone who might tell them how to find

Morton. Their only hope was offered by a ramshackle cabin out in back.

While O'Brien shifted his Spencer rifle to the ready position, Ridge clumped upon the sagging porch with splintery boards that squeaked in protest as he took two steps and knocked on the door.

O'Brien said in a low tone, "Something sure smells around here. Reminds me of the war."

"I noticed." Ridge knocked again, harder. He waited, listening, then thumped vigorously.

O'Brien mused, "Either there's nobody home, or else they're sleeping it off from last night."

Ridge nodded, leaned his rifle against the porch wall and drew his heavy revolver. "I'm going to look in the window," he announced in a low tone.

"Hurry up. This smell is getting to me."

Ridge cupped his free hand against the fly-specked window and peered through the curtain-less glass. "I don't see anybody. I'll try the other windows."

He started to step off the porch when a plank cracked ominously under foot. He grabbed for the two-by-four pillar and caught himself, but knocked off a small board. He picked it up then glanced at it before holding it up for O'Brien to see. "Dick Morton. It's so faded you can barely read it, but this is his place." He glanced around. "Something's wrong here."

"Looks that way," O'Brien agreed. "See if that door is unlocked."

Ridge stepped over, grasped the knob and slowly turned it. "It's open," he whispered.

"Good! Give me a minute to get around in back in case he tries to run out that way."

Ridge rechecked the loads in his revolver, then tensely waited until he heard wood creaking from the back porch. When he heard O'Brien kick in the back door, Ridge threw open the front one and plunged into the sparsely furnished front room with the pistol in hand.

O'Brien called, "In here!"

Ridge ran into the second room where O'Brien stood looking down at a still figure sprawled on the floor.

The men made a very hurried examination and then ran choking into the morning air.

Returning to her hotel room after a fruitless try to catch Ridge before he left, Laurel undressed while trying not to worry about Ridge's safety. Her movements were automatic, allowing her memory to roam freely.

There was no tub, so she used the chamber set decorated with golden California poppies to wash. After pouring water from a large-mouthed pitcher into a ceramic basin, she took a sponge bath, then brushed her teeth. All the while, her memories flowed.

She remembered that shortly after they first met, Ridge had learned about her spying for the North. One of her missions into the South had led to the death of his only brother and his leg wound.

She shuddered, remembering his reaction. "If you were a man, I would kill you with my bare hands."

Yet in time, he had forgiven her. Surely he would do that when and if she confessed that her newspaper role was only cover for her real job as a Pinkerton detective.

Or will he? He might walk off again as he did at the picnic because I've been less than honest with him about two things in my life.

She put on a clean yellow dress, carefully brushed her hair, then tried to read her Bible. The words blurred before her eyes. She was too anxious to concentrate.

I'd better not say anything to Ridge about my work until and if it's necessary. Pinkerton would discharge me if he learns I broke the company rule, and I need this job to support myself.

414

She warned herself, *There's a danger in waiting because he then might not trust me for twice keeping something so important from him.*

She prayed for wisdom for herself and for Ridge's safety before knocking on her aunt's adjoining door. There was no answer. Laurel descended the stairs, planning to have breakfast. She changed her mind for fear that Ridge would arrive but she wouldn't see him. She walked to the lobby corner where they had talked last night and settled down to wait.

It seemed like hours before the two men walked in from the street carrying their weapons. O'Brien had heavy saddlebags slung over his broad shoulders.

Laurel leaped up, a joyous smile of welcome showing. She saw something in their eyes and the smile slid away.

Ridge said, "Morton's dead, but we recovered this." He jerked his head toward the saddlebags.

O'Brien patted them affectionately. "Sure did. Full of greenbacks. Feels like most of it's here."

"What . . . what happened to Morton?" she asked in a small voice.

"Knifed," O'Brien replied bluntly.

A chill raced over Laurel's body, imag-

415

ining again the feel of the cold blade on her throat.

O'Brien added, "It was probably revenge, because he wasn't robbed. Or maybe who-ever did it didn't know to look in these." He patted the saddlebags again.

Ridge said, "O'Brien and I wonder if there might be any connection with the attack on you."

Laurel absently rubbed the goose bumps that popped up on her arms and radiated over her body. "You . . . you really think there's a chance that? . . ." she stammered.

"It's possible, so we have to head it off before it can happen," Ridge replied. "After O'Brien and I check our guns again, we're going to turn the money over to the police, and have them count it in front of us. When they're satisfied that it belongs to the rail-road, we'll have a draft sent to Tomkins in Omaha. Then, Laurel, you and I must go over the details of this whole situation. But not here. Tell your aunt she can come along, but I must talk to you privately."

Laurel relayed his message to Agnes. She surprised Laurel by suggesting she and Ridge go alone. When he returned, the cool-ness of the valley morning had begun to give way to the high heat of mid-day. They strolled down toward the waterfront. All the while, Laurel kept glancing around, making sure nobody was following. She was extra careful, recalling how she had been fooled, leading to Phillips's death.

Laurel told Ridge everything from first seeing Morton in Seymour's office when he handed her the package with the photograph to the last time she had seen him.

She left nothing out about Seymour's assignment, but reluctantly omitted all references to her railroad case.

She concluded, "Now I know why I haven't seen Morton for a while. He was probably dead before the knife attack on me. Apparently he hadn't told whoever his accomplice is that Phillips was already dead."

"But who's the accomplice?" Ridge mused. "And why didn't the one who killed Phillips let the other one know that there was no need to attack you over the picture?"

"I don't know, but it all ties back to the Oglesby murder in Chicago. Phillips told me that Morton was one of them. But who's the other?" She looked back again but saw no sign of being followed.

"The pieces fit so far," Ridge mused. "Oglesby, Phillips, and Morton are dead. The only one who is still alive is Morton's unknown partner. The motive apparently is to keep anyone from finding out who he is." Ridge stopped abruptly and took both of Laurel's upper arms to turn her so she faced him. "Oh, I hope I'm wrong in what just came to me!"

"I'm probably thinking the same thing," Laurel said slowly, fear rising with each word, "that unknown person was with Morton when they murdered Oglesby in Chicago. They knew there was a witness, but didn't know his name. He disappeared to save his life, but Morton and his friend knew there was a photograph of him. Morton knew it was in Seymour's safe, but he couldn't take it from there. But when I had it —"

"I'm afraid you're right," Ridge broke in. "After Morton failed to get the picture in Chicago, he went ahead to Sacramento to wait for you so he could try again. Apparently he had someone try in Omaha, but that failed. When you got to Sacramento, Gardner identified the photo as that of Phillips. You found him, and the mystery of the missing witness was solved."

"Yes, but we still don't know who the second man is. If he thinks Phillips told me so I could identify . . ."

"Don't say it!" Ridge pulled her close and slipped his arm around her. "There may be another explanation."

Laurel didn't believe that, and doubted that Ridge did. She trembled at the closeness, the strength of his arms that held her tight. But her mind wasn't caught up in that emotion. Cold fear kept her brain rational.

"We must not fool ourselves," she murmured against his chest. "We don't know who he is, but it's absolutely clear that he has to make sure . . ." Her voice wavered before she finished in a whisper. "Make sure I can't possibly identify him."

"I'll stay as close to you as possible," Ridge said huskily. "Don't go anywhere without me if you can possibly help it until we figure this out."

We. The word sounded so new, so different, and yet, somehow, so good. Before she could reply, a horse pulled up beside them and Agnes's voice jarred them apart.

"Really, Laurel! And you, Mr. Granger! Surely you could find a more private place to display such emotions!"

Laurel pulled free, dropping her head. "I'm sorry, Aunt Agnes!" Raising her eyes, she rushed on, "We just realized that . . . oh!" She stopped. "Mr. Bodmer!"

For the first time, she became aware of the tall, lanky man holding the reins and sitting beside Agnes.

He nodded gravely, his face somber, but there was a hint of a smile in his eyes.

"Your aunt was kind enough to let me show her some of Sacramento's sights," he explained.

Agnes laughed lightly. "What he really means is that he can be very persuasive."

Laurel blinked in surprise. She had never seen her aunt when she didn't have something caustic to say about someone or something, especially men. Now that Laurel thought about it, she realized Agnes had even been cordial to Ridge.

Bodmer smiled at Agnes, saying, "Sometimes a man sees a prize so rare he —"

"Horatio! Stop it!" Agnes exclaimed, but smiled. She turned to Laurel and Ridge again. "We ran into Mark Gardner on the street a moment ago. He said the police found Dick Morton dead. There were no details yet, but I thought you should know."

Laurel and Ridge exchanged glances. "Thanks, Aunt Agnes," she said. "Ridge and Mr. O'Brien found him awhile ago and they told the police. We were talking about that when you drove up."

"Really!" Agnes exclaimed. "We had better discuss this. Shall we meet you at the hotel in a few minutes?"

★ ★ ★

Laurel and Ridge nodded. As the carriage pulled away, he gently interlaced his fingers with hers.

"I want to have a frank and open talk with you."

"Then we'll do it. But right now your safety is more important. Let's head back to the hotel."

They reached there without Laurel seeing anyone following her. But when they entered the lobby, she caught a furtive movement by the hallway door.

She jerked involuntarily, twisting to look quickly, but the door closed behind whoever had gone through it.

Ridge asked anxiously, "What's the matter?"

"I guess I'm just a little nervous," she admitted. "It was probably nothing."

"You saw somebody? Maybe whoever's been following you? Stay here; I'll go check."

"You wouldn't recognize him, and I can't move too fast in this long skirt. Besides, Aunt Agnes and her friend are waiting for us in the corner."

Ridge took Laurel's elbow and started steering her toward the older couple when the desk clerk called.

"Miss Bartlett, you have a message."

"Thanks," she replied. "Ridge, you go on and I'll be with you in a moment."

He nodded and continued toward the waiting couple while Laurel approached the desk. The clerk handed her a sealed envelope. She stepped away, opened it and read:

"Laurel: I've made arrangements for you to meet Charles Crocker near Cape Horn tomorrow afternoon. It's a long trip, so I will call for you at 8 o'clock. I know how important this is to your newspaper story, so I'm looking forward to our time together." It was signed: Bushrod.

Laurel closed her eyes and suppressed a groan. *I must interview Crocker, but how will Ridge react if I go off alone with Pomeroy?*

CHAPTER 20

Laurel reached a decision by the time she arrived at the corner of the hotel lobby where her aunt and Bodmer waited to discuss the murder of Dick Morton. "Ridge," she said, "I need to speak privately with you." She avoided any possible questions by turning and walking away.

Ridge caught up to her near the front door. "What is it?" he asked. "Something wrong?"

She handed him Pomeroy's note. He read quickly, then asked, "Surely you're not thinking of going?"

"Yes, I am, because this very important to me."

He said patiently, "It's more important that you stay close where I can look out for you. Besides, no interview is worth risking your life."

"This is more than an interview. I can't explain, but I must go."

Ridge's jaw tightened. He said bluntly, "You can't!"

Laurel's independent spirit flared. "Don't tell me what I can do!" She saw him flinch, so she added quickly, "It's an opportunity to talk to one of the famous Big Four and ask him some important questions."

"I just got here, and now you want to leave. Is that interview more important than us?"

She hesitated. They had only been together for a short time since their last breakup, and tensions were already starting. But she couldn't tell him that it wasn't just to interview Crocker for a newspaper story.

The reason Pinkerton had sent her to Sacramento was to find out if there was an organized conspiracy to stop building the transcontinental railroad. So far, she had not done much on that case. Charles Crocker would have information she might not be able to get anywhere else. She had to have that interview.

"Is it?" he prompted.

She kept her voice level. "It's only for one day, and besides, there is no 'us' — at least, not yet."

"Maybe not as far as you're concerned, but I see it differently." His voice softened. "I'm not about to lose you, even if you are the most saucy, obstinate, and . . ."

Indignation in her eyes made him suddenly smile and add tenderly, "and the most wonderful woman I ever met."

She felt her resolve start to weaken, but she quickly stopped it. "I'm trying to be reasonable, Ridge. I can't tell you why right now, but I must go."

"Then I'll go with you."

"That's not possible. Pomeroy has been courting me, so he certainly wouldn't want you . . ."

"Then you certainly can't go!"

"Don't tell me what to do!" She hadn't meant for her voice to rise so sharply, but she resented his high-handed attitude. "I'll go when and where I want!"

He reached out to take her hands but she snatched them back. "You said you're trying to be reasonable," he reminded her. "We don't know who's after your life. What do you really know about Pomeroy?"

"Don't be ridiculous! He's a gentleman!" Laurel felt the conflict threatening to get out of hand, but she was not going to be ordered around. She snapped, "I'm sorry I even mentioned this to you." She whirled around and stalked angrily across the lobby.

"Wait! Where are you going?"

She said over her shoulder, "To get ready for that interview!"

Laurel wasn't very good company on the train trip from Sacramento to Colfax the next morning. She wore a riding habit hurriedly bought yesterday after walking out on Ridge. Bushrod Pomeroy, dressed for horseback riding including high-topped boots, had made favorable comments about the outfit on the hack ride to the train station, but Laurel didn't really care. She couldn't get her mind off of the way she and Ridge had parted.

She was annoyed with herself for haughtily declaring her independence to Ridge, yet she resented his overbearing attitude. It just didn't seem they could get along, no matter how much they were attracted to each other. That aggravation troubled her, but right now she was more concerned about Albert Walker being on this train.

She had seen him run after the train as it started to leave the station. He swung onto the rear car and stayed there, but that didn't ease her mind. Neither did telling herself that he had a right to ride this train.

Yet she was convinced his real purpose was to follow her. His dropped hat proved he had been involved in the knife threat over the photograph. Was he now planning to follow her and Pomeroy into the remote mountain canyons where there would be no witnesses to the crime Walker planned against her? Safety rested in her determination to stay close to Pomeroy. She did not want to alarm Pomeroy with her suspicions, so she waited, saying nothing until she could be more sure.

It was difficult for Laurel to show interest in Pomeroy's narration about all the historic sites they passed on the slow climb from the hot valley to the cooler evergreen mountains.

At first, Pomeroy didn't seem to notice. Finally he said, "Is something bothering you?"

"What? Oh, I've just had a lot on my mind lately."

"Something I can help you with?"

"Oh, no, thanks. It's . . . it has a lot to do with work."

"Maybe some of the questions you asked me the other night at dinner?"

"I'm sorry I took up so much of our time like that."

"I understand. It's your job, and it's important to you. I hope this trip today will give you some answers and also make a great story for your newspaper."

A great story! Laurel sighed, looking back to see if Walker was in sight. He wasn't. *I just hope I don't end up being the story.*

Ridge found Agnes having breakfast in

the hotel dining room. She smiled and invited him to sit down, which surprised him. So far, she had not made one derogatory remark about him being a Rebel, or otherwise shown distaste for him.

"Is Laurel coming down?" he asked, already fearful that he knew the answer.

Agnes looked at him over the top of her coffee cup. "She and Bushrod Pomeroy left for Cape Horn awhile ago."

Ridge gritted his teeth but didn't reply.

"Look," Agnes said, setting her cup in the saucer, "I've always had a reputation for sticking my nose into other people's lives, so let me do it again. It's difficult for a young man and a young woman to work out their differences so they can walk together as one. It takes time to overcome all the obstacles."

The philosophical comment intrigued Ridge. He had not expected anything like that from the older woman.

She smiled ever so faintly. "I can see that you're like my niece; you don't believe I ever knew anything about love."

Ridge opened his mouth as if to protest, but she motioned for Ridge to remain silent.

She said, "The truth is, I once was engaged to a truly wonderful man."

Ridge's eyebrows shot up at this totally unexpected revelation.

Agnes didn't seem to notice. She continued in a low, subdued tone, "We fought all the time, yet we deeply cared for each other. My mother thoroughly disapproved of him, and kept trying to break us up. I allowed her to ruin our relationship, and I've had years to regret it."

Ridge remained silent, unsure of what to say.

She continued, "Anyway, I've lived alone all these years, but you know enough about me to see that it's been an unhappy life. So please don't let that happen to you and Laurel."

Ridge stammered. "I . . . I thought . . . well, that you didn't like me."

"I didn't like anyone, not even myself. But when I saw how my niece suffered on the trip out here, I did some suffering of my own, remembering my own youth. The truth is, I want Laurel to be happy. She's miserable without you, and I'm sure you're the same without her. So don't give up, work out your differe . . ."

She left her sentence unfinished as Mark Gardner rushed across the lobby and straight toward their table.

"I just came from the police station," he announced, sitting down without invitation. "Agnes, do you remember when that

hat was found right after Laurel was attacked with a knife?"

"I'll never forget! It was Walker's. Why do you ask?"

"When the police interrogated him, he claimed his hat was stolen, that he wasn't present when Laurel was attacked. Investigators went to question him again this morning, but he wasn't in his hotel room."

Agnes asked dryly, "Did that surprise them?"

"No, not that. But Duffy, one of the officers who had taken the knife report here in the hotel, came into the station about the same time as the detectives came back from Walker's hotel. He heard them talking about Walker and said he had seen Laurel and Pomeroy get on the cars together."

"So?" Agnes said. "What's that got to do with —"

"I'm coming to that," Gardner interjected. "Duffy said he also saw Walker running to catch that train."

Ridge stood up so suddenly he knocked his chair over. "How long ago was that?"

"About an hour," Gardner replied.

Ridge glanced down at Agnes whose face was suddenly ashen. "Last night Laurel let me read Pomeroy's note. They were going to Cape Horn. Where's that?"

"I don't know." She turned to the news-paperman.

He said, "About fifty miles or so east of here. But if you're thinking about going after her — there are only three daily passenger trains run from here to there. The next one won't leave here for a couple of hours."

"I can't wait that long. Where's the livery stable?"

"There's one on the river by the train and stage terminal," Gardner replied, "but it would kill a horse to push him that far in a short time. A work train leaves for Colfax in about twenty minutes. The boss owes me some favors. Tell him I sent you, and you'll be in Colfax in about three hours. You can rent a horse there for the trail to Cape Horn."

"Thanks!" Ridge spun away and toward the front desk, but Gardner's voice stopped him.

"Before you go rushing off, think about this. It may be pure coincidence that Walker took that same train. After all, there's no proof that he was the one who held a knife to Laurel's throat."

"I'm not going to take that chance," Ridge said grimly. He again started toward the desk.

Gardner raised his voice, "Ridge, if Walker's really after her, there's no way you can get there in time."

"I pray to God he's not," Ridge replied over his shoulder.

He moved rapidly toward the front desk, trying to assure himself that Laurel wasn't in jeopardy. But he could not shake off the alarm he felt for Laurel's safety. If he showed up and she was in no danger, she would be embarrassed and probably give him the worst tongue lashing of his life. But he was willing to risk that because if she truly was in peril, or he got there too late . . . He shook off the fearful thought.

He said to the desk clerk, "My pistol, please."

In Colfax, Pomeroy rented a chestnut mare for Laurel and a gray gelding for himself. The hostler, cinching up a sidesaddle for Laurel, assured the riders that both horses were hardy, mountain-bred, and trail-wise. Pomeroy asked for directions to Cape Horn before he and Laurel rode side-by-side out of the small mining community now becoming a railroad center.

"Beautiful country," Pomeroy commented later as their mounts left the dirt roads and turned onto narrow trails. These had been made by pack mules carrying goods into remote gold mining camps since 1859.

"It certainly is," Laurel replied. She turned as if to take in more of the scenic panorama, but actually her interest was in a lone rider trailing well behind. He was riding a black horse which Laurel thought looked like one she had seen in the corral at Colfax. The man was too far away for Laurel to identify, but she believed it was Walker.

In spite of the rising temperature of the early July morning, she felt a slight chill.

"Look over there," Pomeroy urged, sweeping his hand off to the right. "Magnificent mountains on both sides of us. Very steep, covered with pines. I like the stillness. Except for the sound of our horses' hooves, it's so quiet you'd think there was nobody within a hundred miles."

"It's certainly peaceful," Laurel agreed. She swept the mountains which had closed in around them. There was an ominous stillness broken occasionally by the raucous scream of a jay.

She looked back, but except for the fine dust lingering in the air from their horses' hooves, she could not see any sign of the third horseman. *Maybe he turned off,* she told herself. *Maybe it wasn't Walker. Or maybe he's cutting across to get ahead of us.*

Laurel was feeling uneasy, but she forced herself to ask casually, "How much farther?"

"Not far. But the hostler at the livery station warned that the trail narrows so we'll have to go single file before we get to Cape Horn."

A vision of her ride along the narrow tracks across the face of that awesome mountain flickered through her memory. She could still visualize the river shimmering four thousand feet below.

Stop scaring yourself! she sternly ordered herself.

Pomeroy said cheerfully, "Don't worry. We should be there in plenty of time to get your interview with Charley Crocker."

She could not resist another backward glance. At first, she saw only the increasingly narrow ribbon of a trail over which they had passed. Then, rounding a curve, she again saw the rider on his black horse. This time she had no doubt. It was Walker, and he was gaining on them.

At the top of a hill, Pomeroy and Laurel reined their horses into a wide spot beside the trail to let them rest. The riders slid out of the saddles, stretched their legs, and gazed across a canyon perhaps a half mile wide. Laurel was silently vexed at the delay, and was concerned because they had rounded a curve in the mountain where she could only see a short distance back down the trail. She looked vainly among the pines for some sign of dust.

"Bushrod," she asked, "are you armed?"

He cocked his head slightly to look at her. "Why do you ask?"

"I'm just curious."

He continued to gaze at her with his head cocked. "You must have a better reason than that."

She hesitated before explaining, "This is such wild, lonely country, and I'm a little curious about the rider who's been following us."

"What rider?"

"The one on a black horse." She motioned down the trail. "Don't tell me you haven't seen him?"

"No, I haven't, but you can see by these dusty trails that lots of horses use them."

"On the train coming up, you mentioned pack mules, but I haven't seen any of them or horses. In fact, I haven't seen any animals or people except that lone . . ." She broke off at a sudden heavy dull sound.

"Thunder?" she asked, glancing at the sky above the lofty pines. "No, it can't be."

"Black blasting powder." Pomeroy pointed across the canyon. "Sounds like it's coming from ahead of us. Maybe they're widening the roadbed."

"Between us and Cape Horn?"

"Yes, but I'm sure we'll be able to get around where they're working and make your appointment on time." He moved back to the left side of his horse and put a foot in the stirrup. "You ready to go on?"

She nodded as the last echoes of the heavy blast died away in the distance. With another look down the trail, Laurel remounted and followed Pomeroy's gray.

Ridge rode out of the mountains that clung to both sides of the road and into the flat open area of Colfax with the tracks running through town. At the livery station he was able to get a dun mare. From the hostler, he learned that a short time before, a young man and a pretty woman had rented horses. A few minutes after that, a stocky man with a small mustache and square jaw had rented a horse. All three had ridden off toward Cape Horn.

Spurred by this confirmation of Laurel's danger, Ridge rode out of town, following the directions given by the hostler, fervently hoping he was wrong and this whole hard trip was for nothing. But something inside him told him he was not wrong. Laurel was heading into danger with every passing minute.

Please, Lord, he silently pleaded, *keep her safe until I get there.*

The sound of heavy explosions grew louder as Laurel and Pomeroy emerged from a forest of slender pines and saw a gang of workmen leveling a man-made fill across a cut in the mountains.

The slight but sturdy Chinese workers in their shapeless blue clothes and basket hats pulled wooden wheelbarrows or drove small one-horse dump carts to empty debris into the natural cut to be filled. Laurel guessed that most of them were about her height and didn't outweigh her by more than ten pounds. Yet she knew that Crocker now had about six thousand of them after earlier experiments had proven that they outworked all other men.

A man with a red flag stopped the riders well back from the site. "Ain't no way you two can go through here fer a couple'a hours," he said in response to Pomeroy's question. "Blastin's goin' to last that long, at least."

"But we've got an appointment!" Laurel exclaimed in dismay.

"Beggin' yore pardon, miss, but yonder's the only way 'round, and it's powerful steep." He pointed to the west, away from the work site.

Pomeroy asked, "How much time will we lose going that way?"

"Hour, maybe more. Y'all better hope them horses don't stumble on that deer path they call a trail."

Laurel closed her eyes, trying to blot out the image of what that trail must be like compared to the one they had ridden from Colfax.

"What do you think?" Pomeroy asked her.

Opening her eyes, she nodded. "I must keep that appointment, even if we're a little late."

Nodding, Pomeroy leaned from the saddle and asked the flagman for more details about the detour. As they rode on, Laurel checked behind them. There was no sign of Walker or his black horse.

Where did he go? she wondered with rising concern.

When Ridge topped the rise and saw the workers scurrying about like so many industrious ants, his sturdy dun mare was blowing hard but still going strong. Ridge reined in as the foreman approached, but without his red flag.

"Is it all right to cut through there?" Ridge asked after exchanging greetings.

"Reckon so, Mister. The last black powder blast went off not more'n a half-hour ago."

"Thanks. Have you seen a man and woman come this way in the last hour or so?"

"Shore did. Been a whole passel o' people here today. A man on a black horse came along right after that girl and her beau."

"He's not her beau!" Ridge said sharply.

"No? Well, I mistook them, seems like." He shook his head. "She was some looker, she was. Don't suppose I seen as purty a woman as that since I left 'Frisco."

"Did she seem all right?"

"Looked fine to me, mighty fine. 'Course, she got upset about havin' to go 'round thataway 'cause we was blastin' then. Said she had an appointment."

"That way?" Ridge asked, looking the direction the man had indicated. "How long will it take for them to get to Cape Horn?"

"Cain't say for shore, but I reckon you kin get thar now about the same time's they do, seein' as how you got a straight shot across this fill 'steada havin' to go around like they done."

Ridge smiled in momentary relief, nodded his thanks, and started to loosen the reins, then stopped. "How far behind them was the man riding a black horse?"

"Few minutes. Why?"

"Just asking," Ridge replied, and touched heels to his mount. She responded promptly, heading down across the filled area still swarming with hard-working Chinese.

"Just a little while longer," he said softly to the horse. "Let's hope she's safe."

The detour proved every bit as frightening as the flagman had said. The narrow ridge above the canyon was little more than a game trail. It wound in and out of the pines and brush, but never more than a few feet from the abyss with the ribbon of river far below. In single file, the horses picked their way cautiously through country that would have been breathtaking if Laurel could relax enough to enjoy it.

Laurel raised her voice. "How much farther now?"

"I think I see the summit just ahead. If I'm right, we should be able to see Cape

Horn from there."

It was a temptation for Laurel to close her eyes and trust her chestnut mare to pick her way along the path now cluttered with irregularly shaped rocks. She forced herself to keep her eyes open, believing that if her mount did stumble, she might have a split second to see where to jump to avoid plunging into the canyon and certain death.

Laurel's sigh of relief at the summit was genuine. She reined in beside Pomeroy who pointed. "I was right. That high granite peak ahead of us is Cape Horn. If you look closely, you can see the tracks running along the edge of the precipice."

She nodded, barely able to discern the twin steel rails with the sun reflecting off them as they snaked around the curving face and out of sight. She remembered the omnibus driver saying Crocker's combination office and home was in an old day coach. She turned to Pomeroy. "I don't see any sign of Crocker's car."

"It's probably on a siding while he's riding his horse along the tracks this side of Cape Horn. But don't worry. We'll find him so you get your interview."

"Let's hurry," she urged, loosening the horse's reins.

The trail was wider here and more level,

so they made better time. Laurel looked back over her shoulder. There was still no sign of Walker, and that made Laurel more anxious than when she could see him following.

I wish I knew where he was. He's got to do something before we get down to the cape where Crocker will be.

Pomeroy said, "If we're in luck, we'll get to see the afternoon train coming down from Dutch Flat. It's quite a sight."

She shaded her eyes with her hand to cut the glare. "The countryside is truly beautiful, but that mountain with the tracks clinging to the face of it even looks scary from here," she admitted. She paused, leaning forward in the saddle to see better. "I don't see anyone. Do you suppose Crocker gave up and left?"

"He's probably back in the shade somewhere."

"But where are the workers?"

"Probably moved on to the tunnels."

That sounded logical to Laurel, so she relaxed a little, secure now that solid ground was under her again, and the scenery was awe-inspiring.

"It's too bad that Matthew Brady isn't here to record this," she remarked.

"Matthew Brady?"

"You know, the photographer who took all those great Civil War pictures."

"Pictures can be trouble," Pomeroy said with a tone that made Laurel glance across at him.

He didn't look at her, but guided his horse onto the level area that led to the edge of the massive granite mountain with the river far below.

"It certainly is quiet," Laurel commented, straining to catch sight of anyone. But there was an intense stillness broken only by the soft moaning of wind through the pine needles.

"Yes, it is. Let's dismount and look around. Maybe there's a building or something back under those trees by the tracks."

They tied the reins to a sapling and walked across the open area toward where the tracks started across the face of Cape Horn. Laurel was glad to stretch after the long, tense ride. Stopping twenty feet from the abyss, she slowly started to pivot, taking in all the grandeur of the mountain scene.

"I still don't see anyone," she said. "Should we call out?"

"It's not necessary."

She glanced at him, puzzled, but continued her turn. She stopped abruptly, looking hard back over the summit where they had come. A horseman was just topping the ridge, but his mount was dun colored, not black.

Who is he? And where is Walker?

She turned to voice these questions, but stopped in amazement.

Pomeroy produced a long-bladed knife from inside his boot and held it up. The sun reflected off it and into her eyes. At the same instant, the truth flashed on her.

She instinctively drew back and moaned in sudden terror. "Oh, no! Not Walker, but you!"

CHAPTER 21

Thank God! She's safe! Ridge's silent prayer of gratitude came with the sudden joy of his heart when he topped the ridge and saw Laurel and Pomeroy walk away from their horses. Then he frowned, swinging his head around in all directions. *But where's Walker?*

Ridge drummed his heels against the mare's flanks, urging her to greater speed down the slope toward Laurel and Pomeroy. Unaware of him, they moved slowly toward where the railroad tracks started around Cape Horn.

Passing through the last of the pines, Ridge watched Laurel slowly pivot in a circle. She hesitated a moment when she seemed to be looking directly at him, then she completed her turn. She obviously did not recognize him from this distance.

He blinked as sunlight flashed off of something in Pomeroy's hands. At first it didn't register on Ridge what he was seeing, but when Laurel abruptly drew back, he knew. *A knife!*

His natural instinct was to shout, but he checked himself. If he alerted Pomeroy, he could strike before Ridge could get close enough to stop him. But the sound of the running horse would also draw his attention. Ridge eased the mare to a stop, slipped from the saddle and ground-hitched her, hoping she was trained to stay.

He began moving as fast as his left leg would permit. At every step, he whispered, "Don't do it! Don't do it!"

Laurel could not take her eyes off the knife. "What are you doing?" It was an automatic question because she already knew the terrible truth.

"What I must." He calmly approached her. She started backing up toward the horses, but he quickly moved to cut her off. "You can't get away, Laurel. Running a horse on that trail would probably mean a fall into the canyon, but I can't take a chance that you might live. It's got to be my way."

Her frantic glance showed there was no way to escape except toward the railroad tracks leading around the face of Cape Horn. But she had ridden those rails on a train and knew the terror of what lay four thousand feet down toward the river. She was trapped.

In her fright, she forgot about Walker and

the other rider she'd just seen on the dun horse. She could only depend upon herself, as she had done so often during the war. Her only hope lay within herself.

She stopped backing up and shifted her focus from the knife to his eyes. *Oh, Lord, help me! Stall! Think!*

She asked with forced calmness, "Why me?"

He walked within arm's length before answering, yet she did not flinch or look back at the knife. He asked, "What difference does it make?"

"I want to know."

"You're stalling, but nobody's going to help you. I told you that Crocker would be here because I knew you couldn't pass up an opportunity to talk with him. We are all alone, so just walk over to the edge by the tracks."

So you can kill me and push my body over the side. By the time I hit bottom, it'll be impossible for anyone to know what really happened. That's why he brought me up here. He'll claim it was an accident, and there will be no reason not to believe him.

But her will to live was strong. "No," she said stubbornly as though her wildly beating heart was not about to burst through her ribs. "I must know."

"I think you're forgetting who's in control here."

"Then I'll tell you," she said, furiously searching through her mind for a way out of her situation. Without waiting for him to disagree, she continued.

"Suddenly, it all makes sense to me. You and Dick Morton were the ones who killed Oglesby in Chicago. But you were the brains and he was the drudge. You had him break into my rooms looking for the photograph of the man who saw what happened to Oglesby. As long as that witness remained alive, there was a chance you would also be identified. You couldn't risk that."

Laurel took a breath, trying to swallow the chunk of fear in her throat. She could still feel the frightening point of the knife against her throat in the hotel. But she showed no outward signs as she hurried on.

"When you realized that Morton was incompetent, you sent him on to California, and you got on the same stage with me. You probably wired somebody in Omaha to steal my carpetbag to get the photograph, but that also failed."

She paused, glancing around. If she tried to outrun him into the surrounding hills, he would quickly overtake her. Her eyes probed the other possible escape routes.

Pomeroy was between her and the horses, blocking the way they had come. The surrounding mountains were too steep and rugged to try outrunning him on foot. There was really only one possibility: to dash out onto the railroad tracks and hope he would be too afraid to venture out onto the face of Cape Horn after her. If he did, she preferred a fall to the river over his knife.

Slowly, with great forced casualness, she mentally prepared herself to run.

"You're pretty good, Laurel," Pomeroy said, "but you're wrong about Omaha. That was staged so I could act the hero and you would be comfortable talking to me."

Gaining some confidence in her stalling tactics, she began slowly moving as though thinking of what she was saying. But her eyes were looking for any possible way to save her life.

"I missed that one," she admitted, stopping a few steps away so as not to make him too suspicious. "But I think I've got the rest right."

"I doubt it, but give it a try."

"I should have figured it out before from the two different ways those men died, but I didn't see it until you pulled that knife."

He glanced down at it. "So?"

"So Oglesby and the witness, Phillips,

were killed with a blow. That's Morton's method. But he was knifed, and I was attacked in the hotel with a knife." She looked Pomeroy in the eyes before adding, "That's your way."

"For good reason," he agreed. "Nothing puts more fear into a person than cold steel. I saw that in the war during bayonet charges. Nothing would make the enemy break and run faster than that. Not even this." He reached into his waistband and partially lifted the butt of a revolver where she could see it.

He chuckled, pleased with himself. "You're smart, Laurel; I'll give you that. You figured things out well, but you never suspected me."

"You're right. But that's because I didn't figure out the motives. Now, I think I see them."

"I'm listening."

She began cautiously turning her feet toward the face of the great mountain. Even a half-step might mean the difference between life and death. *A diversion!* The thought hit her hard. *I need a diversion to give me a head start. But what? How?*

"I think," she explained, "that you got tired of Morton's incompetence, and so you put on a mask and came after me in the hotel, thinking I still had the picture. But someone interfered. Walker's hat was left at the scene, making me think he might have been the one with the knife instead of the one trying to help me."

"I'll get him, too."

"For interfering?" Looking for anything to distract him for a moment, Laurel glanced back toward where she had seen the rider on the dun. She saw it then, standing tiredly with head down, reins trailing, and riderless.

Walker was riding a black horse, so how? . . . Oh! He must have traded it for that one. But where is he?

"Not for interfering," Pomeroy replied to her question. "Revenge. Same as Morton deserved for not telling me he had followed you and found Phillips, so we didn't need that photograph anymore."

That horse! Laurel had her distraction, but not yet. Running out on those tracks along the face of the granite mountain was only slightly more preferable to the knife.

She asked, "Revenge against Oglesby, too?"

"Partly. My money was used to start the meat business, but later he got to feeling guilty about selling bad meat to the government. We couldn't make enough money that way. Morton and I quarreled with him." Pomeroy shrugged. "That started all this."

"Greed," she said, nodding, still furtively glancing around for a way to escape. "You once told me that's what the railroad business was all about. But I guess it was also true of your meat business."

"Greedy railroads!" Pomeroy's voice shot up with anger. "They also ruined my wagon road venture, just as they're doing to other businesses, some a whole lot bigger than mine! I tried to get all of us together, but those stupid owners wouldn't cooperate! Now they'll all fail, along with me."

Laurel asked Pomeroy, "So there was no conspiracy against the railroad?"

"The closest we ever came was putting out a thick pamphlet on the *Dutch Flat Swindle*. But there never was an organized effort. Anyway, it's too late now."

He shifted the knife and continued, "I wasn't sure if Phillips had told you enough about Chicago that you might eventually figure out I was involved. When we were dining together, you asked a lot of questions that made me suspicious. It seemed that there was more to your interest than a newspaper story."

"So you lured me into these mountains on

a pretext of meeting Crocker, knowing he wouldn't be here. In fact, you knew that nobody would be here to witness what you planned."

Pomeroy bowed slightly, mockingly.

As long as Laurel could keep him talking, she might have a chance to live. She desperately added, "I don't think you even know Crocker!"

"I don't."

"So back when you invited me to that meeting of railroad men, including Crocker, that was also a lie, wasn't it?"

When he briefly nodded, she asked, "Why? No, let me guess. You thought about murdering me then, but I didn't show, so then you took me out to dinner. But you didn't do it then because it was too risky."

"You're right, but it's too late for you to be thinking of those things. Enough talk! Let's get on —"

Desperately, she interrupted. "Why was it too risky?"

"Don't you see Laurel? There were a couple of problems with that. For it to look like an accident, the Sacramento River wasn't as safe a place for your body as the bottom of Cape Horn. Also, I couldn't risk having your aunt along. I knew that she wasn't able to ride horseback out here, so . . ."

"So you're not brave enough to tackle those men, so you chose me."

Resentment showed in Pomeroy's eyes. "That's not true! You were a threat to me, poking around, asking questions that could have gotten me executed for my part in Oglesby's murder. Phillips and Morton, and now you, then I'm safe."

He shook his head. "But there's no point in going on." He motioned with the knife toward the canyon. "I hate to do this, but I can't take any chances. Let's get it over with."

Laurel's head involuntarily started shaking violently. "No!"

"Don't argue!" Pomeroy snapped. "It's useless! So, move!"

Ridge had circled off to the north away from the horse to crouch behind the only cover he could see: a large pine log. He evaluated the situation with pistol in hand. It was too far for a sure shot. He had to get closer. He shifted his eyes from Laurel and Pomeroy to the open area between them. There was no way to slip closer without being seen if Pomeroy turned around.

Ridge cast an annoyed peek at his game leg. The Yankee minié ball had forever prevented him from running. When he lifted his eyes again, he saw that Laurel was headed toward the canyon with Pomeroy two steps behind.

He drew his good leg under him and tensed, ready to leap up and rush forward as fast as he could.

Now! Laurel told herself, *Make it look believable!* She turned as though making one last desperate look around for help. As her eyes settled on the dun, she started into her act, but suddenly stopped.

Ridge! He rose up from behind a log. In that same moment of delighted recognition, Laurel instantly changed her plan. Instead of distracting Pomeroy to look away from her, she had to keep him from seeing Ridge. She broke into a fast run toward the railroad tracks.

"That won't do any good," Pomeroy's calm voice followed her. "You'll fall and break your neck."

She sprinted across the last of the flat open space and onto the ties between the tracks. She stopped dead still, her eyes flickering a few yards ahead to where the narrow one-track-wide ridge started around the face of the mountain. Far below, at the bottom of the abyss, the river glinted like sunlight on Pomeroy's steel blade.

Instinctively, Laurel stepped closer to the granite face of the mountain, trying to snug up against it. Her legs refused to move forward on the narrow roadbed. She urgently wanted to turn around and see what Ridge was doing, but she didn't dare betray his presence for fear Pomeroy would shoot him. She stood trembling while her mind spun furiously, unable to reach a decision.

Pomeroy taunted her. "Which is it going to be?"

She turned her face to the sky, looking past the top of Cape Horn, past the clouds, past what she could see, past everything but her faith. *Lord, I'm sorry!*

In a splintered second, multitudes of thoughts streaked through her head. She suddenly knew that she had had enough excitement for one lifetime. She deeply regretted her dual life. She regretted not having given up her own willful nature to have what she could have had with Ridge as his wife. She was grieved that she hadn't tried harder to work things out with him.

For the first time, she realized she was unable to handle a situation by herself. If she lived, she would try to figure out what God really wanted her to do. *But I'm reaping what I sowed, so it's too late. Or is it?*

As long as she was still alive, no matter

how few precious seconds of that there might be, she still could do something. She could protect Ridge.

"Pomeroy," she said, slowly turning to face him. "If you want me, come get me." Her eyes sought Ridge, hurrying across the open space but still some distance back of Pomeroy.

"I don't have to," he replied calmly. "Listen."

Laurel frowned, not understanding. Then she heard it: a train whistle from behind her. She spun around. A couple hundred yards away, the empty tracks curved around the mountain and out of sight. But the canyons echoed the engine's warning.

"It'll be here in a minute," Pomeroy assured her. "You want to wait there for it?"

The engineer, guiding the heavy train around the curve and downhill, would not see her in time to stop.

But every second that she kept Pomeroy's undivided attention brought Ridge closer.

"Yes!" she called to Pomeroy. "I'm going to wait right here! And if you wait until it comes around the curve, you'll not be able to do anything to me because there will be witnesses!"

Pomeroy muttered under his breath, then

stuck the knife back in his boot and started toward Laurel. With great will power, she forced herself to move farther out onto the ledge as the whistle sounded again.

Laurel held her breath when Ridge closed the last few yards between him and Pomeroy. Then Ridge commanded, "Don't move!"

Pomeroy whirled around, his hand darting to the pistol butt in his waistband. He stopped at the metallic click of Ridge's hammer being pulled back to full cock. Slowly, Pomeroy raised his hands.

The train rounded the curve behind Laurel, sounding as if it were already upon her.

Ridge yelled, "Laurel, get off of there!"

She started to obey, hearing the engine bearing down on her, the whistle now screaming steadily, and the screech of brakes on iron rails. She didn't look back, but ran with wild desperation toward safety.

Distracted, Ridge started toward her, but Pomeroy's hand smashed down, his fingers closing on Ridge's wrist. They struggled as Laurel tripped on an uneven tie and started to fall. She caught herself, staggered the last few feet back from the cliff face, and threw herself face first into the safety of the dirt.

She jerked her feet away from the tracks,

seeing the engine hurtle past her, brakes still screaming, whistle held down. Curious passengers leaned out the open coach windows as she rolled over and looked toward Ridge. He stood, panting hard, looking over the edge into the canyon. Dust rose from there, but Pomeroy was gone.

Ridge turned and limped toward her, breathing hard, his face smudged and his clothes torn. "Are you all right?" he asked, kneeling beside her.

She nodded, unable to speak. "I . . . I think so. You?"

"I am now," he said, and drew her into his arms.

The next afternoon Laurel and Ridge were with Agnes and Bodmer in the hotel lobby when Walker strolled in.

Laurel asked, "Where did you go yesterday? I saw you following Pomeroy and me, then you disappeared."

"Got lost," Walker admitted sheepishly. "I tried to follow that flagman's directions on the detour, but I guess I'm a city boy."

"Why did you follow us?" Laurel wanted to know.

"I was following Pomeroy, not you."

"Oh? Why?"

Walker smiled. "No wonder you're a

good newspaper reporter. You keep digging deep with those questions."

Agnes prompted, "You didn't answer her question."

"Business reasons," Walker said evasively.

Pinkerton business, I'll bet! Laurel thought. *Maybe he was sent to watch Pomeroy, but I think Pinkerton really sent him to keep an eye on me.* But she couldn't say anything more without giving away her own secret role as an operative.

Walker turned to Ridge. "Sorry I didn't get there in time to be of any help to you and Laurel."

"It turned out all right anyway," Ridge replied. "Besides, you did enough in saving Laurel in this hotel when Pomeroy attacked her."

"I didn't say I did that," Walker protested mildly.

Laurel laughed, now firmly convinced that she was right about him being a Pinkerton. "Well, we're going to give you the credit anyway. Now what are you going to do?"

Walker shrugged. "Go back to Chicago, I guess. How about you?"

Laurel turned to Ridge. "That depends."

Ridge raised an eyebrow. "Oh? I thought

we had that pretty well talked through by the time we got back here last night."

"Something unexpected has come up," she replied.

Ridge jerked as though he had been struck. "Oh, no! We're not going to go through that again!"

"Through what?" Laurel asked. "You don't even know what it's about."

"Then let's find out! Excuse us, please." He took her hand and led her across the lobby and out the front door. The valley heat hit them hard, but they ignored it, standing in the shade of the hotel.

He told her, "I didn't expect another surprise after you told me about your being a detective instead of —"

"Shh!" She said quickly, glancing around nervously. "You promised to keep that a secret!"

"And you promised to resign! Did you?"

"I wired Pinkerton that I wanted to, but he sent this back." Laurel pulled open the drawstrings on her reticule and held up a telegram. "This just came a few minutes ago. Read it."

He read it quickly, then frowned. "There's no problem here. Turn him down."

"It's not that easy, Ridge. He says this

461

case is so important he can't accept my resignation until I solve it."

"You don't need another case! Just quit!"

"I told you it's a problem. You see, I owe him a lot for this one. I spent most of my time trying to stay alive because of my newspaper role, even though he paid my salary and expenses. Then all I came up with was that there was no conspiracy. It's also personal. That's another reason I have to take it. Then I'll quit."

"You told me last night that you would quit today. How do I know that if you take this new case you won't find some excuse to take another one, then another?"

She sighed, closed her eyes, then opened them and replied, "As I told you last night, I love you, but I have to resolve some things in my life before I can plan for a life together."

"Well, I guess I also have some more decisions to make. Like whether to accept Griff's offer of a partnership now that I'll have some railroad reward money to invest."

He paused, but Laurel didn't say anything.

He continued, "I still need to decide whether to rebuild on my family's plantation site. That partly depends on whether I can change my mind and ask President Johnson for amnesty or not."

"Does your pride mean that much to you?"

"It's honor, not pride. I still think the South should have been allowed to remain as separate states."

"Remember, the war's over."

"I know. But my private one isn't. Oh, I'll obey the laws and that sort of thing, but . . ."

She waited for him to finish, but when he didn't, she asked, "What about those house plans you showed me?"

He gently placed both hands on her shoulders. "You know how I feel about you. If I thought you would share that place with me, I'd build it so it would be ready when you are. I'll see that you have all the space you want for your garden, too."

She was touched so that her voice trembled slightly when she spoke again. "You'd do that, even feeling the way you do about asking for amnesty?"

"For you, yes."

"I don't know what to say about that, but Ridge, I have some concerns on living in the South. Your feelings against Johnson are the same kind that some Southerners feel about me, a Yankee. Then there's Maynard, and the fear he caused in me,

knowing that one day someone would recognize me from my war-time missions. That
could ruin both our lives, and that's not
even mentioning Varina."

"She won't bother us again."

"I'm not so sure, Ridge. She has something in her that makes me uneasy, even
now."

"We could stay here in California."

"I like California, or what little I've seen.
But your roots are deep in Virginia. Your
brother died for its soil, and you carry the
wounds. . . ."

She stopped, remembering her part in
having caused that death and Ridge's leg
wound.

He drew her into his arms, ignoring the
people who passed by and turned to stare.
"We forgave each other for what was done
in the war. Let's not dwell on that."

She wanted to stay in the strong circle of
his arms, but she carefully stepped back,
freeing herself. "I'm sure that Brother
Villard was right about reaping what we
sow. I have a lot of regrets about my harvest."

"Put that behind you, too," he urged.
"Start with fresh, new seeds. I'll do the
same."

He opened the door into the lobby and

followed her through. It was empty except for the clerk reading a paper behind the front desk.

Ridge continued, "It'll take several months to get enough money to regain the plantation, if that's what I decide to do. At the same time, you can take this new case for Pinkerton. Then we can see the future better after we come out from yesterday's shadows."

She smiled up at him. "I like that."

"We still face some real problems," he warned. "Oh, if it were just you and me, we could work them out. It's other people and unexpected events that can test us."

A tingle of alarm made Laurel search his eyes. She asked, "Is there something you're not telling me?"

"No. I just want us to be prepared for any kind of surprise. Like that terrible lie Varina wrote you about in that letter. Other things like that could happen."

"I don't want to talk about such things!" Laurel said firmly. "As you said, we'll work them out. Agreed?"

"Agreed! Now, let's see if we can find a quiet corner where I can kiss you."

"Mr. Granger!" she exclaimed in mock shock.

"Don't give me any trouble," he warned

with a grin, "or I might not stop with the first one."

Smiling and holding hands, they walked through the lobby together.